DIARY OF A HUMILIATED MAN

Other books in this series from Lumen Editions:

Too Late for Man
Essays by William Ospina

The Joy of Being Awake
by Hector Abad

Silk
Stories by Grace Dane Mazur

DIARY OF A HUMILIATED MAN

Félix de Azúa

translated from the Spanish by Julie Jones

Lumen Editions
a division of Brookline Books

ISBN 1-57129-029-X

Library of Congress Cataloging-in-Publication Information
Azúa, Félix de, 1944-
    [Diario de un hombre humillado. English]
    Diary of a humiliated man / Félix de Azúa ; translated from
the Spanish by Julie Jones.
        p.   cm.
    ISBN 1-57129-029-X (pbk.)
    I. Jones, Julie. II. Title.
PQ6651.Z76D5313   1996
863'.64--dc20   96-26942
                                                 CIP

Printed in Canada by Best Book Manufacturers, Louiseville, Quebec.

Published by:
Lumen Editions
Brookline Books
P.O. Box 1047
Cambridge, Massachusetts 02238

Contents

Part One

A Banal Man

January 2nd

For a few months now, for strictly personal ends, I've been using a phrase read, if I remember rightly, at the bottom of a painting that has since disappeared from my memory, doubtless to give the words more room. This axiom is (I'm blushing a little as I write it here): "Man is the mouth of God." In the coming year, I'm going to keep the sentence suspended over my head as if it were a sword, or perhaps more like the Roman generals when they returned in victory after one of the usual blood baths. Throughout the whole course of the triumphal procession, they were escorted by slaves whose job was to shout in their ears, "Remember you too will die."

The sentence appeared in my life at just the right moment. I'd concluded that it was advisable to drop out of sight, and I desperately needed the kind of motto that figures on coats of arms. Such mottoes have the virtue of generating a new meaning for each new generation. Simple people, astonished by their accuracy and timeliness, attribute great powers to these sayings. In fact, there's nothing miraculous about them at all. How many fantasies are fueled by phrases like *per aspera ad astram* or the like? Well, this is just how I've used the phrase ever since I decided to disappear from the face of the earth. I resort to it like an amulet when I need good advice about some decision that doesn't really interest me in the least.

At present I'm living here like a stranger, in spite of the fact that I've been an inhabitant of this city ever since I've had use of reason and even though I know its squares, neighborhoods and streets as well as I know my own body — without surprise, of course, but also without tedium. Rather than "like a stranger," perhaps I should say I live here like a dead man. But, in any event, a banal dead man. A lot of people might tend to consider "failure" a more appropriate term — and I would accept and even claim it if necessary — but I think it's more accurate to talk about "banality," since, quite sincerely, there's been no battle and so there can hardly be a defeat. I haven't pursued anything, and I haven't achieved anything. I've been done in by banality, not failure. Far from having the energy and talent to invent an enemy, I can't even imagine a fight. I haven't had the chance to measure up against anything or anybody, so I don't have my own measure. That doesn't mean I'm excessive or immeasurable — good God! no! — it means I'm mediocre. I bear such a modest standard that it doesn't measure anything special, only things that are general and insignificant, that don't stand out, that are hard to perceive, to hear, to touch . . . in short, that are OBVIOUS. I'm the measure of anything. I adapt and accommodate myself to anything without discomfort. I find as much shelter in an elevator as the woods, in the ocean as in a crowd. As I see it, the celebrated, revolutionary proposition of the extreme left, the tremendous, apostolic proposition that says "all men are created equal," isn't charged with heroic and liberating values, but instead with the opaque, flat emptiness of a truism: not only are all men absolutely equal, absolutely the same and alike, I'm the most alike of them all.

Since so much emphasis can give rise to suspicion, I should add right off that I'm having to make an enormous effort to attain the dignity of the perfect stranger. In spite of appearances, all of us modern men know ourselves only too well. We can't possibly give ourselves a surprise. We have a conjugal relation with ourselves in which there's no room for humor. So, as I've said already and I'll say again, this bit about learning to be a perfect stranger can turn out to be painful. I insist, I'm getting there, but I haven't gotten there yet, not by a long shot. Some things still make me mad: people who push, people who shout as if they still believed in the possibility of vanquishing the wicked at this late date. It's hard to break habits that hang on from the days when I still believed I was the protagonist of my own life.

Essential to the perfect stranger is the condition of solitude; without it, everything would be boasting. Here's the reason I have decided to write down everything that happens to me (and I'm convinced that something will happen to me). Only loners and conceited fools write diaries. I believe I possess both virtues. Bear in mind that a man who is isolated from his own kind is without any doubt a new man every minute. So, only by using this Diary will I be able to recognize, to find myself, if I should get lost.

January 3rd

I feel obliged to offer an image of myself. That way, the events that will undoubtedly take place will belong quite definitely to a recognizable object. Voices without a body still frighten me. So I'll describe myself. To do this I have to overcome a sense of revulsion, since by nature I'm quite reserved. In my attacks of euphoria, I invent as much as I can, terrified by the possibility of revealing something I'm unaware of. Here goes.

My body is on the large side and big-boned. My ribs are my most individual osseus section. If I swell up my chest—something I do very seldom and always sadly — I look like a great ape. However, I'm not strong, far from it. My wrists and ankles are thin, almost feminine; my hands, small and with a tendency to sweat; my fingers, brittle as twigs. But my worst part is my hips, which are disproportionate and bird-like, with flat, flaccid thighs covered by a reddish fuzz. My soft, stupid waist is suspended over two bow legs. This gives me the air of a goose.

All in all, I'm not bad looking. Although it doesn't go beyond the ordinary, my face has a concentrated, feral expression that's easy to confuse with intelligence. My eyelashes are long, which arouses women's protective instincts and keeps them from noticing my ears with their droopy, pink lobes, the lobes of a presbyter. I have big feet — size twelve — but they're slender and smooth. I like them a lot. This exaggerated foot doesn't correspond to my height, which is barely 5'10"; their size gives me great poise. The thing about my height doesn't bother me. I've proved that tall men only please people without imagination — children, domestic employees and taxi drivers, people who only notice simple things like "big," "strong" or "black." I have saved the best part of my person for last: my hair. It's straw-colored and wavy. I let it grow down to my shoulders in order to avoid irreparably losing my self-esteem.

This description might make you think I'm a conspicuous individual, easy to distinguish from the rest, the kind of person we use for getting oriented ("on the right of the bald guy," "on the left of the cross-eyed character"), but unfortunately nothing could be farther from the truth. My complexion is very ordinary, the type that traditional medicine classifies as "melancholic;" so I don't attract attention. I console myself thinking that a man with a perfect complexion wouldn't attract much attention either. These days, only the monster does, the person who belongs to a well defined type but who has one feature that is definitely off. Because we can no longer attend to more than ONE stimulus at a time. Our organisms are rotten.

Naturally, as a melancholic, I'm prone to suicide. I doubt, however, that I could kill. If some time, by some chance, I were to subvert my natural inclinations, I would prefer strangulation. A death produced by the body is not as guilty as a death helped along by means that are either mechanical (a dagger, a revolver, a noose) or chemical (hemlock, gas). The intervention of IMPLEMENTS makes one doubly responsible: first of all, for the murder itself, and second, for putting a tool that in itself is innocent and neutral to a perverse use. Because of the peculiar way Germans used gas, for example, there are virtually no sales of carbonized beverages in Teutonic countries. Of course, they won't catch me. Responsibilities are a drag.

January 5th

On my solitary walks, I sometimes feel a nostalgia for collective activities. The ones people engaged in, for example, back when life was determined from birth to death by a profession. A person belonged to the dyers' guild, as it were, in the womb. The streets to the south (they're not EXACTLY to the south, I call them that because of their proximity to the sea) have collective names: Bakers, Tanners, Milliners and Ropemakers Streets . . . Occasionally an individual appears, somebody who stood out in that anthill: the Donkey Thief's Street. The protection of the profession imposed a way of life that was both secret and communal, its visible portion revealed only during Festivals: the banner, the patron saint, the songs with double meanings. The rest of the year was spent in the secret activity of the workshops, the alchemical formulas, the apprentices' training. The crafts formed work battalions, each under its tutelar god, attacking THE WORLD with an oven, a shoemaker's awl, a piece of leather, an anvil. Since then work has become something repellant. Those warriors of work always confronting their age-old enemies, the brutal, lazy horde of soldiers! Now you can't tell them apart. Only on rare occasions are the sheaf and the hammer recognized as the noblest and most civilized contribution we've made to this world of imperial eagles. Signs of labor and civilization confronting the destructive beast and the nihilistic cross of the executed convict. Only rarely. Lately, never.

In the upper city closer to the mountains, in the so-called residential zones, the streets have proper names — posthumous awards to peons who rose in the world. The names of flatterers:

Balmes, Madrazo; the names of go-getters: General Mitre, Alfonso XII; the names of Levites: Valls y Taberner, Doctor Andreu . . . The proper names give the streets a stench of private property, of the estate, that makes you move by furtively and faster.

Following the death of General Franco, many street names were changed. The dead stirred in their tombs. For months you could hear the creak of illustrious bones, the ringing of skulls, the collision of offended skeletons. The scent of open graves floated in the recently baptized streets. The citizens danced drunkenly in the classic celebration of the tyrant's death. The smell of mildew and fresh clay joined in the odor of wine and fireworks. In those fantastic times, you could see Saint Cosmas and Saint Damian riding through the heavens on the western clouds.

Once the celebrations ended, I decided to go into exile from myself and to get my exploration underway. It happens a lot with orphans when they realize that now they've been pushed to the front ranks. They feel like they're walking on tiptoe. Both my parents, simultaneously, took flight.

January 8th

I fill up all the time I can by taking long walks around the city. I imagine looking down on myself from a bird's-eye view, a tiny point moving through urban corridors, between brick walls. Then I see the streets like channels, tilted slightly toward the sea. From up high, the city looks like an amphitheater laid out on a gentle slope. Sometimes I wonder if there isn't some force at work in a port city like this that pushes the denizens from the north to the south. Aren't we always DRIFTING toward the docks without even realizing it? I've invented a number of possible experiments. For example: if a lawyer becomes disoriented, which direction does he most often choose? The sea or the mountains? He's in Consejo de Ciento, but he really wanted to get to Diputación. He doesn't know which way to go. He scratches his head. Suddenly, he takes off. Southward? Northward? In order to be scientific, this experiment would be repeated at least a thousand times.

And here's another convincing piece of evidence: the system of public transportation OBLIGES people to drift toward the sea. The transport system that runs from south to north and north to south is varied, efficient, and managed by uniformed local people who include deference in the price of the ticket. The transverse axis, which is almost nonexistent, consists of an amateurish, depressing tunnel that's riddled with leaks and crossed by trains bought from the Germans in 1927. Many passengers die of electrocution from touching the windows or the door handles of the cars. Others fall victim to crime, which has taken over the aisles to such an extent that in some stations they levy a toll. For many years when I was a boy, I had to travel by this combination to go from the Plaza Lesseps to the University, sixteen stations away. The infamous worm dropped down to the port and ONLY THEN rose up again to the College. It was like going from Paris to Berlin by way of Rome. The plan was obviously laid out with great care in order to keep the working classes shut up underground for as long as possible. There's no point in talking about aboveground transportation; it doesn't exist. It's been bottle-necked for years, and they still haven't figured out how to move the cars that got stuck.

It may seem strange, after all I've just said, that the goal of my walks is to reach the so-called Old Part of Town as soon as possible, allowing myself to be carried along by the force of inertia. I don't even have to walk; I get there floating like a piece of debris pushed along by invisible currents. Every day MILLIONS of citizens like me wind up in the Old Part of Town as if we were laboratory rabbits, and just like the rabbits, if we try to flee, we come even closer to the spot the scientists have designated. Afterwards we return laboriously to our cages, licking the marks left by the electrodes.

On occasion, I've tried to break the spell and walk from east to west instead of north to south; that is, I've tried to go TOWARD the airport or TOWARD the gas depot. I've never succeeded. There's no limit to how far you can go in that direction, but you'll never get anywhere unless you know exactly where you're headed and — more important — why. People like me who don't know where or why get hopelessly lost. After crossing Berber encampments and clandestine airstrips, we wind up flagging a taxi and asking the driver to take us back to the south or the north, the mountain or the sea, up or down, as if we were bears imprisoned by Cruel Forces. And so we go up or down, down or up. Every day. Sometimes more than once.

January 14th

I'm a hopelessly banal man. I absolutely insist on this fact because mine isn't a zoological banality (not like the municipal official of Bombay whose job it is to brush and outfit the elephants), not at all; mine is an assumed banality, a reflexive banality, in a word, a MILITANT banality. Perhaps it will be easier to understand if I say that I'm a man with pretensions to banality.

My shameless insistence doubtless leads one to suspect just the opposite; leads one, I perceive, to take me for an affected man, for someone with an exalted self-image, someone whose efforts to turn himself into a banal man are useless because he ALREADY IS a banal man even though his vanity makes him think he's not. This malicious interpretation can only come from individuals who don't understand the value and the difficulty of banality, individuals who continue to confuse banality with vulgarity.

As far as that "self-image" goes, it's neither big nor little. All of us are governed by the Law of the Two Lenses, according to which everything seems either exaggeratedly big — for example, "I" — or exaggeratedly little — "the world" — so we're constantly changing the focus, horrified by the disproportion of what we see. In relation to my "self-image," then, I'm sick of carting myself around, sick of seeing everything from the level of MY little donkey, but I'm also convinced that any effort to change that level demands an enormous capacity for innocence.

All of this may seem terribly MORAL, but it's not. Not unless physiology is a form of morality, because it's obvious that I couldn't keep on as I was, enduring the unhealthy feeling that I was sitting for an interminable exam. An exam that got underway the day of my birth and wouldn't end until there was half a ton of earth covering my mouth. I was fed up trying to be I no longer knew nor cared what. This enormous self-weariness coincided with the sudden and complete death of my parents. They were coming back from Sitges — driving on a road designed to offset the disproportionate increases in the population brought on by preventive medicine — when they took a leap into the void. It was just off the Costa Garraf. They flew through the air, disconcerting the seagulls for a little while, and then sank forever into the sea. It was at night, and it took three days to find the car. The bill was a relief.

I'm not going to say that their disappearance made me happy. Far from it. We are all prisoners of habit. It's impossible not to feel pain when we lose somebody whose presence in the world we've taken for granted. It's the same pain we feel when we lose any of our habits — whether it's the habit of being somebody's child, of living in one place or another, or of having molars in our right jaw. Every loss and every gain obliges us to perform a laborious feat of gymnastics — being an orphan, living on another street, chewing on the left side. Our distaste for the new identity — because of all the work it involves — makes us feel a sharp pain we confuse with "feelings." That's what shook me up when I found out about the accident: the pain of having to look at myself, again. Franco had just died on me, and I was still trying to figure out how to fill that vacuum, and then my parents do the same thing. Both. Together. All three of them.

Being left an orphan meant acquiring a character I wasn't prepared for. During the funeral service and the burial, I was in a state of stupefaction that could well have passed among my relatives for spiritual collapse. One of my uncles — I'm rich in this particular relationship — approached me during the service in order to gabble something incomprehensible in my ear about foreign cash, property rights, letters of credit. He didn't manage to get my attention at that moment, but he planted the seed of an idea. I knew nothing about my inheritance — in part because my parents and I had never been close, separated as we were by the widest of gulfs: knowing each other perfectly well. But it didn't take much perspicuity to understand that if my uncle went to the trouble of advising me, it must be of some importance.

My father's brother, like all financiers, suffers not only when he sees his own profits reduced, but also when other people's profits are reduced. I once saw him pick up the tip some stranger had deposited at the next table, run out of the restaurant and hand it over to the man, saying: You left this money behind. His indignation was writ large. These people with new money will wind up destroying the morale of our workers, he declared. He was so upset he couldn't finish his haddock. It's interesting. For humans of this type, money represents an obscure form of life. As my uncle sees it, I was as guilty in my carelessness as the heartless fellow who lets a wounded man bleed to death in the middle of a public thoroughfare.

If my inheritance was of the discreet magnitude I suspected, I'd never have to worry about supporting myself again — so long as I renounced every form of HISTORICITY, that is, if I remained a bachelor, an orphan, without children (there's no word for this in our language even though "alopecia" exists, it's shameful), without friends (ditto), without family, business, work, home, dog, concierge . . . in short, if I remained isolated in my nullity, like a toadstool that takes a modest pride in needing almost nothing, in being usually inedible if not poisonous and in decking itself out in gorgeous colors that attract the flies. This destiny struck me then as the most intelligent and honest choice.

Once the funeral rites were over, I had a conversation

with my uncle in order to ascertain, not without a certain uneasiness, just how much would be at my disposition if I sold the two apartments (the one on Muntaner and the one on Ganduxer), the two cars (Eh! said my uncle, Only one car! I had already forgotten the heap of rubble that beast of a coast had dropped from its teeth), the estate in Blanes and a few other odds and ends. Odds and ends! exclaimed Uncle Enrique, red with consternation. He tried to make me see that naked money, bank notes, is like water from a flood; paper money is never real money (he stressed the bit about "real"). Real money is construction, buildings, things, property, PROPERTY. Convert it all into hard cash, and it goes up in smoke. I didn't let myself be intimidated; I insisted on knowing the EXACT amount. When at last, after much insistence, much hesitation and clearing of the throat, I managed to tote up an approximate sum, I realized that I'd be able to become a banal man. I begged him to liquidate all the liquidatable property, and for two months I watched the transactions. At last when everything had been concluded, I showed up in his office in high spirits, after a copious breakfast.

The office on Vía Layetana has its door next to the showroom of Gudiol Coins. When as a child I visited my uncle — and this happened with a certain frequency since he was the strong man in the family, the one who looked after my father's investments — the severe pieces exhibited in Gudiol's window seemed like an ad for the riches that my uncle Enrique (who by now had Catalonianized his name to Enric) kept hidden in his house. For me then those coins had the same function as the enormous slouch hat that identified Prats Haberdashery; they were intended to suggest the riches that awaited the passerby on the second floor.

In spite of every prognostication, there was no such hoard on the second floor. The only treasure there was Señor Torras. Today as usual he opened the door for me. Señor Torras had watched me grow up; he had watched my parents grow up, and the only reason he hadn't watched my grandparents grow up is that Providence only lets you get old in one direction. If that weren't the case, Señor Torras would have gotten old backwards just so he could watch my grandparents grow up. At present he is ninety-three years old. He has labored unremittingly in the office belonging to my Uncle Enrique, my uncle's father and my uncle's grandfather. Showing a smile that barely wrinkled a face as worn as a five-*peseta* bill, Señor Torras expressed the greatest happiness to see me and proceeded to confuse me first with my father and then with my grandfather so that he experienced a triple attack of happiness over seeing the whole family at one fell swoop. At the echo of his jubilant howls, which sounded like the bark of a Pomeranian, my Uncle Enrique appeared. Ah! ah! he said, not to add to Señor Torras's jubilation, but to get him out of the way. Ah! Señor Torras! All right, all right, that's enough, that's enough! With a light touch on Señor Torras's shoulders, my uncle guided him in the direction of the hallway. Ah, Señor Torras, now we have to finish the Inter-Bank thing. Eh? And if there's enough time before we call it a day, the Parallisa board, eh? Ah, Señor Torras, they don't pay us here for slacking off. Señor Torras recedes down the hallway, giving little jumps of joy that grow farther and farther away until he is snuffed out behind a walnut door. That Señor Torras! If we let him, he wouldn't do a thing all day long. The older he gets the worse he gets. I don't know what we'll do when he's old.

There is a library in my Uncle Enrique's office. An authentic library with leather-bound books. It's true that the books are all part of the Austral Pocketbook Collection, but when you think that the binding is the external and visible part of the prop, why spend more on the filling? For some time he played with the idea of having newspapers bound, but he was dissuaded by the quantity of cardboard surface necessary to make them consistent.

Once he was settled in the olive-wood armchair that had heads of conquistadors carved on the back, he got underway. My Uncle Enrique suffers from a nervous condition that forces him to blink continually as though he were blinded by sparks of magnesium; this lends great charm to his conversation. Well, well, you rascal! We've undertaken the request, the charge, the task entrusted to us. We've reconverted the reconvertible and liquidated the liquidatable, eh? discounted the discountable and canceled the cancelable, eh? Then we've put the whole package to work so we expect better than eleven per cent gross for the clean part and eight and a half net for the black part, eh? Everything on demand in twelve months, income accumulated when you cash in your investment. Now we'll call Señor Torras — Señor Torras! — so he can hand over the securities, the sureties, the certificates, the passbooks, the deposit numbers, the endorsements — Señor Torras! — the agenda with the due dates noted down in red — Señor Torras — damned man, he doesn't even hear any more. I don't know what we're going to do in a few years . . .

Señor Torras appears like the projection of a magic lantern. He confuses me with my grandfather again, raises his arms in their oilcloth sleeve protectors, tears of joy fall straight from his

cheek bones to the floor since he has no cheeks for them to
slide down, but Uncle Enrique puts a stop to this touching
scene: Señor Torras! Fine! That's enough! Señor Torras! Bring
me the stuff on Indubán, on the Savings and on Santander right
now; get a move on . . . My uncle accelerates his blink and pulls
his hair, that is, the single hair that with pharaonic industry he
arranges over his bald head until it covers almost the entire
surface. This hair, straightened out, must be about seventy-five
yards long. You can see we keep Señor Torras on here to avoid
adding to the unemployment rate. We businessmen actually
create riches, but the employees . . . I'd like to see what they'd
do in Russia. They'd get a beating there!

Señor Torras comes back carrying a stack of files that
reach his eyebrows. He feels his way gingerly with his toes
like a ballerina, and when he bumps into the massive olive-
wood table, the whole stack cascades over it. Señor Torras,
Señor Torras! Shit! That's enough! What would your father
say if he saw you, eh? Aren't you ashamed? You're an idiot,
Señor Torras! Get out of here, Señor Torras, get out!

In spite of the deluge of winks, I'm the one who gets out.
All I need to know is what banks I have checking accounts
in; I'll get the checkbooks myself. I'd rather leave the rest to
the care of Señor Torras and my uncle, in whose eyes it's
raining hard now. For a second I see his pupils through a fine
film that's stuck there. Good God, man! I appreciate your
trust. You probably know what you're doing, but I'm going to
give you some advice, eh? Just like your father and mother
would have done — poor things. You owe them everything.
You've never done a lick of work in your life, eh? A lot of
literature and a lot of stories, but you've never had a penny of

your own, eh? All right. Don't spend more than five percent of your assets annually or, at most, six. Is that clear? Because you've got to reinvest at least what it takes to restructure the annual money supply. And don't run around on me with whores — or if you do, make sure they're high-class. And be sure to put the next day's date on your checks, even though you're not supposed to, because every little bit helps. If you need a doctor, Medina, who has always taken care of the family, is excellent, and he charges about twenty-five hundred *pesetas* a visit . . . And so on.

Once I'm in the Plaza de San Jaime, I stop at Gudiol Coins. A Roman collection rests on a grey velvet background. The imperial profiles look at the backs of each other's heads, waiting in line for eternal rest. The last coin belongs to the epoch of Suetonius, a skeletal bust with a chicken neck that vaguely suggests Señor Torras, his contemporary. You only need a LITTLE money in order to stop existing, to perform no part at all in this comedy whose author has discreetly steered clear of the stage and even refused to sign. Here are the ingredients for a "personal disappearance": the desire, the aforementioned money, and a big city. It doesn't have to be a great city, but it does have to be a city. That's critical because disappearing out in the country just means getting lost, with subsequent efforts on the part of the Civil Guard. And it's impossible to disappear in a village, where everyone has his function and there are barely enough people to go around. Anyway, now that I've gotten the money — I already had the desire — all I need is a squalid apartment in some ridiculous hotel in the northern zone, where I can keep this notebook.

January 13th

In spite of their inconveniences — and there are tons of them — big cities, ALL big cities, are well made. And they are well made because we don't know how to make them any other way. There's no point in comparing the differences between Vienna and Ciudad Real. They are two fatalities, two throws of the dice without a player and, worst yet, without anybody to place a bet. So all big cities, along with the societies they shelter, are the best cities and the best societies possible. This is due to the fact that cities, like the men who inhabit them, have masters. And the masters do and undo within the narrow limits that allow them to keep on being masters. In the final analysis, a city is a piece of ground, and every piece of ground has a master — even the desert. The masters of this city decided to put the poor down below and the rich up above. The proximity of the port created an unhealthy semicircle that, considering its labyrinthine and semi-explored condition, is hard to control and useful for illegal business. As a result, down there in the southern zone a really remarkable zoology and microbiology have been mounting up. It's the border between East and West. There are corners straight out of Naples, but if you turn another corner, you may sink into the stench of Turkey. It's there you find the dead churches, like specimens of the taxidermist's art.

The owners of the city live to the north, far from the sea they've always feared or despised; most of the are immigrants from the interior, and they preserve an archaic terror of unlimited space, of the uncontrolled, the indefinite, the indeterminate. They are a people accustomed to high walls and fences, to protecting their garden plot blunderbuss in hand. And so the city is divided into two symbolic zones that should be respected by anybody who is making a will. The partition, however, is strictly symbolic. The northern part is a narrow corridor that's choked by a ring of mountains, asphyxiated like a house crammed with junk; it has never attained the coherence and solidity of a real neighborhood. Not by a long shot. Spurred on by envy, the masters sold the modest houses with little gardens that were all they'd managed to put up during the turbulence brought on by workingmen's movements in the nineteenth century. In their place but up on higher ground, they erected the neutral blocks of apartments where they live today (blocks that are hard to distinguish from blocks of workingmen's apartments. In fact, the only differences are the price, the tiles in the bath and the concierges' caps). The result has been chaos. Many masters are scattered over different neighborhoods, all equally sordid, or hiding out like ferrets in the chicken coops where their servants dwell. Being scattered like this has deprived them of any but a purely economic consciousness since they have no meeting places, social centers, accepted dress code or identifiable accent. It's very easy to confuse a master with a common criminal, and easy as well to mistake the criminal for an aristocrat. The city only respects gold. So its masters fight among themselves like Arabs and jackals. The basic weakness of the masters has led to foreign enfeoffment. Bereft of clan consciousness, they obey the orders of foreign lords. For centuries the city has been a colony of old fugitives from the Castilian system of justice. Yet the tragedy of being colonized has in no way made the masters more compassionate toward their servants. On the contrary, it's precisely because they have to answer to their feudal lords that they exploit their fellow countrymen and treat them cruelly.

As for the penniless hordes, they in turn live isolated within their tribes, barely mixing with outsiders. For them the city is a passageway. They come here to escape from hunger, and they're on their way to death. So all the physical elements of the city are in ruins, like the railway stations and the state hospitals and those other hateful places where the poor pile up on their way to somewhere else.

On summer days when there's not a hint of a breeze, the smoke from factories, the stench of trucks and buses, the sweat of the busy masses, all this forms a greenish cloud like the air in times of plague, when corpses burn slowly in public squares.

This is a no man's land. The masters serve ruffians from foreign parts, and the servants are foreigners who've been rented out by salesmen. This quality gives the city a nihilistic, delinquent and alienated life. Nobody cares about anything but immediate satisfaction. Crime and chimeras reign. Civic life is reticulated in sects, castes, tribes and secret societies that wage a mutual war of extermination. When the last bonds break, the mistreated hordes will hoist black flags aloft, and scarecrows will hang from lampposts. Mummies will rise from their tombs to liven up the festivities, and the vengeance of the Castilian ruffians will leave five or six generations of workers without progeny. In the almost interminable years of defeat, women will earn their first money when they are twelve or thirteen as they did in Byzantium, where livid priests prayed continually for invasion because things are so much better under a tyranny. For their part, men will take their first corpse for pay before they shave the adolescent down from their faces.

January 14th

Although it's true that I don't lament the death of my parents, considering that their unfortunate accident is going to make it easy for me to prolong a fiction of independence, today I recalled my mother with unpleasant vividness. This means that she still grasps the floating plank of my memory like a castaway. I was eating breakfast at the corner bar by my hotel. This is a noisy spot, staffed by waiters with Mexican moustaches, an adornment typical of the turbulent soul. Years ago the police used to arrest people who had them, noting down on their dossiers: "The subject has a moustache like a queer." These days a lot of policemen wear them, which suggests customs are easing up. While I was sipping my coffee, a lady beside me rejected a serving of apple pie with this expression: "I don't want it; it doesn't look very Catholic to me." It was the same phrase that my mother and her friends used when something or someone did not coincide in its external aspect with what they expected.

Like my mother, this woman also adorned her ears with two gold hoops about an inch and a half in diameter and her index finger with three rings: diamonds, emeralds and rubies. It was like seeing the Totem again. "This shop isn't very Catholic." "These oranges aren't very Catholic." Expressions inherited from the French Neo-Catholics. I was depressed. In the terrible years of her decadence, my mother spoke, moved and dressed exactly as she used to after Franco's victory when she and her friends saw the country as THEIR tennis court. Her words evoked figures on horseback, their chests crossed with cartridge belts, the histrionic sons of unscrupulous pharmacists, who were getting rich selling penicillin on the black market. Theirs was a world of blood and tinsel that, fortunately, lasted scarcely a decade, just enough time for the real beneficiaries of the bloodbath — who were even more ruthless, but less bourgeois — to assume their positions and take over the country.

Those obscure foremen brought with them an exaggerated interest in genealogy so that my mother and her friends — even though they were absolutely divorced from any real power — were convinced they belonged to a magic circle. Many years later when they had all become indigent, they continued to ask about uncles, nephews, sisters-in-law and sons-in-law every time a family name came up in conversation. Carner? I know who you're talking about. His father married a Moixons (when in fact it was his grandfather). He has a cousin that is the Bofarulls' son-in-law, and they've assured me that he's not very Catholic. Meaning the cousin *cum* son-in-law was a member of the Athenaeum. My mother's youth and her maturity were taken up entirely with conversations of that sort. At an advanced age when she was fortunate enough to run into another survivor, she still talked about the Aixelàs or the Borredàs as if they were the Saxe-Coburgs.

Those ladies said "no"; they said "no" a lot. When the negative was resounding, they held on to the initial "N" and then let themselves slide with a smooth modulation: N-n-n-n-noooo. No, she's not a Sistachs; she's a Camprubí. Their favorite form of denial was the kind that would emphasize a character trait that was original and striking. So, when her sister Teresa told her that Uncle Oríol, whom she greatly esteemed, had been admitted to a clinic, my mother answered that she didn't intend to go anywhere near him. Whyever not? Teresa asked her. Because I have never visited sick people, Teresa, n-n-n-never in my life. After these negations, she would wait for an astonished "ah!" from an invisible biographer. They were like survivors of some novel written by the head of a provincial section of the Falange, a starched man with bluish cheeks and a little moustache like a bit of adhesive tape. The kind who used to kiss the provincial bourgeois ladies on the hand in order to get a good look at their rings and decide if it would be worthwhile pursuing matrimony.

My father, on the other hand, was a surgeon with some expertise, a capable man, who figured out very fast where true patriotism lay. He built a gynecological clinic in which it was possible to extract money from each and every part of the feminine anatomy. Once women with big checking accounts signed into that deluxe butcher's shop, they were treated like a malleable material, a kind of pork, transformed and quartered so it disappears as a unit, cut into so many pieces that nobody can put it back together again. True, not a week passed without a victim, but the cadavers were written off as work-related accidents.

My mother's celestial music and my father's robust pragmatism served as a real symbol of the nation. It explains almost everything: I'm the son of the jackal and the little Pekinese bitch.

January 15th

I confess that I dedicated myself to the banal in my flight from poetry. Before undertaking the conquest of banality, I wrote poetry. Naturally, all of us used to write poems. I would write poems until the first light of dawn. On tiptoe, genuflecting, on all fours, prostrate, our lips pursed, we would write poems. To the stars, the moon, the Ebro River? Of course! To Luisa, Marisa, Rosa, Lisa? Of course not! Love poetry was pro-Franco. To the fall of the Roman Empire, an Iberian urn, a worker on strike? Worse yet! No, the amazing, the incredible thing is that we would write that we were writing that we had written! As a famous French critic said, we kept the motor of language running *au ralenti*. *Le moteur, la langue, la parole, sursum corda!* That was only one of our revolutions. In a very carefully studied process, commonly referred to as the Terror, we learned to savor the seductive nature of Chinese thought. A butcher in Shanghai insisted that he beheaded goats with greater efficiency after reading Comrade Mao's *Little Red Book*. We composed celestial symphonies inspired by the same beacon. And we also drugged ourselves with the cruel incontinence of a seamstress addicted to her rosary. After a couple of years, our active idiocy had turned into stupefaction.

"Individual" actions that enjoyed great esteem — suicide, conspiracy, vice, literature — were practiced on a massive scale. Individuality had died in the embrace of individualism. Today, you only die of these things if you live in the slums, but the dregs of these ideas remain, only now this sediment has drifted into the decorative: pantries stocked with syrup, plaster casts, Austrian water colors, English gardens and Viennese chairs. More rheum, more little drawings of flower vases. Many people have started going to the opera. The Opera! Popish, gallinaceous hopes! When I run into them, I see things. I see the concentration camp at Mauthausen with an emaciated Jew paddling in the mud, showing off an exquisite hairdo that sets him apart from the common herd.

January 16th

I always end up on the Ramblas, that intolerable, common, extra-common, arch-common place. In the old days, that boulevard was a series of gutters through which the water ran down from the Tibidabo, from Bellesguard, from Collcerola, from San Gervasio. These days, it has a similar function: it's a human sewer. Night after night, a current of citizens squeezes inevitably into the conduit to be carried down with the neap tide. Hundreds of blood vessels lead into its principal artery. Innumerable bars, taverns and inns prick each one of these capillary conductors like tribes of lice infesting an old wool blanket. In one of the capillary vessels of this alcoholic web, the Boa has made her nest, a bar that bears the name of its mature proprietor. The Boa has enormous breasts covered with freckles and hands as spotted as cowhide. She usually sports a helmet-shaped wig, the color of egg-yolks. Reflected in the mirror behind the bottle rack, it lends the bar a magical light. Whenever I think about the hardness of the universe, it comforts me to remember this mote of dust, loaded with drinks and commanded by a woman with rigid eyelashes. In moments of ecstasy, death doesn't really matter. When nothing but burnt-out suns and cold stars remain, when we can no longer see our sweat turn green and pink under the neon lights, this frail bar built out of scraps of tin and wood will lay low until divine vengeance has passed. In the corner, the no-goods of the Roman Empire drink to the Boa's health while toga-clad scorpions and pontifical owls build temples and massacre peasants. Here the interminable sermons of Virgil's public verse are greeted with skepticism. From time to time, a drunk throws a piece of rancid bacon to the dog and then shifts his weight to the other elbow.

But what am I writing? Our nails grow. Our hair grows. We are gardens without gardeners. Every year we have to extirpate a piece of gut that has come uncoiled, to sew, hit, sink, perforate, perhaps add on here and there. Here's my empty head. Why does everything seem too big to me? What does that smile mean? Resign yourself! We melancholics sweat a lot, but we don't get tired. We're agile and nervous. We spend hours as quiet as mice and then, suddenly, without any apparent, outside reason, we spring into action. Prince Hamlet, in spite of his fat, flabby look, was a very competent swordsman. I am almost as fat as Hamlet.

I turned forty-seven a few months ago.

January 17th

First effects! Talking about the Boa! Here's what happened: I go down to the Boa as usual and ask for the usual. The wig sparkles, as shiny and full of spikes as a gold reliquary. The Boa is talking with a friend of hers about a television program in which assorted citizens subject themselves to humiliations they would never dream of putting up with in real life. The odd thing is that they do it because they are humiliated in front of MILLIONS of eyes. I can't contain myself — why should I? — so I too remark on how extraordinary the whole business is: that a lot of people will tolerate humiliation only if the audience is big enough. The women turn enormous, hippopotamus eyes on me. They take me for a cop. A normal citizen doesn't stick his nose in other people's conversations. Being mistaken for an agent of law and order has its advantages in a neighborhood like this one. They immediately tell me their names and fill up our glasses. The Boa withdraws to attend to the bar, and the girl sits down beside me.

She is thin — probably about a hundred and ten pounds — with a vehement expression. She says she's studying languages. What languages? French. The French language. Then, in fact, she is studying A language, I tell her, opting for the kind of wit they toss around in police stations, but she still doesn't follow me. I try to make out her figure under the black sweater and the leather skirt. Her legs are not very muscular; that almost guarantees there will be no surprises in the lumbar and pelvic zones. She has a long, smooth neck. There is something bird-like about the way she moves her hands and twitches the ash off the end of the cigarette. Her heavy eye makeup gives her the air of one of Franco's Moroccan soldiers. I pay for the drinks. Hers was an Alexandra. I figure I'd better invite her to an establishment that suits my profession, so I take her to the Drugstore del Liceo. The floor is covered with cigarette butts and pools of beer. From time to time, someone crashes noisily on top of one of the Formica tables.

I order spaghetti; she goes for chicken. I wasn't expecting the chicken. For obscure reasons I can't examine at the time, I feel touched that she has ordered chicken. It's the first amorous sign of the night. I begin to look at her in another light, almost affectionately. I insist she order vanilla ice-cream with whipped cream and a slice of canned peach on top and slices of banana on each side. There's a photograph of it on the wall. She absolutely refuses. No way. She speaks very fast. About herself. The most important thing in the world is good manners, refinement (refinement!). If people had manners there wouldn't be so much crime because crime is a problem of behavior, everyone agrees about that, but — nobody has manners anymore. Oh, it's not just a question of money. She knows guys with a lot, a whole lot, of money, and, hey, they're scoundrels, they're no better than criminals, because there are criminals and criminals. She could introduce me to people that I would NEVER suspect what they get up to, authentic gentlemen (an offer of confidence?). The real criminals are involved in drugs, but, poor things, they suffer enough as it is because of their habit even though, it's true, they really scare her. They haven't attacked her yet, but ALMOST ALL her girl friends have had problems, serious problems, rape, abuse . . . The conversation doesn't stray out of my area of interest. She admires us. She understands that, considering what we're paid, there's no reason we should risk our lives. They pay us quite well, I say, in a spurt of honesty. Well, it doesn't make any difference. You shouldn't put your life at stake for money. She used to know policemen who risked their lives because they had PRINCIPLES, beliefs, faith in human beings, but now . . . And what would make you risk your life? She would risk her life in order to see Paris. Oh, yes! She's wild to see Paris, especially the Tuileries.

She doesn't like my apartment at all. This asymmetrical niche quite obviously upsets her. It doesn't fit in with her notion of a policeman's home. By way of excuse, I tell her I just got here, they just transferred me from Rentería and I haven't had time to get settled in yet. She doesn't know exactly where Rentería is, but when she finds out, she makes a face: the Basques. She doesn't even want to see them in the movies. But she's not speaking now with much conviction. Even she realizes that there are a lot of strange things in my house. Considerate, she straightens up a bit, emptying the ashtrays, piling up the newspapers, arranging the cushions on the sofa, where she sits with her legs pulled up under her. I pour out two beers. Do you want yours with gin? With gin? Did you work in Germany? I explain that I don't have anything else; I usually add some anisette, but there's none left. Now she's convinced that I'm NOT a policeman. Hey, you're not trying to trick me, are you? I haven't done anything to you. I like you whether you're a policeman or not. I calm her down. I'm a clerk at a bank. But she doesn't believe anything I tell her now. In a way, she doesn't care. Since she has figured out that I'm not a policeman, she feels more comfortable, calmer. They make me a little edgy. They're good people, but you never know how things will wind up. But I like to stay on good terms with them, because I free-lance. We're in such agreement about all this that we decide to have our beer with gin.

She shows me a book she's carrying in her purse. It's the method recommended by the academy, but on her own she has also bought a book of poetry because she likes poetry a lot and she's dying to read French poetry. She shows it to me: the poems of Jules Laforgue. Incredible! The thought of it still affects me. Do you know who he is? No, it *is* poetry, isn't it? I open the book and read out loud: *Lune, Pape abortif à L'amiable, Pape.* Oooo, that sounds terrific. What's it mean? Never mind, the important thing is the pronunciation: *lun-e-papabortif-alamia-blepap-e.* The *papabortif* bit leaves her spellbound. She's crazy about it. For a good while, we take turns repeating it. Tears of laughter roll down our cheeks. It's a true miracle. This is the spark, the cataclysm . . . how little it takes! The *papabortif* has left us alone in the world, has shut out everything that's not related to the mechanics of copulation.

She's sweating like a horse. My hands slide all over her body and get tangled in the rumpled sheets. The pillow is stained with spots of mascara. Her movements are abrupt, but she's flexible and, because of the color of her skin, I deduce she's from Málaga. I feel a euphoric sense of empathy with her now. I like her ears, her scant breasts, her thighs and even the mixture of smells she gives off: merchandise, pigment, dried seaweed and acetone. We've gone to bed together because of the *papabortif*. There's no doubt about it.

The next morning, she has me buy Bimbo Bread and milk. She never goes out without breakfast. When I get back, she has washed the dishes. But I want to get rid of her. And soon. The *papabortif* is of no avail. I'm burning to read the newspaper. When I put her in the taxi, I feel a surge of relief. Back at home, I see that she has forgotten the volume of Laforgue between the slices of Bimbo. On the edge of each slice a border of green mold glows.

January 19th

It's true. For the last twenty years I've behaved with delightful cruelty. As a protection against experience, my spirit formed such a thick shell that even the most modest invitations broke up on it like little boats against the rocks. I have the feeling now that I spent my whole life surrounded by castaways, but that's because I myself was a castaway. This explains why for such a long time I didn't see anything but other castaways and sharks.

But now I want to prepare a beach fit for any vessel no matter how shallow its draught. It's taken me too long to realize I'd become a pious hypocrite! Yes, sir! A hard-hearted hypocrite whose only pleasure lies in measuring the distance between me and the sinners. My vanity made me think that if I handled things right, I could save myself for sublime undertakings.

But what hurts the victim, kills the hangman. The cruelty that's born of intelligence — albeit a bastard child — finally turns into sheer rancor and then into frustration. Now, all is different. Now I want to be invaded by the unassuming, the unimportant, the base, by everything I once disdained. I don't want to save myself for anything now. I'm betting heavily on the ephemeral. In this void, the revelation may take place.

I've taken an extraordinary dislike to Diogenes, a hypocrite from the land of black olives and goat cheese! His exemplary conduct, his display of spirituality — and so cheap (a lantern, a bushel) — were bound to win the emperor over as a client. It's the hypocrisy of someone who has absolutely nothing, who shows off his poverty, his trust in nature . . . a petty official! I feel so ashamed! Years ago, I too counted myself as one of the righteous! I didn't let my beard grow, but I just missed it by a hair's breadth.

January 20th

Lately, especially when it's raining, I don't let myself drift down to the Ramblas. I try to stop halfway, like somebody who grabs a handful of reeds to keep from being dragged along by the current. I must say I feel a new and surprising fascination with the enormous quadrangle that separates the lower city, down by the port, from the upper city, rising toward the mountains. This checkerboard is the net that catches the part of the middle class that sees itself as middle-class. The middle class that sees itself as upper-class digs in on higher ground when it can, from the Plaza de Molina on up. And the middle class that sees itself as lower-class settles south of the Plaza de Cataluña.

The Ensanche is a bastion, a fortress of Moderation that keeps the animal spirits of the humid zone at bay and softens the savage greed of the dry zone. It's an intellectual and industrious flatland, whose enormous extension makes it very hard for the two enemy castes to meet in a head-on collision. A criminal from down south, thirsting for revenge, will get bored before he reaches his victim, the boss from up north. When the Ministry of Development's accounts were made public, it was confirmed that the most expensive item in the Billy-Club Squad's budget was public transport. On some occasions, hit men heading north even had to break their trip overnight when they got as far up as Urquinaona because they couldn't cover the trajectory in a single day. By the same token, a businessman who devotes himself to the white slave trade, for example, will have to lay out a huge sum in tariffs and duties before reaching the marketplace in the south. In this way, everything is balanced out and tempered. That's the function of this miraculous neighborhood. It's not just a city in itself; it's the best of cities!

The inhabitants of the Ensanche are geometrical, orderly, neat as newly minted coins. The tiny handful of mathematicians, entomologists and numismatists who were born in the city and who have not died of hunger still live here. You'll also find a great number of Kantians, vegetarians, Masons, Darwinians and urban planners. It's a museum of learned fossils, the poor inheritance the Enlightenment prepared for this unloved daughter. Living alongside these luminaries in a surprising state of symbiosis are the little merchants, the little manufacturers, the little employees and almost all the little citizens, the average height being a few inches below the statistical average. To sum up: gathered together here through a process of *Einfühlung* is the part of the population that, being apportioned no leading role in the history of humanity, has had to come up with a way to order, regulate, stamp and dominate everyone else's life.

If a freighter docks in the port with, let's say, a hundred million *pesetas'* worth of goods, the trajectory of that fortune provides us with a very clear idea of the catalyzing function of the Ensanche. Naturally, the profits must reach the investors in the north of the city, but not directly. They take a roundabout route. To start with, the poverty tax must be paid: 10% of all goods that enter the port are stolen, according to official statistics. This sum is recovered later through the administration of houses of prostitution and the drug trade. The remaining 90% is spread over the Ensanche like the waters of the Nile over its delta. It irrigates hundreds of commercial streams, each of which consumes a tiny bit of the flow, all at tremendous speed, as long as the flood lasts. Finally, by means of a network of banks as well concealed as the circulatory system and, like it, only visible in case of injury, the money winds up in the hands of our northern residents.

With sidereal intuition, the denizens of the Ensanche have baptized their streets with the names of places: Aragón, Corsica,

Valencia, Mallorca . . . recognizing the intellectual ambition of a neighborhood that wants to be every place, a map of the world on a small scale. It's the last sprout on the superannuated Renaissance tree, a sickly offshoot, but of good stock.

In this platonic micro-city, there are bars where the alcohol is truly enlightening: it evokes notions of Cartesian meditation by the light of a little stove and of drunks who totter around with a theodolite or a royal measure in their hands. On the rare nights in June when the cloud of gas has dissipated and the tropical heat doesn't sully the atmosphere, from a vantage point in the Ensanche a person can see the severe and harmonious movements that Newton imposed on our dreams. On those nights, it's possible to forget the carnage that came later. And so, like a balloon batted about by two contrary winds, I give up my usual descent to the Ramblas on rainy days to sink instead into this backwater, this purgatory for the middling soul.

January 21st

That's the way it is! Today, after reading the paper and smoking my first cigarette (the day looks a bit green), it came to me in a single image. To get to the point: my life is reduced to a single passion because that's all I can keep going. Having two passions, three passions, FOUR PASSIONS! That would be sheer excess! With one, I have more than enough. However, I *have* known multipassionate individuals. One of them, a Mexican, used to go into fits of rage at the mere sight of his girlfriend, a lass from Valencia with a cow-like character. Yet at the very moment when he was raising a huge fist to strike the poor thing, he would freeze, his eyes popping, and then his arms would fall, his hands open, he'd drop to his knees and embrace the girl's legs shouting, You bitch, you bitch. He loved her, he used to tell us, but hopelessly, because a woman always wrecks an artist's life. Then, still on his knees, he would notice that Amparo had not gotten rid of the ring an old rival had given her. Overwhelmed by a new and more furious attack of rage, he would floor her with a horrible blow. We would try to restrain him, and he would calm down, an expression of beatific serenity in his eyes. Don't get mad at me, don't get mad at me, he would tell us, looking toward the window where the light of the afternoon was fading. He would drop beside Amparo as though struck down and embrace her laughing and crying. That's what faith in God is like, he would shout, and redemption — don't you see, mine and yours too, will cure all our ills . . . In those transcendent moments, you could see him shine like an allegorical painting of Charity. I was profoundly envious.

I've also had friends who have surrendered to their passions — who've become saints, criminals, heroes and traitors — without ever essentially changing. You could spot them through every transformation, like a mountain through a veil of mist, a thick cloud, the noonday sun or a curtain of rain. Their unity admitted a plurality. Not mine. I've limited myself to a single passion, and I've been working on it patiently without taking much interest in the results. This passion has no name, but it's not short of adjectives: it's a vindictive, sullen, bad-tempered sort of passion, and it's not even remotely amusing. I need hardly add that it's a modern, urban passion, unadorned by classical tradition. A dry, bristly passion, the color of industrial light, the luminosity of neon, a dead light whose brilliance reveals a mercantile soul — that is, a MALIGNANT light. It was created so that false nights, nights for men, not for animals or for plants, could exist. On my strolls and wanderings, I'm choked by a sense of sexual oppression every time I cross a beam of that dead light.

January 22nd

The greatest invention ever is the furnished apartment, a revolting place where we can mistreat the fixtures, the furniture and the fittings because we don't give a damn; they're not ours. And yet we pay a scandalous price for them. As far as mine goes, it's a niche that forms part of the Ovidi Apartments (on Ovidi), a building intended for couples making quick stopovers, for long-term affairs and for free-lance prostitution, a place no one plans to stay. Because of some caprice on the part of the speculator, the building was thrown up on a narrow, pentagonal lot. As a result, there's not a single right angle in my apartment. The walls reach the corners as if by chance, like those *chekas* where so many unhappy souls had time to examine their consciences. For me, the red hordes are still active, and their name is Ovidi. When I wake up with a hangover, it takes me a long time to shake off my nightmares, and for a good while I make a pointless effort to straighten out the walls.

I feel bound to this *cheka* for a reason: it's stimulating. No matter how late I've fallen asleep, I can't stay in bed in the morning because a tremendous racket of horns honking and people cursing inevitably wakes me up. My only window opens on a narrow street (Ovidi) that is jammed every morning, afternoon and night. Starting at seven-thirty, thousands of motorized employees confront thousands of motorized mothers who are trying to deposit their children at schools in San Gervasio and Bonanova, that cradle of Catalonian pedagogy where hundreds of thousands of education centers have accumulated, taking advantage of the low prices, fiscal advantages, pious inheritance and brash swindles, in short, of everything that underlies a good Catholic education. As a result of these advantages, between seven and eight o'clock every morning hundreds of thousands of Catholics honk at each other in order to assert their right to be tortured. And they do it right under my window.

My living-room is also my dining-room and my bedroom. It's amazing that it's not my bathroom as well. All this unification of functions leads to a considerable savings on heat. On top of the table are piles of newspapers — almost all copies of *El País* — a container of ATO brand milk (gone sour), Bic pens (with and without caps), a package of dried-up Bimbo Bread (with green edges), assorted socks, a key chain from Renault (no keys), the volume of Jules Laforgue's complete poetry, the laundry bill, various bottles (purchased late at night, as the labels suggest: Toreador Gin, González Vodka), a nail-clipper case, a bus pass (issued by our excellent municipal government), three packets of Alka-Seltzer . . . That's the table. The floor is more highly ornamented.

The apart-hotel, as it's called, has a cleaning brigade — complete with handkerchiefs on their heads and green-striped aprons — that works from ten until twelve, but for the reasons I cited earlier, by that time I've already come back from my morning stroll and am either sleeping or writing these notes. As a result, the apartment hasn't been cleaned in the last twenty days, and it's beginning to look the way I like. The lavatory (I use the bidet) and the so-called "kitchenette" are even better.

I'll never be able to leave this place. It suits me perfectly. It keeps my adrenaline level high and never lets me get a good night's rest. To top it all off, if I stay here any longer than three hours at a stretch, I run the risk of going absolutely crazy. So I'm forced to keep a modern, Spanish pace. Right now, it's beautiful: the racket produced by the honking horns, my indigestion, the wire that cuts through my head, the instability of the room all inspire me with a wild enthusiasm. Through the window I hear someone yelling our popular Catalonian expression: *Malaïts seguin els sacraments!* (May the Sacraments damn you to Hell!).

I walk to the bidet, wash my face, put on what I wore yesterday and the day before and the day before the day before and so on for a count of seven, and step out to buy tobacco, because it always runs out on me before I go to sleep.

January 23rd

The poverty of the great cities has, on occasion, the grandeur of a vanquished empire. Today I saw a decrepit but dignified old man seated at the inexhaustible entrance of the Cataluña-Ramblas metro station. In his hand was a sign on which he had written in pencil: "Shoelaces tied here." Beside him was his upturned cap. This fellow is an emperor of poverty. All he has left are his fingers and an ability that, unfortunately, is widely disseminated: he can tie shoelaces. I remember seeing a similar case in Istanbul that was so majestic it took my breath away. Squatting beside a rather beaten-up, modern bathroom scale, an ancient man sold your WEIGHT. It took me some time to nose around the market, and during that time not a single soul needed to weigh himself. After a few hours, the old man put the scale under his arm and headed up the street, maintaining an uneasy equilibrium. Business was not good, but that ancient Turk at least had a machine; he was an INSTRUMENTAL beggar, and so he enjoyed the same hierarchical level as guitarists and accordion-players. I also saw magnificent examples in Mexico: Indians wrapped in blankets, sitting next to a stretched-out piece of rag; on the rag there would be two matches, a toothless comb and an empty box of aspirin. No matter how minute their business was, it gave them something to fall back on before making the decisive leap to riches.

When the big day comes, the Christian cities will provide spectacles of poverty far superior to Bombay or Port-au-Prince. Oh, we've almost forgotten her fangs now, but Mother Nature will be waiting for us around the corner when the great democratic idyll comes to an end and the wolves are separated from the sheep by something more than a vote. A childhood friend of mine, Bartolo, turned off in the direction of poverty. People even saw him going through garbage cans and dipping the crusts he found in puddles of rainwater. I talked to him when he was in the last stages of his descent. It was remarkable. He was convinced that his was an intellectual experience.

January 24th

To avoid falling into doubt, I answer my own question — "Why am I writing this diary?" — at least three times a week. Each time the answer is new, different and cumulative. These days I have a real arsenal of NEEDS that I can satisfy only by writing this diary. As a consequence, then, writing this diary is

— or if it's not, it should be — my only obligation. It's the only obligation of a trivial man. This week, for example, my answer to the question "Why am I writing this diary?" will make it possible for me to keep on writing for at least six more days.

In general (let's make concessions, let's be kind) there's a *modern* tendency to respond in the following way: "I'm writing this diary because I'm writing just for myself and enjoying absolute freedom of self-expression." But this week at least, my case is just the opposite: not only am I not writing for myself, but I'm also writing with the express intention of not allowing any of the multiple My-Selves that inhabit me to encroach on or to tyrannize over me. The hard part is to prevent an ephemeral section of my soul from taking over and turning me into a "man of great character." So this week's answer is: I'm writing this diary because I have nothing to say to myself — and who needs it anyway.

January 25th

Now I'm going to explain why I detest poetry. I shove the packages of cigarettes aside, and the free spirits appear. I scratch my three-day beard, and the Great Artists remind me of pirates in an operetta; I see them brandishing swords made out of tin. Were they all like that? Did anyone ever manage to make a huge effort and raise himself above the level of this trivial city with its silly streetcars and bad brandy? There was one. Someone whose sword could kill. But he always believed that he was playing at pirates. His naked blade whistled over our heads without his even remotely suspecting that he could decapitate one of us. It's true, he had an iron will sus-

tained by a catastrophic physique. Because of his long neck
and his Palestinian nose, he had always been known as the
Buzzard, except for a brief early period (with the Jesuits) when
he was called Bone-Breaker. He was the son of an architectural assistant who had made a fortune in conjunction with
Mayor Porcioles by using materials from the city dump to
build cages for large families. He's responsible for a lot of the
buildings that have ruined this city, giving it the look it still
has of an ox decorated by Franco. During the fifties, everything was high-rise, from the most ordinary military headquarters to the main office of a savings bank.

I first met the Buzzard one day when he was stealing books.
He was with the Wise Man, an equally extraordinary character
that I don't feel like talking about now. I came upon the two of
them at Señor Daroca's, a peaceful little bookstore, devoted to
old and secondhand volumes. All the book thieves in the university (which lay close by) were familiar with Señor Daroca's
toupee. Over a period of many long years, Señor Daroca had
elaborated a philosophical cosmology that allowed him to explain absolutely everything according to two principles: (a) the
velocity at which the Earth moves through the universe, a velocity calculated manually with phenomenal strings of numbers,
and (b) the mixture of blood and hybridization of race, an element that invigorates any culture. Señor Daroca had a weakness for explaining his cosmology to anyone who fell into his
clutches. He had published it under an assumed name and at his
own expense, and he would mix a few copies of the treatise in
with the books that were always piled up on tables in the store.
From time to time, he would pretend to notice a copy by chance.
Good heavens, he would exclaim. I believe it's Aníbal Asdrúbal's

philosophical cosmology (that was the pseudonym), an edition that's *ex-treme-ly* hard to find! If the person who was there to buy books or just to have a look-round didn't know Señor Daroca, he would fall for it. In this way, Señor Daroca had been selling the books one at a time for fifteen years.

There is a delightful little trick lions use when they hunt gazelles: the lioness frightens them, and just as they start thinking they're getting away from their executioner, they fall into the jaws of the lion, who has been waiting for them quite comfortably, couched in the grasses, humming a little tune. In the same way, while the Buzzard and Señor Daroca were discussing the possibilities for invigoration that might be realized by crossing a black pygmy and a peasant from the Ampurdán, a possibility that years later would turn out to be quite practicable, the Wise Man was stealing a gigantic cloth-bound copy, complete with gilt end papers, of *The Spanish and Spanish-American Enlightenment.* The Wise Man had managed to insert the huge volume under his blue plastic Piuma D'Oro raincoat, but unfortunately, without his realizing it, the seat of the coat was tucked up and the book obtruded like a tail. Señor Daroca could not be deceived with the same impunity as the gazelle. The Buzzard said good-bye with exquisite courtesy and began to make his way toward the door, giving little pats to a pile of Coyote stories, leafing casually through a history of Spain, in short, covering up. I was on the opposite side of the book laden tables so I could see the Wise Man's scandalous rear-end and even relate it to the ferocious grimace that was extending from Señor Daroca's chin up to his toupee. When the bookseller shouted his characteristic "eh, *malparit!* You little son of a bitch!" the Buzzard and the Wise Man took off at full speed, and I joined them out of a sense of *esprit de corps*. Once they had made the corner on the Calle de Aragón, the Buzzard and the Wise Man turned to look back without stopping, but when they spotted me, they sped up like meteors. I caught up with them at the Ronda Universidad, not because of my speed, but because the Wise Man, exhausted by the weight of *The Spanish and Spanish-American Enlightenment*, got tangled up with the volume and fell flat on the ground. He looked like a ham wrapped in newspaper. I was very young then, and the only comment that came to mind was the legendary "Don't worry. I'm one of you." The Buzzard responded by grabbing me around the neck with pincer-like hands. Not only was he strong, he was also a pioneer of the martial arts in Spain, and he would certainly have crushed me if it hadn't been for the complaints of the Wise Man, who couldn't get up on his own.

I was taken aback by the nature of the object they had stolen. What dark design impelled the two of them to pursue that huge volume? Why didn't they go for books by Camus, Pratolini and Franz Fanon, like everyone else? It has taken me years to understand the transforming mechanism of poetry, to understand that a miracle produced from insignificant elements — a piece of necktie, a postage stamp, the smell of a certain dry cleaner's — can bring the dead to life. But the Buzzard and the Wise Man were already poets even though they hadn't realized it at the time. Years later, in the late sixties or early seventies, the Wise Man would come to that awareness and would exploit it with the terrible tenacity of a mining engineer. But not the Buzzard. The Buzzard never did.

Their choice of *The Spanish and Spanish-American Enlight-*

enment was justified on poetic grounds, which are as eccentric and tyrannical as scientific grounds and just as futile too. On page after page of that volume, absurd prints of, say, a sugarcane worker on the Mendoza Plantation would nestle cheerfully up against equally mad plates depicting, for example, the wedding of a colonel with royal connections. Here the mechanism that makes things come to life was working full-steam. That picture of dirty, emaciated natives gathered around a Belgian explorer in full regalia had the same effect as a ball of opium; it felled the addict, admitting him to a world of pain and caprice, God the Father's historical zoo. Take the case of a certain Señorita Pallarés, who was married to a government lawyer named Gómez Tortajada. Pictured in that volume, her face, which was somehow both nunnish and a bit donkey-like, leaped out from oblivion into the infinite space of memory — a memory of someone who never existed — and took on the romantic beauty of gala balls and deaths in childbirth. Consigned to nothingness, Señorita Gómez Tortajada née Pallarés, came back to life in the intoxicated brains of two Catalonian zealots. And so, the residue of history, that garbage dump of the collective memory, became the raw material for a desperate and amoral art.

The Buzzard was the master-of-ceremonies, the Wise Man and I, the novices. Each of us learned a different lesson, since effective teaching — the kind that relies on example rather than theory — shares the virtues of water: it fertilizes what lies deep in the seed-bed, but slides over the stone. We learned to eat by watching someone devour his food. Our classes took place in a bar in the Plaza Letamendi, a bar made up of two iron tables (unpainted), a number of barrels, and a cal-

endar (compliments of Mateu's Long-Distance Hauling) picturing a typical figure from the Canary Islands: a water-carrier with
African thighs and huge Galician tits. Here the Buzzard began
to point out the veins of ore hidden beneath the asphalt. I'll
never forget his chortles of laughter when he saw me with a
book by Jorge Guillén, whose poetry enjoyed great esteem at
that point thanks to his status as exile. He also forbid me to
read Lorca ("with his little business in castanets and
mantillas"), Alberti ("a peddler"), Neruda ("an infamous deco-
rator"), León Felipe ("a braggart"), Unamuno ("he choked
on a cassock"), Ortega y Gasset ("a whorehouse that reeks of
stew") — in short, all of Spanish literature from 1680 on.
The foreign authors he demolished by using authorized quotations: "Tolstoy is a satyr crushed by the weight of the Cross,"
"The real ideologue of the Third Reich is Kafka," and so on.

On one occasion, I interrupted his iconoclastic delirium
with a timid "How about Proust?" — Proust was familiar to me
because a high school friend named Cucurella had lent me the
first volume of Salinas's translation, complete with an enormous
egg stain that had soaked through as far as page 648. The Buzzard replied with a terrible expression: "Zero," and underlined
his remark with a magnificent gesture that could have produced
its full effect only in an amphitheater. The opposite of "zero," a
category applied to only the most amazing works of genius, was
"God." In the hotel reserved for the immortals, far above the
places assigned to the common lot, reposed Guido da Verona.
You *had* to read Guido da Verona. Each time his name was
pronounced, the Wise Man, who was a few lessons ahead of me,
confirmed: Yes, yes, he's God, he's God.

Reading Guido da Verona was no simple task: no matter

how Godlike he was, you could only find copies of his works at the secondhand book dealers; not the ones on Aribau, those aristocrats of the used book trade, but the ones who presided over stands in the port, the dregs of the business. Generally these copies had lost their covers and were falling apart. But to the Buzzard this was a mere detail; covers were for women's magazines. The first almost complete copy I found was titled *The Book of My Wandering Dream*. A locomotive crossed the cover from left to right. Under the iron wheels a dead girl was giving birth to a rose that lay over her stomach. The inside jacket blurb began: "Something of the fever of the gambler shines in his eyes." It ended with this extraordinary sentence: "Not one of those miserly writers who give a poor return on your investment, he is a living capital." The editor put his name to it. Later on, I got hold of other masterpieces: *The Man Who Was Two; Let Down Your Hair, Mary Magdalene; The Woman Who Was Found on a Train*, and others.

At an immense distance from Guido da Verona, we had permission to read a Peruvian translation of Macpherson's *Ossian*, treatises on teratology, Hoyos y Vinent's *feuilletons*, Herrera y Reissig's poetry, the memoirs of a postal worker whose name I've forgotten, London's *The Pilgrim of the North Star* (but only that novel), some very carefully selected D'Annunzio, like *Maybe So, Maybe Not: A Novel about Aviation* . . . This last work had an unforgettable opening that can only be compared to the chords of some heroic symphony: "Maybe, answered the lady, offering up a faint smile as she pressed on heroically into the wind that whipped her long veil so that it shimmered like the silver willows on the fleeing plain down below." Reading these books took your breath away.

Confronted by the will to power, a stench that infected the work of those severe intellectuals and artists of the post-war period, the Buzzard had opted for defeat. We pursued it with a warrior's zeal. Later on, I came to know more poets, and in all of them I felt I'd once again glimpsed that deep and desolate game. Ten years later, for example, I made friends with a Philippine poet named Leónidas Melilla. Melilla only read old volumes he'd bought for a shilling from the outdoor book stands on the Charing Cross Road, where they display goods no one even wants to steal. I still remember two of his finds, both of them treasures: a history of the banana, and a manual describing the practical uses of the icebox. History books recount only the acts of destruction; they say nothing about what's been destroyed — who cares? This, then, is the poetic passion: to restore what has been destroyed and to mock the kind of people who always have to be on the winning side. Including God. Bartolo Madera was another one, a poet who opted for destruction. I never saw him read anything but *Esoteric Cuisine* (Cutrecases) or *Solomon's Navel* (Azencot). Filtered through his brain, these wretched works were transformed and endowed with life. In the same way, the history of the banana, once intended for speculators, horticulturists and merchants, acquired its real meaning only when it fell into the hands of a man for whom it was not intended. And this man saw in its pages nothing useful, practical or moral, nothing but a wild joke dreamed up by the Absolute Being. So the banana becomes a prank carried out by a God that's *loco*. Today I'm drinking the Orinoco. Sweet Jesus! What rubbish!

January 26th

Monotony. When it rains, especially if it only rains a little, poverty really stands out. I have to keep an eye on my appearance. Today I caught myself by surprise in the mirror of a public lavatory. I'd accidentally dropped my Bic, and when I straightened up, I came across my own gaze. It took me a while to recognize myself. I haven't cleaned up in a number of days: a few sprinkles of water in the bidet, a few scrapes of the toothbrush (there's no toothpaste left) . . . Between the shape of my head and my bristly, grizzled beard, I look like some sort of efflorescence in the desert. This is what I would have looked like had I been of humble birth, hmmmm. I could also be Professor Umrat a few months after he enjoyed the favors of the splendid Lola-Lola. But I don't want to look like this. It's just an effect of the first feeling of euphoria, a beginner's slip-up. Tomorrow without fail, I'll go to a drugstore and buy razor blades, soap and a brush. Or better yet, to a barbershop, that most humane of all public establishments. I'll have the barber trim, shave, wash, rinse, rub, perfume, and grease me. My head will feel like a hairy plaything in the hands of a child, like something that has nothing to do with me. I'll be both sovereign and decapitated, a French monarch at high noon. I'll glance through a pornographic magazine, study the cabinet ministers' shoes, their wives' necklines, the great Amazons' bathrooms, the highly honored magnates' gardens . . . that's the ontological substratum of the barbershop, preserved these days in its basest form: the glossy mags. All of the great cultures, from Imperial Rome to the absolute monarchies, have spoiled their hairdressers. It's an unequivocal sign of moral grandeur and victorious oppression.

But not yet. I'll spend a few more days nestled in the warmth of this beard, this dirt, as if I were bundling myself up in what I could have been. In what I can be as soon as I decide.

January 27th

Mid-afternoon, the city's dead. I'm killing time in different cafes. Especially (very especially) the Velodrome. It hasn't stopped raining. When I see the wet streets, I feel an impetuous nostalgia for the bells. For time in its musical aspect. The people around here have a peculiar way of measuring time because of their bells. They tell it according to how much of the hour has passed, always jumping ahead to the next hour. So: when it's ten-thirty by Castilian time, it's half of eleven here; and when it's ten-forty-five there, it's three quarters of eleven here. This predilection for fractions, for quarters and halves that precede an hour instead of accompanying it, fragments our existence, makes it baroque and creates an almost Islamic sense of finitude. It's essential to bear in mind that the inhabitants of this city spent ninety years, from 1773 to 1865, without a clock because they were being punished by their Castilian masters. For ninety years — decisive years involving the urban expansion, social solidification and psychic composition of the city — they told time according to quarters and halves without any official help. The shock was so strong it's doubtful if we'll ever be able to tell time any other way.

The punishment neatly defines the brutal aridity of our feudal lords. Depriving a whole people of the sound of their bells! The punishment was imposed on May 4th, 1773, after a peal of the Honorates bell that went against all orders. An insolent, subversive peal that the hirsute functionaries of the crown just couldn't stomach. From then on, time was drawn and quartered. When a bell finally struck the hour once again — the Eulalia bell on the Day of the Dead, 1865 — it no longer mattered. Everyone who needed to know the time had already gotten a watch — back then they were called "repeaters." But by that time, too, the city's soul had been formed; it was stamped with a fractured sense of time.

Just to prove my point, I ask someone in the street what time it is. The passerby hesitates, perplexed. He looks at his watch, vacillates, doesn't know which method to go for. Finally he settles for pointing at the dial with his index finger and looking me in the eye as though he'd been forced to reveal a physical defect. The gesture means "figure it out for yourself."

January 28th

Overwhelmed by the weather, which is leaden, unpleasant, *inhuman*, I continue my memoirs of the banal and evoke, once again, the Buzzard, who had no money but lots of resources. That's what people used to say: "he's a boy with RESOURCES." If instead of that they said "he's a boy with MONEY," the fellow might be suspected of having acquired wealth by means of his own efforts, and that was equivalent to the horrifying characterization "new rich." It's not at all easy to explain the Buzzard's singular opulence unless you realize that in the sixties only laborers worked. Worse yet: if you weren't a laborer, you would never even see a real laborer. It was impossible. Oh, a few people — overseers, architectural assistants, social service doctors, two or three ecclesiastics, a handful of clandestine political organizers . . . in short, very few — did manage to see them, but only when they were gathered *en masse* and (to put it in simple terms) raised to a very high degree. Moreover, these people could never see things clearly. They either insisted that the workers were a terrible nuisance *period*, or they decked them out in so many fine-sounding adjectives that they sounded like the best and the most misunderstood people to walk the earth since Christ had died on the cross.

Considering, then, what a reduced and squalid world we lived in, it was relatively easy to guess the origin of everyone's spending money. But the Buzzard had no money — I mean he didn't belong to the order that has its expenses paid — and yet he spent money anyway. For a while it was a deep mystery, a mystery that hit me between Guido da Verona and Guido da Verona and which I discussed at length with the Wise Man, who was also completely in the dark. Until we finally found out where he got his money. He won it playing poker.

A guy who's not yet twenty, who reads Guido da Verona and earns his money playing poker is a pretty dangerous character. The influence he exercised over the Wise Man and me was enormous, devastating. I made my discovery on the day he beat me out of two thousand *pesetas* that should have lasted until the end of the month. At the same time, I found out he cheated. On that occasion, he was using Silvano Cafetti as a confederate. Cafetti wasn't his real name, but a nickname he had gotten because he was crazy about coffee and car races. Boys don't usually like coffee, but Cafetti ingested it by the gallon. He also spent a lot of time making noises with his mouth and moving his arms as though he were changing gears and holding on to a steering wheel.

Even when the Buzzard was exposed as a cardsharp, he still refused to return my money. Instead of getting mad, I begged him to teach me his tricks. Youth has this great virtue: confronted with true nobility, it doesn't stand on a sense of dignity, but humbles itself with gaping mouth. The Buzzard was the noblest person I had met in that city of black-marketeers and, fortunately for me, he reacted favorably. Over a period of three exalted months that summer, we left Tote Romeu, Pep Fontanella, Jordi Loberdos, Quim Vilaplana, Andrés Pantaleoni and Nani Puig-Xicoy — all of them owners of Seat 600s — in a state of complete ruin and desperation. In a series of exhausting and glorious games, I played the part of Silvano Cafetti (simultaneously cultivating the jewel-like expression of a Guido da Verona hero). I have to admit that the Buzzard would have won even without cheating, so it was hard to convince him afterwards to give me my part of the take.

When classes started again, we stopped seeing each other, but in early October the Wise Man called a meeting. He was shrewd and tenacious, and these gifts, which he would employ artfully later on, had paved the way for him to become a member of the jury of the Maresme poetry prize (we never referred to it as anything but "Marasmus"), which was financed by José Félix Guardiola, the director of a publishing house that brought out his own books. According to the Wise Man, the time had arrived to make off with eight thousand *pesetas*. He himself couldn't enter the competition since he was a member of the jury (not one to give up easily, even on

apparently impossible possibilities, he had submitted the problem to a minute analysis before admitting as much). I couldn't
see entering my work, and this opinion was rapidly and roundly
seconded by my cohorts. But the Buzzard had only written A
poem: he had never dreamed that in order to be a poet he
would be expected to write verses. However, eight thousand
pesetas was a goodly sum; so the Buzzard decided to write a
book of poems that very night and enter it the next day. The
Wise Man and I were a bit stunned by his decision, but we
never doubted for a minute that he was serious about it. The
Wise Man told him timidly that he had twenty days to turn
it in, but the Buzzard refused to waste more than one night
on such a useless business. The next day at noon, he handed
us a book entitled *Criminal and Martial*. The poems were all
there, sitting on top of a table in the Boliche Bar. We devoured them on the spot, accompanied by French fries and
San Miguel beer. We were wild about them; he was God. If
he won the prize, the Buzzard said, he would keep five thousand *pesetas* and give each of us one thousand five hundred.
The Wise Man protested. In the end, it was as important to
have a jury as to have a book, both were essential, and so he
refused to take any less than the Buzzard. Finally they reached
the following agreement: four thousand to the Buzzard for
having written the book, three thousand to the Wise Man
for giving him the prize, and one thousand to me if I typed up
the poems. No one doubted that we were going to win. With
a remarkable intuition, the Buzzard declared that only bach-
elors make the cut in these competitions, so the Wise Man
needed to make sure that only married poets got to the finals.
And, in fact, that's the way it worked out. In November we

divided up the money, and at the end of a year the book was published with a beautiful, cobalt-blue cover. At the last minute, the Buzzard had changed the title for commercial reasons. Now it was called *The Dwarf Bride*. You still see copies from time to time in the used book stores. It's as arrogant and enigmatic as *The Divine Comedy*, but shorter.

The Buzzard decided those eight thousand *pesetas* were only the beginning. With that kind of money we could risk a "grown-up game," that is, a high-stakes game with profits running over twenty thousand *pesetas*. He chose as his objective the casino in Sitges, a spot frequented by merchants who'd gotten rich in the Civil War and by corrupt policemen. I didn't think I had enough training to play fast and loose with those jackals; so I refused to go with him. Anyway, my uncle Braulio, a nut who had signed more than a hundred execution orders in 1939, staked whatever money he could steal from his wife there. Even Guido da Verona would have exulted in that scene. The Buzzard headed off toward the railway station like an arms dealer, with eight thousand *pesetas* in one pocket and a book by Jean-Jacques Pauvert — pictures of naked women — in the other. His last words were: It might go as high as fifty thousand. And then, looking at the Wise Man: In that case, count on getting a copy of Cansinos's *One Thousand and One Nights*.

We didn't see him again for many years. I don't know the details, but they caught him giving himself the bottom card when he was dealing. An understandable arrogance must have pushed him to disaster; the temptation to deceive the biggest sharks with the commonest trick would have been almost irresistible. Fortunately, illegal society is much kinder than legal society. Each crime has its tribunal and its punishment, but they take into consideration the difference between a wastrel and a potentate. The Buzzard was fined three hundred thousand *pesetas* and banned from all the gambling houses in Catalonia. Obviously, he couldn't pay such a sum. The situation was dire: in case of delay, these people would resort to a physical form of compulsion that involved a series of warnings and culminated in a tumble near the curve where my parents sailed into the sea. But the Buzzard had an aunt who owned a stationery shop, an aging, pious woman, armored with the kind of pathetic love for her nephew that often occurs in people who have no descendants. It was God's will that this aunt should belong to the Opus Dei. Through the mediation of a priest who had connections with the Virgin of Padua Residence, she managed to place the Buzzard in the order's refuge in the Huesca Pyrenees. This center was officially dedicated to biological research, but it might well have been a clandestine biochemical laboratory. Hidden in that remote spot, the Buzzard escaped from his pursuers. And that's where he conceived the passion that was to dominate the rest of his short life: ornithology. Years later he contracted matrimony with a well-heeled widow from Zaragoza and settled into a hamlet a couple of miles from Egea de los Caballeros. He led a peaceful life, played gentle games of cards in the Military Cultural Center, studied Pyrenean biotopology, and founded the Association for the Protection of Scavengers by means of a series of agreements with the Environmental Protection Agency and the Ministry of Government. In early 1980 they found his dead body in a buzzard's feeding place near Calaceite. He had apparently slipped off a cliff even though it was an area he knew like the palm of his hand.

I recall the Buzzard with the greatest pleasure. He just escaped becoming an artist or an intellectual. For me, he will always be the NATURAL incarnation of poetry. The Wise Man, like females in classic tales, sacrificed his life to flesh out his friend's intuitions. His first published work, the one that would launch him on the last page of the newspapers, was a brilliant book of poetry entitled *Guide to Verona*, a book so rich in surprising images and unexpected music it seemed like the work of a guitarist. It was, to make things simple, an homage to Errol Flynn, who formed an essential part of the Buzzard's pantheon. He also published an anthology of D'Annunzio's work with a prologue praising the poetry of Ramón de Basterra and Agustín de Foxá that provoked the ire of leftist versifiers. This sentiment was aggravated by the fact that they couldn't publish a single verse in the Franco press without using so many euphemisms and simulating so many bows and scrapes that they wound up sounding like Ramón de Basterra and Agustín de Foxá themselves. For months you could hear them rattling about pointlessly in their hiding place at the Ministry of Information and Tourism, that little bastion of liberal ideas, like beetles on a hot frying pan.

Impelled by his memories of the Buzzard, the Wise Man launched a meteoric career. In his first interviews, he only talked about obscure Mexican poets and swore that he read nothing but sixteenth-century Japanese poetry: an early indication of his great talent for conning people. In two years' time, he had dethroned Gabriel Celaya, Pureza Canelo, Mario Angel Marrodán, all the Adonais prize winners, the poets published

or showcased by *Insula, El Cierro, Indice, Poesía Española,* by
every ministerial or paraministerial, episcopal or paraepiscopal
review, and he was beginning to assault the bastions of university poetizing. He grew until he fulfilled his intellectual
promise. When it was opportune, he backed off from his pyro-
technical origins, got a grip on himself, renounced everything
he had ever written, published a work of negative theology, and
was immediately proposed for a chair at the Autonomous
University of Bellaterra here in our bucolic suburbs.

Lately in my disorderly morning walks when I flee from the
sound of honking horns, I've seen him heading toward the
Tibidabo metro station. He doesn't recognize me any more, but
he has hardly changed. He still has the noble cranium he had
then, and the straight, silky hair that brushes his shoulders like
those romantic visionaries who once dreamed of getting elected.
Everything he publishes is interesting. It's the public form of an
ongoing monologue inspired by guilt, the voice of Segismundo
legislating in his ergastulum. I am deeply sorry that he no longer
devotes himself to poetry. The last volume that came out, back
in 1973, under the title *Ser Deserto,* involved a single, violent
scene. The cold light of the dead illuminates a nasty, bourgeois
parlor. On a nineteenth-century bureau is a crucifix without a
figure, resting against a pack of Ducados. The blurred luminosity of dawn comes in through the window. At the door, his back
to the narrator, the Wise Man is trying to force the lock. He
can't get out, but he's afraid to look through the window. He
tries to open the door by using the crucifix as a lever. At that
moment, a voice is heard. The book ends there, when the Wise
Man hears the voice and asks himself in a rush of terror: Sweetie-
pie? Did it say Sweetie-pie? It's a philosophical poem whose

dazzling metaphorical richness sparkles against that dark background like tropical fish against a black lacquer wall.

January 31st

For twenty minutes I've been contemplating the volume left behind by that girl who said she studies languages. Or rather A language. I don't even want to think about feeling like reading it. It's the complete edition (*Complete Poems*, ah hah!), the one that has it all . . . and that always bothers me. On the cover, next to the author's name (Laforgue, *furca*, our names condemn us) are some handwritten verses and caricatures by Laforgue himself. The first verse in the book is so French that it makes you laugh: *Nous nous aimions comme deux fous.* The fall of the Bastille left the French, once and for all, in the hands of their *coeur. Écoeurant!* I read Laforgue a long time ago, following the Buzzard's lead. I remember him as a Baudelaire in rags. More burnt-out than Baudelaire. Rags, fits and rancor confronting richness, calm and pleasure.

Books are powerful enemies. Books of poetry are the MOST POWERFUL enemies. You reach out your hand, open it, read *tout m'ennuie aujourd'hui. J'écarte mon rideau,* and you can say good-bye to your work for hours and maybe even days. But I close it with a dry snap like the Protestant ministers close their Bible once the victim is condemned. Let others poke around in it. Women and books. Those two words have cost me much too much.

February 2nd

A tremendous hangover. A red wire that cuts through my neck and comes out at the top of my head; invisible fingers move it up and down while a ball of tar dissolves in my stomach. When the need to vomit seizes me, everything in sight sizzles, and a pearl-grey stream spurts out onto the Formica of the table. But I mustn't blame this sad state on the excess of drink, far from it; this affliction is due to commercial folly, a greater source of suffering than asylums, hospitals and prisons. They put trementine in liquor in order to give it more body! Thousands of modest drinkers of both sexes go blind or die squirming like worms thanks to this small savings on the part of the hospitality business. In our society, which still shows the traces of Islam, resistance is a vice we scarcely tolerate: we see ourselves as creatures bound for death.

Yesterday I walked around the little bars in the area known as Raval until I got to the Santa María del Mar neighborhood. I started, however, at the Boa, a more grandiose relic of Latin colonization than the thermal baths at Caracalla. Protected by the sparkling helmet of her hair, the widow was serving mixed drinks. It's obviously not coquetry; it's baldness. People say that in the throes of copulation, the widow deposits her wig on top of a wooden head. In the red half-light, the unsettling wooden gaze sinks into the seducer's spine, inducing an uncontrollable impotence. But there I only drank two vermouths that were almost rustic in their honesty.

Later I headed down toward the port, bumping into vendors selling garters, tobacco, drugs, condoms, newspapers (out of date), socks, fancy combs, who knows what-all, until I reached a little liquor store. It has been set up for serving drinks by the ingenious method of resting a plank across two sawhorses. It's a black-market place, not very far from the old Borne Market, and it has an intriguingly bucolic air that recalls those anthropophagous Catalonians who used to wander around the backwoods with a blunderbuss in hand and who ate nothing but crucifixes that had been dipped in the cold waters of the Cerdaña. At any moment, some guy with enormous biceps tattooed by the painter Sert may show up and kick everyone out into the street. Sometimes it's open; sometimes, not. There's never an explanation. You can only drink what they have on hand, but it's always the best quality and absurdly cheap. Yesterday, for example, we got champagne, not that Moët the Philistines drink, but a thick, dry broth with a bite, served as cold as beer. They're all consignments either stolen directly from the docks or traded for other, equally illegal, merchandise. Underneath the three light bulbs hanging from their cords naked as Jews in news photos, the unlabeled bottles danced the brown-shirt polka. The habitual drunks, serious consumers used to *orujo* and kerosene, turned up their noses at the bubbly. An ancient fellow, who floated inside his baroque rags, a bit of plaster stuck in his ear (it's interesting to note how many odd bits a vagabond accumulates in his ears), whined, It's getting to the point where nobody will come here; you only have drinks for whores. Next to him, a giant with a neck like a chicken's, an acromegalic sprung from a deep Andalusian belly, held a minute glass in his huge hand with the delicacy of an entomologist. He nodded his huge papiermâché head fraternally, his eyes closed and a grimace on his lips. And on Thursday, it was Calisay! he added with an air of *that's that*. It's inhuman!

The back of the place is barely lighted. The wall is covered with ceramic appliques that look old, tiles with motifs relating to guilds or some other Gothic silliness of the kind that's abundant around here. But when I got closer, not so much to look as to stretch my legs, which had fallen asleep, two good-looking, olive-skinned lads with elaborate coifs cut me off. They didn't say a word; they didn't have to. I realized that behind the improvised counter there's a sort of office, like the cubby-holes once reserved for colonial bureaucrats. Seated in an almost Phoenician aura, an Oriental presided over the establishment. Our eyes met, and I have to admit that he made an impression on me. This must be somebody who's involved in the underworld. With a gesture of great elegance, as though he were brushing aside an unpleasant thought or arranging the fluid silk of mandarin sleeves, he signalled for the bodyguards to withdraw. I just wanted to see the tiles, I said. And repented immediately. Why was I apologizing? What memory of enslavement did that unpleasant bit of submission come from? I looked around more calmly (it was a false calm), mastering the situation, but the only thing I managed to do was to see that he wasn't really Oriental; it was just the atmosphere he created around himself. In that state of uneasy equilibrium, I pretended to examine the tiles, feigning valor but on the verge of smiling or doing something else despicable. I returned to the bar slowly, sweating profoundly like those grotesque *hidalgos* from Toledo who are eaten up with lice. I counted out my money and stepped into the open air, feeling as though I'd had my hand on a high-tension wire.

I was in a bad state, a condition of spiritual disorder. I felt subservient, vile, contemptible, a mere scribble compared to the rigorous geometry of that firm, magnificent crook. It's not respect for life that stays my hand, it's servility, I thought, picturing myself confronting the body guards with a switchblade. If it were a pistol, I still wouldn't shoot. It has nothing to do with loving kindness; I just don't have it in me. Like poor Babel facing the cossack who had his guts hanging out. I was so furious that I went back to Raval and drank foolhardily at Casa Ginés, a spot also known as El Mengele. Drinking there was tantamount to poisoning myself, but I needed the one poison as an antidote for the other. The other, of course, was a desire to return to the liquor store and show the kind of violence that converts cowards like us into toughs.

February 9th

I waited so long to go to the barbershop that they almost wouldn't let me in (they would, of course, have slipped a coin into my hand before sending me away). My insistence, however, must have been a bit threatening because the barber stepped back and showed me to one of the empty seats, a stupendous pump-operated machine with an adjustable headrest. I was taken care of not by him, but by a younger and leaner employee with enviable coffee-colored sideburns and an abundance of gold necklaces sporting pacifist, Hebraic, amorous and mystical charms. He dealt with me only after making me wait and change places three times by dint of gentle nudges with his elbow as he dragged his broom over the locks that were spread over the green-tiled floor. And yet we understood each other, and the results were good. His bony fingers manipulated the scissors, the razor and the comb as though they were drum sticks, and I dozed placidly to the sound of the clicking shears. It must have been the smell of talcum power, the fortuitous mixture of perfumes, shampoo, sandalwood, cologne, brilliantine and hair spray that gave the atmosphere a Levantine, almost druggy quality. Once his work was done and he had showed me my occiput in a portable mirror, he shook out his apron with something of the coquetry of a toreador. I paid with great satisfaction, and then something unexpected happened.

This barbershop is located next to a wholesale appliance outlet on Tallers, one of the main streets in the Ramblas. It's a glass box lined with mirrors, with Viennese hat-racks on the walls and a tin parrot at the entrance. To go out you have to pull on a sheet of glass that only opens inward; as a result, people often, quite literally, bump into each other. There's a sign above the knob that says "Pull," but over a period of many years, I have verified the incapacity of our citizens for reacting in time to the subtle difference between "Pull" and "Push." I, for my part, pushed. And I would have kept on pushing if — even before the barber came to my assistance — another client had not installed himself in front of me on the other side of the glass door. Both of us remained silent, waiting for somebody to resolve the dilemma. But my silence was determined by another cause: the client planted opposite me was the pseudo-Oriental I had met the week before in the liquor store. I could see him clearly, and a vague uneasiness assailed me once again. What was so irritatingly peculiar about those eyes that were as thin as eyebrows? I was suddenly struck by something extraordinary: he wore glasses. Round, clear, steel-rimmed glasses. Once you noticed them, they were obvious. But they were such a part of the shape of his cranium that I had no more registered them at first than his nostrils or the five fingers of his hands.

I don't know how long I would have taken to react, sunk as I was in contemplation of that face I REALLY DIDN'T SEE, but soon I felt a soft yet determined pressure, and I began to back up, not without resistance. The door was being opened from outside even though I continued to hang onto the knob. The man didn't make any show of force; he entered slowly, greeted me with a nod and went to the vacant seat. Once I was outside on the Ramblas, I realized that I had known him a long time before our meeting. Perhaps it was only his phenotype that was familiar, but I knew very well what I needed to watch out for: a rabbit doesn't have to be PERSONALLY acquainted with every fox; one's enough. And yet this realization in no way diminished my desire to return to the liquor store. I was driven by a puffed-up, almost prurient desire to assert myself, to blot out that awkward moment, as if history could reverse itself, as if I could really study the tiles next time after thrusting the body guards aside with one sweep of my hand. That, however, is not going to happen. The body guards already know my M.O. Worse yet — I just don't have that kind of class.

February 14th

I'm watching the volume of Jules Laforgue out of the corner of my eye as though it threatened to attack me at any time. A lamprey eel that could suck out my whole substance in order to fatten itself up. That's the way reputations grow. They leave their admirers bare as bones. I don't have the strength to eliminate the volume from my sight, but I let the newspapers pile up on top, and I make sure that the stray spark from a cigarette and the odd splash of gin will get to it so the tome will slowly rot away. Still, I know it's lurking in ambush, there in its hiding place. I have a cervine, or should I say CERVICAL, fear of books. Why are they such terrifying enemies? It has to do with a conviction, that is, an IDEA — but an idea understood in its sensate definition: the forgotten corner of a terrace that suddenly becomes meaningful when we remember having kissed a cousin in that very spot years ago. Anyway, the fear of books has to do with one of those ideas that clearly separates youth from maturity, the idea that gauges the effect of reading on an educated citizen.

In the opinion of every grown-up, right-thinking individual, no matter how much knowledge a consciousness acquires, its possessor continues to be stupid and wicked if that learning was sown on acidic or rough terrain. No stupid man ever stopped being stupid because of a book. A countless number of stupid men have read tons of books. In their youth, however, people have an almost African faith in books. They read with the exaltation of nuns. They even reach the point of penitence, suffering through sublime treatises they don't remotely understand in a kind of ritual of ingestion. The young (including those who are old enough to qualify for retirement) believe that the written word is a potion that will transform the chemical conditions of the soul, producing an immediate benefit in what they usually call the "intelligence." And, in fact, THAT'S THE WAY IT IS. This is the terrible danger they represent. Terrible.

Reading is like manure; it can only stimulate growth that is alive on its own, that is autonomous. Increasing the quantity of fertilizer can increase natural production up to a certain point if the quantity is DISCREET, but an excess burns the shoots and

stifles the free circulation of minerals. Any increment above
this critical point spells ruin. There are frequent cases of brains,
like Unamuno's, that have been laid waste because of their
imprudent optimism about how much fertilizer they could take.

The young believe they can augment the capacity of their
consciousness indefinitely by means of an ascetic program of
cerebral gymnastics when, in fact, all they manage to do is abort
the ridiculous seed they started out with. This explains the degree of silliness rampant among teachers (eternal youths subject
to the most painful acne), obliged as they are to spend their
lives swallowing manure. Knowing the exact limits of our consciousness is an essential condition for learning to read. But
since this planet is governed by a system of adulation, things
work just the other way around. Outcome: a world full of dwarves
hauling around giant corpses on their backs in the conviction
that they'll grow taller that way.

When I, for example, stopped reading, it was already too
late. I had destroyed all the sprouts that could have made my
spirit bear fruit. I had been reduced to a salt lake, laid waste
by fertilizers that had suffocated my spirit. And I held that
sterility in great esteem! Nevertheless, when I stopped reading, when I stopped "increasing my knowledge," as they say, I
felt the same sense of peace someone has when he pulls out a
thorn he has lived with so long he'd forgotten about it. At
the same time, I stopped seeing cultivated people of character. I realized I had aged and now that I'd overcome these
tendencies, I'd be like the old men who sit on park benches
in the sun, reeking of wine. I'd find my only consolation in
the company of animals and children, watching their evolu-
tion from a safe distance and establishing no more contact

than a handful of crumbs tossed into the air.

I'm reminded now of a great philosopher, a friend of my youth. In his whole life, this man read only one — very important — book, and he read it with such intensity that he managed to substitute the author's gears for the cerebral gears he was born with, like someone who exchanges his milk teeth for teeth more appropriate to the life of an adult carnivore. Although it retains a few contemporary peculiarities, his head basically functions with the artificial regularity of that other head. There's no doubt at all that he can resolve any metaphysical problem related to the worries of the inhabitant of a small Prussian town in the 1800s, but he is utterly incapable of dealing with problems that come up every day. This has not presented an obstacle to his happiness, or to his unhappiness. For example: he has managed to avoid taxes with a certain dexterity, but he drives his car like a Tartar, holding on to the wheel as though it were a pair of reins and using the accelerator like a whip. He talks to the car like an ox-driver to his team, urges it on, laughs at it and hits it on the bumpers. He adapts his speed, not to the kind of street he's traversing nor to the density of the traffic, but to the running argument he carries on with himself — or rather, with the artificial head of the Great Departed. If the polemic excites him or makes him mad — which happens with suspicious frequency, as though both heads had not quite managed to get themselves together — the automobile advances at top speed, shudders when he hits the brakes impetuously, and leaves behind a trail of terrified pedestrians. But if he sighs deeply and falls into speculation about the golden sheen of Creation, the car ambles along at twenty miles an hour, giving rise to truly amazing traffic jams. The terrifying honking

of horns that shatters the air is to the philosopher's ears as
the lowing of oxen and the tinkling of cattle bells.

Inserting a complete orthopedic support system into the
soul can only lead to ruin. But it's unavoidable BECAUSE
NOBODY HAS ANYTHING INSIDE until they put something in. So, between an inheritance that crushes you and impotent poverty, there's only one road — one Calvary — you
can take: you must squander your inheritance. First you stuff
your brain full. Then you empty it like a sawdust doll with a
good-sized hole the rotten stuff pours out of. As long as you've
got something left to forget, there's hope. Everyday something
should be eliminated from the memory. This is the famous process known as the Self-Erasing Mind. A method, system and
receptacle that prepare us for dismemberment. Dis-mem-ber-
ment. Everything, inside and out. What's not dismembered, what
clings together, has only a social alternative.

In order to understand the present situation of dismemberment, I'm falling back on an excuse: history has no imagination, and in the absence of ideas, it has decided to repeat a
drama it feels comfortable with. We're re-living the immense
yawn of 1850. A few believers — who have the air of ortho-
dox priests with their unmistakable smell of rotten sardines
— drift about aimlessly. Just like all those people who were
disillusioned by the Commune, these fellows look askance at
the masses, that is, at "everyone who's not like me." The
shrewder ones retrench in lairs with the intention of provid-
ing themselves with a cheap, sterile life. The ones who are
not too sharp, who are a bit thick, go to ruin majestically like
ships whose boilers explode due to the engineers' negligence.

Sometimes, in the street, in the metro, in the National

I.D. line, two old grenadiers run into each other. One of them is now a Hit Man, the other a Burnout Case. Both of them have reached an age when they confirm the hypotheses of the past in order to prove that they WEREN'T JUST HYPOTHESES. The Hit Man sums up the Burnout Case succinctly: he's going to ask me for something. The Burnout Case is just as hard on the Hit Man, whom he always regarded as an idiot. Seeing each other now makes them sick. With a little luck, they can still make THE OTHER ONE pay for their failure. Their old quarrel, they see clearly now, was a grudge between clans. They believed they were joined together out of necessity, but it was suspicious that they did everything on behalf of THE OTHERS, considering that both of them had surmounted — that's what they say, "surmounted" — Christianity and they knew that all sacrifice disguises an even more insidious selfishness. For a few years, they strutted tragically on the cutting edge of freedom, but now, terrified, they recreate the snare that thrust them into the world in the first place.

We're moving into a universal yawn. The weak will be crushed as usual, but a little more than usual. The not so weak will be muzzled as usual, but a little more than usual. The strong will be in demand, as usual, and they will rely on the weak to exist, as usual. Bound hand and foot, the old colleagues are there for the allotment of parts. The masses join in the allotment, grateful for the reappearance of masters and lords who can put things in order. The ones who are left feel let-down when they realize that only one enemy confronts them now: their friend. The same old game is underway again, and the cosmos scratches an insignificant itch. Ho hum.

But I'm generalizing. My own cell keeps me from seeing the

bars. The first step toward getting the little drama underway again is the desire to see things clearly. That's what the sentence consists of: setting myself off from "people who are not like me," that is, people who don't need to see things clearly, who can do without testing since they are their own proof.

Anybody who tries to see things clearly is an enemy, a hired lackey bought off by the Church, a toady who is trying to find solutions (solutions! uh-huh) even though he knows the so-called solutions only amount to hypotheses about a new defense, a new difference in relation to the "people who are not like me," the non-seers, the self-evident.

I'm exaggerating. The night is interminable. It's better to drink. This rage is suffocating me. All of us are abstract at the beginning, that is to say, innocent. You can't live by satirizing the innocent; the satirist is a worm in need of cadavers, but there are dead bodies that still shine in this universal night while no worm ever gives us light.

I must also take into account the people who are never wrong, the people who never lose out through any fault of their own, the people who know what you need to know from the tenderest age — if they ever had a tender age, the people who inherited the black hood and the hatchet from their parents and then settled around the chopping block to jubilant shouts of *bring on the next victim!* They are the strong, and there's nothing you can do about them.

I need to be cold-blooded if I'm really going to achieve banality, if I'm going to answer the question "How can anyone endure these times of ABSOLUTE poverty?", if I'm going to do all this without hiding a single fact from myself. So then, making use of INVALUABLE reports, I answer today that our primordial obligation if we truly want to achieve the dignity of banality (and as long as the light of the world lasts) is to speak well of the animal kingdom.

Laforgue's volume lies breathing under the pile of newspapers, feeding on the spilt gin and coffee. It's a bladder charged with acid, tricked out as a little shepherdess. With amazing innocence, thousands of adolescents inject those rhymes into their thoughts and then doze off in the lap of the ogre. Once infected, they reproduce.

February 15th

The liquor store is on a street with black pavement that winds alongside the apse of Santa María del Mar. It leans against little stands that are manned by old pilgrims from Thailand. With long hair and beards framing waxen faces on top of incredibly thin shoulders, they could have been torn from that same Gothic portal. These peddler-mystics sell papier-mâché dolls, carnival masks, writing implements, puppets . . . in short, goods as innocent as their opium-consumed souls. One of them might have played the flute in Kampala less than ten years ago; after exuding an archaic, yellow outfit complete with ribbons and silks and cheap cotton prints, the notes dried up in his heart. There, in a remote Asiatic corner, his soul crystallized, and there, too, it died for good. The dolls are like their owners, either extraordinarily thin or extraordinarily fat — or should I say "plump" since it's the women who suffer from this glandular inflammation that affects those of a Buddhistic turn. All of them, dolls and humans as well, have a Mongolian air. I examined the dolls carefully, one at a time, without buying a single thing, but neither the dolls nor the owners seemed to care. The fact is, I was only killing time while I waited for the liquor store to open. Hours before, I had studied the great Gothic nave in detail, the pews, the slender columns, the arches and, outside, the buttresses, the figures in the entablature, each acanthus leaf, the rose window, the repulsive pigeons that whiten the grey relief, the Grecian fretwork, the cornices, the metopes, the portals! . . . The truth is, I was bored to death.

From looking at it for so long, I began to think that the basilica was like a garage. For cars. German to be precise, and surely from the Bauhaus. In fact, once you've torn the soul out of it, there's no great difference between this frugal and ascetic Gothic and an industrial construction. If we took the hangars, metro stations, garages, bus terminals and workshops and cut a rosette window in their facades, we'd practically have Catalonian Gothic. In these thoughts I immersed myself while waiting for the place to open.

At six in the afternoon, a tall, fat, blond man, a real Titan, raises the heavy screen with the help of a hanger. He turns on the lights and busies himself inside, laying out planks and barrels — they serve as tables — and a row of glasses on the bar. By seven, half a dozen customers have gathered, and I'm shivering from the cold. To keep from freezing, I start circling the church. I move fast so I won't miss the pseudo-Oriental's entrance on one of my rounds. At eight, I'm half crazy with impatience, fatigue, boredom and hunger. I enter the liquor store and ask for the specialty of the day: a thick, muddy gin. I've never tasted anything like it: it's so viscous that it sticks to the glass like milk. That's when I see the pseudo-Oriental exactly in the same place I first saw him, the far end of the bar, seated like an

Egyptian scribe. He must have come in when I was on one of my Gothic tours. So I didn't manage to catch him by surprise. He may have been sitting there for hours.

I approach him, and this time the toughs don't jump me. Maybe my assured, firm, determined expression has inspired them with trust. So subtle is the boundary that separates the criminal from the cop, and vice-versa, that guards frequently mistake the enemy for a colleague. I situate myself opposite the stranger and greet him in my own good time. He responds courteously. It seems they've been observing my trips around the church for quite a while; perhaps I'm looking for somebody? As I don't respond, he asks if I'm a regular client at the barbershop on Tallers. I still don't answer, because the truth is I don't know what to say, nor what I'm doing stuck there as though I'd taken root. It would take a long time and probably be pointless to tell him that I don't have anything to do all day except for following up the signs that cross my path. Don't you recognize me? he says. Yes, of course, from the barbershop. Then you have a bad memory; don't you remember Cucurella or Podiol?

That was thirty years ago. Podiol, Cucurella and I were in school together, in the same class and the same group, for eleven years. Podiol was a quiet, introverted boy with a tendency to scratch himself. He was always at Cucurella's beck and call. I hadn't heard anything about Podiol since we finished school. Cucurella's case was different. Just the opposite in fact. Brilliant, aggressive and predatory, with a hint of carefully controlled madness, like a Russian epileptic, he was a cool, tough ringleader. I continued to see Cucurella after we started university. At eighteen, he behaved like an adult with criminal tendencies. Crime was the only field that offered any scope to an intelligence so poorly adapted to the legal system. I mean, to *any* system that was legal. One of his more outrageous acts — the systematic robbery of all the blind lottery vendors in his neighborhood — got out, and his family decided to shut him up in a country place they had near Matorell in order to force him to examine his conscience and come to terms with them. During the winter months, shut up with firewood and books — an enthusiastic reader of Rudyard Kipling, Curzio Malaparte, Luys Santa Marina and Folch y Torras, with a taste that inclined toward the picturesque — Cucurella was building up steam. He trained his dog, a mastiff named Chamberlain, with an asbestos glove and a club until it became completely unpredictable, a wild beast with the sidelong gaze of a peasant. In January he went out hunting and shot everything that moved until he had used up the two dozen boxes of ammunition his father had stored away after the Civil War. He even killed cockroaches with those Mauser cartridges. I think he was completely crazy.

In April his father showed up in order to talk to Cucurella and negotiate diplomatic terms: either study engineering or get ready to work in a trucking business the industrialist had set up around Campo de Tarragona, using leftovers from both armies. He didn't have a third option in mind. And we'll never know what the outcome would have been because they didn't exchange a single word. As soon as he raised the entrance beam for the Dodge, Cucurella's father heard the voice of his son urging Chamberlain on. Then there was a leaden-colored mass at his throat. Raised in the country, sturdily built and used to the worst brutality, he had enough strength to seize the animal's head, force open its jaws and kick it into submission. With his neck torn open and his hands mutilated, he got back into the car and managed to reach Matorell, where they stopped the bleeding.

The family was one of those tight-knit, unfriendly tribes so abundant in the Franco era. Under threat of prison, they forbade Cucurella to go near the hospital where his father was convalescing. His three brothers were making sure he'd be cut out of his inheritance. But the father didn't die. Although he was left practically mute, the mastiff hadn't had time to sever any of the interesting little veins and arteries that run up and down the neck. Cucurella, of course, showed up at the hospital. In a repeat of the scene with the mastiff, his mother threw herself at him with her nails out, resorting to a violence one can only admire in a parent. Cucurella had to grab her by the waist and sling her onto a chair as if she were a bale of hay. Then he approached the bed where his father, choked with rage, lay panting and trying to curse him, and showed him an enlistment order from the Captain General's office. I only wanted to tell you good-bye, he said; I'm off to Africa. Later the news got around that he had deserted, and also that he was running a boys' brothel in Melilla. For ten years nobody heard anything about him. Then one fine day, I had a phone call. It was Cucurella, but I didn't recognize his voice. It sounded hollow and abandoned; no, not just that — it sounded as though it had been produced by an electric battery. The conversation was dry and to the point. He arranged to meet me at the Cafe Monza, on the upper part of the Rambla de Cataluña. I waited for him there for more than an hour without quite believing what was happening. By the time I gave up, it had gotten dark. I was just about to take the metro at Provenza when I saw a man who vaguely resembled Cucurella heading down the boulevard. Ten years had gone by! I kept quiet, feeling almost afraid. As he passed beside me, the man looked at me out of the corner of his eye and then pointed to his throat with a sardonic expression that froze my blood. He kept on down the street, and I did nothing to stop him. Even today I'm not sure it was he. It's a confused scene. Two days later I began to think the whole story was too absurd; so I called his parents to find out if they had any news of him. One of the brothers answered the phone, the youngest I think, a fellow with a lot of nerve who wound up destroying the competition from without *and* within the family and who now owns the paternal abode, where the mute father vegetates, shut in like a prisoner. The brother told me that Cucurella had died two months ago in Tangiers. In view of my surprise and confusion, he added, Cancer of the throat, it was all very fast; let's see what he gets up to now in hell.

I've always been convinced that Cucurella feigned his own death in order to punish his family or to prepare the way for a timely reappearance or, more innocently, just to escape the law. I suppose that I must have been part of the plan. Cucurella — I'm sure of this — had gone over the edge long before deserting the legion — if, in fact, he ever deserted.

You know Cucurella, then? I asked the stranger. Yes, I got to know him very well, intimately, in fact. Where? In Africa? The pseudo-Oriental smiled gently, waved his hand with that gesture of brushing away flies and added, On more than one continent. Because of that pedantic answer, I decided to drop the conversation. I was being humiliated again. But he hadn't finished speaking: I know you as well, and you know me. The situation was becoming intolerable. I made a move to leave but without much conviction. I was indecisive, perspiring.

The man smiled: Drop in more often; if you don't see me, ask for me. Who do I ask for? Ask for the Chinaman. Goodnight, friend. The drinks are on me.

It's obvious that he's the Chinaman. And it's equally obvious that I must never go back there again. But an important part of my present work consists of not sawing a single branch off the tree of knowledge. A fruit may grow on any one of them — or a hanged man. There's more: I was much too insistent about paying for my drink, an insistence that only exposed my lack of character. No smiles. No apologies. No obsequious behavior. My God, I'm still trying to improve myself!

February 16th

I can illustrate a variation on the Self-Erasing Brain motif with a pair of opposites: hoarding and squandering. Wealth involves either spending or accumulating. So, for example, my uncle Enrique, surrounded by his leather-bound paperbacks, is feared because of what he has accumulated, but it can't be said that he's rich. In fact, nobody knows if he is or not. The law of the accumulator is to keep his assets secret in order to obtain loans secured against the hidden treasure. This explains the frequency of EMBEZZLEMENT among people who either fail to keep faith with their creditors or are betrayed by somebody who leaks their actual net worth: NOTHING. On the other side of the coin, however, are cases like Virgilio Muelas's. Muelas was an old barroom brawler, long since disappeared, who spent his entire inheritance in two nights. During those two nights HE HAD EVERYTHING HE WANTED. Brief though it was, it is the only example of real wealth that I've ever known. It's absolutely impossible to have wealth without waste.

If you accumulate knowledge, like money, you corrupt your wealth in the interest of converting it into a SENSE OF POWER. But intimidation only provides provisional relief. When you've reached the limit of stupidity, as I have, the only thing that matters is making music with your intelligence and not worrying about the score. The same enigma that underlies *The Critique of Pure Reason* illuminates a sheet of newspaper that's been left behind on a park bench. Sometimes the spirit, tense as a violin, needs only a single word to achieve UNDERSTANDING. I stopped accumulating a long time ago. Now I try to squander. I spend the day playing my brain like a concert musician plays his piano. Not that I claim to be a virtuoso: I play by ear.

February 17th

Everyone who squeezes into the city's narrow ravines becomes aware of the anguished impossibility of changing to a different time. The sensation of escaping from our own time, of inserting ourselves provisionally into a TOTALLY DIFFERENT TIME is vital if we're to avoid falling again and again into mental confusion, even madness. That change from one time to another demands specific places, privileged spaces, but there are no such places in this city. In London, the Burnout Cases take refuge in parks and churches. There they withdraw and pull themselves together, literally; they pull together the dispersed bits of themselves and manage to go on a few more days before committing suicide. In this city, however, there are no parks or churches where you can collect yourself. Our parks are thrifty little bits of ground that seem to have been shipwrecked. No one knows what to do with them; here's a found object called "a piece of sculpture," further on, a rectangle of dirt drenched with wine. Everything is accidental. Everything — and this is critical — is in plain sight. In our temples, it's equally impossible to pull yourself together, to rest and to have a different experience of time. Most of them are mercenary places of worship, dedicated to administrative religiosity. The historical temples like Santa María del Mar seem never to have served the population as refuges from pain and anxiety, but rather as status symbols. And so the unnameable steers clear of them, suspicious of the kind of attention it would receive there. But this, of course, is why the city is so modern — modern, I mean, in the old sense of the word, as it was once applied to Chicago and Montreal: there is not a single space here that escapes modern times.

The same thing has happened in cities that were crushed by the last European war, cities like Rotterdam or Frankfurt that lost their sacred spaces and that now have only commercial monstrosities instead. Here, too, the spaces that lead to contemplation have disappeared, but without the intervention of war. They have been levelled by the free will of our citizens, or SOME of our citizens — the most important ones by definition, since it's the shape of *their* spirit that has determined the shape of the city. Every space here is clinical, exterior. Every space is subjected to the pressure of time present. In moments of enormous tension, there are a few underground stations where by a process of exponential elevation, you can intuit what these sacred spaces used to be like. In the Plaza Cataluña station, for example: an immense nave criss-crossed with greasy cables and illuminated by a chill grey light, the light of mechanized death, the grey of the slaughterhouse.

I imagine the kind of mud the Jews walked through on their way to the gas chambers: woolly, officious mud. The Burnout Cases, too, spread out in underground stations. But I mustn't despair. Maybe that space exists, and I just don't know how to find it. Maybe it will shun me until the day I stop contemporizing, the day I give up forgiving.

February 18th

Today, taking advantage of the rain that leaves the pavement looking like patent leather, I visit the squalid streets that lie to the right of the Ramblas. The greasy tiles and walls smack of family life, the domestic circle: stews heated up on wood stoves, clothes hung out in streamers on the line, matrons spying from the shadows of doorways. In their quilted bathrobes, they looked like a strange cross between an owl and a mattress.

Every hundred yards there's a misshapen bar. Many are now called "cafes," but they retain the darkness, the foul sawdust, the water basin cut in limestone, the old, dented-up zinc bar, the flies suspended in the air like minute solar systems in motion. Spurred on by curiosity, I drink gin after gin in one bar after another. I want to investigate all of them, to make out each one's individual history, its biography, the need it answers. In the Barcelona-Galicia Cafe-Restaurant, a woman of about sixty or seventy serves an espresso to a young man who's quite suited up. There's a grey felt hat with a brown band on the table. The young fellow is pale with albino eyebrows, and he holds himself very straight, keeping his knees together like a condemned man in an electric chair.

Both of them look at me without seeing me. At the far end of the room, a door is half-opened. For a minute I think a see a face gesticulating, but because of the darkness, I can't decide if it's a retarded relative or some sort of insinuation. In any event, I'm excited. The place seems paralyzed. The woman hasn't moved, and the man hasn't touched his coffee. I feel as though I've been thrust into the frozen world of Sleeping Beauty.

Later on I spot a set of huge, wooden doors that have been left ajar. I push them back, cross the old coachyard and go up an unlighted stairway with shallow steps. On the first floor, I knock. I'm dying to see who lives there. The door opens, but only a hand's breadth. I can just make out the eyes of somebody who has neither sex nor age. The only thing I can discern is the fatigue. Even though I have an excuse ready, we remain silent. From a room at the back, someone yells, Is it him? Is it him, Sweetie-pie? I can't speak. My voice has frozen. I keep on staring at the tired, mute eyes that float in the crack of the door. The person who yelled inside must be an old man or a little boy — or someone imitating them. I don't know how much time passes, but the door closes very slowly as though it were in a dream.

Going down the stair, I bump into the finial at the end of the handrail. I must be a bit stupefied by gin. My arm is paralyzed, dead, and a carillon of bells sounds in my ears. When I get to the street, I break into a run, almost afraid. There's a sense of threat in those doors that were opened to me today, one by one, without ever letting me in. I don't know how to read these signs yet because, until very recently, I didn't pay attention to them. I was taken in by solid appearances. Now it may be years before I learn to decipher them. This is where my disdain for science has gotten me.

Do something about it even if it's hopeless.

February 22nd

For the third time I ended the night at the liquor store, having decided to do just the opposite when I left my apartment. A classic knight's move: two squares up and a square over. The first two squares take me to the Boa, where I have the good fortune to be caged in with animals of the same species. There there's no fantasy of cross-breeding threatened by sterility. Sometimes I don't know if I make myself understood, hmmmm. For example: a rabbit and a ferret don't mate, not because they don't feel like it — animals aren't bothered by that kind of consideration — but because such a cross won't produce a rabbit, a ferret or even a rarret. The unions between different species are sterile. And unions between very similar species, if they do bear fruit, bear fruit that's sterile: the mule. Wicked men with uncontrollable appetites have been known to cohabit with female chimpanzees. At the moment of their arrest, they claimed they were motivated by scientific interest. No pregnancy was ever produced as a result of their experiments. The same thing happened with the desperate love of a schoolteacher for her German shepherd. The only thing she managed to produce was a public spectacle: she was lowered down the staircase of her apartment on Aribau, laid out on a stretcher with the shepherd (who had been named Article in honor of the study of grammar) securely wedged between her legs. Anyway, in the Boa I feel sure that I will only meet MY OWN KIND. I know that any union contracted here will be generative even if it hasn't taken place yet.

But then the lateral part intervenes. One of the customers or customeresses at the Boa pronounces a line that contaminates my drink, a line that reminds me of the existence of poets, artists, and intellectuals. I overhear something like "green skin, hair of green, and eyes of cold silver" or "I can write the saddest verses tonight" or some other obsequious, high-flown sentiment (I'm inventing, but it's ANALOGOUS) that cuts my gin, and I leave the bar, sunk into bitter reflections about the nature of artists, poets and intellectuals — degenerate animals, all of them, whose destiny quite frankly is rather tiresome.

That does it. The night begins to go awry. I drink anxiously as I get closer and closer to the fateful Vía Layetana. With no strength left, I cross that ridiculous artery — the abortive dream-child of a peon who made it rich — and wind up ON THE OTHER SIDE. It's inevitable; no one who crosses the Vía Layetana resists the lure of that siren made of stone, glass and lead: Santa María del Mar. That's how I reach the liquor store, all my senses torn to shreds, telling myself — but it's a pious lie — that there I'll finally be able to have a drink that's not too badly cut with lye.

This has happened three times now, and all three times I've been received with cool courtesy by the Chinaman. All three times, I've provoked arguments with the other customers, almost always by defending the warrior-like valor of the Italians, especially the *bersaglieri*. All three times I've suffered the humiliation of being led to a taxi. All three times I've sworn I would NEVER EVER go near the place again. But it's destiny; I'm condemned. I keep thinking I can blot out the ridiculous impression I've made the day before. That's how I've been getting into deeper and deeper trouble.

Maybe I should reverse the process, begin at the liquor store and then make the lateral move to the Boa. But this wouldn't be easy. The city imposes a natural direction on the night, an imposition that has been developed over a period of almost a thousand years. A THOUSAND YEARS since the Arabs strolled around here, leveling everything in exactly the same direction. Except for victims of fascist tour directors, nobody starts the evening on the other side of the Ramblas. It would be absurd, it would be ridiculous, it would be un-Catalonian. The only exception is the businessman on an expense account who dines with a woman — business or not — at one of the indescribable restaurants in the area, in order to take off later to some spot on the north side where he can rub up against his date until she gives in. Fine, but a drinker would NEVER start there.

February 23rd

What's the Chinaman like? All of us have some trait that identifies us from infancy. This trait is responsible for all our humiliations and all our nicknames, which are our TRUE names, names like the Tortoise, Timex and Kryptonia. It's also responsible for the brief instants of passion and pain that our animal warmth allows us. In the Chinaman's case, the essential characteristic, the one that identifies him at a single glance, is the fact that he's short. But not because of a shortage. I doubt the Chinaman has ever considered his height a deficiency. He must imagine that the rest of us identify him by some OTHER pecu-

liarity. Wearing glasses, for example. And it's true that he wears
them even when he's not wearing them. It's as though he were
looking through mirrors. He's always walled in, always protected.
The glasses give him a double meaning, an emendation, vision
"n" plus one. He uses steel rims that underline the blue pupil
parallel to the eyelid. And yet in spite of the remarkable influence that gaze has had on his life, it's not his determining quality. What can't be helped, his destiny, is the fact that he's short,
with a small body that's wider than it's long. This disproportion
is due to a lack of space; he's compressed. If he'd been taller —
at least a third taller — his head would have been too big. But
because of a geometrical phenomenon common to Mediterranean countries, the small size of the trunk and limbs disguises
the excessive size of the capital.

His hands, however, are exquisite, with small, pointed nails
very different from those square, striated nails that are so shocking in their abundance. His wrists are fragile and bony. The
hands of a lyrical simian. Although I've never seen his feet, I'm
sure that they are real miniatures because I'm convinced that
some day his extremities are going to give way and the Chinaman
will just tumble over. He's only confident and firm when his
body's center of gravity and his soul's center of gravity coincide.
That explains why he panics in the presence of anything involving manual dexterity or sports, his fear of excursions, his
contempt for pottery. It also explains a few positive aspects —
haircuts, card games and fishing, activities that are sedentary
but passionate, activities that befit a Mandarin.

As far as his hair goes, it's abundant, even thick, but at
the same time somehow dead. He could be a flexible sculpture of very high quality. All of his features are simultaneously

infantile and worn. Under the weight of his hair — which at first glance doesn't look heavy, like those streams of lace carved in marble — his face sinks into an orgy of crevices and wrinkles; at any moment it might crack in two like a loaf of overdone bread. But wait! This hasn't happened YET. I'm only saying that it MAY happen any time.

I should add that his gestures are deliberate, if not exactly elegant, since he avoids excess with an almost pedantic moderation. But this doesn't keep you from having an uneasy feeling as if suddenly and without warning he might poke his nose into your business without the least embarrassment. If he did, you'd probably say: I *knew* this would happen!

You have in him a combination of qualities that would have made for success on the banks of the Yellow River five hundred years ago, when the great warriors saw almost no difference between a good watercolor and a successful impalement. The Chinaman is obviously well equipped for both things.

February 26th

In a place not very far from the liquor store, a place identified by a neon moon inscribed with the words "Barbas de Plata," I run into an old friend. He has barely changed. A Belgian Catholic fantasy has induced him into letting a line of black hair grow along his jaw, and this underlines his Saracen appearance even more incisively. The little hair he has is as kinky and hard as a curry comb, although the most African things about his person are his long eyelashes and the humid gleam of his eyes, which are like two buckets of tar. It goes without saying that he's from the Balearic Islands, from Felanitx.

Years ago when we saw each other from time to time, he used to talk about "giving it all up." There was nothing to give up, but it was a period when we were fascinated by the use of words like "all," "nothing" and the perennial "them." We referred with special delight to giving up "work," but nobody was working yet. And giving up "security and obligations," which were absolutely non-existent. We wanted to live in poverty and to occupy house-squats. My friend had a special talent for summing up our desires in a few choice words, pronounced with the fascinating paleolithic accent of the islands. We only found out much later they were lifted from Hölderlin. Occasionally he invented his own. The last time I saw him, he characterized that happy moment yet to come when we'd be swimming in poverty with a memorable epigram: *quins poemes escrivirem!* What poems we'll write! People from the Balearics pronounce it *excrgivirgioem*, in the timbre of a Soviet bass. That same day I decided never again to write a single verse, and I initiated my investigation into banality. It's true that I still lacked the means and the resources, but I had been awakened to my vocation, and I owed it to the bard from Felanitx.

It is this man I now see seated at one of the window tables next to a girl with a look of concentration on her face. When the sign lights up, his expression is barbaric and monotheistic. When it goes dark, he looks like an archimandrite. From the bar where I'm sipping my gin, I watch him perform a ritual of sexual proselytism. How well I know that air of grave conviction, that sublime wave of the hand, that gaze suddenly lost in the contemplation of Poetry. He's an exalted prestidigitator, spinning his web around the fly, drawing her in with his greasy "r"s and borrowed quotations!

He finally notices I'm staring at him. At first he looks at me distrustfully. He's very short-sighted; but he's not wearing glasses, because he's with a woman. Then he raises his arm and invites me to come over. He's in a state of euphoria, not quite drunk. It's the perfect moment to share everything before he's prostrated by boredom. Now I can see the girl better. Obviously a student, done up in a pound or so of brass and several yards of black cloth that go with lips she has painted the color of liver. She'd be attractive if you could forget what lies in store for a nose that's already bulbous and sweaty. Her skin, on the other hand, is very white and lightly freckled. This model will only survive twenty-five if she can afford to spend a gold mine on cosmetics. For now, however, she has been taken on as part of the Balearic poet's lyrical orgies for a fee of about four thousand *pesetas*. He never pays. It would be humiliating FOR HER.

The guy combines glory — he still writes poetry — with power — he's a professor of literature and language at a secondary school. He takes advantage of the absence of a wider public (which, alas, is awaiting his death with the laudable intention of giving him the recognition he deserves then) in order to transmit his compositions by oral means, generally to his female students. Including this one. Laura, she herself tells me. In order to seem independent and free of burdens, of obligations and responsibilities, the poet never introduces his dates. Even when he's enthusiastic, as he is today. You'll see: Laura is hyperaesthetic; it's unheard of in a person who has no education. This pleases Laura, who nods her head as though recognizing a virtue she didn't have to work for. Perhaps it's because she's an Aquarius TOO — remember Luisa? Luisa was an Aquarius and absolutely brilliant . . . before she killed herself. But killing herself wasn't worthy of her, and she knew it: "Without my consent," she left written on a piece of paper next to the ashtray — an absolutely brilliant line. Aquarians have UNFATHOMABLE potential. They light up the dark even though there are no eyes to see the light because on those heights where the danger is acute, everybody is blind (he finishes the word off in a sharp "t" sound like a slap), don't you realize? We're all blind; I'm blind myself. You know perfectly well, we poets are always blind: Homer, Borges, (he hesitates) M . . . Milton? Wasn't Milton blind? But suddenly I meet Laura, an unfathomable fish with lights no one can see (he slips his arm around her shoulders and his hand rests on her left breast as if by accident), and so I understand that there are others like me — not necessarily poets, but blind as well — wandering with a light hanging from our heads, and we can't see it, that is, we can't see it IN ourselves, but we can see it IN others, eh? Do you understand?

I don't understand very much, especially since he insists that nobody can see these lights and on top of everything else, he says, everyone's blind, but Laura has understood. These things come naturally to her. For her, it's *natural*. It's always been that way; ever since she was a little girl, she's SEEN things this way, suddenly in a group of people, a light IN someone, and she's never been wrong. She knows at first sight if somebody does or doesn't have that light. It's a gift that some people have from birth, and she was gifted that way at birth. She sees the light some people have, but only if they have it, and then she sees it clearly. Exactly! exclaims the poet, interrupting the hypnotic recital, because YOU HAVE IT TOO, understand? and that allows you to see, because you see with your own light, a beacon and a torch, but not a mirror of mirrors, understand?

I don't understand anything by now, and I move to get up, but he holds me back with his naked claw, the free one. You know? I'm going to kill a dragon, he says with a transcendent expression that is definitely unfathomable. He is still inflamed, waiting for the fiery chariot. The situation is awkward. I can't leave him like that, like a prophet who's out of a job, so without sitting down, I ask him, How do you know you can kill a dragon? The man is suddenly perplexed: Well, I don't know, I don't even know if I can FIND one. In fact, I think it will have to find me itself (the word comes out sharp, like a sneeze).

We're both disconcerted because what we've said we haven't exactly said ourselves. Our words are not our own. Our mouths are not our own. I sit down again. It's not that I know a lot about dragons, I say, but my understanding is that dragons don't look for people, they run into them. So, says the poet, you have to move around then, in order to be run into. My head clears. Without any profound doubts and without raising my voice, as if I were talking to a sacred apparition that has come to me by chance, I put the question that really does matter to me, the one that could change my life: It would also run into you if you stayed still, wouldn't it? And I listen to his answer, stunned: Yes, but it might think I despise it then. It must find me in motion. I at least have to look as though I'm searching for it. We are both in a state of consternation. We drink from the tall, vapor-covered glasses. Laura doesn't know what to do, but she intuits that she'd better not open her mouth. She has recognized the ancient goat's mask grinning from its humid grotto, and she's as quiet as a mouse. We remain frozen for a minute, and then hesitant, he asks, That's what you wanted to know . . . ? That's it exactly . . . . I get up and leave without saying good-bye.

Oracles tear the voices out of their bodies, and the sinister and corrupt depths of the mouth of God appear, leveling everything so that a word in monologue with a dead cosmos will be left behind, floating over our corpses. Inevitably I end up, once again, at the Chinaman's. The conversation, however, is more serene than it has been on other occasions. I don't provoke any altercations with the clientele, in spite of some unacceptable insinuations about the behavior of the Arabs and the young officers during the Civil War.

February 28th

That voice from Felanitx still buzzes around me like a fly. The pre-banal world — even though it is preparing itself for banality — still forces you to undergo a tedious ritual of initiation. It is a world run by artists and intellectuals. This is true of all the Christianized West. Those who are lucky enough to have been born into the working world, the people whose fathers and grandfathers were crushed in workshops and factories or whose families moved from a gelid hole in the country around Teruel to another gelid hole in the Perona neighborhood, those people have never felt obliged to give into banality. They've been freed from original sin by virtue of the mere fact that they belong from birth to the human community. I've suffered a lot from these insulting comparisons! The working masses boast incommensurable privileges, far greater than those enjoyed by the feudal lords during the Dark Ages. The most important is being regarded both by others and by themselves as single unit.

The world of banality, on the other hand, is heart-breaking because it doesn't form a unity of any kind at all. Nobody

bothers to unravel that piece of knitting. And this leads to
an extremely peculiar phenomenon: artists and intellectuals
presiding like dictators over fragments of a hare-brained population. Their tenure never lasts more than a few months or,
at most, a few years. But their fall doesn't alter the relations
of power. The ones who are in today won't be in tomorrow,
but someone will always be in. This is the inheritance of the
Terror. It spawned an ambiguous sphere that belongs neither
to the decision-makers nor to the slaves, a sphere that can
achieve universal dominion by resorting to terror. When that
happens, God Himself will tremble! It is the artists and intellectuals who have designed every bloodthirsty machine. The
greatest artists and intellectuals in the pre-banal world were
an Austrian painter who produced watercolors that received
little attention, a Georgian linguist who was a movie fan,
and an ex-librarian from the University of Peking who read
French. All of them were consummate artists and intellectuals. That's why they were convinced that the great work of
the twentieth century wasn't a watercolor or a treatise on
linguistics or an ideogram, but the construction of a world
that would itself be a work of art. Art no longer makes sense
in private houses and lifeless museums. Art is only legitimate
now when it works directly ON HUMAN FLESH. In this
way, the cycle of art that started with tattoos comes to an
end. At the beginning, artistic signs were inscribed on the
flesh of the privileged body. At the end, that same flesh piles
up in slaughterhouses, immense funeral monuments raised to
the greater glory of the artists and the intellectuals. The History of Art: from the tattoos on a Polynesian to the hill of
false teeth at Auschwitz. And new universal designs are still

being prepared for today's flesh. There are a lot of poets running around in the world.

I, of course, never had access to the higher levels of art and intellect. I've only sampled the offerings of this wretched land of ours, and a painter who favored landscapes adorned with deer had his own designs on it. When I was in the press office of the General Headquarters, fulfilling my obligations to the Nation, I used to glance through the Civil Guards' magazine: *The Guardian Angel*. It was filled with poems dedicated to the morning star, which apparently inspired these guards as they marched two by two between cork trees and stubble, wrapped up in their cloaks with their rifles on their shoulders. The sense of stupefaction I felt then was to be the seed of my apprenticeship in banality. There are many, many poets still loose in the world.

In spite of everything, beautiful, unique beings, struck down by some misfortune like stars in a bed of worms, are swimming in that pompous puddle. All of these beings are women, on whose reproductive organs the intellectual and artistic world exercises an incomprehensible influence. Some of these women succumb and wind up quoting poetry as naturally as the bard of Felanitx. Others are married to architects, an intermediate species that has access to the world of decisions but has not lost its license for hunting big game in the pastures of art. A few, the really superior ones, resist these temptations. In fact, they don't even *realize* that they're being tempted. It's as though the devil had tried to tempt St. Jerome, a vegetarian, with pork chops. And they don't realize it because they have no instinct for domination. They love and consent and wear themselves out loving and consenting.

A superiority that's so obvious subjects others to cruel humiliations. More than one artist and intellectual has been
reduced to a shambles because of these creatures. Of course
they're absolutely unaware of the damage they're doing, and
so they keep on with this destruction like battering rams
moved by an external and quite extraordinary strength. They
are always tall, but never haughty.

Like one of the Balearic poet's ancient conquests back
when he was younger and could hunt really big game. I'm
thinking now about a prehistoric, better-made Laura. He wasn't
satisfied until the girl had read *The Iliad*, an ornament essential for any lyrical Mediterranean. She was a third-year student with a tan, a real aquatic tan inlaid with salt and iodine.
Her first — and last — public comment, when the poet
urged her to give an opinion, was that Ajax reminded her a
lot of Peralta, a boy from school who used to hit everybody
and who was, oh, a real animal. The poet-professor filed her
away before I had a chance to get hold of her myself. I did
everything possible, and impossible, but she escaped scot-free
and became engaged overnight to a furniture designer. Before
that, the poet-professor used to apologize for her by assuring
us that the girl read a lot and that she was trying to make up
for time lost on the beaches and in the discos. In my eyes she
was like an exile's first sight of home. I loved her with a
primitive passion. She smiled, smiled in general, smiled at
one, smiled at another, lowered her eyes modestly as though
she were saying, Am I doing this right? Her name was Luisa,
and it's not true that she killed herself, although as far as that
goes . . .

Second Part

The Dangers of Banality

March 3rd

Even though I was expecting it, it still surprised me. The fact is: I'm working for the Chinaman. In truth, I can hardly call it "work" since I doubt that he'll pay me for it; perhaps it would be better to call it "symbiosis." What am I doing, and more important, why am I doing it? I don't know. From the very first, I could discern a playing field between the two of us. And, in fact, this playing field is now official. It has been agreed on, like a card table that's been improvised on an orange crate. Fine. But I still don't know what game I'm playing.

It's not strange that all of this has come about in a casual, banal way, like lower forms of animal life that breed by brushing up against each other when the ocean currents bring them together. It happened yesterday or the day before. No, it was exactly the day before yesterday. The pressure of the nights and the emptiness of the days have me confused. I was fulfilling my obligations at the Boa, killing time before eating supper in the Egypt, a place that serves stuffed sardines. My favorite spot in the Boa is the far end of the bar where they keep the phone. This poorly lighted corner provides me with a vantage point for inspecting the clientele without having to look away every time somebody picks up on my curiosity.

I saw them come in. They had that unmistakable way of moving that men who are sure of themselves physically but uncomfortable in their suits have. I immediately recognized the prominent cheekbones, the tubercular color of the skin, the hair like asphalt. I was terrified by their gold watches, gold rings and gold chains, all shining in the neon lights. Under their linen jackets, under their coffee-colored pants, beat the hearts of hired killers, hearts accompanied not by flowers and lace, but by pointy-toed, two-toned shoes and multicolored handkerchiefs sticking out of their breast pockets. Descendants of anthropophagi with a passion for the guitar and the knife in their blood.

They stood beside me, daiquiris in hand, speaking slowly, hissing with the fatigue of many generations of slaves behind them. From time to time, their impeccable teeth twinkled like stars. They talked and talked, their Andean accents watered down by a rudimentary trade in corncobs, basket work, jugs, alpaca and rot-gut alcohol, the kind that comes with a lizard at the bottom of the bottle. I could hear everything they said perfectly clearly because nobody could have made sense of their words. Nobody who wasn't familiar with the key to the code. And I was familiar with it. So they spoke quite openly, the way we do on the London metro, without dreaming that any other traveler might understand our language.

When they paid, I paid. When they left, I left. In their eyes, I was an ordinary man, like everyone else, not worth remembering. They hadn't recognized me. But how could I forget them? They had been my guardian angels. I knew where they were going; so I speeded up.

I think it's of the utmost importance to make clear that my decision at that precise moment was BANAL. I consider this a triumph and one of the first fruits of my new life. That's why I'm anxious to get it down. I didn't stop to think it over, I didn't hesitate, nobody inspired me with pity or special interest. I was moved by the most perfect indifference: a supper or a crime, it's all the same to me. I didn't think for a minute that I was "going to help" anyone, much less that "someone was going to pay dearly for it." Complicated criteria about "race" and "sexuality" make me laugh. I would have done exactly the same thing if it had been two canons from Aragón conspiring against the Vicar General of the armed forces. To sum it all up, the most important thing to me was that I HADN'T TAKEN A LIKING to the two killers.

When I got to the liquor store, my heart was beating the way it used to during exams. Having spent so many years without feeling that emotion is a sure sign of despair. Only when our heart gives us this kind of warning do we know we're still part of the living tree. I advanced calmly as if I were (in fact, I was) an *habitué*. I didn't let myself get involved in the theory someone was developing about derelicts who spend twelve years sipping malt whiskey as if it were wine, and I ignored one of my innumerable opponents, who was trying to provoke me by saying the President of Catalonia was from Castile. No, I wasn't going to fall for that obvious a trick. At the far end of the bar, like a Tibetan seminarian, the Chinaman was listening to the barman, a giant with rolled-up sleeves.

I was on the point of doing something that would have

ruined my scene, being sorely tempted to stand at attention. But I got a grip on myself, although my high spirits were hard to contain, and simply recounted what I had heard: that the killers were on their way to the liquor store. This gave rise to a misunderstanding since it was perfectly normal for killers to show up for work. But the pig-eyed bartender apparently had already had some misgivings. Are they stupid enough to yell about their plans? the Chinaman asked me. One of them, I answered, the yellower of the two, the one with a braided watchband, didn't agree. They talked about "doing it" and said "it would have to be done," but the one with the watchband kept insisting "do it yourself, do it yourself" as if it were the other one who was really affected. I may be wrong, but . . . there you have it. They also said that somebody was going to beat their butts if they didn't do it, or was it their cunts?

The bartender seemed more nervous than the Chinaman. By the time I'd gotten out two or three phrases, he was repeating in a low voice: I told you so, I told you so, and he rocked back and forth like a bear, with his hands behind his back — a gesture I've noticed in professional football players. The Chinaman was undaunted, looking at me with a certain distaste. Then he blinked his eyes and went into action. In spite of a fragile appearance he shares with mammals like the ferret and the weasel, he moved with surprising agility. He shifted the table where his mysterious bills were piled up, ordered the bartender to keep an eye on the door from behind the bar, pushed me toward a baize curtain that covered up a toilet, took something like a pistol out from under a pile of newspapers and put it in my hand, and then wound up cramming me into that hole that reeked of lye and ammonia.

This wasn't the first time I'd ever had a pistol in my hands, but it was the first time the pistol was directed not to ornamental or instructional purposes, but to a single, concrete piece of business: an agreement that under certain circumstances I would fire at a living person. It seemed odd that I should have acquiesced so readily in that part of the contract. It was as if I had divined sometime back that this situation would arise sooner or later. The pistol had come to me from the distant future, like a movie shown in reverse. In the next few minutes, I could kill somebody, and from that point on I would be a person who has killed somebody. In other words, I would be a very special type of person who is subject, in turn, to the caprices of very special powers. It was strange!

Holding the baize curtain in one hand, the Chinaman showed me a grooved button on the left side of the pistol butt. This is the safety, he said, don't take it off. Put your finger on the trigger, and that'll be enough. When you see them come in, watch Diego behind the bar, and if he puts both hands, I mean *both* hands on the counter, come out and aim at them. Don't say anything, but make some kind of noise so they'll hear you. A noise? Yes, a noise, a sneeze, a cough, a burp, got it? Stand here. Right here. You have to look through the crack. The Chinaman moved my arm and turned my head as though I were having a fitting. The situation had lost its drama. I can't kill them? Not even one of them? But the Chinaman was busy, and he wasn't in the mood to listen to my exercise in bravado. He kept on giving me instructions patiently as if I were a retarded child: Pull back the curtain on this side with the barrel. Like this. They'll have their backs to you. They only use knives so there's no problem. The likeliest thing is that they'll try to take me when we close; so keep your eyes open, but stay calm. I asked if I could have something to drink, and he pointed to a case full of bottles that was propped against the lavatory wall.

Out of childish stupidity, I had always judged people who carry arms as inferior. That opinion crumbled when I found myself holding a pistol I didn't intend to put back up in the closet. I never thought seriously about firing it, and yet I'm conscious now of the fragile barrier that saves us, miraculously, from the catastrophe that lies in wait under our beds. I suspect that in some subtle and barely conscious way I felt more complete with that iron prosthesis filling a vacuum I hadn't even been aware of before. It's well known that mechanical interventions modify the nature of the inventors. Something similar must happen to the dispossessed and the humiliated who, by some chance, find jobs that oblige them to wear uniforms. As soon as they don the cap and the epaulets, they become aware of the horrifying nudity they lived in up until that time. From the moment of that initial shock on, they forget they were once men; now they'll never be anything but the uniform they wear. The experience of pure power, however, has a disadvantage. At any moment, they may have to abandon their comfortable, plastic fantasy in order to fulfill their function. They may have to stop being glad rags and start being efficient machines. And that's the end of that.

I looked through the crack in the lavatory door from time to time and confirmed that things hadn't changed much. Big Diego was serving the customers, the Chinaman was fooling with his papers . . . I reached for a bottle. As usual in this house, it had no label. In spite of its amber color, it wasn't whiskey. The light and the shape of the bottle had tricked me. It was *orujo*, and it cut a path through the labyrinth of my intestines. I have never experienced a sense of hatred solid enough to consider killing somebody DEFINITE, just vague ideas of a general sort of revenge against "them." I've always admired those figures, usually feminine, who throw themselves at the enemy and sink an ice pick into his liver, but the best I've managed in that field is an inconsequential rage, a short-lived fury I've contained because of moral scruples. After a fit of ineffectual rage, you feel dissatisfied, vulnerable, tired, and hungover from consuming so much rotten fury. Something very different from the volcanic satisfaction that springs from hatred and revenge taken in hot blood. These reflections made me thirsty.

The passage of time was dissipating the impulse of violent good health with which everything had begun. Now the *orujo* was producing *Christian* effects. I was overcome by a morbid sense of pity. I saw the hit men as victims, underground men born in the stinking pits of a tin mine and raised up by some miracle to the domain of the linen suits. Time brings everything to an end. I opened the curtain suddenly, ready to throw in the towel, fed up, humiliated once again. The Chinaman stopped me with his hand, like a municipal guard from classical times. Then, shaking his finger, he ordered me to go back inside. And I went. But a little later, from behind the curtain, I yelled, I'm leaving. He didn't even answer me. I pushed aside the curtain with the barrel; the butt was sweaty. From behind the bar, Diego smiled at me with his plantigrade scorn. I kept on drinking *orujo*. Now I felt ridiculous. I put the pistol in the pocket of my jacket and sat down on the toilet. The tedium was undermining my nervous system. It's the cycle that runs from exultation to apathy that's so familiar to anyone who has loved, has managed to get a date in spite of a thousand obstacles, has showed up tense as a drawn bow and has waited hours and hours, brain empty, spirits frozen, until at last, when the one we thought we were in love with appears, she turns out to be a real dog. That's the way I felt, and so I was overwhelmed by a sense of warmth, of homey, domestic peace, and I fell asleep. That's the absolute truth.

A veteran of the RAF told me once that in London during the German bombing raids, old men, women, and children slept peacefully underground in refuges that were constantly shaken by explosions. Apparently people who have been condemned to death also sleep soundly hours before their execution. A delicate mechanism protects us from desperation in our moments of greatest danger, disconnecting our consciousness and cutting the body's cable so it will float out with all sails set. I myself, when I was very young, suffered from an unhappy romance, followed by a high fever and suicidal impulses. The night I'd planned my immolation, laying out tubes of methadone on the table next to a bottle of Font del Regás still mineral water, I fell asleep out of boredom. The telephone woke me up with a start. A classmate was inviting me to spend the weekend on the beach. After that I just forgot to kill myself.

This is a kind gesture on the part of the animal, who only acts when the soul demands too much and threatens to take over entirely. The animals of our body are our salvation; they are our liver, lungs, heart, stomach, kidneys, pancreas, brains and a nice collection of glands that join together with the sole aim of protecting the intangible and invisible thing that generates our life and unifies us. When the soul — damned, desperate and sick of itself — wants to end it all (and this happens a lot), a handful of animals gets together with a single, common goal: survival. And the wretched consciousness, on the point of leaving them all behind, is anchored down, screwed into place and even consoled with all kinds of good juices and humors.

The animals can't speak. They are silent and benevolent; so they only manage to put that subtle creature the consciousness to sleep in order to let it rest and to avoid discord, at least for a few hours. The livers, the kidney, the pancreas, the brains keep on working; for them life and work are one and the same. They filter the blood, dissolve the food with good doses of acid, oxygenate, dream . . . but that invisible something that holds them together and guarantees their survival sleeps. Who or what, exactly, sleeps at that moment? I don't know. I've only learned one thing: some questions answer themselves. So if a person asks me seriously: *What* is sleeping in our unconscious body? in a way he already has his answer, yes.

On this particular occasion I'm telling myself about, I came to with a start. I hadn't dreamed at all. It's true that my head hurt. The Chinaman was busy with his papers. Diego was pushing the last customers toward the door, sweeping them out with his huge hands as if he were taking the broom to wood chips and sawdust. The most recalcitrant, a sickly, little thing with transparent ears, was trying to gain time by piquing Diego's interest: Let me tell you, Señor Diego, I had quite an experience with the troopers. But the manager dragged him along with his pole as if he were a tuna fish. The hit men hadn't shown up, and I was nauseated. The half bottle of *orujo* was gurgling around in my empty stomach, which was sustained in turn by a pair of legs that were numb after hours of staying still in the lavatory. I was obsessed with two ideas: first, not looking like a drunk, and second, not doing anything I would be ashamed of. But I could barely walk (both feet had fallen asleep on me so I moved like Andersen's little mermaid) and felt sillier than ever. I would never be able to erase my humiliation. With every passing day I managed to increase it geometrically. To my surprise, the Chinaman had a satisfied air about him, like a shopkeeper who's had a good day. Diego, too, came over full of smiles, his pole at rest like a Lancelot of the tavern. Let's close up, he said jovially. I felt my pockets to confirm what their weight had already told me: I didn't have the pistol any more. The Chinaman asked me if I was hungry. I was very nauseated. I had to eat something. It was two-thirty in the morning.

The pavement was wet and the fresh shine felt wonderful. A globed street lamp dispersed its acetylene light over the corner of the Plaza del Borne. There was a slice of a moon. The Chinaman walked behind me. The car's over there, he said with a vague gesture, his voice too loud. Diego followed us, a bit behind. I wasn't very sure which way to go, but when I said so, the Chinaman motioned for me to be quiet and keep walking. He was as tense as a cross-bow. Suddenly he raised his index finger and then waved his hand palm outward as if to say "charge." Diego caught up immediately. It finally dawned on me: the hit men hadn't shown up; THEREFORE, I was right. I felt immensely relieved. A real paradox considering it was then that things were getting dangerous. The killers were lying in wait, and I didn't have my gun. Worse yet, we were in the street, and the streets always belong to the killer. But consciousness had taken the initiative again, and the confident, benevolent animals turned over the command post. I took a deep breath of damp air. My hair was curling like a gypsy's. The Chinaman was insisting in the same loud voice that I should be careful not to bump into anything, that the area had been set aside by the authorities for putting the shocks onto trucks since one of the main truck-shock factories belonged to the Catalonian Minister of Culture, and so on.

Even though my legs still hurt, I felt terrific. Now we were following the string of trucks parked on the Avenida del Borne, a kind of dry dock illuminated by yellow lights whose chimerical appearance is intensified on humid nights by the prisms that whirl around each resistor. The old market, on the right, continues to draw truckers even though it's not very welcoming these days. To compensate for their mobility, truckers are so conservative that they seem to be governed by the same inertia that made the pagans return again and again to temples that had been razed by the Christian militia. An imposing nocturnal panorama. In spite of the wide sidewalks, you seldom see night people, just trucks, semis, moving vans and machinery in an interminable procession on both sides of the walkway. Only the ragged cats that infest the port break up this sulphuric atmosphere.

I was walking alongside a Trans-European eight-wheeler covered by a grey tarp with handsome Walloon lettering when I noticed a shadow move. The speed of motion, at night and even just before dawn, tends to decrease. It was, in fact, one of the killers. He didn't come out from the cab of the truck, but from underneath, whirling his knife so that it hissed like a whip. Without thinking, I windmilled my right arm out to such good effect that it clipped him hard between the eyes. I didn't even know what was happening. It was as though I were waving away a wasp while driving my car. Now I see that the Chinaman had been keeping me in front of him like a shield and that while the killer was trying to get to the Chinaman, I knocked him down without even meaning to. It's very sad. The killer had tried to avoid me in order to get to the Chinaman. From his point of view the consequences were fatal. That's the way it went: the Chinaman thrust his knee into the fallen man's neck while Diego ran behind the semi looking for the other guy. The knife lay on the asphalt shining like a dead fish.

The subterranean life we carry inside us is so rewarding! The little burlap bag with our ancestor's bones! The dangerous killer was once again a slave, defeated. Just like a dog, his instinct told him it would be pointless to waste his energy. Diego came back to report that the unfortunate soul had acted alone; that's what he said: "acted." Then, while the Chinaman held him down, Diego planted his foot — about a size twelve — on the unhappy fellow's face. I could hear a noise like dry wood snapping; it must have been his nose. But the Indian didn't let out a scream, just a soft, feminine groan that was very sensual. He had fainted. Diego kicked him until he disappeared underneath the semi.

The Chinaman walked off with his hands in his pockets, and I started vomiting until threads hung from my mouth and my eyes were full of tears. I couldn't bring up anything but a kind of spinach-colored juice. He reappeared behind the wheel of a Citroën. Between the two of them, he and Diego dragged the Indian to the car and dumped him on the floor by the rear seat. Then he told me to get in. I sat in the front, with Diego behind, his foot still on the unhappy creature's neck. While we were going up the Vía Layetana, I could see his yellow eyes floating in a mass of dough formed out of flesh and blood. In the neon lights, the beautiful linen jacket looked like a piece of chintz printed with big, blue flowers.

He didn't offer the least resistance even when we stopped for the traffic light opposite the Layetana police station, where there are always cops smoking and shooting the breeze while the people around them are busy hacking each other into shreds. He was done in by the fatalism of a people who have been humiliated for centuries and who can no longer rally when something important goes wrong. It takes them so much energy to come to a violent decision that if it doesn't work out, they're set back for decades.

It took us over half an hour to get where we were going. We didn't talk, and the Indian didn't complain. The Chinaman kept an eye on Diego in the rear-view mirror. That trajectory is as clearly recorded in my memory as if I had been branded with it. We crossed the city from the sea to the mountains along Urquinaona, Lauria, Diagonal, Vía Augusta, Balmes and Paseo Bonanova, a classic route for transferring prisoners from the south to jails in the north, a trajectory as sanctified by history as the navigational routes across the North Atlantic. It was like traveling in one of the Güell family's galleys with a cargo of slaves. The car stopped in front of a bungalow on a street next to the Jesuits of Sarriá. It was the Chinaman's house, or at least one of his houses. I can't keep on writing. My fingers ache.

March 7th

It's been a serene day, filled with memories of childhood, like that sea "filled with masculine memories" that the Buzzard liked so much. In his pantheon, Leopoldo Lugones came right after Herrera y Reisig, followed closely by Valencia. Neither Guillermo nor Luis Valencia, but the city of Valencia in its totality. If it didn't quite rank as living God, it was almost God. So too was Oliverio Girondo, author of one of the most renowned verses of the century: "Sodium pentothal, what for?"

At this very minute, I'm newly washed and ironed. I only need white gloves to feel totally First Communion. I've even asked them to change the sheets. The dwarf Mime has worked his way through a little crack of satisfaction and has injected me with the desire to read Lugones's stunning poems again — preferably sitting on the terrace of a cafe. Another immortal verse, this time by the poetess Sarah Bun (although underrated because of her name, she was often quoted by our artistic and intellectual youths) forces itself on me: "Her scarlet clamide, draped o'er her arm / Was like a folded wing. Oh, alarm!" I resisted, however. Somewhere in this *cheka* Laforgue's volume still lies panting.

The day is sunny and very fresh, so I've gone up to the funicular station along the Avenida del Doctor Andreu, a real ruin. This is where the most solid mansions in Catalonia were erected. Now most of the ones that remain standing have been converted into clinics, elementary schools, German secondary schools and dog houses. Only a few fossils still live in these gelid, damp houses. They are dominated by one desire: to ruin the lives of the people in Pedralbes, new rich accused of having made their money on the black market. All of the fossils on Doctor Andreu are half-crazy. A year ago the police discovered that one surviving patrician had eaten his cook.

My intention was to visit the automatons in the Tibidabo.

Years ago, in the fifties, thousands of children were forced to undergo the same experience. From May on, every Saturday or Sunday they were packed off, with or without a paid companion, to the so-called Amusement Park. I always associate the Tibidabo with the discovery of oil. We had a fat-cheeked chaperone, a chemistry student, who took us on for the afternoon in exchange for twenty-five *pesetas*. After we'd seen "Dallas: Frontier City," he explained to my cousin and me what oil really was. From then on I was convinced that the Tibidabo mountain was filled with dinosaurs and giant ferns rotting away in hopes that someday someone would perforate its intestines. Was it because of the similarity in structure between the Jungle Jim and an oil well?

Since the Jungle Jim and the Roller-Coaster were the only two amusements forbidden to us, we always started with the Jungle Jim and the Roller-Coaster. Then it was time for a hot dog and a Coca-Cola, items which had first appeared as great novelties at the Montjuich Fair. Afterwards came the Haunted House. Since we knew it by heart, we always got scared at the same places. And then the Hall of Mirrors, where it was so hard to get lost that you really had to work at it. Finally, when it was getting late and we were in danger of reflecting on our wretched childhoods, we would enter the Gallery of the Automatons.

These were mechanical devices of a shocking technical simplicity that had been constructed at very different times. The oldest ones — the Chignon, the Poet Falls Asleep, the Simian Orchestra — were porcelain models with bright eyes and Greek smiles, conceived as a lyrical expression of positivism. I figured that they must have been imported from France and were no older than the *drôle de guerre*. Other, more modern ones were made of cloth and represented the Catalonian National troops' homage to General Franco, with scenes like a street fair in Madrid done up in GHQ style.

But we, meaning my cousin and I, weren't interested in the rotten inheritance of Verlaine nor the barracks fish fry. As upright sons of Catalonia, we were interested in the representation of the Modern: the "Mechanical Workshop" (a factory made of pleistocene) and the "Firemen Putting Out a Fire." But most of all (and for understandable reasons) we were fascinated by "Hell." Here, moved by invisible pneumatic belts, souls hurled themselves into a sea of flames surrounded by devils brandishing their pitchforks. At the same age and for the same reasons, I felt a marked preference for Siennese art of the Trecento, an art I detest today. The fact is children are tremendously attracted to hell, and they yawn over celestial visions. This hard truth demonstrates the complete failure of the Church and gives a clear indication of what we really are. Of course, occidental philosophy has tried to cover it up with coughs and clearings of the throat that have reached such a level of virtuosity they almost compete with the abomination known as Italian opera.

Well, the automatons were all still there, but — in keeping with the decadent era the city has entered — they'd been converted into museum pieces. In fact, though, they hadn't changed too much. The ones in worst shape had been replaced by machine-made models whose faces looked like biscuits full of buckshot. But they were all still there, and there they will be still when worms are breeding in my eyes.

To take advantage of the last light of day, I also went out onto the terrace with its remarkable panoramic view. The city was a grey marble headstone, covered with inscriptions and cut up into niches like a necropolis; the pines supplied a Roman air. Threads of lethal, yellow smoke floated over the whole mass. Any bird that ventures across these mercurial frills is struck down instantly, plummeting onto the citizens' heads. It's a protective covering that keeps life out.

It was almost night, that clear night of nothingness that lends such dignity to things. Once again the funicular, once again the Blue Streetcar, once again the afflicted plaza with its monstrosity of a Rotunda, heraldic symbol of the city. Like the ruling class, this building is a gaseous mass petrified in the basement of our consciousness; the pretty flourishes won't be able to contain the eruption that constantly threatens. A tip of the hat here, a "how are you" there, a landscape of the Olotine School, a grand piano and then, without any warning, the attack of blind rage, the zealot — blunderbuss in hand, gut full of wine, eat your children alive. Today, luckily, things have changed. Now people are thrown together every which way.

I'm not planning to spend my night at the Boa. Nor at the Chinaman's either. Instead, I'll finish my notes about the events that took place four days ago. I haven't gotten around to what happened to that unfortunate soul, the misguided hit man. As soon as we got in the house, Diego started beating him in order to find out who was underwriting them. The bothersome thing was that the boy couldn't talk. His face had swollen up so that even his eyes were shut, and his gums showed between his livid lips. But Diego, who seemed unaware of the problem, kept on hitting him with a mortar on the most swollen areas, short, sharp blows. I must confess that my attack of good health had abandoned me, and I was again on the side of the victim. My heart was insisting loudly that it wanted to return to its comfortable, Christian bed. Nothing mattered to me any more, and I'd even forgotten the part I'd played in these proceedings. Nothing of the Indian was left but a pile of aching flesh laid out on top of a plank trembling as if he were being electrocuted. He kept trying to shout a name without managing to get it out. I couldn't ask the Chinaman to let him go, since his own life was at stake; so I retired to the living room, chose a sofa covered in burgundy velveteen, and tried to sleep.

Diego's questions seemed to go on for hours, but I must have fallen asleep since I also heard — or thought I heard — sharp, regular blows that no one could withstand for that long. Later on I fell into a deeper sleep, but I woke up from time to time startled by the silence. When the sun began to come in through the living room windows, I stepped out on the terrace. I looked out over a professionally landscaped garden, whose rosebushes, hydrangea beds, boxwood hedges and pepper-plants showed more technique than love. The mimosas were starting to turn from yellow to green. The sparrows were making a racket trying to drive off the crows. The Chinaman's waxy face appeared with an offer of coffee. How are you? I asked him. Fine. That beast Diego didn't realize the fellow couldn't speak. I let him rest a bit, and then he wrote it all down for me with a marking pen. He's getting cleaned up now. It's incredible what those people can take. If we'd gone through half of what he got, you and I'd be dead.

He was wearing his glasses, and he took them off with a flamboyant gesture. I suppose you understand what happened. If it hadn't been for you, he would've hurt me. I didn't suspect anything. He picked the perfect spot, and he's no slouch;

in fact, the boy's very good at these things. He messed up because he didn't stick it to you. He had to get around you to get me, and he didn't make it. These things are tricky, even in the dark. I listened to him indifferently. Dead Indian, live Chink. Dead Chink, live Indian. I was tired. I've no idea why you warned me. I don't know anything about you. You probably did it because you were bored. But don't kid yourself; for me it's a work-related accident. I'm going for coffee.

Diego calmed me down about the killer's fate. They considered him harmless, a greater danger now to the one who had sent him. And stranger yet, they were going to save him from his own client; that's what they'd agreed to. And it must have been true because there were the three of us drinking coffee while the Indian coughed and spat in the next room.

The Chinaman picked up the phone and dialled a number from memory. He asked for a certain Chicharro, wanted by "the secretary to His Excellency the Bishop." Alberto? I'm sorry to bother you at this hour for something trivial. The thing is: two men tried to get in the house last night, but Diego heard them and got one of them, a South American. The other got away. Would you be kind enough to pick up the one we have here? I'd appreciate it. Thanks! You don't need to do anything to him. I'm not going to press charges if you get my drift. Just give him the usual.

Diego served more coffee. The cups were minute and almost transparent. The spoons had a dainty design on the handle that reminded me of my grandmother and almost made me laugh. Who's the bishop's secretary? I asked the Chinaman when he sat down again. He looked at me with an indescribable boredom. I am, of course. Listen, do you have anything to do in the next couple of days? I'm pretty busy, but I like to talk while I work. Come by before closing any night, and we can have supper together. I suppose you don't need anything, he added, but tell me if you do.

A half hour later, the door bell rang. Diego came back with two very young, almost childish men, dressed in coat and tie, their hair recently combed, smiling. The Chinaman called the Indian. It was pitiful to see that handsome lad with his face swollen, his lips cut up and his eyes like two wrinkled prunes. Don't do anything to me, he jabbered; he sounded as though he had his mouth full. They're going to take you home, I already told you. The Indian didn't move, and the men took a step in his direction. I'm fine, thanks, he said with an amusing arrogance. Then he held out his hand. The Chinaman shook it and wished him good luck.

Out of sheer inertia, I drank two more cups of coffee. From Diego's comments I deduced that the second killer would be working for the Chinaman. The sun felt warm on my legs. I was very sleepy, and I wanted to go back to my apartment. Before leaving, I received paternal advice: rest up this week, take a lot of Vitamin B and Fosgluten and come by the liquor store next Monday or Tuesday. And buy yourself a suit. Once I was inside the taxi, I opened the manila envelope with curiosity. It contained 300,000 *pesetas*.

March 14th

In the first few days of my collaboration with the Chinaman, I established that he uses the liquor store as a general headquarters. That's where his associates, clients, creditors, co-conspirators and hit men show up. It's not a crowd, just two or three a night, but always a variety of types. Some belong to the field of bacteria. Today he dealt with a vagabond, a dry, elusive, bearded fellow with a bit of a swagger. He was dressed in the uniform of poverty: shiny, patent leather shoes, no socks, pants hanging around ankles thin as pencils, a jacket with narrow lapels emblazoned with a Chilean Nitrates crest, a hat. These days hats are only worn by beggars, who form a much more conservative group than we usually realize. Under his arm, he had a bundle of papers that the Chinaman slowly and painstakingly unfolded as if it were one of the Dead Sea Scrolls. Each piece of paper was different: El Galgo brand legal sheets, a tape from an adding machine, teletype ribbons, pajamas, a perforated strip. The Chinaman gave him twenty-five thousand *pesetas*. I couldn't suppress an expression of surprise, and after our dandy left, I began to take an interest in the garbage trade. Every cubic centimeter of trash is valuable. Some people know how to read in the garbage what journalists will never write. That guy had risked his life gathering together refuse.

Predators rely on the odor of excrement for their sense of direction. The best information about this city turns up in the feces of power. There was garbage there from the Cros, from the stock market, from Asland, from several hydroelectric plants, from a certain Ferrer's residence, from two law offices connected to the March Foundation, from the Model Prison, from the Banesto bank, from the civil government, in short, a heap of offal.

The job is not unlike the Buzzard's, venturing out on cliffs and descending ravines to take care of scavengers, making a great effort to save the few families that had not yet determined to leave the country. But it's in a different key. In the final analysis, buzzards wheel at a great height with their wings outstretched, drawing slow, astral circles, but the Chinaman feeds urban buzzards, scavengers who work at ground level.

Our suppers are silent. I don't see my situation very clearly. I have no obligations, but I don't want to ask any questions. In a way, I've wiped out my old humiliation — unless the Chinaman is keeping me on out of *gratitude*. That would be troublesome because, if it were true, I'd have to get in a fight with him. For the time being, however, I'm just waiting.

I'm fascinated by the monstrous inertia with which he ritualizes every act as if he had accepted the bureaucratic constrictions of a confused and negative administration. It's impossible, for example, to find out what he plans to do about whoever it was that paid to have him murdered. Not that he hides anything in my presence. He talks with Diego openly as if I didn't exist. In fact, I don't exist. All he says about whoever instigated the attack is "he has to be moved" or "he has to be taken home." He doesn't seem too worried about it. The efficient cause, I guess, is that "he found out about the electrics." I haven't the vaguest idea what the phrase means: a stock portfolio? chorus girls? Diego asks, Should we wait 'til next week? And the Chinaman answers, Correct. He tends to use that word "correct." It makes me frantic. I try not to ask any questions he can answer with "correct." I suffer as intensely hearing this as I do when somebody says "to the delight of the audience" or "it's absolutely exquisite" or something else along those lines. Should I take him home? No, wait and see what happens. We could send him to the other guy. No, let's wait a bit, and then we'll take him home. Don't you feel sorry for him? If we let him alone . . . ? The Chinaman has had enough. In a threatening tone, he adds, Next week you'll take him home, is that clear? Whatever you say, whatever you say; it doesn't matter to me.

Diego doesn't seem very convinced; however, I've discovered that Diego has some disconcerting traits. He feigns absolute obedience but belongs to a ferocious pro-Catalonian group that is violent and clandestine at the same time. He doesn't really speak a word of Catalonian, limiting himself to a few expressions ("guaita," "la mare que el va parir," "s'acabat el bráquil" — *Guaita*: Look! *La mare que el va parir*: Son of a bitch! *S'acabat el bráquil*: That's enough! — and so on) and a keychain with the crest on it. And his argumentation is explosive. If, for example, someone mentions the customs post at Port Bou — and this happens pretty often since the Chinaman has a contact there, a cop who drops in on us from time to time but never gets out of his Volvo — the thought of all the territory that should rightfully be *ours* and has been wrongfully occupied by the French for over three hundred years — this thought has a dramatic effect on Diego. He swells up until his face looks like a purple wine skin and the madness of a Sicilian cut-throat glitters in his eyes. He doesn't doubt for a minute that the Spaniards have brought about a change in the climate of Catalonia by the costly means of burning and cutting down forests: all this in order to invade our principality with rabbits. In my part of town, he assures us with absolute conviction, three Catalonians have already died of myxomatosis; at this rate, within ten years there won't be a single patriot left south of Perpignan.

On some nights, select followers from the cell come to visit him. The group calls itself *La Farem Petar* —Let's Blow It Up. It has very good connections with hiking centers (which they use for smuggling in appliances from Andorra) and with the Employers Union. The followers come in two types: the real Catalonians, chubby and blushing with fine hair like cotton; and the nouveau variety, blackened and rachitic, with shapes like carrots (one is even called Carrot Top), sideburns and strong Estremanian accents. Whenever they come, they attract attention because their heads, eyes, eyebrows and ears are always in motion; suspicious of everything, they're constantly looking over their shoulders. They talk a lot about the great times they had when they were doing target training on a chicken ranch out in the sticks. Carrot Top came in yesterday, covering his face with a newspaper (*Ya*) and ran head-on into a post. Blood of the Virgin! he yelled, and one of his fellow drinkers (a cripple from Seville, your typical southerner with deep Catholic convictions — this one carries around a silk-embroidered picture of the Virgin del Rocío inside his military service papers) hit him so hard that his cane broke. After they'd stitched up Carrot Top's mouth at the emergency clinic, he looked more like a rabbit than a carrot. Well, to get to the point, not only did his leader not defend him, Diego decided to expel him from the militants for letting himself to be caught off guard and wounded by an outsider of an inferior race. Later, he pardoned him benevolently.

March 20th

The Chinaman loves math. Actually, it would be more accurate to say that he loves *numbers*. The sympathy some painters feel toward pigments, in which they see such pure colors that we seem blind in comparison (Cézanne, for example, classified one hundred and eight shades of green in a ripe lime), that sympathy is what the Chinaman feels for numbers. It's a sensual pleasure, probably his only one. In the afternoons, he spends hours drawing interminable strings of equations in a tight, little handwriting. The sterile offspring of sterile Señor Daroca. He's not trying to solve any problem; he's not even developing and verifying any hypothesis. He's like a musician improvising at the piano, letting his fingers run free and unrestrained until they hit a seductive chord. Then he plays with that chord, searching up and down until he comes on something related or complementary. After hours of playing, his joints aren't tired, his hands don't seem like parts of his body, but extensions of his imagination, and that's where the melodic delirium of numbers and equations begins. In this inebriated state he throws up edifices and later dissolves them into clouds that become new architectural forms reflected on a quiet pond. The inverted image provides another combination, the negative, superimposed on the earlier combinations in a complex harmony that infiltrates the fugitive labyrinth of the positive forms and travels through these mackled conjunctions in search of a way out that can be a new beginning, and so on. He enters a trance-like state, and his eyes cross ferociously.

As long as the impromptus last, the Chinaman is a motionless figure. His hand advances over the paper with the neutrality of a seismographic needle, unconscious of whether it points to calm or catastrophe. His thoughts are not his own; they are universal, cosmic and, in spite of all this, insignificant. They drift along the master lines of the universe, coming on the same crossroads where Oedipus and Orpheus trembled. But on the sheets of paper and in the notebooks, like the piano once the lid is down, there's nothing left behind. Once they're covered with ciphers, they slide off the table. Sometimes I pick them up off the floor and look at them. Like stone tablets dug up by Cretan workmen, they're inscribed with obscure doodles. Nothing. The indecipherable deafness of the cosmos, the encephalogram of God. Nothing. Nothing at all.

If a pro were to examine these notebooks, what would be his professional opinion? He'd probably sum it up as BANALITY, since it's just another way to kill time, but I'll never find out because the Chinaman invariably gathers together his papers at midnight and tears them up according to an inflexible order: first he tears them in two, then he tears the halves in two, then the halves of the halves in two and so on until the thickness of the bundle stops him. That process puts an end to his vespertine exercises, and a metamorphosis takes place. He is entirely transubstantiated in body and soul when he turns to the bills, letters of exchange, IOUs and accounts. What was lyrical improvisation before crystallizes into HIS TRUTH, just as an architect's subtle drawing is later transformed into a machine that will grind up and digest the unfortunate residents. I told him, but he was ahead of me: Because what you see now, he pontificates, is the ani-

mal zone, and so it's susceptible to all sorts of sickness, ampu-
tation and rot. But here, there's no room for unhappiness,
and he taps his head with his index finger.

I suppose that for him each number is a *species* with its
own pattern of behavior, morphology and set of instincts. He
has the musician's capacity for distinguishing between a sustained E minor and an A flat — perceptible, carnal figures
that are as different from each other as a bear from a stork —
or the writer's capacity for deciding whether to use past perfect, imperfect, preterit perfect, past indefinite or past ante-
rior, any one of which will lead him to a different destina-
tion. I've deduced all this from his comments; from his ani-
mosity, for example, toward the number nine, which he considers disappointing and on the verge of extinction.

I've also told him about my first impression when he
reminded me of an Egyptian scribe officiating over bills and
bad debts. I assumed that, like all hieroglyphics, he came
from the Orient, but once I realized that, in addition to the
bills, he carries a free accounting of time and space, I began
to worry that the mystery would turn out to be a simple
paradox.

There's no such thing, no such thing, he answers. I've
been sure ever since the time of Cucurella that our only
sustenance is numbers; they're our last allies. Everything has
been destroyed; virtues and vices, churches, nations, arts, letters, honor, dignity, everything, even war, has been destroyed.
We're left with Kantity. And he motions toward the papers
scattered over the floor. Every time he uses the word "quantity," he stresses the first syllable with a certain scorn as though
he were saying "Kantity." I'm sure this abomination of quan-

tity gets mixed up in his dense memory with the egalitarian consequences of the French Revolution. Since the universal imposition of equality, he adds looking at the ceiling, every political strategy is numerical; morality is now a question of pure Kantity! But nobody takes the trouble of finding out what numbers are, what they think, what they feel, where they take us and why . . .

For me, these lucubrations are just nutty, but he delivers them in a priestly tone that I haven't heard in a long time, maybe since the death of Pius XII. You think a bill makes *sense*. Obviously so much is owed, somebody owes somebody else a certain sum, etc., etc.; whereas a Kantity written down by chance seems insignificant, senseless. For example, if I just write down, without giving it any thought, one, five hundred and eleven, one hundred eighteen thousand ninety-seven . . . these signs seem opaque, arbitrary, mute. And yet, they establish networks of relationships and laws among themselves. There are maximums, multiples, exponents; there are series you can only see by paying very close attention. They are like time-bombs, waiting for someone to defuse them or — just the opposite — put them to some use. They've undone even famous mathematicians. Charles De Mora went crazy before he could divulge the secret of prime numbers. It CAME to him one night, and he lost his head. He didn't even have time to scrawl a farewell. Look, in this case, the series responds to the exponential sequence two times n to the eighth power minus one. It's odd, isn't it?

He rests his arms on the table; they flutter down like big sheets of silk. The bright lenses of his glasses have a sinister glitter. Yes, I tell him, but everything changes as soon as you bend over your invoices. What goes before seems like whetting the knife; when your scalpel is ready . . . He makes a scornful grimace that wrinkles his whole face, sunk under the weight of his hair. When you look at an invoice, he says, you're like a peasant who's looking over his property: he sees the Kantity of trees, of sheep, of manure and of children that he already has or that he needs: he only sees money. But a painter would see something very different. He would see that it's essential for everything to be IN THE RIGHT PLACE, to be in a precise location, with an inexorable color, volume and disposition. Which of the two is closer to what you call "meaning"? The farmer doesn't care if the cow is fat or thin, white or brown; he would go along with a green cow with no hooves if she gave him the Kantity of milk he wants. That's why he would go along with mechanizing everything — even himself, since his spirit is nothing but a thin, gaseous coating. All he sees are ghosts with price tags on them. The meaning of ghosts is interchangeable; you can substitute a cow for a sewing machine with no sense of loss. But those of us who pay attention understand the danger that lurks behind every change, and we're getting ready for what comes next. I see numbers as my property. My property is symbolic; its return isn't dependent on the Kantity.

Although I enjoy watching him officiate with his remote, pompous manners, I don't trust him or his numbers. What can we possibly find out from animals that can reproduce infinitely but that always begin and end in zero? All skulls are the same, but every face is a broken heart. Numbers are dry as dust. The Chinaman takes to them because he's essentially cold. The minute he leaves his arpeggios and turns to the accounts, he looks different: his mouth is pursed, a deep frown line forms above his glasses, a big vein throbs in his neck. He's the very image of a banker. He amputates, reduces, levels, ruins, with a simple computation. He moves living beings from one place to another by adding and subtracting; he's like the bubonic plague, conveyed by the invisible hand of the wind that kills from afar.

March 29th

Another cheery night on the Ramblas. I'm a cork floating on a sea of gin. Ocean liners, white and pedantic, sink; corks float on. Today corks of every size were afloat, a golden dross from the gallows. Because the Ramblas were the first jungle, the first no-man's-land. In the old city, they fell just outside the wall. That was where your candidate for a hanging foraged about for his living. And there they remained until the wall was demolished around 1820. The wall wasn't damaged by a single obus; instead, it was brought down by the progress in questions of artillery and ballistics that rendered such things obsolete. The noble blocks fell without a single cannon shot sounding; the *idea* of the cannon shot did the trick. Ideas, like impetuous winds, leveled walls all over Europe; they were stronger than cannons! But up until the idea-of-a-cannon-shot, the Ramblas were external, outside, insecure, open country.

For those who haven't yet reached the Idea, a walk along the Ramblas is still an extramural walk where whatever is uncivil, whatever doesn't admit monastic constrictions, persists. It was in this uncivil area that inch-long corks were floating today. Here venereal infections reach the highest quota in the Mediterranean. The ports of Marseilles, Genoa and La Goulette are Swiss clinics compared to our blenophilic puddle. Tonight the Catalonian Aphrodite was mounted on an Andean llama who had digested two generations of pig-keepers in service to the Crown. Tonight every smile (to-night EVERYBODY was smiling) was a dental specimen of the agricultural and livestock sector. Stench of gasoline with whiffs of manure. A drunken bumpkin was hoisting aloft his gigantic prick and singing the Riego hymn — O, Catalonia! — at the top of his lungs until he ran into the police. From the ground, his head split open, he was still shouting *"bon cop de samaler al bisbe."* The bishop needs a good thwacking! One of the cops stuck a nightstick in his mouth, and that shut him up.

I argued about prices with a very thin Argentine girl. She had no talent for bargaining, and the way she said "love" smacked of the university — as if she'd just read Paul Geraldy. The minute she accepted my terms, I was overwhelmed by an intolerable sense of revulsion; it was as if she'd been running stats for me. I took off fast so that I wouldn't throw up on her, but I got some on myself. I still smell. My stomach can't take anything now. I'll wind up losing my taste for these dragnets and investigations. If I'm not mistaken, what ails me is sheer nostalgia for the liquor store, for the *boredom* of the liquor store. Tedium ties us down more than anything. This explains why the matrimonial bond is so successful.

April 4th

Our suppers take place in a restaurant with pretensions to grandeur: the Peratallada, situated near the Vía Layetana, a spot where the folkloric elements (Ibizan arches, Maresme beams, rough brick walls) clash with the current architectural demands, all of which are based on a sense of humor and pastel tones. Even when the three of us are at a table together, the Chinaman and I are usually the only ones who talk. In spite of his craziness, Diego is a man of great dignity, and he seldom opens his mouth unless it's to satisfy himself that the produce is local. He doesn't accept anything foreign, but fortunately his imperialistic ideology allows him to include the entire peninsular with the understandable exceptions of Old and New Castile and Andalusia. He's proud of the Rioja wines, for example, because the Basque country is a sister nation. If, in the Chinaman, there are traces of the malign Orient, home of Fu Manchu, Diego preserves the inclinations of the benign Orient: plump, greasy females snoozing on pillows in lascivious nakedness, merchandise perfumed with basil tea, masculine chats about the best way to wield the scimitar when you're chopping off heads.

But our conversations are consumed by interruptions, not only to make room for the series of typical dishes that come our way — the *escalibadas*, the *espardenas*, the *esqueixadas* and the *empedrats* — but also to allow the Chinaman to engage in six or seven asides with individuals who approach him as if this were a second administrative seat that's showier and more important than the first. The clientele here is homogeneous: young men with good wool suits, no ties, wide pants and jackets with exaggerated shoulders. I would guess they pull in half a million *pesetas* a month. I have the greatest sympathy with these trustees of the Franco inheritance: they've left the rhetoric behind but haven't renounced the lack of scruples. Scoundrels are easier to tolerate without lyrical additives. Whenever I see them together, I try to guess which one will be the next hangman.

During the oases of tranquility today, the Chinaman kept on talking about numbers, but one of the things he said sounds like a threat. To me. I had made fun of mathematics. From the point of view of those in power, I said, math is a trivial adornment of the juridical system. I don't really know why I said it, nor what profound meaning I attached to the sentence, but the Chinaman drew up like a spring and then told me in a flute-like voice that really powerful men had to choose between the world and eternal life. You, of course, think that a person can live without making the choice, but not making the choice is the same as giving up, and only slaves give up.

His pedantry is extraordinarily irritating, and sometimes I can't contain myself, especially when I'm dealing with a baked vegetable medley. It's a mistake to interrupt him; the best thing is to let him talk. A man who's worked up is no longer very convincing. But today his excitement led him to his enigmatic threat. I argued that animals live in the world and that there are no grounds for assuming the obvious superiority of eternal life. There are grounds even though you're not aware of them, he answered. Animals and slaves live in the world, but their masters enjoy eternal life. Well, I don't see what's so shameful about being an animal or a slave, I say. The Chinaman sketched a gesture of pity like the police chief who understands the powerful motives that have inspired the purse snatcher but has no choice except to apply the law to him and turn him over to his destiny. You still prefer animals and slaves because you still feel a nostalgic need to love the victim. You're infected with Christianity and a horror of life, eternal life, but surely you're not so simple as to believe that all men are equally alive . . .

He can freeze his face until it's absolutely flat and expressionless, a mask put on to intimidate people. He plays dead just like a crocodile waiting for its prey. When this happens, he builds up such internal tension that an equilateral triangle appears over the crown of his head and strings of phosphorescent numbers follow each other across his eyes. At the end of a few seconds, a bell rings, and he comes to.

Diego, on the other hand, looks at him scornfully: I'm such an animal I can only deal with these things, pointing at the plates of beans and pig's feet and fish. Right now I'm stuffing them in my gut, but later on they'll eat me up. The Chinaman finds this very funny: See what I mean? And he adds with a warning hiss: But Diego isn't animal enough; one of these days, I'll show you a real animal.

Great. One of these days he'll show me a real animal. So what?

April 10th

In front of the cutler's shop on the little plaza of Santa María del Pino, a company of puppeteers sets up its stand on holidays and when the weather's good. It's a modest net thrown out by humble fishermen with the idea of catching any coins that overflow from the parishioners' pockets. This cutlery enjoyed great prestige before the quality of its blades was discredited. For the last few years, it has looked like a museum. I buy a beautiful switch-blade in the shape of woman's leg with a bronze shoe that serves as the release. It's a present for Diego.

Along with the façade of Santa María and the knives, pruning shears, files and pincers in the shop window, this little theater retains the Gothic fluidity, the sense of time standing still that has disappeared elsewhere. I stay there for quite a while, my hands behind my back in the canonical posture of the on-looker. The scarecrow. The marionettes move and form diagrams of great simplicity, the most basic grammar of our fatuous survival. If the spectacle is to be a success, the bodies, the hands that hold up the marionettes must remain invisible. The true protagonists must keep out of sight. If the real body were visible, the public would disperse. A judicious attempt to show the body would provoke scornful, even violent, reactions. Can you image any drama that permits the shameless presence of the one who pulls the strings!

In spite of what the Chinaman says, being a puppeteer or being a legislator, for that matter, and hiding behind the law, isn't really worth the effort. It's a job that's done in the dark, squatting down. I'd rather live on all fours, as Diego says, then on my haunches. A likeable fellow, Diego. When he's not busy, he asks me for real Catalonian expressions. I've just given him two good ones: "we've just drunk olive oil" and "she's a limp cabbage." He writes them down carefully in a lined notebook and pencils in neat parentheses afterwards:

"we've really blown it" and "she's a real dog." He's sharpening the rhetorical weapons of his blushing follower with the aim of infiltrating him into the Catalonian National Guard.

April 30th

I'm eaten up with boredom. It's stupid, I know. Because of course I know it's thanks to this routine that I can tell the difference between dead time and living time. I try to make sure that ALL time is living time, and, not surprisingly, I'm left with nothing but ashes. Drink has a greater effect on me now. You shouldn't cut back on the amount you drink, because it's very painful to get up to your normal level again. Youthful variations on the theme of purity (stop smoking, take cold showers, get up at dawn, read Popper) are understandable as a preparation for old age, but in a corrupt man they're disgusting. What lesson are they trying to teach us, those fitness nuts? By the way, the Chinaman really bores me with all his purity. Diego bores me too, with his eternal copy of Pompeyo Fabra's Catalonian dictionary.

Yesterday the second hired killer showed up. He came in like someone who'd been resurrected from the dead, and he went to work without saying a word, except for greeting me with exquisite politeness (Good evening, how are you? Well, thanks, how about you? Not bad, I can't complain. I'm glad to hear that. Thank you.) before opening up a sports paper. His black shoes were shining like polished jet, giving his well-oiled head a lot of competition. Nothing happened. Well, yes, something did happen, but it can't be helped; so it's not worth talking about. The question he asked, before closing the bar, sums it all up: Excuse me, please. Can I have my month's pay? The Chinaman turned his plaster mask on the fellow. They are so entirely different that they seem to divvy up the same ground — both of them firmly planted — on opposite sides of the Earth. Three weeks, the Chinaman answered.

Because, in this duo of wolves and lambs, there's a certain rationale that never quite disappears: the working day. It's a fiction, but one that's convenient for both parties. Otherwise, they'd have to work out their positions with knives. I find this just as amazing as the fact that bankers are reimbursed as soon as the war they've financed comes to an end. But there would be no civilization without bankers. The semi-delinquent life form we have here, this fodder for the gallows, comes down to a bureaucracy as well. It's all a barracks. The liquor store stinks of the barracks, reflects the colorless light of the barracks, evokes the apathy and decay and meanness, the latrines with obscene drawings. It's a nucleus of degradation, like depots, railway stations, sacristies, hangars . . . places where the pools of blood are cleaned up with a good swipe of the rag. Life is in a coma here.

What does the Chinaman's work consist of? Supplementing the national administration. Some birds clean the crocodiles' teeth, and some men clean the REAL CRIMINALS' hands. These subalterns, these affable parasites, live in the shadows of their masters.

Great. But what does the Chinaman do? The usual: he finances blackmail, I suppose, buys merchandise, adulterates and sells it, expedites false driver's licenses, traffics in the adoption trade, hides runaways, runs bars in his own name or someone else's, peddles influence, raffles off information, fixes bids, distributes products. Does it matter what you call it? I can't see how it differs from the usual perfectly acceptable commercial, industrial and administrative practices. Who decided it's okay to sell aspirin but not dynamite? And that *only a few people* can sell it? Where can you buy tungsten? The Chinaman is just performing a public service. Thanks to him, operations that are usually hampered by democratic-egalitarian hypocrisy run smoothly. He's INNOCENT.

There's no real difference between day and night. It's only an idea; the substance is the same. That is, they are made of the same substance but perceived by an animal who's obsessed with differentiating, with dividing that substance in two. Why shouldn't we accept the social value of illegality, then? Why not admit that the Chinaman makes the same contribution to the empire of death as a bishop or a stockbroker? I'm not going to find anything new at the Chinaman's. Everything's rotten to the core. Criminals and great men have both agreed to SUPPORT the law. And to think I once believed the hired gun was a noble soul! Talk about naïve! Talk about misguided! The only way you can make profits is *outside* the law. The enterprising man NEEDS the criminal! The history of the world boils down to the collaboration between criminals and legislators. But this delicate truth mustn't fall on innocent ears. Hitler tried to make everything clear, and look where he ended up. The criminal has to keep his place in the shadows, just like the rat, out of sight but always ready to provide his services.

May 2nd

A grotesque scene! We were stupefied, mired in our fish and our baked vegetables, chewing on, half-dead, full, when suddenly all hell broke loose! Shouts of *maître* at the Peratallada's door, waiters in motion, guests uneasy. It's impossible. I can't believe it: Señor Torras, Señor Torras with all his ninety-three years, locked in hand to hand combat with the restaurant manager, who, in a desperate effort to keep him out, is holding on to the arm of his jacket. The waiters don't dare intervene. They watch from a distance like urbanites at a traffic accident. Señor Torras is emitting rat-like screams and jumping up and down with both feet. *Deixam anar, recony!* Let me alone, you cunt! you can hear him shouting. The *maître* doesn't really get down to it; he's terrified of breaking one of that apparition's incredibly fragile bones. At last Señor Torras slips away like an eel, and the manager is left, disconcerted, with the jacket hanging in his hand. Señor Torras' agility is astonishing. He makes his way from table to table with the speed of a hare, scrutinizing the guests and revealing a set of *esparto* suspenders that keep his pants up at the level of his sternum so that his tie hangs from his collar like a third limb of the same egg color, the same texture and the same diameter as his arms. Two waiters try to cut him off, but Señor Torras avoids them with a pretty taurine pass while continuing to inspect the clientele, who draw back in shock every time he leans down and nails his eyes three inches away from someone's face; at any greater distance, he can't tell a dog from a buffalo.

As you can well imagine, I was engaged in an inner

struggle, trying to decide whether or not to make myself known. I was convinced that, thanks to some miracle or supernatural power, Señor Torras not only was looking for me but even knew where to find me at that late hour. Much to my surprise, however, once he reached our table (he arrived at the same time as a waiter, who was trying to block him like a football and wound up running head-on into a pillar), instead of recognizing me, or my father or my grandfather, he addressed the Chinaman with an intimidating smile and screeched: *ara si que t'he enxampat, malparit!* Now I've got you, you son of a bitch! — at the same time he seemed to scratch his flanks as if he were overcome by a sudden itch.

But he wasn't scratching his flanks; he was looking for something in the pockets of his jacket, and his jacket, like a Republican flag captured by the *fascio*, was still hanging from the *maître's* hand. Desperate, Señor Torras turned his cranium in different directions, cursing shrilly: *M'han fotut la jaqueta! m'han fotut la jaqueta! lladres! policia! me cago en la mare que els va parir!* They've stolen my jacket, they've stolen my jacket! Thieves! Police! Shit on the mother who gave birth to them! — and so on until the manager gave the rag back to him, convinced that it's better to abandon yourself in the arms of destiny than to struggle against a force of nature.

Relieved, Señor Torras wept a few tears (*molt agraït, senyor, no sé pas com li ho hauria explicat al meu pare: la jaqueta es seva, sap?* Thank you, sir. I don't know how I would have explained it to my father. It's his jacket, you know?). Finally, right under the nose of the honorable *maître* , he produced a battered envelope ornamented with a big stain that must have come from sardines packed in oil. This he handed over to the Chinaman with an almost eighteenth-century flourish. *Vosé és el paio que li diuen el Xino, oi? Doncs tingui, de la part del señor Enrique, i que li aprofiti!* You're the guy they call the Chinaman, eh? Well, this is for you from Señor Enrique, and I hope it's useful to you! The envelope didn't tremble a bit in those gnarled fingers. The Chinaman took it and, without opening his mouth, much less the envelope, put it in his briefcase pocket. Then he asked the *maître*, whose unnecessary presence was making Señor Torras very uneasy since he obviously suspected the man of being a coat thief, to accompany the elderly gentleman (that's what he said, "elderly gentleman," hmmm!) to the door. And offer him a drink, please, he added majestically. *Això sí que no! Si fos una dona, encara, pero d'alcohol, jo, ni gota.* Absolutely not! I might still be interested in a woman, but I won't touch a drop of alcohol! Well then, offer him a woman. Diego, it's out of our hands. *Home, moltes gràcies! Mira quin noi més trempat! Gràcies, maco!* Thanks very much. What a nice boy! Thanks, kid! And happy as a lark, Señor Torras went out, escorted by Diego on the way to some brothel. Hey, grandpa, I heard Diego say, When you were young, did you know Prat de la Riba? *Un putero, aquell sí que ho era, de putero!* A real fucker, that one was, a real fucker! And what a president!

I suppressed my curiosity. I'd bet the Chinaman is well aware of my relation with "Señor Enrique." All he said was: What a repulsive old man! Imagine eating canned sardines!

May 15th

Softened up by the repetition imposed on me by my *idle occupation*, I return to the land of alcohol without taking the

least precaution and immediately win a prize. The incident
took place in that peculiar bar, the Malvaloca, seat of the
city's sublimest lyrical and artistic traditions, a hangar with
naked light bulbs hanging from greasy wires. On its dance
floor, elderly people of both sexes exhibit themselves in a
half-dressed state. They're not just egged on by poverty —
that would be too natural for the taste of the public — but
intoxicated by GLORY; you can tell from the gleam of sacred
madness that dances in their eyes. A satanic vanity nests in
the straw-filled brains and flowers on the faces of these artists; it's like a green fly flashing over a tasty pile of excrement. The spectacle is part of any young person's ethical
initiation. No one who has seen an eighty-year old woman
vibrating, strutting and wheedling while her toothless mouth
intones a ditty that goes "they used to call me Tomato 'cause
I'm from the farm," no one who has seen that can ever look
at his grandmother with the same eyes again. Grannies are
very big in this ethnic group.

Well, it was in this very place last night that I came upon
my onetime professor and longtime friend, the old and well-
loved Leandro Bonet, who had been drawn, undoubtedly, by
the bar's connotations. He was seated on a green plastic stool,
engaged in animated conversation with an Arab. We hadn't
seen each other for five or six years, but he wasn't anywhere
near as old as I'd imagined he'd be. A big glass of what looked
like Coke and turned out to be brandy may have been his
fountain of youth. He still has a full head of hair, pulled back
at the neck with a fancy comb of embossed leather, an exu-
berant rat-colored cascade, furrowed with countless white
threads, that provides him with a kind of electronic nimbus

and makes quite a show. His clothes, an ornamental medley gathered together from the most unlikely sources, provide a synopsis of the history of occidental attire. From the fourth century B.C., represented by the huge, thick-soled buskins that elevate him majestically like a Peloponnesian tragedian, to the *incroyable* style of the late eighteenth century, embodied in a vest with lemon-colored flowers on a cream background and in a sequined shawl: an example of every single European fashion for the last twenty centuries finds a niche on this welcoming body.

Now that those times have passed when lads and lasses covered themselves from head to foot with ornaments and flowers and left their arms looking like Swiss cheese, the sight of Leandro Bonet arouses the sausage-maker's ire and the teenager's empathy. Both reactions are dear to this philosopher's heart, and he encourages both. The Moroccan, for example, a young man about twenty-something, had stopped selling his watches and condoms in order to solve a few elementary problems. His eyes were as wide as saucers. But it's true, you say, that Allah is less God than God?

Leandro has dedicated his whole life to a pugnacious pedagogy (imparted through abundant body movements, swinging of arms, making of faces, twisting of hips and flexing of limbs) that he inherited from those severe anarchists who used to indulge in their affection for nudity and lettuce in an atmosphere perfumed by TNT. From the top of his heap of apparel, Leandro's head continued to release ideas with more feathers to them than the savage lances that once hummed past scrawny colonizers with pointy knees. Yes, of course! He's less than God because he came later, and the more Time that passes, the less God is God. The Arab scratches his throat with a hand the color of chocolate.

During my years of apprenticeship, after I was separated from the greats of old — the Buzzard, the Wise Man and Cucurella — Leandro was my guide. He was an intrepid and vehement leader, but the generation he modeled with a potter's hands has been destroyed now, and he has had to make do in an unfriendly environment where it gets harder and harder to distinguish between the disciple and the live one who pays for a drink, a meal or a trip to the brothel. I'm sure that when he dies he'll be just about to say something, his insolent, Velázquez gaze still intact and his passion still at fever pitch. I've heard him argue with the dexterity of a baroque duelist, waiting until it's CONVENIENT to undo his opponent. Nowadays, nobody dominates this technique. And I've seen potentates of the intellect tremble with terror and fall to their knees before one of his sophisms.

The minute he recognized me — even though he's the enemy of all sentimental effusions — he clasped me to his chest, crushing me with the mass of necklaces and sharks' teeth that hang from a neck swollen with greenish veins. He completely forgot the Moslem, whose expression was so perplexed that the slightest breeze would have blown away eyes, eyebrows, moustache, lips and nose, leaving nothing behind but a smooth ball. Leandro liquidated his glass of brandy in two gulps. What time is it? he asked the Arab, consulting one of the watches and then strapping it on his wrist without a thought. I'm starving! he added and pushed me into the street.

The man I'm remembering is baroque in nature, affected to the point of exasperation, twisted as the sacristy in Granada, a man who never takes questions up in what we've come to think is the only possible order but tackles from the opposite end instead. As a result, his attacks tend to defend exactly what he's attacking. If, for example, he starts a diatribe against the persistence of religion among the simple folk (this often happens when he hears flamenco, as was the case tonight), he does so with the intention of demonstrating the marvelous presence of desire even among those people whose ferocious, daily poverty keeps them from reflecting about anything at all so that they've never been able to reach a conception of the divine character of mortal beings. There they are, living vicariously off the triumphs of others, real guardians of Death, aptly administering that phantom born of the noblest aspirations. Shall we go in?

Pushing me all the time — when he walks he elbows you without interrupting the flow of talk for even a second — he led me to a cafe with a pink plastic sign. Written in white wash on the window was a list of exquisite, alimentary possibilities that were monopolized by the avian and the porcine. We sat down at a Formica table covered with pools of beer and ordered a gin for me and the "Ipanema Special" (a quarter chicken, salad, croquettes and a hard-boiled egg with mayonnaise, anchovies and olives) for him.

Naturally he didn't ask about the friends we have in common. A man who's busy penetrating the causes of our ignorance can't let himself be distracted by substitutes, and it's well known that friendship is one of the most insidious disguises for laziness, as big a waste of time as cards and billiards. Instead, Leandro Bonet started analyzing an ad for sausages that's printed on the napkin dispenser. He does it with the mastery of a surgeon whose scalpel separates elements that to the uninitiated seem indistinguishable. Leandro's versatile talent takes on a satanic brilliance when it's applied to linguistic problems. In one of his most famous discourses, he analyzed a proclamation issued by the municipal government of Madrid and dictated by a mayor notorious for his atheistic pretensions. Leandro demonstrated that the use of certain syntactical peculiarities revealed beyond the shadow of a doubt the author's unconscious belief in the eucharistic hypothesis.

Leandro's life has evaporated in the diffusion of brave messages whose effect would only be perceptible if they were understood by the enormous masses of citizens whom, in principle, he addresses. However, the extraordinary elegance of the argument gives his messages a luxurious, alexandrine form inaccessible to anyone not possessed of universal knowledge. His ideas can only be effective if they're shared by the disinherited of the earth, but through no fault of their own that mass of humanity is incapable of understanding him. That's why his followers are limited to a handful of privileged pariahs who are unable to put even the simplest of his moral notions into practice.

He's not a Don Quixote or Fermín Salvochea sort of idealist, an idealist defeated by that pitiless stupidity called realism. Leandro, in fact, advocates no change; instead, he pushes for a complete acceptance of the *status quo*. But this acceptance involves Great Rebelliousness. This extraordinary doctrine will never reach the masses although Leandro is their true leader and guide. But it doesn't matter because — even if it had reached them — it wouldn't have changed anything. That's the very crux of the doctrine.

However, its effect on the *lumpen* aristocracy that follows it has been very different. If you take the doctrine from an individual point of view, applying it to ME and not to the MASSES, its results are catastrophic. Salt, which is essential for maintaining ocean life, would have terrible consequences it were concentrated in a pond. When it's applied individually, total rebellion in favor of the *status quo* has provoked countless cases of suicide, idiocy and catatonia. Sometimes all three.

Leandro is completely innocent since he always addresses mankind in general rather than this or that more or less insignificant individual. But we, his followers, found it impossible to imagine that our master and friend was not referring to our own special case, our own special problem; so we got intoxicated breathing in at home stuff that should have been administered to a multitude in a football stadium. Over a period of years, then, Leandro's doctrine has had two consequences: on the one hand, it's followed by the masses, who have never heard of it, and on the other, it's betrayed by people who are totally undone precisely because they *do* understand it. The only people to benefit from his doctrine are totally unaware of its existence.

All this time Leandro was devouring the drinks, the croquettes, the salad, the hard-boiled egg with great voracity and without dropping his analysis of the sausage ad. I was touched. His output of energy was so great, and the wild cuffing he was giving the phantasms of material thought and invincible reality was so admirable, that the real importance of a pedagogical method like his suddenly dawned on me: THE SHOW. That is, the show of faith and passionate belief. It doesn't really matter whether that faith and that passion are directed toward a concept, a state, the universe, eternal glory or a basketball team. From the master you only learn to love the fight. Nothing else matters. Seeing him move about the stage, brandishing his wooden sword, aware of the superior powers flying overhead that are ready to crush him in a moment of caprice: that was the content of his lessons.

In an unexpected moment of silence, I mentioned that I was working in an office that formed part of the underworld. Ah, work! he exclaimed, work: that's the only theological system left us. There's no God now except the Job, no Time but the Hourly Rate! When I see these brainless heads rolling along the Assembly Line, these little cream tits subjected to the Progress of Death, I wonder if that other Lord who threatened us with his Ire and his Destruction wasn't better at least than this new one whose splendor has been tarnished by Profit and Progress. The old one didn't make any promises, and the boys and girls fucked in the Spring sun and danced on their own graves because Death nourished their dances like a Stepmother. Now they neither fuck nor dance; they're too busy building Paradise, and now Death has lost its sting since between them they've all plugged it into tubes and electrodes in the Hospital, which is just another form of the Factory and the Movie Theater. So, the State is Paradise now! There you have it. Since they're all the Same, they vote for the Other, and they keep right on progressing because nobody slows down Progress, not a lion in the path, not a spanner in the works, not a goddamn thing!

Recently Leandro has developed a vocabulary he thinks typical of the common people; it's full of capital letters, diminutives and the rural lexicon of around 1898. He's convinced that by means of this simple literary subterfuge he will reach the hearts of the masses with amazing ease. The masses, however, no longer know what an adze or a sharpshooter is, and the diminutives evoke nothing so much as a nunnery, but this doesn't discourage Leandro.

Crime isn't what it used to be, Leandro, I told him. If you want to go in for murder, first you have to get credit at a Savings Bank. Last week they sent a guy to Bayonne to play Shoot at the Basques, and they had to take out an insurance policy on him.

Dawn found us in the Plaza de Cataluña, steadying ourselves shoulder to shoulder in order to avoid being swept away in the early morning tide. In the poisonous green light, we felt cold and bored. Evading the anthropophagous taxis, I took Leandro by the arm and led him to the boarding house on Pelayo where he rents an inside room. His eyes were still darting about like a hawk's in hopes of finding an open bar. The old guy is as tough as a buffalo. When we said good-bye, I lit out like a bat that takes flight, beating its big bony membranes. His last words were undoubtedly produced by fatigue: Do you come around here often? They were a modest appeal for help, inspired by the ancestral terror of turning up dead on a corner some day without a familiar hand to hold on to. The petition was dignified, but essentially contrary to his Doctrine. No, I answered. Hardly ever.

May 16th

The Chinaman wakes me up at four in the afternoon. Stupefied by fatigue, I at first confuse the sound of the telephone with the honking horns. Then I overturn loaded ashtrays and old newspapers in my effort to reach the machine.

He arranges to meet me at his house as soon as possible, and in my bewildered state I don't even realize that I'd never given him my phone number nor told him where I live. Catching sight of myself in the mirror, I feel repelled by my body, my filthiness, my very self. I leave at top speed.

He receives me with an onslaught of affability. We sit in leather chairs on the terrace. On the table: the sempiternal sheets of paper covered with ciphers; on the papers: the minute coffee set. I nod, half dozing, and if I don't fall asleep, it's due to the nausea brought on by my hangover. I didn't even shave. My hair is sticky, my clothes sweaty, my hands swollen. But he's as shiny as the silver coffee pot, polished by I know not whose hands. Diego's? It would be amusing if Diego also performed domestic chores. The coffee burns my palate, which has already been flayed by alcohol and tobacco.

I can't pay much attention to the Chinaman, and he has intuited as much, so he's speaking slowly, refilling the minuscule cups as soon as they're empty. He seems to be touching on something I don't understand, something personal, although he hasn't asked for my opinion. I'm not following him, perhaps because of the dissipation of the last few days. Or is he referring *directly* to me? Because finally he asks, How do you think a man who has no dignity can put up with life? It's the kind of question we used to ask during recess; so I respond unwillingly, without much enthusiasm. He doesn't move a muscle, just keeps on looking at me, inviting me to come up with a more satisfactory answer. What do I know about dignity? You need will power and determination even to kill yourself, and I think that's giving yourself too much importance. I imitate the animals; they make themselves small when they're in danger. Correct, the

Chinaman says in odiously soft tones, but animals don't kill themselves. You're wrong there. It's not that they don't kill themselves, it's that they don't make decisions, and so we think animals ONLY kill others. The Chinaman makes a characteristic gesture; he lifts his thin hand and shakes it with his fingers open while he nods majestically. I have the uneasy feeling I'm taking an exam, but I'm good at exams.

To kill you need enemies. Do you know how to make enemies? I've never had one, but if I come across one, I think I'll know how to recognize him. Out of animal instinct, I suppose! You can't say that the Chinaman smiles, but on certain occasions like this he's capable of producing a fairly close imitation. The truth is, I don't hold anything against him, I just feel irritated. Okay. You're right. I don't know how to make enemies. Is that why I have no dignity? Do you have to humiliate me over and over again? The anteater doesn't let a single ant get away; not a single rat escapes the cat, but NOTHING AND NO-BODY that arouse my appetite have passed in front of my eyes yet. So I still don't know if I'm an anteater or a cat. It can't be helped. Ah, you sound very puffed up for someone who has been humiliated! he answers. Because you're forgetting one possibility: what if you're neither the anteater nor the cat, but the ant or the rat instead. You're lucky nobody has eaten you . . .

At that point I really did feel vexed. Because the Chinaman is absolutely right. In my foolish vanity, I still thought I was the hunter when, if anything, I'm the prey. The ridiculous prey of some insignificant animal. What would I have done with the pistol in my hand and the hit man in front of me? Wouldn't I have felt more NATURAL in the opposite situation, the hit man pointing his pistol and me crestfallen? Wasn't I born to be somebody else's *aperitif*? The hangover was overcoming me with its malignant, mortiferous gases. Finally, furious, I yelled: Well, if somebody catches me, I hope he gets poisoned.

I think it's the first time I've ever heard the Chinaman laugh. It's quite an experience. First he produces a whistle like a balloon that's losing air, and then he cackles very slowly. It's sinister. Let's visit the zoo. I think that'll calm your nerves, he says. The zoo? Now? Yes, the zoo. I have to take care of something. He's in good spirits, and by the time we're heading down Bulnes, I'm beginning to come out of my state of self-pity.

The zoological garden is included in the Ciudadela enclosure, very close to the north docks and the Estación de Francia. It's a corner of the city that is hardly related to the rest, an *almost* civilized zone that by some miracle has survived the successive generations of patriotic speculators. Its origins are characteristic and instructive: the Spanish army razed more than a million houses in this area as a retribution against the citizens for having been so fickle as to choose the Austrian archduke's party in 1705. It was a kind of *corporal* punishment, which is the highest level of intelligence the national militia ever reaches. Once the ruins were cleared away, they built a citadel on the site — that is, a fortress — so that the Catalonians could see who's boss. Later the fortress gave way to gardens. It had served its purpose: they had seen. It's almost comic that the only worthwhile park here should be inhabited by animals, but that's the way it is; they've kept the best part of the capitol for themselves. Here the least of the gorillas lives in greater comfort than the mayor himself.

We entered the park by the Avenida de los Tilos, and I parked opposite the National History Museum. We're not going

to visit the zoo after all, but its taxidermic form. The Chinaman
heads toward a side door painted English green; in the middle of
it are a bell in the form of a nipple and an administrative label.
Soon after he rings, the door is opened by a round — I was
about to write "spherical" — individual about thirty years old,
clean-shaven, smiling, attentive and mellifluous. He has soft,
sweaty hands and limps slightly like Byron. The huge, cork sole
of his left shoe reminds me immediately of Mussolini's girlfriend.

We follow him along a corridor that opens onto the ground
floor, an immense nave that is dark now because the museum is
closed to the public in the afternoon. The Chinaman stops
when we come to the mammoth. The piece can barely be made
out in the dark; it's an immense, smooth shadow. Did you also
put this one together bone by bone? he asks. The cripple nods
his head, but then corrects himself: Well, it's not actually ours;
it's a French installation. A complete fabrication, I think. Who
knows . . . And then he comes up with a wild theory. According
to his scientific opinion, prehistoric animals are shamelessly
reconstructed from unrelated fossils. The bones and remains
are gathered together higgledy-piggledy: a reptile's head, a
mammal's rib, a saurian's tail, it doesn't matter. They use
everything they find, and then they baptize whatever comes
out. A monster! How can a diplodocus have a head like that?
That's a snake's head stuck to a dragon's body. That's what
it's like with all museum animals. An absolute exploitation
of the child's innocence. A swindle! What I do is *completely*
different, he concludes dramatically.

We reach a little stairway with an iron handrail. A
patched-together, provisional piece of work that looks like
it's been there provisionally from the time of Primo de Rivera.

On the first floor is a study filled with books on comparative anatomy, the odd one opened to show big, steel engravings. There's also a twisted goose-neck lamp and a stool, where it's easy to imagine the cripple going over the drawings as if they were works of pornography. He opens a little door of unpainted plywood at the end of the study, and we're in a room full of bones. It seems like a funereal discovery, a Sicilian catacomb or the charnel house of a Trappist monastery, except that here the bones are put away, labelled and ordered in cardboard boxes that range in size from shoe to cider barrel.

In the corner to the left of the entrance, the dusty, dried up skin of a crocodile hangs from a nail. The cripple proudly shows it to the Chinaman. Eh, what do you think? The Chinaman examines it without touching it. It smells of formaldehyde, and the yellowish glow that hangs from the ceiling tinges it with diabolical reflections. The Chinaman takes five thousand *pesetas* out of his pocket and gives them to the cripple bill by bill. The cripple doesn't take his eyes off the bills, but he seems disappointed when, once five has been reached, the distribution comes to a halt. Hey, this isn't enough; this is a pittance. You can get four purses out of this at the very least. This is worth at least half a million, and at five thousand *pesetas* a pound . . . But the Chinaman cuts him off, I'm not paying you for the skin, but for those other things . . . Go on, show the skeletons to my friend. The cripple hesitates. He's not happy, but he's afraid to complain. He smiles compliantly and, after a submissive grimace, pockets the bills. Then he signals me to follow him.

The second floor is a bare space with a floor that feels like clay and a big window that provides air and light opening onto the park. The room is as big as a garage, a grove of skeletons that have been wired together, some complete, others half finished. A bear, a deer, a wild boar, two horses, a vicuña . . . along with smaller ones that might be weasels. The cripple smiles with satisfaction as he names them to us one by one. He strolls between the skeletons like an overseer at Dachau, his hands inside his pants' waist and his thumbs on his belt. What do you think of this? Done without any help! I taught myself! I have all of Cuvier in here — and he strikes his bulbous forehead so hard that his glasses jump like a frog. There aren't many left now since it's the season. If you'd been here a few months ago . . . And there's a lot more to be done! All those boxes downstairs! There's no rest for the weary!

The Chinaman looks at him straight on. Tell us the truth. Do you kill them with your own hands? The cripple starts, flaps his hands, opens and closes his fish mouth, screams in soprano. What are you saying, Señor Chino! They die, they die of old age and what people throw at them — screws, nails, balled-up bread with bolts inside, tubes of glue — people love to poison animals because when they die, they move around a lot instead of being still, half asleep and bored like they usually are. Why should I kill them? I don't need to! Fine, fine, but once they're dead, do you skin them yourself? Again he smiles, calmed down and proud of himself. He puts his hands back in the waist of his pants and stands on his toes. I wouldn't dream of skinning them. There's only one way to do it. There's only one system! A scientific system!

He doesn't tell us what it is; he just looks at us scornfully. Now he's going to show us something magnificent, something that few people have seen. He leads us across the room to a landing. He points to a lock. What do you think? Should I open it? The lock secures a trap door that obviously leads to the terrace; the many damp spots (traces of antediluvian leaks) testify that the museum is flat-roofed. But when the cripple opens the hatch, and we peer in, an unexpected, penetrating buzzing makes us jump. I manage to see a thick, black cloud that rises like a magic carpet. It turns in on itself, spreads out, draws together. I think I'm hallucinating; in two seconds it has disappeared from sight. Flies! The best, the most SCIENTIFIC method! Meat flies! They eat everything and leave it clean as a whistle! Now I see the partially decomposed bodies of three unrecognizable animals spread around the floor. They're dromedaries, he says. They were born dead. The doughy mass of skin is being mined by white larva that move frenetically like the fingers of a violinist. A pungent, sweetish smell hits me in the face. I back up sickened, unconsciously drawn by the rosary of larva. I've just had time to see the eye cavities. I start throwing up. Bah! says the Chinaman. I've seen this kind of filth in Africa time and time again. And I know even better methods!

The cripple closes the door, and we go down the little stair. I have to grab the handrail several times. Everything looks blank to me, and I'm soaked with sweat. Before we leave, the Chinaman comments calmly, Do they already know about it in Health? The cripple jumps. He moves his mouth. If he could turn pale, he would, but it's impossible because he's already the color of a stingray's belly. Well, you should be careful. If anyone goes to the authorities, you could have a bad time of it. Be sure to let me know when one of the bears dies on you; I'll be needing a coat soon.

While the Chinaman is taking me home, I start shaking as if I had fever. I feel dirtier than ever, and I keep imagining

I hear flies buzzing. He takes me to the apartment building, but I don't even have the strength to ask him how he got my address. I have a weak stomach. I'm a weakling. The crocodile skin lets out a sinister crackle from the back seat. See, the Chinaman tells me, you never know who finishes off whom. When we think it's all over, then the flies begin. One of these days, I'm going to show you an extraordinary animal, one of the strangest in the world. And, stranger yet: it's mine. It's my exclusive property.

I get out of the car feeling really sick. Do you have your wallet? he asks me. No, I don't have my wallet. I wave goodbye and slam the door of the Citroën. I just catch him saying that we have work to do tomorrow. It's very clear that the Chinaman feels a visceral antipathy toward my banality and that he wants to teach me a lesson. With that idea in mind, he keeps me under control, tries to humiliate me. But his teaching method is corrupt. He doesn't even use fear, just DISGUST. I feel sorry for the animal that has fallen into his hands. Everything in this man is experimentation. The world was created to provide him with guinea pigs.

May 17th

Obeying orders, I turned up at the liquor store at opening time. But nothing worth mentioning happened. Far less anything related to the "work" he had announced yesterday. The night went by quietly with few interruptions. We kept on talking about animals, animals and more animals. In any event, the interruptions are sometimes funny. Today a member of the forces of law and order showed up in his tobacco-colored uniform, his pistol in his belt, his cap on and sporting gold braid on his jacket. Instead of getting upset, Diego slapped him on the back (It's been a long time! It's great to see you! How's the wife?) and they toasted each other with one of the bottles of malt whiskey that are still left. The Chinaman devoted a long time to him without either one of them being in the least disturbed by my presence.

This highly remarkable official works in conjunction with a couple of trusted associates to strip those estates that contract him or some private security business to protect them. The operation is elegant and profitable, since the only people who ask for protection are the citizens who keep goods of some value in their "second homes," as he himself calls them. He had left a van parked outside the bar, and while he finished off his business with the Chinaman, the two helpers unloaded half a dozen televisions, an equal number of stereos, carpets, two telescopes, VCRs, short-wave radios, satellite dishes, fur coats . . . in short, the usual garbage of the rich. As far as jewels and foreign currency, the Chinaman doesn't deal in them; it must be another department. He paid six hundred thousand *pesetas* for the whole load.

I was delighted with the public official's good manners, and while the Chinaman inspected the load, I exchanged a few words with him. Apparently, he had gotten the idea for his little enterprise from the French security teams that work the Côte d'Azur. They've become fabulously wealthy. What we have here, of course, is like everything we do: puny in comparison. The Costa Brava isn't Monte Carlo. I asked him if they also requisitioned paintings, but he assured me it's not really worthwhile because the rich people around here have no taste, all you'll see on their walls are things they've gotten on sale at some chi-chi gallery like the Parés. You can't imagine what awful taste our wheeler-dealers have! If you could see the things they collect! Hey, I'm not saying that if I run into a Morandi some time I'm going to leave it behind, but usually the best you'll find is a bad imitation of Dalí, the kind you find in the book stalls by the Seine. My wife, Amparo, has a degree in art history. I used to take her along at first to help out. Talk about misguided . . . Have you ever found a Mont Blanc pen, one of those big, black ones? I could really use one. Count on it if I run across one. You're absolutely right. We never pay any attention to details, and they're really what we get the most pleasure from. The other day, you wouldn't believe it, we were taking out a fax machine a Delegate had installed in his house — I don't know why he needed one since he's Autonomous. But anyway, imagine, out of everything he had what caught my eye was a book by Stevenson, *Treasure Island* — have you read it? It was bound in blue leather, a real beauty. I don't know . . . I've been fond of that book ever since I was a kid.

I'd bet a lot that reading Stevenson as a child pushed this guy into spending his life looking for treasure — and he doesn't even realize it. A charming man, tall, strong, about thirty-five, with an energetic head, like the profile on an Italian coin. And beautifully educated! He has a law degree. He reads French and English, and he only joined the police force when his first child was born in order to make a little money. Once we were alone, the Chinaman agreed with my panegyrics: A real professional! he said. It's the first time I've ever heard him praise one of his employees.

Then we went back to talking about animals. I don't know why, but we only talk about animals of late. Today we got onto hunting. I, of course, have never hunted anything in my life, and I told him so. I don't have the moral health to go around the countryside blowing up rabbits and partridges with buckshot. The Chinaman isn't interested in that kind of game. The interesting thing, he says, is to hunt live, whole animals in order to set up an EXCHANGE. In captivity, animals adopt an artificial behavior. I want to get hold of the animal as it is, without losses. I want it to turn itself over of its own free will. That's real hunting! The most intricate and arduous part is convincing the animal to hand itself over, considering that you can't offer it advantages over its natural state. The line of argument consists in letting it know that it's in possession of something valuable it doesn't even know it has, and then in convincing it to hand this thing over to you voluntarily and free of charge. As you'd expect, this kind of hunt only involves the capture of a very special animal, a highly unusual animal. And have you caught one of these animals? I ask him. Correct. I've caught one of these animals, my favorite animal. Once again the promise of showing it to me soon.

I don't really understand a hunt that doesn't destroy its prey. One summer on Ibiza, I managed to establish a solid friendship with the lizards that are the principal — if not the only — resource of the island. There were many different species: there were malachite green ones with pink bellies; others had skin like moiré; some were huge, dusty saurians with incrustations of graphite; the most abundant were just plain, little lizards with their heads always up sniffing around; but there were also haughty lizards with pretensions to iguanicity, lazy leftovers from the

Carboniferous Era. Every one of them, without exception, used to come for me to give them their food and drink at my retreat, a whitewashed hut, very cool and dark inside, that was up in the hills. They ate everything from rotten apricots to leftover macaroni in tomato sauce. I used to shower with ice cubes in order to alleviate the Palestinian heat, and the lizards would crowd around my feet, licking the puddles with tongues like pumice stones. They were more faithful than dogs. At dusk, for example, they would climb all over my body while I read or wrote, and even though they rushed off if I made any sudden movement (as a result I turned each page so slowly that, by the time I finished turning, I forgot what I'd just read — probably not a bad thing), once their instinct for survival was satisfied, they would come back to doze on my legs or arms until the moon had risen. The country people flatten them with a whack of the hoe.

Since then I've developed an affection for lizards that is impossible to satisfy in this city. They are extremely decorative, much more so than canaries, parakeets, squirrels and tropical fish. Their meat is tasty, better than chicken, and they're cleverer than chickens at laying eggs too. It's very clear that the practice of domestication has been in the hands of idiots who've developed a rustic, parochial sort of method bereft of imagination. Whoever could imagine domesticating chickens and pigs when they have lizards so close at hand? It's inconceivable. On top of it all, there are nocturnal and diurnal lizards, and this doesn't happen with chickens or pigs. Take the gecko, for example, that little character with protruding eyes and suckers on his feet who hovers round the street lamps at night looking for insects. He's obviously a superior being! There's no up or down for him: he walks vertically, horizontally, on the floor, on the wall, on the ceiling, and he's always ON HIS FEET. He's never underneath anything. They can't HUMILIATE him. He has no definite color; he can be grey or white or just dirty. His color is the absence of color, the color of the earth as a blind man imagines it.

The chicken and the pig, now, have brought a whole host of disasters in their wake. Think how many violent deaths have been provoked by the insult Pig! Swine! Porky! SOW! How many murders! And remember what most people think about the biological link between women and chickens, both of them shameless hussies! If our ancestor who was so obsessed with the chicken and the pig had only domesticated the lizard instead, he wouldn't have died of malaria, and he wouldn't have infected his life with animals that are always in competition with man. Oh, but domesticating lizards is not so simple, not such child's play, as domesticating a stupid pig or an imbecilic chicken! It takes talent, admiration and COMPROMISE. You have to accept them as they are. The Chinaman wouldn't like this hunt at all: lizards and humans sharing the joys and sorrows of life in mutual, fraternal curiosity . . .

May 18th

I've been thinking about it, and it's quite true: I don't know how to make an enemy. This failure, which I share with my entire generation, has led me to banality, the sole refuge for my humiliation. The few exceptions to this rule stand out a mile! Cucurella, for example. It's not just that he put great ingenuity into making enemies; he treated it as an art, he tried to murder his father, not with a pistol or a knife or cyanide, but by ACCIDENT: by the casual encounter of the paternal throat and a dog's jaws. Now that's grand! He won't be forgotten, whatever became of him. That's how the men of old acted. The great Bertram de Born set the son against the father, set HIS dog, his animal, against the good enemy. That's why Dante refers to him in the *Divine Comedy*, not because of his verses, which are a secondary attribute of interest only in a humiliated epoch like our own.

Cucurella and the Buzzard were classical men, survivors of the Golden Age. I, on the other hand, am a contemporary, the definitive embodiment of my own time. And this is a time of humiliation and destruction. I remember the kind of ice cream that had no name. With the help of little donkeys, the people who made it used to sell it in the street. Suddenly, an ice cream with its own name appeared on the scene, an ice cream named "Frigo." It was upsetting. We were disconcerted. How could ice cream have a proper name? It was like baptizing apples or water (and this didn't take long either). The following year, we were in for an even bigger shock. It was bad enough to have to call ice cream "Frigo," now there was *another* ice cream. It was just as ice cream as the other, but *this one* was named "Camay." It was intolerable. We could understand that a river might be named the Ter or the Miño, but we couldn't believe that ice cream should have more than one proper name. Now that everything has a proper name — now that everything is PRI-VATE PROPERTY, in other words — I see that my contemporaries were born of that terrible shock. From Cain and Abel down to us, there had never been a break; kids always played with marbles and pistols made out of clothes pins. But with the multiplication of proper names for every single thing, an abyss has opened at our feet.

Humiliated people are recognizable at first sight. We have the blasé, Ciceronian gaze of someone who has seen the universe sink beneath him without a single shot being fired. The ancient Earth has become a phone book. It says nothing at all, but it opens the way to a cosmic charlatanism. And it's pricey. Very pricey.

May 22nd

I have lived through a little incident with ominous consequences. Now I'm more disgusted and dirtier than ever. My stomach pulverized. Moral collapse. A moment of distraction is enough to embitter your life. Silly me. I go to the Boa in a confident and cheerful mood, because tourists are starting to appear on the Ramblas, a fine sight. For several months, the number of Spaniards will drop to half in relation to the number of foreigners, a splendid program, this. It suggests the possibility that maybe some day THE SPANIARDS WILL DISAPPEAR. Too beautiful to think about. On the fourth vermouth, I see the girl from Málaga accompanied by a good-looking young fellow. It's a magnificent opportunity since I've just reached the point of brotherly love. I send a benevolent greeting, but it is received with august indifference; so I approach them and confirm that either I didn't leave the girl satisfied or she demanded a little attention later on that, in my stupidity, I hadn't understood. Because she says to her companion, Look, this is the guy I told you about who passes

himself off for a policeman in order to get women. My back
feels like ice. The man looks at me with an expression that is
unambiguous and eternal. It's unmistakable. This man belongs to the profession; he's the real thing. Anyway, I defend
myself: I didn't say I was a policeman, you did. Oh yeah! Do
you think I'm deaf? She moves her fingers as if she were
playing a guitar. The policeman doesn't seem very anxious to
complicate things. With a little luck, I can even make a
friend. So I address the girl from Málaga in an extremely
respectful tone. I just wanted to ask you the name of your
academy for a friend of mine who's French and who's looking
for work. I thought that they might need teachers there . . .
The young man, very formal, finds himself obliged to intervene. Is her work permit in order? Well, not yet; she's seeing
to it, of course, but since they don't issue permits if you don't
have a contract and of course you can't get a contract if you
don't have a permit . . . Right now she's studying symbolic
logic (ah, alas). The poor fellow doesn't understand a word.
She'd better be careful; they keep a close eye on that now.
There's a lot of unemployment, and foreigners are taking what
little work there is. This man is a patriot, all heart. I look at
the girl from Málaga as though my life depended on her capacity to keep me informed. I don't think they'll give her
work there. They have plenty of teachers. She should look
somewhere else. All right, but she can try, can't she? Well,
it's the . . . Language Academy. "Language?" Yes, "Language."
Are you deaf? Suddenly, she seems distracted; she looks for
her lighter, doesn't find it. Her friend doesn't take his eyes off
me. And where is the Language Academy? Uh, around.
Around Balmes, no, around Vía Augusta, around Gala

Placidia. And then I make a mistake. A mistake born out of
resentment. Thanks very much. Oh, by the way, I have to
return your book. It's a little stained. What book? (The two
of them ask this at the same time; the operetta is getting
underway.) The one you forgot at my place, the *papabortif*.
What are you talking about? Your place? What place? Nerves
are contagious. She's nervous, and I'm nervous thinking how
nervous her friend is getting. All right, bye. Listen! Wait a
minute (identity card?)! Don't try to get funny, and don't
come back here again, or you'll be sorry. Leave him alone,
Víctor, let him go. I just want him to know that if he tries to
be funny again, I'll break him in two. Let him go, Víctor,
please. But it's very hard to stop a hero in his star turn. Víctor
is raring to go. So now you know, buster (the passage from
formality to familiarity is like crossing the Rubicon). The
next time you'll know me, and don't even think about looking at this girl again. And then my second mistake. Instead
of walking though life with our minds fixed on the infinite,
sometimes we amuse ourselves by killing a cockroach or buying stamps, and it leads to our ruin. Thanks for the advice,
Víctor, good night. Hey! What do you mean? Hey, you! I had
already turned my back on him, not supposing that he would
follow me out of the bar. I hadn't made an adequate appraisal
of his virility. If you try to get tough, it's going to be worse for
you, you understand? Look, I'll break your ass right now, you
hear me? I don't take back talk from anybody, not even God.
You got that? A crowd is forming. A narrow street. He has
me by the arm. Pay attention to her, Víctor. What do you
mean pay attention to her? Didn't she tell you to leave me
alone? Well, leave me alone. Don't get familiar with me,

man. The girl from Málaga joins in. A scene out of Quintero.
A real farce. Let him go, Víctor, come in, people are looking.
See! Don't laugh at me. Let him go, Víctor, for God's sake.
I'll take care of this guy. Come on, Víctor. Let go, you fucker!
Let go! And so on.

We're nothing but a parody: waitresses imitate waitresses;
police, police; victims, victims; negroes, negroes. All we needed
were candy apples, an organ grinder, a monkey. Switchblades
didn't flash; the patent leather hats of the Civil Guards didn't
shine; nobody met a dramatic end. Nothing happened. The
shouts died down, the adrenaline thinned out, the gonads settled
down, then the red and gold plumes turned back into the worn
skin of a flea-bitten nag. The beauty withdrew with a hiccough,
and the stench of Spain floated in the air. Beside himself, the
Guardian of the Peace shouted, I'll get you!

Not even all the tourists in this blessed land could drive
the night away. I kept on drinking in one dive after another,
trying to avoid the liquor store, sick of myself. So many months
of rigorous and SCIENTIFIC banality just to lose it like an
idiot at the first opportunity. A tough guy! A tough guy with
pasodobles on his brain. A coward and therefore a tough guy.
Now I have to cross the Boa off my itinerary because next
time, inevitably, Víctor will sink a can opener into my spine;
it's in his nature. I've been dejected for three days. I had
never slept in a bed covered with vomit before. They'll even
end up throwing me out of *this* place. Well, I'm glad. Grotesque. I'm grotesque. And I'm getting fat.

May 25th

The afternoon is suspended, crystallized. The pepper plant is glowing from within like the burning bush. On the table the minute coffee set has been shrinking until it's about the size of a doll's toy. Both of us know that things are coming undone for lack of attention or out of apathy, and that in a few days the real reasons for this work exchange will surface. We've gotten far enough along that the repetitions bother us, but not far enough — and we never will — for them to amuse us. Inevitably we've reached the boiling point, the sacred instant that determines destruction and oblivion. The Chinaman is slowly becoming still as stone as he sits there on a chair covered in English chintz in an ornithological pattern. His rigidity portends an attack of epilepsy in the distant future. It seems as though I hear the whirring of his joints because now, like an automaton, he's beginning to lean over with an exasperating slowness while his hands squeeze the armrests. His effort is so intense that it makes his knuckles turn white and produces a seismic shock that rattles my silver coffee spoon. But he keeps his head perpendicular to the ground with his eyes in a straight line, like a cobra. What hidden key is being turned in his brain? I prepare for an assault, but before he launches his speech, I notice something: the birds, that had been making a racket, have fallen silent; the wind, that was moving the branches of the pepper plant, has stopped blowing; the twilight is no longer setting in. The whole world is waiting to hear the Chinaman speak; even the sun stops in its tracks before the prophet's outstretched arms. It's a monotonous murmur, heavy and sorrowful as a Maronite chant. Now nothing is human but rather "human" as if there were nothing left but the institution, like astrology which keeps its rituals and clientele even though the stars themselves have become dead stones. Not many people are willing to believe it, but it's no less true for that reason. A few of us have decided to put the obvious into practice. Only a few people can admit IT: human thought has been exterminated. It's a field that's been burned by too much fertilizer. Whipped on by Asia, we're galloping backwards toward the biological plane. Soon sacred tyrants and huge, tribal families will be back. The frontier has come on at an incredible speed; WHAT WE ALREADY KNEW ABOUT has happened so fast it shocks us. Forces that were restrained for millennia are sweating fire and blood. When the seams give way, an irruption of physical power will erase the human from the human. In times like these, times of paralysis, the best of us have killed our maternal inheritance. Its belly swollen with blood, the democratic beast sleeps off dinner placidly. Now everyone is Hitler: bishops plan murders, judges steal their clients' property, doctors rape their patients, ministers practice blackmail, nuns sell newborns, generals run the drug trade, magistrates handle brothels, union leaders finance kidnappings, hospital directors sell fetuses, presidents of financial consortia exploit gambling dens, police chiefs steal the cadavers of torture victims, the authorities — the ones in charge, the Powers that Be — provide a bulwark for their employees. The thieves, the blackmailers, the murderers, the rapists, the kidnappers: they couldn't devote themselves to their professions without the protective aura of AUTHORITY. The ones who practice crime without that kind of protection, the amateurs, the newcomers, swell the jails and the cemeteries; they divert the rage of the brutish masses, but real social life, the social life that matters, is CRIMINAL. It's above the law, above the voting urns, above justice, patriotism, brotherly love, our children's future, merit raises: all that circus invented for the scum. A magnate will never be imprisoned by another magnate; a banker has never been tried without the consent of another banker; it's impossible to sentence a military man who hasn't been denounced by other military men; no bishop ever falls unless there's another bishop who covets his position. Only the police denounce each other, and even if they're tried, they're never condemned unless their condemnation is essential to protect the life of criminal society, which is to say, Society. There's nothing human in social life, nothing social in humanity. Humans are beasts in excessive numbers who mess up their own kills because they're overcrowded. And finally the destruction, the torture, the humiliation: all that for nothing, for nothing at all, less than nothing, food for passing time, stimulants for murderers with long fingers who prefer killing to playing the piano, toys for dead children. Universal suicide would give us a rest, but it's impossible.

I decide it would be rude to interrupt him because his expression is becoming more and more concentrated, like a balloon that grows darker instead of fatter. With the word "impossible," he'd reached deep purple, but the position of his arms and legs hadn't changed from the beginning: his arms straight out on the chair arms, his body tilted slightly forward, his eyes fixed straight ahead, an offender tied to the garrote. The word "impossible" exploded in his mouth like a soap bubble that leaves a myriad of luminous points in the air. I couldn't resist the temptation: At first you said, "what we already knew about." Which of us knew about it? He didn't answer. Slowly his spinal column returned to the back of the chair, and his hands, which had been clutching the edge of the armrests, gradually released their prey. He looked at me with a bucolic sweetness, the kind of look we thanked the Virgin of Lourdes for when we were children. His head (for a few minutes it had been emitting an intense buzz) nodded gently like a top just before it loses momentum and circles on the floor in a last pirouette. A Da Vincian smile illuminated his words: You know very well which of us knew about it. The ones who've always known about it; no matter how much you try to avoid taking the consequences and responsibilities of knowing about it seriously. But who are you talking about? The Christians, of course. The ones like you who go along with the butchery without getting blood on their hands. You Christians forget the most important thing he said, what it shocks you to think about, what annuls you and pushes you aside, what leaves you at *our* mercy. Who? What did he say? You don't even remember: I will spew the lukewarm out of my mouth!

Could I have seen a crown of thorns on his head at that moment? But it was the fringe of lank hair that sketched little vertices, forming a zig-zag pattern of shadows on his waxy skin. As soon as he was quiet, the night fell with a crash like a loose tile.

May 30th

Worse and worse. Out of sheer boredom I've been helping Diego tend bar for the last few days. I help him serve and still have time to sweep and wash up. If I see anything out of the way, I approach the Chinaman's table, but I hate him with greater determination every day, and I prefer to align myself with the regulars. They wind up carrying me home like a sack of potatoes because of my disgusting habit of toasting the victory of the Italian army in Africa. Lately it only takes two or three drinks to put me under the table. And the shipments are becoming increasingly eccentric. Today it was Calisay. At this rate, we'll wind up destroying the business. So what? Who cares? The most faithful clients make faces, but they keep on drinking. Who else is going to give them half a bottle of Calisay for three hundred *pesetas*. And where else can you get a glass of anything — Chinchón, malt whiskey, Parfait Amour, Mumm's — for a hundred and fifty *pesetas*? A tumbler? One hundred and fifty *pesetas*? It's an imperturbable clientele. We could give them cement, and they'd drink it.

Diego isn't happy with me. Could he have gotten ideas about my patriotism? Everything's falling apart. A few days ago he even talked to me about his mother, whom he accompanies some afternoons to play bingo. She usually loses everything Diego gives her, and it's a good thing, too, because when she wins, she gets the idea that it's an auspicious day, and she goes into debt buying reams of tickets for every kind of lottery, for lotto, for the football pools before she finally unloads the last few coins in a slot-machine. The majority of Spanish women over forty ruin themselves gambling. It's an

Islamic vice. Diego's mother lives alone and carries on conversations with her dog, an ancient Pekinese. The animal suffers from a nervous condition that gives his muzzle a Parkinsonian tic as if he were speaking. The old woman "reads his lips" to figure out what he's saying, and sometimes she gets mad because the dog votes for the Socialists.

At the high point of a delirium brought on by the Calisay — which, to tell the truth, is a little darker and thicker than normal — a mature man dressed in an impeccable vicuña jacket and a little Tyrolean hat enters the bar. A smiling, affable aristocrat. He and the Chinaman are dealing with a mess related to the electrics. Lately a lot of people have been coming about the electrics. Apparently the Chinaman has them, and everybody else wants them. It must be the only way to invest in atomic bombs. Through a veil of Calisay, I notice something strange. The Chinaman stands up. The aristocrat stands up. Did you give them to Guardiola? How dare you? My whole debt is in that man's hands now! The Chinaman doesn't raise his voice. He lets the aristocrat, who's purple with rage, vent his fury. There are no words to describe you! You're a rat! The Chinaman doesn't like the bit about the rat. He tilts his glasses slightly, and the Indian starts to move. But the aristocrat is very aristocratic. Behind him are at least three generations accustomed to domestic help, and that's the one thing that distinguishes a gentleman in this country. You're taking a lot of risks! I'm going to talk to Alegrete! The Indian takes hold of one of his arms, but the aristocrat frees himself by elbowing the Indian sharply. That's when the blow falls — a slap full in the face. The aristocrat steps back, but he's more surprised than frightened.

He leans against the bar and looks at the Indian as if he'd just come upon his wife eating a fried egg with her knife. The Indian hits him in the stomach. The aristocrat is very close to me — an older man with a blushing bald head that has a brownish design on it like a piece of chintz. Doubled over, he looks as though he's going to throw up into his Tyrolean hat. The Indian lifts him by the ears and drags him to the door while the Chinaman gives the hat a kick. The aristocrat looks in from the street with his eyes full of tears. What is he going to tell the people from the Savings Bank? His wife? His poliomyelitic son? The administrators? That he's been tricked? Fifty million? Forty? Seventy-five? He must be counting it up in his mind, because he's not leaving. He tries to come back in again, this time with an air of supplication. Please! Listen! Don't do this to me! We regulars watch the scene, with our glasses in our hands. It's amusing. It's fun. This man has been happy all his life. What's he going to do now? For God's sake, don't do this to me! The Indian grabs him by the collar, and while he's being dragged, the aristocrat shrieks like an hysterical woman. Then he gets a kick in the legs, and he collapses onto the wet, garbage-strewn ground. The regulars turn back to the bar and start talking cheerfully about the scene. What a drag! Talk about pretentious! Is he still there? Right there, crying like a baby. Give him a Kleenex! As if there weren't enough idiots to go around!

I feel very peculiar. The Calisay makes me go all sentimental; it's a tearjerker. The aristocrat reminds me of my father, who also wore a loden hat on rainy days. The thing is: these people aren't made to be humiliated. They're vile, but they don't know how to be humble. Feeling a little sick, I go out into the street, not without noticing the Chinaman's sardonic smile. The aristocrat is leaning against the wall now. He has a handkerchief in his hand, but he's not using it. He's staring at the ground with great concentration. I'm overwhelmed by a propensity for drama; I can't help it: Could I give you some help, sir? He looks at me from a great distance, straightens up, puts away his handkerchief with great care and sniffs loudly. *Charnegos!* he shouts suddenly. Wogs! Outsiders! He's looking right through me, but I can tell that he's working himself into a fit of rage. I'm worried. If Diego hears him . . . Go home, please. Scum! he shouts again, beside himself. Sewer rat! He takes a step, his arm raised, and tries to hit me. He tries to hit me without knowing who I am or what I want! We get twisted up together and tumble grotesquely to the ground. The regulars peer out to see what's going on. I help the gentleman get up before Carrot Top comes out, but he shakes me off and limps away as fast as he can until he disappears into the humid night.

I keep on drinking Calisay until I can hardly see the glass. I suppose the Chinaman has come up because somebody whispers in my ear, Sewer rat! I don't know if it's a joke, but just in case, I grab him by the lapels, or maybe he grabs me to keep me from collapsing. You think you're a man? I shout without being very sure who I'm shouting at. Well, it's time you figured it out: Man is the mouth of the Lord. The mouth of the Lord, that's what! And the sewer rat? I hear before sinking into a sticky, brown sleep that I've just woken up from. The sewer rat is the mouth of Señor Guardiola, I try to answer, but I only manage to say it to myself. At least, that's how it seems.

June 2nd

Well heeled? Of course, very comfortable! Great! No. Let's be frank about it, brutally frank: my investigation can only meet ALL the scientific requirements if it's undertaken without a safety net, that is, without a cent, with me naked as a jaybird. The dangers of banality on a tidy income? That's for parlor revolutionaries, for the premature ejaculation school of radicalism! After this noble reflection, I decide to renounce my income (forsake all else, and follow me), I decide to get rid of the net, to experience my banality without any protection. I was going to have to pay dearly for so much sublimity.

I can't deny that to a great extent I aspired to higher things: to exalt and ennoble myself, to expunge the humiliations meted out by a harsh environment, to crush Uncle Enrique with an imperial, a colossal, gesture of martyrdom. In my fantasy, it was going to be like PAYING A RANSOM. My hallucinations ran along these lines: I go and tell Uncle Enrique, I don't want my money! He's shocked, paralytic. He falls to his knees and cries out: Oh, noble being! Oh, exalted spirit! What a lesson you have given me! I'm stunned! What spiritual strength . . . ! Fantasies.

But I didn't direct my steps to his office on Layetana. I opted for a surprise attack at home, during supper. That way I would save myself the usual tonic encounter with Señor Torras, and, I could probably check out some details of his business with the Chinaman as well. So, there I was at 8:30 in the evening, light-hearted and feather-brained, pressing the door bell on the Paseo San Gervasio, having practiced my opening lines on the way over: I don't want my money!

I'm carrying out an investigation into the deepest abysses of the spirit now, and this work is incompatible with a sense of security and with the boring life of the remittance man. So do what you like with my money. Donate it to the Domund Fund, to the Red Cross, to the San Pablo Hospital, or keep it — in fact, that amounts to the same thing. What naïveté! Sweet Jesus!

It wasn't Uncle Enrique but Aunt Belén who let me in. This lady weighs about two hundred pounds; she has eyes like cabbages, and she doused herself with Arpège for so long that even now, eight years after she gave it up completely, she still emits clouds of an asphyxiating Parisian stench. Alongside Belén, Cousin Tony — the only OFFICIAL mental retard in the family — appears out of the blue. I hadn't seen him since childhood. My aunt and uncle keep him hidden away from malicious — that is to say, Catholic — eyes that would attribute such a misfortune to the parents' syphilis, alcoholism and general depravation. By way of greeting, Cousin Tony receives me with his famous question: Is it Thursday yet?

The whole family knows that, for years and years, they have paid a professional to come every Thursday in order to keep Tony, who's over forty now, quiet for the rest of the week. Over the years, Conchi has become part of the family. She's very affectionate, she runs errands for them — Buy me some suppositories, Conchi, I just don't know what's wrong with me; Bring me a little Manchego cheese, Conchi, you know what to look for; See if you can find a button like this one, Conchi, there's no place around here that has them — and she has charged the same price since 1970, adding on just the Increment in Consumer Prices (ICP), after religiously consulting the Official Government Bulletin (OGB). The little fellow is doing fine, and everybody's so pleased. What neither Conchi nor his parents have been able to eliminate is a sentence that passes the unhappy soul's lips every two or three minutes, that Is it Thursday yet? anxiously muttered in the most diverse tempos from *andante grave* to *allegro con fuoco*.

Hush, Tony! Of course it's not Thursday! What a tiresome boy! Come on now. Go play with your Barbie doll, and leave your cousin and me alone. And what's brought you here, dear? Do you want to see Uncle Enric? I don't know . . . I think he's here, but I'm not sure, that is, I doubt he's here, do you understand? He hasn't felt very well lately — muscle pains, weakness, his age, and so, of course, when he feels like that, he's not here. Well, of course, he's here, but it's as though he weren't here. So, come in, come in. You've gained weight, haven't you? Why don't you sit down while I ask him if he's here. Do you want to look at a copy of *Hola*? Fine, I'll go right now, this minute . . . Did you want to see him about anything? What a silly question! Of course you want to see him about something. Shall I tell him what you want to see him about, if he's here? No? This is a strange family! You're just like your mother and Uncle Enric! All of you — stranger than a purple cow! We Balaguers are completely different, com-plete-ly . . . Yes, yes, I'm on my way, on my way!

She doesn't have a chance to be on her way. Uncle Enrique appears in the entrance hall, rudely pushing an impeccably dressed gentleman who's topped off with an amusing, little Tyrolean hat. Somehow this gentleman has managed to get kicked around by the entire social spectrum. Uncle Enrique

is dismissing him as if he were a maid: Fuck off! I don't give
a damn about your family, you son of a bitch! If you've been
as stupid as I have, just grin and bear it! It's cost me a fortune
too. And if you think I'm going to spend another just so you
can keep on buying yourself hats, that'll happen when pigs
have wings!

Uncle Enrique's peroration, quite admirable in a man
suffering from aching muscles and weakness, is interrupted by
the presence of my remarkable cousin, who, with a gleam of
hope in his eyes, comes to ask if it's Thursday yet. Thursday?
Thursday? Shit on the divine light! I'll show you Thursday,
you little son of a bitch! And he pushes my cousin so hard
that he falls over the caramel-colored sofa. Once that little
obstacle is eliminated, he goes on to suppress the life-sized
one. As to you, get out of here! I don't want to see your face
again, you idiot! And though the aristocrat keeps threatening to tell Alegrete, Uncle Enrique roars with laughter until
he runs into Aunt Belén and me. Good God! The whole
family! What is it now? What in the hell does this lay-about
want?

This lay-about maintains a dignified silence, and Aunt
Belén, who's accustomed to Uncle Enrique's business style,
opens the front door to let his clients out. Her success is only
relative because nobody retreats but the aristocrat, still evoking Alegrete. And this character? Why doesn't he take off?
Aunt Belén, who is basically tender-hearted and bovine, a
woman with an only husband and an only child, looks at me
with curiosity as if she were, in fact, asking herself why I
don't take off if it's really for the best.

My dear uncle — I attack with great resolution, irritated

that I can't work in my well-rehearsed speech — I don't want
my money! Uncle Enrique interrupts me violently, crossing
his arms and nodding wisely. That's great! He doesn't want
his money! That's terrific, because I'm not giving you a cent!
Shit! You don't have a cent, so it's a good thing you don't
want it! What do you mean I don't have a cent? I ask him,
disconcerted. Just what I said; you don't have a cent. A threat
of intervention on Cousin Tony's part sends us into the sit-
ting-room where his father apparently decides to employ strategy to get him out of the way. That's right, baby. It's Thursday now, it's Thursday now! As soon as he has him cornered
in the closet, Uncle Enrique employs a manoeuvre as deft as
Frégoli's best tricks: he buries him in between overcoats and
raincoats and locks the door. Good, that's two out of the way
now! Holy Virgin! Let's go for the third! So, you don't want
your money, eh? Come over here. I'll show you a thing or
two.

Sitting in the dining room, far away from the closet and
the heart-breaking howls that keep reminding us that some
day it will be Thursday for every man on earth, Uncle Enrique,
Aunt Belén and I look each other in the eye. A bit of Dry
Sack? asks adorable Aunt Belén, who's always on the lookout
for ways to make everyone happy. We also have *garnacha*, she
murmurs modestly as if to sweeten my silence and her
husband's furious glare. Oh, well, I'll leave you two alone and
take the little one with me so you can talk in peace, man to
man. We women don't understand a thing about this sort of
business. We just know about the home, love, feelings . . .
I'm on my way, I'm on my way.

My dear nephew, we're all losing out here. Uncle Enrique

gets under way energetically. On Conchi's birthday, we were eating the Surprise Cake, and it turned out that I was the one who got the surprise. A gypsy — or South American — looking guy with his hair all greased back, in short, a crook, shows up here and advises me, as a friend, to insure my cargo. He must have thought I was a live one. How did he know about the *Sanfaina*? I have no idea, but he was on to everything. He knew that the cargo was toilet paper, fine lingerie, Lladró porcelain, Mandelmans dolls, bathing suits from the Corte Inglés, perfumed soap . . . in short, all that kind of stuff. He knew that it was already on the dock, stowed and ready, that it was going to the Arab Emirates, where they're wild about that junk, and that we were planning on making about twenty-five million, give or take a few cents. They probably got the information from that idiot Gomés. Can you understand anybody wearing a hat in June? I'm sure he doesn't take it off even to bathe. And who do I need to insure it with? I ask this fellow. With me, he answers. As your agent, I'll take care of all your problems. And just how much is this little policy going to run me? I act interested. Five million, the honorable agent informs me. Did he think I'm an idiot! I ask you! I kicked his ass out of the house just like I did that stupid Gomés. Well, the next day, they arrest the captain of the *Sanfaina* on the grounds that he had caused a public disturbance in the Liceo metro. The police chief assures me that the captain was wandering around naked, wearing nothing but a cap and hurling insults at the wife of the president of the Generalitat when people were coming out of "Il Tabarro." Then they tell me the customs agents are inspecting the cargo. Then they find a bunch of cured hams that have gone bad (for the Arabs? I ask you) and the Health people come in . . . and so on. I keep quiet, of course. I start moving the people I've paid off — they've cost me a fortune. I move the people I have in the Civil Government, I move the people in Development, I move heaven and earth, and I manage for the *Sanfaina* to set sail and get away from this den of thieves. All right then, the minute she anchors in Genoa, the port authorities confiscate the cargo. I know when it's time to give up! When the South American comes back to visit me without anybody calling him, just to let me know the insurance has gone up from five to ten million because in Genoa everything is very expensive, et cetera et cetera, I offer him a contract: three million if the insurer is killed off. The South American looks at me. You say three million? Yes, I'll give you three million if you kill off your boss. He turns around and leaves.

At this point, I was on pins and needles. I was slowly beginning to form some idea of the secret relation between my uncle's cargo, the administrative career of the Chinaman's hit men, and what my poor parents had bequeathed me. I couldn't deny a feeling of admiration and respect for private initiative. To be absolutely fair, considering the going rate, three million for stabbing somebody was a generous payment.

I didn't hear any more about it until suddenly, a few nights later, ANOTHER South American or gypsy or crook, just like the other but a different one, shows up and tells me that his colleague and friend (that's what he said) has had an accident and that now the insurance had gone up to twenty million. Twenty million! So, I make my calculations, and I tell myself: Enric, you've fucked up. Enric, these guys are no amateurs. Enric, if you give twenty, you've still got five left, but if you don't give twenty, they'll skin you alive for trying to kill off their boss. Enric, this country is based on compromise. Fine! No sooner said than done! We agree that Señor Torras will hand over a check to him at the Peratallada — do you know the place? near Santa María del Mar? they've got fantastic pork jowls — on such and such a day, at such and such a time. And that's what happened. Everybody did his bit, and right now the *Sanfaina* is on her way to Kuwait, happier than a pig in shit.

My uncle put his hands together as though he were going to launch an Our Father, but instead he cracked his joints, producing a racket that sent chills up and down my spine. Now he's getting to the point, I thought. Now he's going to tighten the screws. And, in fact, he did. My dear nephew! he said. The world of business, which you know nothing about — although I've noticed you have no objection to collecting your income as long as you can do it elegantly, without getting wet or dirty, so that your conscience is as pure as the driven snow — the world of business is full of sons of bitches. Yes, it's true. I'm the first to admit it, may my granny forgive me, I'm a businessman, *ergo* I'm a son of a bitch. Put yourself in my place. See, if I let myself lose twenty million, it would mean that I'm as stupid as Gomés, and the minute the shareholders found out, they would finish me off like Gomés. But I'm not going to end up like Gomés! Far from it! I'll get my twenty million back, or I'm as good as dead. And I've gotten it back. How about a little Dry Sack? Oh, come on. It's best to keep these things friendly. I'm going to tell Belén to bring us a couple of glasses of Dry Sack. Belén!

Aunt Belén appears as if by magic, round and smiling, a real little light bulb. Ay, Enric. You frightened the boy and me with that yelling. Do you really want a drink? I'll bring it in right away. I'm so pleased you're getting along. Sometimes I get so scared . . . ! Do you want some corn nuts too? With that she sailed out as if blown away by the horrid blasphemy her husband uttered.

Look, my boy, Uncle Enrique tells me paternally. When you signed all those papers, you also signed documents giving me the usufruct of your inheritance for investment, with the understanding that you were in for a third of the profits and all of the losses. It's very simple, eh. It means I agreed to give you a third of the profits, but that you would take the losses if there were any. I know, I know! But usually there aren't any losses . . . Anyway, it's all your fault. You have to look at what you sign. You have to read what you sign with a magnifying glass! It's so easy, by God, you sign, and everything's great. It's so easy to let other people get wet and dirty with your money and then you, the great gentleman, sit back and wait for your profits! But that's not quite the way it works. Money belongs to whoever makes it work. I shit on the saints!

Don't say such things, please, Enric. The little one will hear you, and then he'll repeat it all to Conchita. Here are the glasses and the bottle and the corn nuts so you won't drink on an empty stomach. Is everything all right? Do you agree about everything? Remember the family is all we have left in this world of terrorists and drug addicts. We Balaguers (there's a Valencian branch called Borjasot from the Borgias of Florence) got a hundred and seventy guests together for the golden wedding anniversary of my . . . But she stops short when she meets Uncle Enrique's eyes with their placid, serene, warm and benevolent expression. An expression that recalls what Hitler's must have been like every time he ran into Isaac Sharon in the street.

In short, summing things up: You footed the bill for the entire *Sanfaina* operation. I was only a proxy. You bought the goods, paid the bill of lading, made the consignment, paid the insurance, and you'll collect the profits if there are any. That's what business is like: sometimes good, sometimes not so good. This time you cut a pretty poor deal; it's hardly surprising, given your lack of experience, but, who knows, next time you may make your fortune. Oh! By the way, don't get any ideas about going to the police. As you can well imagine, I had everything notarized. I have at least six notaries who'll swear on the Holy Virgin that . . .

I refuse to listen to any more. I also refuse to explain to my Uncle Enrique the difference between interest and profits. Hadn't I come by in order to give up my money? Was there any difference in giving it away *after* it had been stolen? I was too confused to go into moral considerations. Didn't I want to be poor? Well, now I was poor. What profits do you think I'll get from this deal, dear Uncle Enrique? I asked him calmly. Well, if everything goes well, and I think it will, well . . . Let's see, let's see, about five million, and a third of that is yours, so . . . about one and a half million. That's all I have left? No! Oh, no! You haven't gotten it yet!

When I got up from the armchair, I was dog-tired. I felt absolutely indifferent about the money that had been lost — or, rather, transferred to the Chinaman's coffers — and at the same time, I was overwhelmed by a surge of warmth for Uncle

Enrique, who was so much worthier, nobler, braver, more *classic* — right? — than the guy who was stripping me indirectly. I told him as much: it's been a pleasure doing business with you, Uncle Enrique. We parted company like good friends. Next time, come see us on Thursday! Aunt Belén begged me at the door. The little one is always in such a good mood on Thursdays!

June 4th

The real pro comes back with a ton of gadgets, the whole of modern electronics, a duty-free syndrome, right here at the liquor store. We have lots of fun with a dictionary that not only translates in beautiful electronic letters, but also talks. Ask it how to say "bistec" in English! a famished, broken-down regular with a yen for beefsteak pleads. When everything has been stowed away, I greet the official. How's your wife? Oh! She's fine. Thanks for asking. Of course, I remembered you. Oh? Look here. And he takes a wonderful Mont Blanc out of his pocket. How do you like it? For me? For you! What do I owe you, then? Don't mention it; this is private, between you and me. Was it hard to find? Harder than you'd think. As soon as you decide to look for something, it disappears. If you focus on something, it goes up in smoke. I've worked at least twelve residences, all of them belonged to notaries, dentists, stock-brokers, heads of personnel, aerosol manufacturers . . . no luck. The best I found were Parkers, most of them cartridge pens and all of them, *all* of them in French designs like . . . Like a whore's? That's it, just like a whore's. Fancy? That's it, fancy: silver, gold, all of

it real, Chinese lacquer (Chinese lacquer!), lapis lazuli . . .
don't make me laugh. Not one Mont Blanc? Not one! But at
last, ah! We hit a house . . . and what a house! A gentleman
of the old school! No velvet. No Dalís. No brass. No pink
marble . . . A real gentleman! Real! His desk, his ceiling
mirror, his little red lamps, his Bernat Metge, in short, a
gentleman! And what tapestries! No Subirachs? Not one!
No Mirós? Of course not! Everything was first-class, even the
piano! I came this close to taking it. Imagine. I had so much
respect for the man that I only took the pen and a volume of
Calderón for my little girl — she's studying Golden Age literature now. That's all? I swear it's true! On the bureau, he
had a Club Español flag, and since that's my team . . . It's the
first time I've ever worked another fan's apartment. When
I'm in one of the Barça Club places, I don't even leave the
ashtrays. Don't tell Diego. No? Why not? Never mind; it
doesn't matter. Can I stand you to a drink? Some other time.
I have to sign the receipts now. Tell me how you like it.

After signing the receipts, the real pro says good-bye at
the door, waving a fistful of bills. It's the first present I've
gotten since I finished high school, but as you can see, I've
kept on using my ballpoint. I can't pull myself together enough
to buy an inkwell. Buying an inkwell requires a great deal of
hope. It's a move reserved for tranquil spirits with long years
ahead of them and everything in its place. It's a potentate's
move. A move that smacks of after-dinner coffee and cigars.

I'm consuming a novel substance administered by Diego.
Straight olive oil that smells like Scheherazade. It's been mixed
up in the belly button of a fat, musky bayadère. I'm practic-
ing a SUBSTITUTION cure for alcohol. Giving the ulcer-

ated fabric a little respite. And, changing subjects, I see a lot more clearly what they're trying to hide from me. The most hidden things are becoming obvious. So, for example, from the Vallcarca bridge, I have a BOLIVIAN vision: the heap of buildings climbing the hill is a slum in La Paz even though the inhabitants think they're in a LOVELY RESIDENTIAL AREA, ahhhh. The metro station, which was dedicated less than a month ago by presidents, mayors and ecclesiastical dignitaries whose pockets were stuffed with invoices, outstanding bills and hate mail looks like a cave now. The escalator, which hasn't moved since Day One, is flooded. The ticket-seller has covered some of the steps with sawdust so it's like one of those bars where the customers throw up on the floor. The wood shavings have formed deep mud puddles. In dark corners, youthful scholars are assaulted by ragged gangs that steal their pencils, their shoes and their t-shirts. Vallcarca Station! Opposite it lies a villainous slum criss-crossed by cables, posts, rusted oil drums and fallen electrical lines. Women wearing typical Andean derbies are filling up green plastic buckets on the garbage dump.

I venture down under the bridge. A strange taxi with neither license nor wheels — it's raised up on bricks — is rotting there. Its unlikely owner is rubbing the body of the car with a piece of chamois. I assume this mental case abandons the carcass at night to go sleep in the metro and then returns the next day to apply the chamois to the taxi-skeleton once again. Diego's novel substance allows me to see more clearly what I always see: THE ATOMIC BOMB. But once the effects have worn off, I also feel more abject than usual. If I hadn't broken off, and I mean BROKEN OFF, with the Chinaman, I would tell him that the Kantity of our vision is limited. If we go beyond that limit, we have to pay for it with hours and days of stupidity.

Today I'm superbly stupid. I can go to the liquor store when I feel like it. I can go in WHEN I SAY SO. Now I'm a regular. I see Diego, say hello to him, hey, how's it going? I don't say a single word to I KNOW WHO. I ask Diego with great courtesy if he has some substance left. I go home without saying a word to WE KNOW WHO, and I wander around my neighborhood, south of Repúlica Argentina, without putting a foot on the infamous Plaza Lesseps — I'd sooner be dead. I go back to the Lovely Residential Neighborhood of Vallcarca, ahhhh. The women with their derby hats and their plastic pails have babies on their backs now. A mere detail. Babies like piles of rags. And condors. The condors sketch wide circles. Sometimes they get as far as the antenna of the Tibidabo. Essential. A gnu: blue stone encrusted in the Turkish beak. I'm going to visit my friend, my GOOD FRIEND, Diego, to see if he'll let me sweep out the place.

June 6th

I'm overjoyed to discover the poet from Felanitx, this time in severe solitude, at a little table in the Barbas de Plata. Urged on by an essentially foolish sociability, I feel like drinking in company. A big mistake! He's leaning over his drink, absorbed in solemn meditation, his angular face chipped out of stone, his beard like a Belgian priest's, his eyelashes as black as anthracite. A sinister image for a lyric poet! All that's missing are the skull and the candle with its column of smoke blackening the ceiling. I approach him, but he doesn't notice my presence. Then: surprise! perplexity! He's weeping. His eyelashes aren't DAMP, they're SOAKING WET like little paint brushes. It's as though the guy were possessed by a silent film queen.

Unfortunately, I don't pull myself together in time to get away. (I've lost my reflexes, I've lost my vision, I've lost.) He looks up suddenly, jumps and . . . Amigo (*amik*, he says)! Come here. Sit down for a minute, please! Your company does me a lot of good. Don't think it's the drink. It's something more intimate, a misfortune. It's the light; the light has become thought and made me blind. Do you want a drink? Can you understand a blind man who speaks? Listen to me. My life isn't HUMAN now. Do you understand? I thought it was until yesterday or the day before. I built my life as a cathedral of words until yesterday or the day before, but now it's a ruin. There's nothing to be done about it. The cathedral was a coffin. I was wrong from the start, and now there's nothing to be done about it. I believed in myself. I was an alexandrine or a quatrain, but I wasn't HUMAN. A life filled with conventions, a waste, after so many years . . . the most elevated ideas, the highest poetry. From childhood on I sacrificed everything for art. At fourteen I consecrated my life to arts and letters — it was a real priesthood. I've had no friends, no family, no children — do you understand? — no descendants. I am my own dead man. Tortured by perfection, rhythm, the breath of the language, its beating heart, its disconcerting tempo, the highest, the noblest aspirations . . . And that's how I lived for thirty years, thirty years! Producing works like *The Crow and the Well*. Suddenly I meet Rosa Sadurní, and I discover the other side of the mirror. What mirror? That's the way the expression goes "the other side of the mirror" . . . I'm absolutely, COMPLETELY in love. I've overcome primitive fears: will she ruin my work? Will she destroy all those years of sacrifice to art and philosophy? Ah, I realize she won't. On the contrary! She's a window opening onto infinity. Yes, of course, a mirror and a window, too. I continue. She's the eye that sees through the dark. In her gaze I discover A NEW WORLD. I write *The Modern Corner*, win the Jiménez Prize, win a grant from the Ministry of Culture . . . We set up housekeeping on the coast in Palop. It's an eternal spring, burning emotions, an EXTRAORDINARY sensitivity. The sea surges in my brain and floods it with MEDITERRANEAN poetry, with MEDITERRANEAN intelligence. I translate my work into Spanish for Editions 62 — it's my personal contribution to our national literature! My style may vary, but my thoughts remain close to the eternal sea. I pass my qualifying exams! I can now teach in secondary school. My thoughts soar higher than ever. And so it went for two years, two years spent carving out the abyss! And then, suddenly, I separate from Rosa Sadurní, who is more beautiful than ever, more poised, an odalisque. I love her deeply, sorrowfully . . . Our last meeting! We arrange to see each other in my house. Trembling with emotion I must contain, I am writing my verses of farewell. I know what terrifying solitude awaits me, but I am happy FOR HER, happy that she can realize herself as a wife and a mother — she's going to have Pep Junquera's baby, didn't you know? — happy because she found SALVATION. She arrives at eight P.M. She's wearing a black knit suit with a gold belt. Eve! Pandora! I feel over-

whelmed, overwhelmed, but I pull myself together FOR HER
SAKE. I stick to the conventions . . . Oh, she's brilliant, she's
splendid! Earth, air, fire, stone! Water? All right, water. She's
beautiful! The best! Two hours go by. It's an incredible conversation between two spiritual twins! And then, the end,
good-bye. You won't see her again, I think. I tell myself,
You'll never see Rosa again. It's as though she were dead to
you, had died here in front of you. It's too cruel. I'm very
moved — very. In a surge of tenderness that's overwhelming
but natural, I beg her to take some souvenir of OUR home, a
wedding gift, anything she likes, something imbued with
memories of our years together, a piece of our history . . . Ah!
Rosa looks at me in surprise. Do you understand? She's perplexed! She looks around the room. "Well, except for the
Etymological Dictionary," she says. Then it dawns on me, and
I cave in like a tower built on the sand, I crumble RIGHT
TO THE GROUND. Do you understand? There was nothing there, nothing at all! Rosa — that superior soul! — had
sacrificed everything for my art. What could she take with
her? Books, of course, tons of books, oceans of books, deserts
of books, old chairs, a sofa, the worktable covered with my
creations, the bath, my razor. Do you understand? There was
NOTHING AT ALL, garbage, less than zero. I didn't even
have anything to give her AS A SOUVENIR. So I collapse,
like a dead elephant, like a dead whale, and Rosa gets up,
gives me a kiss and goes out the door. From then on, I feel
useless, as bare as a billiard ball. I don't have a minute of
inspiration; it's a meaningless life . . . I offered her the Mediterranean, but she was already in the elevator.

He has a sonorous, almost braying wail, and the customers are looking at us with curiosity. I'm ashamed to think that I'm ashamed they think that I'm the cause of his woes, so I ask him in a very loud voice: You haven't seen HER again? with emphasis on the HER, but he doesn't even answer me. He's still sniffing. How about Laura? I venture. Who? Laura, don't you remember? The girl who was here the last time we ran into each other, the one with antenna for detecting the abyss. He doesn't remember Laura, but I do. Humble, modest Laura, listening to the most elevated ideas and the highest poetry produced by this fallen tower, this dead whale. She was an Aquarian, I add with a touch of malice, and you decided to kill a dragon. Oh, shut up! How could I have been so INHUMAN? Now I can't create a sonnet; I can't even write a single verse . . . And he starts to weep again, loudly.

I decide to go to the bar for a drink, but thinking it over again, I just keep going. Out in the street, I take a deep breath of the night air, saturated with humidity and gasoline.

June 7th

Now I too have a secret: I'm keeping a sewer rat in my room in order to carry out scientific investigations into questions of similarity and difference, questions of fraternity . . . It must be very old because it has lost an eye and it's covered with bites. I found it pitched out by the dry-cleaners on Lucano, next door to my apartment, and I brought it back wrapped up in a copy of El País. There are millions of rats swimming in the sewers of this city, better than one per inhabitant.

I watch it carefully to see if it's hiding some secret that

would allow me to expand the opinion I'm forming of the Chinaman, but the truth is that once they're dead rats lose all their charm. It's heavenly to watch them run, attack or screech, showing their tiny fangs. In the Mira quarter a man was bitten by an enormous, bald rat. Startled by the broom that the man had taken to it, the animal started climbing up the man's pants or, to be exact, up the man's leg since he'd confused the trouser with a drain pipe. In his terror, the man kicked violently, but the rat kept on going, keeping a tight hold on the man's flesh. Finally the man had to hit it again and again with a Coke bottle — to give it a real pounding — before the mass stopped moving. In the hospital they took note of a rosary of black spots, like needle marks, in the shape of a half moon, near the groin. The man died twenty-one days later; he had a big tumor under his arm. No one had diagnosed the disease because no doctor nowadays is familiar with the bubonic plague. A black cleaning man who saw the cadaver by chance threw in the towel. Nobody has seen him since. The Health authorities hushed up the incident in the interest, as they put it, of averting panic, of maintaining public safety and so on.

When they're discovered and threatened, rats hide in cracks and crannies and under furniture. In olden times, women wore long, full skirts that swept the floor. Rats would often scurry to find safety under those pseudo-tablecloths. They'd climb up the women's legs and even slip into the vaginal conduit, provoking deaths that the Church refused to consecrate. That's how the feminine custom of jumping up on chairs in the presence of rats got started. Keep this in mind! A scientific method for ascertaining if the Chinaman is a sewer rat: find out if a woman jumps up on a chair in his presence.

I've seen horrifying rats among the garbage bags in the San Gervasio area. In less opulent neighborhoods, the rats devour newborns as soon as their mothers step out to buy detergent. I give my rat a few light kicks; it's still soft. Its eyes are two black buttons: an expression of panic. I pick it up by the tail and put it away in the refrigerator. I'll get back to it in search of wisdom and comfort. It's a first-class specimen.

June 8th

This place is filling up with animals. The head, covered with honey, sticks out of the sand, and the ants eat it. Yes, there are ants too and cockroaches and fetal beings that tap thousands of heels like a militarized flamenco show. But more than anything, there are lizards. Right now, at this very minute, believe it or not, I have one in front of my eyes, advancing across the table with great care.

I get closer, with the idea of reading his spots and patterns. They say it's the handwriting of God in its FLAT form. There is another, two-dimensional, handwriting on the Tablets of the Law. I want to learn the lizard's language. I put my ear against his snout. The lizard opens its toothless mouth — a characteristic of the senile that you also see in every survivor; think of Auschwitz and Dachau, where not a single Jew had any teeth left — and speaks. It's incredible. Although minute, its voice is full. It produces a LITTLE sound, like a Japanese radio designed for scaled-down ears. It may be very powerful (deafening!) but in any event it's a powerful littleness. Other examples: Atom Ant, Mighty Mouse, Jerry, and all those other metaphors for atomic fission. Little with a lot of noise.

It's time we understood each other, says the lizard, or the lizard's brain, a white worm in the shape of a spindle. The voice is so tiny that even though it thunders, it's impossible to make out the almost invisible LETTERS; so I get closer. My ear brushes the top of his snout. Then he turns into a bullet, fires and cuts through my cranium.

When I wake up, there's a clot of blood on the pillow. Where did it come from? Did it well up from my ear? Did I hurt myself? What with? I hear very clearly.

(illegible date)

Hung around the port, for quite a while. That's for sure. I mean, around the effluvium and the humidity, soaking wet, my socks dripping . . . In an out-of-the-way spot, I have a paschal vision of a little street carpeted with flowers. Corpus Christi? In Sitges? But they aren't flowers, they're scraps of paper covered with fish scales. They shine like sequins under the street light. I sink my feet in the papers and drag them along like dried up banana leaves. It's autumn, and I'm on my way to school. The cats jump, arch their backs and hide in the garbage like paunchy rats. Their eyes are mirrors.

A man stops me. No, he doesn't stop me; he only points with his finger. A hard time remembering. I'm not well. A tube? A thermometer? I can't take my eyes off him. If I'm not careful, he'll bite me in the neck. I understand! It's because his teeth are ON THE OUTSIDE OF HIS MOUTH! I think it's time now. I'm truly dead. But I'm a busy man, extraordinarily busy. I don't have time to lose. I keep on. I pay no attention to him. My diary, I have to write this in my diary. I keep on without moving. I have a look of keeping on, an intense expression of keeping on. That man's teeth float in the air. I walk without budging from where I am, and the teeth pursue me, beating wings with the click-click of dominoes. They're going to bite me at any moment. I employ the well known TRIUMPHAL move, turning sharply so I can hit them by surprise. But I collapse between bits of paper and cats. I'm covered with garbage. Over my head a mother-of-pearl light glows; in fact, it's the Carnival in Venice interpreted on the accordion by Annie Cordy. By the light of the music, the teeth dance a waltz like a big yellow butterfly. They sketch two spirals, one ascendant, the other descendant. They're going to take advantage of my weakened state to bite me, but instead they explode into a guffaw of stars.

I feel much better now; I must remember, must not forget. I can get as far as the Ramblas and take a taxi. An intense smell of fish. On the Ramblas a group of blacks with their lips painted red are examining a match box, totally absorbed. I cross the city by cab, a glass submarine. The city is submerged in a green and gold liquid. I float between big, opalescent balloons the color of money.

Home. I look at my teeth in the mirror. Extraordinary. They're little rabbits nailed into a watermelon. I'm beset by the imperious need to wear my hair in a bun, to feel my whole face pulled back and ATTACHED TO MY SHOULDER. No, it's not that: I want to have my head shrunken. I pull my hair as hard as I can. Do I have to keep on like this?

With my face to the front? As if it were looking at something? And how about my rat? I open the refrigerator. The
rat's not there. Police! I look for it on the floor. I'm on all
fours. In the bed. Ah! What a relief! It's under the pillow. I
feel much better. We sleep together, and I wake up at the first
honking horn. I write my notes fast. Every day I forget more.
My duty! If I'm not here, where am I? Is it you? Is it you,
Sweetie-pie?

(no date)

Literature! Littttteratttture! The little cafe is a box of
SONOROUS smoke, whose coils and spirals are words that
— thanks to a miracle, divine intervention, or the holy spirit
— I can see in their real PHYSICAL form even though it's
opaque. Like the sound of the organ that is a "submerged
cathedral," sunk in an opaline, *sfumato* sea (Opalino and
Sfumato! Bertoldino and Cacaseno! Tweedledum and
Tweedledee!), the sea before a storm. One of the spirals of
smoke curls around my neck, and then I hear the voice of
Leandro Bonet, good, kind Leandro Bonet, talking to a churl-
ish, fierce-looking animal. I paid for supper, I say. I paid for
supper. I keep on insisting, I swear that I paid for supper. I
weep noisily. Leandro's guffaws issue forth from an enormous,
toothless mouth, a saurian mouth, a SURVIVOR'S mouth.
It was splendid, he says. I've saved a few slices of the omelette. And then, like a conjurer, he whips out a fan made of
seven pornographic photos the color of fried eggs. I take great
interest in one of them that shows a drowned man who's
floating between two currents with beer froth coming out of

his ears. Immediately, as I'm wont to do of late, I throw up all over Leandro Bonet's lime green vest. Literature! he shouts. Littttteratttture! Look for me at the cafe, Mr. Pink-Cheeks. But Leandro doesn't say this, because I wake up with a false beard in my hands. Feeling the raspy texture of the hairs, I think I have a rat in my mouth, and I throw up again.

It seems like daytime now. I don't know . . . I think my eyes see as well by night as by day now. A raw wool light.

(no date)

The poet from Felanitx has committed suicide. Remember this well. The lights on the cop car. The fat woman beside me: How awful! she says. Under the wheels. Her fat, purple tongue: a rat in her mouth. It's the same thing. Remember this well. A Dutch semi. Its wheels skid over the puddle of guts. He's an Arab, the cop says. I laugh so hard that he hits me in the kidneys with his nightstick. Get out of here, you son of a bitch! An Arab! Remember. *Quins poemes escrigvirgiaoem!* It makes me laugh. You can't help it.

(an impossible date: February 26th)

Your honor:

Taking advantage of the general improvement in my physical and chemical state and in memory of a lyric poet whose life was cut short by a public — in fact, a municipal — vehicle and also taking into consideration (taking into consideration!) the pity I feel for the poplars, whose rachitic SPIRITUAL existence is determined by their being a branch

and not a tree even though everyone believes the opposite
(an extraordinary destiny, it is true, to live as a branch when
everyone takes you for a tree!), not to mention the absence
of seeds, fruit, flowers, in short, anything that is not pure
BRANCH cut from another branch that in turn was cut
from another branch and so on back to the primogenital
poplar, the Ur-poplar, from which all the other poplars de-
scend AS BRANCHES, I explicate for your consideration
the case of the SPERMATOZOID, the only being that one
can truly say is a man since only the spermatozoid endures
while ephemeral human beings (human beings!) succeed each
other, transferring their burden of spermatozoids from one to
another so that the spermatozoid may survive in one and in
another and so on while every one and every other, all of us
ACCIDENTAL carriers of the spermatozoid, tear ourselves
apart with pain and humiliation in order to placate that idiotic SPERMATOZOID, who is ready to finish us all off as
long as it can keep on hopping from one to another, and so it
has lived, quite comfortably, ever since Adam, and I have
absolutely no interest in determining the origin of the first
spermatozoid (the Ur-spermatozoid) when it first installed
itself in that zoological protuberance that was Eden; I could
care less if it sprang from a monkey with illusions of grandeur, from a Martian or from a joke on the part of Providence, but in any event I think the moment has arrived to
put a stop to such a wicked little creature, and for that reason, I shall explicate, I AM EXPLICATING, my proposal:
having learned through the press about the existence of sperm
banks to be used for industrial purposes of which I highly
approve, I now believe that it is possible to transfer ALL

SPERMATOZOIDS IN THEIR TOTALITY to a bank or to multiple banks so that, distracted by a synthetic and until today technically impossible prolongation of life, they give us time to empty each and every one of the so-called virile organs since once all spermatozoids are enclosed in one or multiple banks without time to reflect or react in self-defense, it will be extremely easy to finish them off, and I am firmly convinced (firmly convinced!) that in this way we can spend the last days of so-called humanity in perfect happiness and peace, compelled to celebrate the last act with bagpipes, streamers, sack races, Italian crooners, raffles, piñatas.

Thank you for your attention . . . It would be absolutely pointless to extend my proposal to the ovum; I have exempted that department from my consideration (just because I am incompetent in that field), and I am convinced that you would do well to work out an alternative model (an alternative model!) that will propose administrative solutions for unmarried ova, since they are apparently unfit for hibernation; at this moment, I am too busy to devote even a minute to anything that does not concern me DIRECTLY; this does not preclude, tomorrow when I have recuperated and all this has come to an end, when I am calmer and more peaceful, My God! wouldn't it be wonderful to be calm! I haven't been calm for ages! I don't even know now what to tell myself, hanging on to the table, to the paper, because if I let myself go now I won't find myself again, the flying carpet, ah, it's coming back now, I'm losing my head, but who . . . ?

Third Part

Killing a Dragon

June 29th

Here I am again, dear Diary. The sensation of finding myself in my own notebook is terrifyingly pleasurable — you might even say vertiginous, like the sexual shudder when you drop down at full speed in a swing. When pleasure is really intense, all the liquids seem to escape from the body: tears, mucus, saliva, urine, semen, sweat, all of them flee from the sweet, private heat.

Many days have passed; a lot of things have changed . . . Now, shielded by my ballpoint, I withdraw into the peace that all returns provide. I've come back to myself, and what I'm writing now is the offspring of what I wrote before so there's a simulacrum of order where, in fact, nothing but chance and confusion really obtains. Writing in this notebook is a way of gathering myself together: it's my Church, my arrested time.

Now it's easier for me to understand people who fill their lives with this business of writing. I don't hate them any more. Many things have changed. I don't hate them any more. The people who write are, inevitably, the ones who are afraid of losing their identity or who have already lost it during a moment of carelessness or, perhaps, who know that we don't even have an identity to lose while everyone else lives on in the rashest unconsciousness, believing they are SOMEBODY. In fact it's quite mysterious that the man of yesterday should also be the man of today, that the man of tomorrow isn't transformed into a stranger looking over his shoulder for the distant, perhaps hostile, figure that he himself was just a few days or months ago . . . I've found myself again here, and some meaning will persist in spite, or because, of the tales I tell.

Once again, I'm the one who's writing. There's no doubt about it. And because I'm the one who's writing, last week's page and last month's page are believable. It's as though, when I turn on my bedroom light before going to bed, I simultaneously turned on all the lights that brought me this far: lights on streets I've walked, headlights on buses and taxis, lamps in bars and taverns, tracks of lights that sketch the complicated map of a day, of a whole life as convoluted as a scribble. Other street lights, other headlights could have gone on as I passed by, but these were the ones that actually did, and now I'm stuck with them.

I wrote "my bedroom" above, and this could lead to a misunderstanding. I'm not in my bedroom now, not even in my trapezoidal apartment. I'm living in a house not my own. Yesterday I installed my things here or, to be precise, they were installed for me — among them this notebook and a volume by Laforgue that looks at me as though it were an undeniable proof of everything that happened. I don't live in my old house now, but I'm not very far from it, just a discreet number of streets higher up in the direction of the Tibidabo. However, this feels more like "my home" now than the other one, since we're always putting together the right spot for the next nightmare. These projects are what we call "property." In fact, the time we devote to dreaming is so important in our lives that it's easy to confuse the place we want to dream in with the place we want to die in.

I, at least in the immediate present, want to die here even though I feel like a stranger in this room that doesn't belong to me. I'd like to suppress the difference between us as soon as possible even if I have to change from top to toe to adapt to it. Actually, I'm using "bedroom" and "room" for something which is bigger but not so grand. Bigger because, to sum things up, I've settled into one of the Chinaman's other houses, and I occupy all of it. It's a cottage with an interior garden, situated on a street that runs parallel to Doctor Andreu in a quiet neighborhood perfumed by flowering acacia. I don't know the function of this retreat in Chinese strategy, but I can imagine what it is.

When I say I can imagine what it is, I mean — let's make things clear — that I assume it, considering the essentially feminine character of some of the domestic details: the dominant pink of the toiletries, the collection of perfume samples, the baby soaps and shampoos, the luxurious bathrobes, the shower caps with garlands, the sponges, the cotton balls, the powder puffs, the talcum powders, the creams, the sachets, the lotions, the colognes . . . But even if I didn't know about this treasury of the feminine body, the smell of houses inhabited by women is unmistakable.

In spite of everything, what I've just said is a mere inference: I've yet to see a single woman in the house, and I can't help shuddering when I think that she's probably totally unaware of my presence. It's possible — almost certain, in fact — that the Chinaman has told her nothing. It would be just like him. I wrote earlier that it was "bigger," and I think I've clarified that, but also "not so grand." That's due to certain insinuations the Chinaman has made that lead me to believe the famous animal he promised to show me *also* lives in this house, and I'm harboring a suspicion that both inhabitants, woman and animal, are one and the same. This would be intolerably vulgar; it would destroy all my expectations, reducing the Chinaman's threat to a locker-room joke. The possibility saddens me, and for that very reason, it gives an edge to my desire to finally meet the woman who lives here.

I may be exaggerating. It's possible that after setting me up in this room, the Chinaman moved his lady friend to the house on Escuelas Pías. That would mean I've now taken her place . . . or the animal's. It would be another cheap trick. No, it can't be. In the end, what brought me here wasn't one of the Chinaman's plans (he only intervened in one chain of events) but instead a conjunction of causes and effects that he has brought to a provisional conclusion. Considered on its own, each incident that took place in the last few days is meaningless, but if they're taken together and given a conclusion, they become coherent. It's the same thing that will happen to this notebook.

One thing is clear: a few days ago, I was a bit confused. I think I may even have become a little crazy. My impatience intervened decisively in my confusion or craziness. Did I try PRECIPITOUSLY to put an end to that humiliation and banality? Was the very word "collapse" ordering my moves as if it were a magnetic field? I don't know, and even when I reread what I wrote days before (I've torn out a few pages), I don't understand my seizure now. I think I suggested it before: I can understand what happened based on what I'm writing now, but that's it; I don't understand another word. You could say the same thing about the stars: they're an arbitrary handful of crystals until someone uses them with perfect freedom to draw the figures of Scorpio, Gemini and so on.

During my period of obfuscation, I visited the Boa with great frequency and without protecting myself from the dangers to which I was exposed there — or maybe that's why I went. Why not? I wouldn't act like that now, but at that point I was bumbling around, trying to find a way to get someone else to undo the knot that was strangling me. There can be no doubt that Diego's drinks and chemicals had drawn a curtain over my instinct for self-preservation. Like all curtains, it had the virtue of uniting what's separated and separating what's united. After ten or twelve glasses and a couple of pills, what kills us can also prolong our lives and keep us, if not exactly alive, at least IN life. It's like the theater: by virtue of theatrical conventions, the actor who's speaking IN another spirit, who's sunk in a foreign soul, acquires a SECOND MIND that allows him to observe the stage and the prompter, even to wink at a member of the audience, all with a detachment and coolness that would be beyond him if he had only ONE soul.

As the night came to an end and I found myself in the company of other drunkards who were impossible to individualize, I dissolved into words that were not my own, and in that way I lived up to my motto. I spoke like a lover whose partner has just died in an unexpected and stupid accident, like someone who's bearing up at the critical moment but who hasn't forgotten for one second that the worst has only just begun. The strangest thing was that *I* was the one who'd just died in the unexpected and stupid accident.

No idea how many nights I wound up sleeping in the corridors of the metro, collapsed in the doorways of department stores, on top of the benches on the Paseo Marítimo, set upon by the guards. The pain, the humidity, and the hangovers, the horrific hangovers. I think I let myself get into pretty bad shape. I made it to the apartment only on rare occasions. This was due not so much to the mechanical difficulty of the operation as to the great satisfaction I derived from my lamentable state: destruction exercises a far more voluptuous attraction than development.

The reactions of pity and repugnance I provoked in our good citizens were proof enough that I looked repulsive. The beggar, like the actor I mentioned above, enjoys a cooler and more subjective second sight that allows him to see people from an extraordinary angle. Behind his repertory of expressions — anger, conceit, rejection, indifference, submission — the honorable citizen is paralyzed by fear. Poverty produces terror among the Christians. There's panic behind the gestures of piety, universal love and philanthropic goodness. It's not surprising that the Church should be so obsessed with economic gains. Everybody who gives alms, all the charitable souls, are terrified of poverty. The only people who escape this panic are the few who have actually experienced the horror of poverty. They give alms with the greatest simplicity, as though they were buying a newspaper.

But these little amusements only filled the day. When night fell, I joined people in the same condition I was in, people who respect the law. Then the performance would begin. Everything was conventional, even the hostilities. Baboons never get hurt because one of them always surrenders before any damage is done. We derelicts also followed the rules of a very carefully designed system. The same dramatic art that is essential to begging for alms also allows you to be thrown out of a joint without losing your dignity. If you haven't tried it, you don't know what I'm talking about.

During the day, the performance demands that you remain almost invisible, revealing nothing but the hand that falls on the money or the twisted leg that justifies the act of charity because it's essential to BEG FORGIVENESS for being in such an unhappy situation. At night just the opposite is true. You have to be noisily conspicuous, to importune customers in taverns and inns, to bounce around the streets with a bottle in your hand, to open your fly in front of groups of young ladies, to hurl obscenities at the government . . . it's the law.

But I wasn't a real professional in the art of abjection, and my lack of practice showed. It's not surprising, then, that some nights I got a beating when I begged for a bite to eat in a cafe or that I was pushed down by a waiter on the third shift who'd just come in and was fresh and anxious to make points. These things would never happen to a real professional in the art of poverty. But they were unimportant, and I endured the little setbacks with pleasure, trying to learn a new role. Yet in spite of all my enthusiasm, God hadn't chosen that road for me. A few days later, it became obvious that I just didn't have the talent to enter into a swift decline and reach an abrupt end.

My desire to bring my investigation to an end by means of hunger, cirrhosis, or a heart attack that would allow me to die in some alleyway like a dog — this desire was cut short brutally on the night that once again (it was destiny) I ran into the girl from Málaga and Víctor in the Boa. It was inevitable. Since I was trying to panhandle a drink and avoid the waiter at the same time, I either didn't recognize or didn't see them. They were the ones who found me: the dragon is the one who finds his hunter. I can affirm that Víctor was overwhelmed by pity on seeing the state I was in and deducing the intensity of my humiliation. But he couldn't help it. Leave him to me, he told the waiters. It was in his blood. He was really going to indulge himself in his hatred.

I remember the girl's protests quite clearly. In fact, they were a lot more intriguing than the claw that grasped my neck. There was an element of excess in her protests (oh, poor thing, don't hurt him!) that went beyond a merely selfish interest in keeping Víctor out of trouble or making sure he'd be able to perform that night. In her protests I discerned the balsam that the Virgin Mary applies to the victims of Purgatory. I stretched out my hand, trying to reach that rosary dangling over the flames, but Víctor dragged me out of the place and backed me over a red car that was double-parked outside. That's where he hit me for the first time, not very hard, on the kidneys or maybe a little lower down. Then he opened the door and pushed me in. I didn't know where he was taking me, but I didn't care either. Every time I breathed in, I felt a sharp jab in my side, so I restricted myself to short, well-spaced pants. This little business took all my strength. While he was driving, Víctor watched me out of the corner of his eye. It was a childish precaution since I hadn't the slightest intention of doing anything. I couldn't contain an idiotic laugh. I'm sure it infuriated him.

He parked in a curve on Montjuich behind the old stadium, got out of the car and lit a cigarette. We waited that way for a good while. He would lean on the hood, smoke, walk a few paces, come back. Against the yellowish glow of the city, the line of cypresses that bordered the edge looked like a marionette theater. Once he'd put out his cigarette, he opened the door and hauled me out vigorously by my hair, my long blond hair. I fell to my knees and got the first kick, right there, on my side again. Now that I was on the ground, he kept on kicking me, but I protected myself with my arms. I saw powder flashes, lightning flashes, and felt vomit pouring out of my mouth. Sometimes a kick caught me in the face. I also remember, because it was so close by, one of his loafers resting on the bumper of the car. He was cleaning off the blood with a piece of chamois. Then he got down to work and kicked me some more. I wanted to sleep, and I think I really did drift off or, at least, the part that holds us together went out for a little stroll to avoid witnessing the blood bath. But I woke up again, shocked by a vile knife running up my body as if it were cutting a channel. My poor consciousness came racing back to see what was happening.

Víctor had opened my fly and thrust his hand in like a snake sliding into a rabbit warren; he was squeezing my testicles with his ring. A profound, electrical pain that doesn't affect your muscles but your nerves, cuts off your breath, and sends blood flooding through your head. Between my eyes and Víctor's — we were looking each other over from head to toe, and our faces were probably the same shade of purple — there was a lilac explosion that sizzled with the peristaltic rhythm of my viscera. I felt my sphincter loosen up with a dry crackling sound, and an acid stream of excrement enveloped me like a shroud. I must have fainted, but not before I heard Víctor's voice repeating like a prayer: What a goddamn miserable life this is, what a goddamn miserable life . . .

Next came a cement room with a light bulb hanging from the ceiling, in other words, a jail cell. I didn't identify it right away because the door had no bars, no peephole, none of the details cinematic fantasy has accustomed us to. The pain in my side was so intense that I woke up crying without knowing why. As soon as I moved, my head was blown away by a flash of pain shooting from my crotch as though it were fired from a musket. I couldn't breath, and when I touched my nose, a disconcerting stream of black sand poured out. Later on I realized it was dried blood, but for a minute I felt like a sawdust doll, losing my stuffing through a ripped seam. It took me a while to figure out that every time I moved I howled in pain, but once it dawned on me, I kept still.

I felt real tenderness for myself in my sorry state. In the final analysis, how long had it been since I'd cried with such eagerness and such a sense of relief? I couldn't remember. I did remember that the pleasure of emptying out my tear ducts

had one or two precedents, but I suspected they had been
caused by vaguely amorous sensations of a perfectly vulgar
nature. The enormous relief of self-pity began to produce
good effects. I felt close to the kind of liberation the great
saints and martyrs experience, the overwhelming conversion
that wipes away the sins of the past. St. Augustus gambling
in dens crowded with blacks, Arabs and Roman low-lifes before writing the greatest treatise in Christian history. Now I
saw an ingenuous, loving future so close at hand that I felt
exalted by universal pity. Once again the passionate fusion
with the Eucharist, the solitary conversations with God, kneeling on a wooden bench while the other students silently take
communion at the high altar, all of us enveloped in a Saint-
Saëns score winnowed out of the organ by the *solfeggio* teacher.

Focused on the all-powerful inner voice, the child is a
god who converses with another, slightly older, god. How
many years had gone by? How could I have forgotten that in
times past I had been God? No, I hadn't forgotten; that long
lost memory was precisely what had brought me to this point
although my constant humiliation had made me almost forget the intense, tortured, exalted, voracious, absolute life of
(what else?) a god! I would never regain that state of divinity
in which you don't think, you live! When everything around
you is a resounding YES! In view of this loss, I had no alternative but going crazy, losing sight of myself. I was the residue of a season in Paradise. What was left of me was a source
of irritation now, a scrap, a cosmos of remorseful boredom.
At last I knew what I was looking for. Not only that, I had
found it. The emblematic phrase, my motto, had acquired a
new meaning. Here is what the mouth of the Lord says: You

will live an eternity of humiliation because you once lived in Eden, AND IT WAS NOT ENOUGH.

I had to get out of jail fast. It was extremely important for me to put my NEW nature into practice. And then the miracle occurred. Just when I realized that divinity is PHYSICAL, just when it became clear to me that everything that happens is miraculous and that there are no miracles that aren't material and even MATERIALISTIC. It's not by chance, incidentally, that scientists, the real atheists, deny the existence of miracles. Of course they do! Science is nothing but a selfish effort to finish off matter. Scientific truths (truths!) are printed pictures that hide MATERIAL EVIDENCE, in other words, miracles. To sum up, "matter" and "miracle" are synonyms; like "fire" and "hearth," they point to the same object, in the first case with the eyes and in the second with the heart. From now on, I was only going to live by miracles. Not by miracle, but by miracles!

The first miracle that took place at that unfortunate juncture was this: someone opened the iron door, and a man dressed in brown asked me if I would be so kind (so kind!) as to follow him to the office of the Honorable Chief of Police. I assumed my bureaucratic Calvary was about to get underway: the fines, the seals, the birth certificates (to prove a person has been born, ah hah), the memoranda, the contentio-administrative petitions, the wait, the togas, the ushers, the courts of law, the appellate courts . . . but to my amazement, when the guard helped me (I could hardly walk and had to hold up my genitals so they wouldn't stab me at every step) into the office of the Honorable Chief of Police, I saw the Chinaman, who else? the Chinaman unfazed, the Chinaman, faintly smiling, the Chinaman, his arms crossed, the Chinaman.

They settled me in an armchair with the seat and back made of embossed leather, one of those chocolate-colored pieces of furniture that always have Don Quixote on them somewhere, and then the guard said he was going to find the police chief. When I sat down, I heard the crunch of my pants clearly; they were covered with dried excrement. I found out later that the Chinaman had been combing the city for me, but at that point I thought I was seeing the apparition of the Risen Christ; at any time, he would unbutton his striped shirt so I could touch the wound in his side. You're a loon, he said, but he said it gently as if he were talking to a dog that has come back in a sorry state after making its spring rounds. I pulled my jacket shut and kept my feet crossed tightly while my body, indifferent to my inner glory, trembled on the chair, shaken by delicious emissions that endangered the brass tacks of the fancy trim.

The Chief of Police turned out to be a man with an ample beard and a tobacco-stained moustache who controlled his gestures and liked to get to the point. Víctor came into the room first. At the sight of him I gave a little start from where I was sitting there on top of my excretions. The chief greeted the gathering with a Japanese nod of the head and addressed me with a speech that required no response, except at most agreement. This man, he said, motioning toward Víctor with his chin, has committed an indescribable outrage against you. I say "indescribable," but, in fact, it is describable since it's referred to in our constitution or our code of human rights or whatever the hell it is, but I have to make

clear that this doesn't involve one of our agents, I mean, one
with a diploma; he's short a judo course and he flunked first-
year grammar, both of them disciplines, that is, the course
and the discipline, that he'll never finish because we're throwing him out on the street right now — shut up, you! and
thank this . . . gentleman for not making you really pay for
what you've done because this . . . gentleman is not going to
lodge a formal complaint — are you? None of us would benefit from it, these things cause a lot of trouble and then the
judges turn the perps loose the next day, and in the final
analysis, you can be sure that this lost, or black, sheep will
never be part of the flock again, and that's definite — so you!
you can start asking this . . . gentleman's pardon right now
. . . yes, you, this minute — and I beg you to forgive this
barbarian — get on with it! Beg his pardon, Morales! Beg his
pardon, dammit!

Now it was Víctor who was swallowing the bitter pill of
humiliation, but he wasn't a bad kid. I'm convinced he had
the simple strength of the peasant. Sturdy feet like his have
carried us through all our glorious wars, like the War of Independence, all of those wars fought for reasons of honor. It
must have seemed totally bewildering to the poor monster
that a drunken wretch should be treated with exquisite courtesy. As a boy in his hometown, he had thrown rocks at
drunks with the same innocence with which he popped the
eyes out of newborn kittens, and now he was losing his job
for the same reason his superiors had applauded him up until
that incomprehensible moment, that is, because he knows
how to give 'em a good beating, maybe that'll make 'em
mend their ways. His look sears me with the Hispanic fire of

his grandfathers, common men who cut down French soldiers, beat women and lapidated queers. Speak up, or I swear
you'll remember me for the rest of your life, Morales! Víctor
looked up, held his hands behind his back and emitted a
short sentence between clenched teeth that fainted as soon
as it peeped out of his mouth. Fine, Morales, fine. See how
easy it was? You can go now; we'll talk later. But Víctor didn't
go; he kept on looking at me with eyes like darts, unable to
digest the injustice that his bosses — who had seemed like
reasonable substitutes for his grandfathers, his father, the ruddy-
cheeked, hard-drinking vicar and the mayor — had committed. I alone was the source of his bitter misfortune. The Honorable Chief of Police waved his right hand palm up like
school teachers when they are urging slow scholars to leave
the classroom, and he even added something appropriate to
the occasion, Go on! Get a move on!

But as soon as we were alone, the weight of his position
fell over us. The Honorable Chief of Police addressed the
Chinaman without the least cordiality, with a bit of consternation in fact: You're satisfied now, aren't you? Well, tell
Señor Chicharro (where had I heard that name before?) that
we didn't need his warning; we'd have done the same thing
anyway for the sake of the corps. This kid Morales was okay,
but now he'll go to the bad. You'll see. He'll wind up back
here again, on the other side of the trenches. Not that I want
to justify him, eh? Far from it. But I'd like to know what
REALLY happened between these two (directed at me) that
got him into that state. If the police hadn't gone by on their
rounds, he'd be dead. When they stopped Morales, he was
half crazy. Ah, and if it were true that your acquaintance was

passing himself off as a policeman — although I can't believe anyone who's a man of honor and a friend of Señor Chicharro would defend such a person — I swear that I would give him a beating myself. As if we didn't have enough trouble fitting into this fucking wonderful civil society of ours.

From the door now, the Honorable Chief of Police reviewed me from head to toe with such Olympic disdain that I was glad I'd had it out with Víctor and not the Honorable Chief of Police. Then, addressing the Chinaman as though I were about as important as one of the ashtrays in the room, he added: And get him to clean himself up a bit, dammit; he's left this place like a pigpen! I have to admit that in the conjunction of circumstances I've just described, the Honorable Chief of Police shines like a parenthesis of rectitude and goodness. So much so that once I'd been released, I felt I'd lost someone close to me. It was like saying good-bye to a father who's entering a clinic or a grandfather abandoned in an old folks' home. I tortured myself wondering if that grandfather, that father, that Honorable Chief of Police would ever know how good I was going to be and what high grades in math I would get from then on.

Let's go. I'll take you home, the Chinaman said. I assumed he meant my asymmetrical apartment, and I was on the point of refusing to go back to the dirty clothes, the empty bottles, the blocked-up toilet, the Bimbo bread, the honking horns, the rat . . . the rat! What had become of the rat? Where had I left it the last time we saw each other? I stopped short, because that rat was my life, the one I'd chosen freely for my investigation, my life of scientific banality, and it would be hard now to exchange it for another. But when we reached the Avenida Tibidabo, we didn't turn onto the Paseo San Gervasio; instead we went up Doctor Andreu and pulled into the garage of a cottage with a pitched, slate roof. The Chinaman accompanied me to this room where I am now and said: Take a bath, clean up, sleep all day, and tell me about it tomorrow. Your stuff is outside — here's the key to the trunk; take it all up yourself. Naturally, they didn't let me take the rat, but if you like, I can get you another.

I confess I only washed superficially, mainly my nether parts. When I felt the fresh sheets against my body, I fell into a deep sleep even though I was assaulted once again by the nervous spasm, the pain in my throat that had shaken me from head to foot in jail. But this time it overwhelmed me for entirely different, even diametrically opposed, reasons, from which I deduce that physiological reactions respond not to the content but to the intensity of the emotion. The fact is, I pissed on myself out of sheer pleasure.

Up until yesterday, I hadn't put my things in order: a pair of pants, a sweater, a razor . . . Here there's a closet, a table, a chair, a sun . . . I'm completely recovered and alert, ready for the miraculous life that awaits me. Everything would be wonderful if an obscure sense of anxiety didn't gnaw at me every time I think about the woman, the HYPOTHETICAL woman. I would consider it a real fraud, a cruel trick, if this newcomer replaced OUR animal, the one that's been laboriously constructed over so many long and tedious conversations.

July 2nd

I'm not moving from here. The sun shines in through the windows and leaves orange reflections on the ceiling. The lace curtains sway with the coming and going of summer. The total silence of the siesta hour is filled with the music of the sea. It's been years since I was with things, near things and IN things! The desk I'm leaning on is cherry wood with markings of a pale pomegranate color. On top of it, a proud and useless radio from the fifties sports a mythical sign: *Transoceanic!* It used to resound at two in the afternoon with the BBC's spectacular symphony orchestra interspersed with brief but forceful newscasts about the streetcar strike. My aunts and uncles would gather around it, listening for the hidden truth so they could save their jewels in the (unlikely) case that Franco failed to use the necessary force. All of them ought to be killed, Uncle Enrique would shout, beside himself over his vision of all the union workers in the country strung up from the scrawny trees that line the Paseo de la Gracia.

A heap of perfidious memories form the nebulous universe of those years. The convulsed faces of Hungarian officers condemned to the firing squad, the white plastic Dual record-player, the red and grey covers of *Life Magazine*, the sports section of the movie news (music of "Images" superimposed on a montage of the German Olympics), the smell of Imedio Glue, Luis Mariano's operettas, the Hoover, the third-class seats on the metro, the impossible choice between two armoires: in one, hidden beneath a pile of *foulards*, a copy of *Common Cause* filled with the numbered and frighteningly disfigured cadavers of those who had been killed by the Reds; in the other, under the shoe boxes, copies of *Cinémonde* with photographs of Diana Dors and Mylène Demongeot. And all those empty rooms, when aunts and uncles took off for the summer, leaving us in the hands of our grandfather, a man who modeled himself on Mussolini.

Laid out for me here is the difference between two ghosts, the person I was and the person I am now. The old me was fascinated by pictures of torture chambers, these *chekas* where, they said, the aristocrats of the city were tortured to death, the old me was as taken with that image as with the tableau of "Hell" in the Tibidabo automatons. The person I am now looks at the same photo of the *cheka* with nothing but a kind of bored surprise at the dictatorial influences. Did Malevitch invent the *chekas*? The distance between the two ghosts is easy to sum up: the vision has GOTTEN COLD. In the past, every detail, no matter how insignificant, was part of an august and mysterious design. Each detail was a REVELATION; I lived in the world of miracles. In the present, even important, significant things seem perfunctory. But these material objects haven't changed; I'm the one who has withdrawn from them. Only if I can keep the Jailhouse Vision, only if I strain my optical nerve, only then can I return to MATERI-ALISM. Take, for example, this very room. The little bed with its caned headboard, the vanilla-colored parquet. It's the antithesis of my trapezoidal room, of my private *cheka*. Utterly impossible for a rat to live here! And so, utterly impossible to cohabit with animals inferior to the lizard. Here or in any other part of the house.

Not that I've seen it all. On the second floor, which I've explored only superficially, there's a spiral stair that leads to an attic? a studio? a terrace? The whole house, I mean, is a stage set for feminine ritual. The kitchen, glowing in ivory and olive tones WITHOUT A SINGLE ARTIST, is like Dr. Barraquer's Ophthalmology Clinic, but it certainly wasn't designed for a blind woman (I have proof: the multiple mirrors under pink festoons; does she look at herself here and there, from over her shoulder — How does this pleat fall? — from the front — What's this mole under my breast?), an apple-green carpet with copper cross-pieces on the stair, a nightstand in the second-floor bedroom with a lamp that hides a jewelry case made of sandalwood (nothing in it), a rose-printed silk robe and slippers, a clothes closet that's perfumed but almost empty . . .

I search eagerly for a photo, an album, a driver's license. A portrait done in oils? No way. That would be fatal, fatidic. I don't want to meet her in a portrait done in oils. Magazine clippings, creamy white girls in tennis shorts, a racquet on their shoulders, smiling at the photographer with their radiant teeth — is she one of them? Impossible. SHE'S NOT LIKE THAT. Not at all. Nothing like these omens of a bovine future. In any event, I'll make a concession: an image of the Virgin Mary done in the Languedoc style. But no, that's not right either.

It's intolerable not being able to give some sort of physical support to this house, an enchanted house whose ghost plays with my ghost (two), leaving me (three) out of the fun. So at night when the Chinaman finishes his accounts and drops by for a drink while he talks on and on about animals, a feminine specter wanders around making the curtains ripple and eclipsing the moon like a shadow . . . a Chinese shadow!

My protector (why does he protect me? or rather, what for?) has acted with supreme elegance: not a single comment, much

less a reproach, has escaped him in relation to my melancholy
police rescue. Out on the terrace, his emphatic voice, underlined by administrative gestures, assumes such flute-like tones it
sounds like the chirping of the blackbird that makes a racket
every morning. He seems more opaque and more pedantic than
ever, except now he has a new ritual that's more Byzantine than
Mandarin. The Sacred Form is hidden behind the veil, and the
priest with his stikarion, his epitrakelion, his epimanikion, his
felonion and his camilafkion of black wool and heavy gold,
peers out through the curtains of a beard that's curled and
anointed with scented oil, hinting, praising and insinuating as
though he were peddling transcendence.

Now he's insistently evoking Sunday afternoons devoted to
skating on the Diagonal when it was undeveloped and you could
still see donkeys grazing. That's where he saw his first neon sign;
it was over the door of the Río, a sinful cabaret owned by the
Captain General's mistress. That neon light — more than artificial, it was false through and through — seems to have had a
decisive effect on his understanding of the world. As did his
undefined relationship with Cucurella. But since I'm fearful of
undermining his trust — what's all this trust about anyway? —
I don't ask, I don't insist. Without our ever being aware of it, the
Chinaman used to watch us from a corner of the schoolyard. A
pea-sized Chinaman studied Cucurella's solid superiority, his
natural nobility, with a view to usurpation. He had even skated
on the Diagonal! But solely with the aim of imitation! Making
a superhuman effort, behind his father's back (his father was a
provisioner for the Espulgas Barracks), he bought his own skates
(what money did he use? was it his first dirty money?) and
studied the liturgy of skating on the Diagonal.

For him, the action of skating was neither a form of training nor a sport; it was an incantation that would deliver the forces of evil into his power. The rest of us, careless kids with bubble brains, EVEN GOT BORED skating on the Diagonal. We didn't know he was already beginning to store up strange experiences that would one day come in handy. This willful act of mimicry must not be understood as the kind of ostentation that leads a shopkeeper's wife to occupy a box seat at the opera, where she must endure an avalanche of stupidity in Italian in order to show off copies of the rings she keeps in the safe. No. It was more like the anthropologist who is eager to learn the steps of Hottentot dances in hopes that they will help him take on the Hottentot's strength.

While his father was working his way up the service stairs, hopping up the residential ladder from La Sagrera to the Ensanche, from there to Llave de Oro, and then on to Nuñez y Navarro until at long last, in the seventies, he reached that exquisite paradise of dwellings identifiable not by construction and building firms but by the names of architects whose green and blue wool ties topped off by the cupola of their English tweeds (copied in the mills of Igualada) had stood the small world of the Catalonian press on its ear. While his father was doing all this, the Chinaman was following a parallel but darker path, busying himself with the study of animal behavior, the HIDDEN ZONE, Ur-society. If his father, black marketeer, overseer, head of personnel, supporter of the Regime, head of services, managing director, vice president, if his father ascended by fair means, making use of the diurnal work surrendered to him by Catalonian aristocrats, who were brought down as much by their own weaknesses as by others' machinations, the

Chinaman, in neat complementarity, took an interest only in nocturnal work, in nothing but the sewer.

He must have studied a lot in those years. What crime laid the foundation of the Bellvitge development? What secrets are hidden in a Provincial Traffic Court? Why do you never see any brand but Fred Perry polo shirts? What magnet draws weddings and baptisms to the Pompeya parish? What sexual transgressions lay behind the passage of the Corporations Law? What form of slander do these Hottentots fear the most? Who's their witch doctor? Who do they listen to and why? When do they look the other way? What keeps them awake nights? His father's power was worth its weight in GOLD, but the Chinaman knew how little gold is worth. His power was worth its weight in BLOOD.

But the strangest thing is that he has failed. Like his father. These days a rich man, a powerful man, is little more than a deluxe laborer. The Chinaman, then, doesn't crush, doesn't flatten, doesn't pulverize, he simply SUCKS. He's no superman, just a superflea. He's the usher of death. Because there's no room for soldiers of fortune, *condottieri*, guerilla leaders, the Chinaman administers the poverty of the powerful. He's not a bird of prey, not a predator; he's the bacteria that arrives on the scene just before the curtain falls so he can finish off what the vultures disdained. This explains his expression when he saw the carnivorous flies on the roof of the Museum of Natural History: they're his competitors.

Today he was saying, The only things that get my attention are things that don't follow the rules, things that BREAK THE LAW. Diamonds, for example, are repulsive; they're willing slaves. The bodies of people who collect diamonds obey foolish laws that are as monotonous as the desert. How about pearls? Pearls are ridiculous! The women who wear them are perfectly SPHERICAL. Amber, on the other hand, now there's an enigma! Things that are misshapen, that are deformed, those things are glorious. And then, after a yawn, motioning vaguely toward the night: Stars are grotesque; the only acceptable thing up there is the clouds.

July 5th

Today is the third day I eat breakfast, lunch and dinner and get bored all alone. Obeying his instinct for drama, the Chinaman has disappeared. Not a note, not a call. Silence. With the exception of some presentiments, nothing has changed in the house. But I mustn't be vain; the presentiments are the result of an evil action. Up until now, I'd never *ever* tampered with the mail. The fact is that every morning postcards signed with an initial arrive in the mail. There are dozens of them, and the initial is always the same: "M." It's almost certainly not the vampire of Düsseldorf. I deduce that from the text. They fall from the mail slot right onto the parquet floor. Alerted by the sonorous thud, I pick them up, gather together the letters, municipal magazines, political flyers and the incredibly abundant junk mail. I keep piling them onto the shelf over the radiator, and they're in danger of sliding off now. The Chinaman hasn't read his correspondence in months. But yesterday they brought a telegram. The doorbell. What a shock. A boy with a ballpoint between his teeth like a rose. Signature. No change. Don't worry. Hunting around. Not a cent. After giving him a can of tuna fish that was lying out in the kitchen, I had the telegram in my hands. I was shaking like an autumn leaf.

I leave the house before lunch time and go up Doctor Andreu as far as the funicular station. The concrete on the avenue is in bad shape, and the cracks are filled with weeds and trash, but the ample views of the city fill me with love. Yes, I have to confess: *je t'aime, ô capitale infâme!* I've changed a lot since my Jailhouse Vision to get to this point! Then I eat something silly in the restaurant they've fixed up by the funicular station. Fixed up from the decorative point of view, because the comestibles bear absolutely no relation to the red-hot prices that apply now. But you pay for the air and the bougainvillea, which forms a lilac-colored curtain over the high russet wall. Surely it was planted and watered by Gauguin before he moved to a similar place in the Pacific. If you stare at it and then close your eyes, phosphorescent forms flit through your brain, lighting the darkest rooms of memory.

I return with a delicious sense of uneasiness (in part self-induced, a real indulgence this), like a high school student at exam time — will it be the first-degree equations I know or the Pi Cosine I can't make head or tail of? Will she be there? No. She's not there, and it's the Pi Cosine. I pick up the telegram again. Hold it in my hand. To read it or not to read it. That is the question. Perfectly justifiable to read it. Urgency must be dealt with urgently. Look, I opened it just in case it was urgent so I could let you know right away (where?), so I could let you know at the liquor store. A telegram MUST be opened immediately. Urgent. Top secret. Reasons of State. The submerged, cloacal, vile state. And, therefore, all the more fragile, weak and vulnerable.

I don't have the strength to open it. I leave it on the unstable summit of the shaky pile. I reread a few postcards whose content is frankly disconcerting. "Got here Thursday. The weather's awful. Kisses. M." And one from Geneva with a picture of its great fountain, its swans, its Swiss flag — so esteemed when it flies over hospitals, clinics, hospices, asylums and chocolate factories. Or: "The Cathedral is shrimp-colored, but the whole city reeks of sausage. A kiss. M." Strasbourg. And: "What a surprise. It turns out they've opened one of those great French book chains. I'm going to be left without a cent. All the better. That way I'll come back sooner. Kisses. M." Montpellier. Any relation between the (sudden) desire to come back and the move from "A Kiss" to "Kisses"? A transitory fit of good humor? "I'm at the Gabarrós' house. We took the boat out, but there's always a lot of wind. Yesterday it was from the south. The Gabarrós send their love. Kisses. M." Cadaqués. So she came back, but not quite. And another: "This place is crammed with secondhand book stores. I saw the latest Bergman. The Gabarrós send their love. M." Toulouse. Not even a kiss! And in Cadaqués again! With winds from the east or the west! "Sun! Sun! Sun! Millions of flowers. Even the cows here are more virile than in Switzerland. The Gabarrós want to go back Saturday. I'll let you know. Big Kisses. M." Baqueira. Problem solved! A question of mood. If she's in a good mood "Kisses," in a great mood "Big Kisses," in a bad mood "A Kiss" and in a really bad mood, Get Lost. And now, the last one: "I don't feel like going back. I'm sorry. I really like it here, and I'm in a much better mood now. The Gabarrós are coming up this weekend. I may go down with them. I'll let you know something. M." Baqueira. Either she's an idiot or a queen or an idiot who thinks she's a queen. It doesn't matter. Between the first and the last postcard, there's more than enough time to decide if she does or doesn't want to come back. This queen thinks slowly. Because she must be a queen — mustn't she?

July 7th

I've dropped my outings, my strolls to the funicular station, my forays to the tobacco stand for Coronas. I'm not leaving home. I've stored up enough food in the refrigerator and the pantry to last three months. For me, the Third World War has broken out. I'm in a state of acute excitement, panting like a gas meter. My only relief comes from the television set, a tool that's foreign to me, but that's extremely useful for measuring the implacable destruction of humanity. World power is now in the hands of a gang of sickos who are going to self-destruct via the spiritual annihilation of the masses. I'm wild about the game shows. They're like police interrogations complete with torture but spurred on by an audience that laughs and claps. There's also a really amusing informational program accompanied by images that are either out of date or unrelated, with a preference for alpine scenes and butterflies fornicating. Often characters called "politicians" come on in order to explain what they've had for breakfast, how they feel, whether they're going to buy a new pair of pants and so on. It's more educational than all the moral philosophy from the seventeenth century on.

On the few occasions when I'm not frozen in front of the television (in fact it's on right now; over the top of my ballpoint pen I can see the fifth little blond boy drinking milk, an obsessive image that is obviously produced by sexual perverts), I pace back and forth like a bear, totally unable to do anything. You can imagine how much I've changed when I say that I've even cracked a book! Disaster and disgust. I looked at *The Swindler* by Quevedo, thinking it would be funny, something to regale my skeptical spirit. Wrong. It's a string of stupid locker-room jokes. And then a little book by Azorín, *The Confessions of a Small-Time Philosopher*, thinking it would be balm for my excited brain. Wishful thinking! Its intellectual poverty is on a par with its hokiness. And those "poetic prose" pieces of Juan Ramón Jiménez. That stuff was ejaculated by a pea-brain with little pursed-up lips! Enough! That's it! The Buzzard was right — and how! This country is good for nothing but choirboys and garlic-eaters!

My attack of nerves is easy to understand in view of the content of the telegram that I opened for URGENT reasons. A text as laconic as the postcards, but much more disturbing: "Decision reached. I'll be there at any moment. M." It's dated five days ago; so she may arrive at any moment. And that ambiguous "decision reached." A woman who has geared herself up? Or a man used to "reaching decisions"? In that case, not a feminine M, but a disgusting, hairy, sweaty, pretentious, smelly, masculine M! What anguish! *Ay*, my poor little bark destroyed on the cruel rocks!

And talk about projects that come to nothing! The Jailhouse Vision has changed the direction of my investigation. To attain real banality, it's necessary to do without will power, but doing without willpower demands AN ENORMOUS EFFORT. For example, while I was tearing open the blue envelope from our incompetent Telephone Company (an operation that took about twelve minutes), the cornices, beams and capitals that buried Samson fell on my head. A truly banal man would never have opened the telegram. Let's not kid ourselves. A truly banal man is free of desires and projects; he lets himself be carried along by any breeze that blows. He improvises according to the weather. He DOESN'T PROVOKE. And I've fallen. I've sinned. Once again, just like I did in the formidable fight with Víctor at the Boa, I've acted like a spiritual — instead of a material — tough guy. Failure. Humiliation.

It's true that last night, after many days and nights without a hint of sex, I started thinking about fornication again. I was probably egged on by the television, which talks about virtually nothing else. However, it was a brief visitation WITHOUT ANY REAL EXCITEMENT. It came to me the same way school songs like In a Cottage in the Wood or Ladybug, Ladybug, Fly Away Home come back to us forty years later when their luminous meaning only serves to remind us how many senses we've lost with the passage of time. Now, there's a woman in the buff advertising garden tools . . . let's see, what's that?

July 10th

I can hardly sleep at all; I'm a mess! I put off going to bed as long as possible, and I manage to push it back to just before dawn when the birds are getting started on their repulsive little struggle to see who has the fattest crumb. The television programs end with the flag floating over the national anthem, and that really wakes me up. Then the screen is covered with a swarm of bright dots that manage to keep my attention for another half hour. After three quarters of an hour, it becomes quite frankly intolerable because — as I see it, and that's why I watch so much — it's like the last vision of someone who's in the midst of death throes brought on by a cerebral tumor, the cerebral tumor being the REAL *raison d'être* of the television set (a huge increase in the number of cerebral tumors in remote mountain villages dates from the installation of television transmitters), that is, a systematic destruction of the human fabric. When I can't stand the cerebral-tumor-vision any longer, I don't know what to do with myself. I wind up opening some book, but only to close it immediately. Yesterday, for example, a little *Faust*, but instead of wisdom and beauty and Olympic grandeur, I got cold cuts, a beery porker fattened up on swinish pomposity, locker-room jokes even worse than Quevedo's. Coarse and brutish, all of it. Crap, fart, a worm disguised as part of an Athenian frieze. Nuh-uh. I shut it with infinite distaste.

And this goes on in a house with a truly demented literary selection, all of it enclosed in bright, cheap bindings. There are a lot of peasant novels — Fernán Caballero, Pereda, Father Coloma — and a few volumes of "philosophy" with ineffable prologues — one of them starts like this: "From Descartes philosophy has inherited the habit of asking itself 'What are we conscious of?' and answering that we are conscious of *the content of our consciousness*." The italics are his, the author's . . . These are practically the only products of humorous literature that we still have. But they make me sick. For some reason that I don't quite understand, a third family of books here belongs to the scientific genre: animal etiology, biochemistry, programming . . . They're most amusing. I spend another couple of hours glancing at the illustrations in them. A comparison of rabbit, cat, monkey and human brains, for example. It's an absolute torrent of hints and lofty ideas! The relative size of the olfactory bulb decreases dramatically as we get closer to man; so the disproportionate influence that smells have on our behavior is not surprising. What we used to call "thought" (or "the content of the content of the content of our consciousness," as the prologue humorist would put it) is so tediously familiar that we don't even notice it, but as soon as we SMELL an idea, we go half crazy. The same applies to the somato-aesthetic field.

By about five in the morning, I've managed to get into a really sottish state. In this stable stupor, I enter the bedroom, trying not to make any abrupt moves. The bed is a pile of wrinkled sheets that give off the unmistakable stench of the nocturnal smoker. I amuse myself a while longer, listening to the clock radio and the voice of a terminal sicko who claims so insistently that she loves truckers and taxi-drivers that everybody knows just what she means except for the truckers and taxi-drivers. They phone in as if she were their mother. The men who run big machines are always naïve. Result: incredibly powerful nuclear missiles in the hands of mongoloid kids. I also look at drawings of things like the so-called "oblique long call sequence" in two kinds of seagulls. This is a sequence of expressions that are OBLIGATORY if these poor, little animals have any intention of surviving. It leaves them with the horrible burden of repeating the oblique long call sequence like a broken record until the next oblique long call sequence just in order to keep the charade going a bit longer! And we do the same thing, brother seagull, *mon semblable, mon frère.* Well, yes, but this is a SPIRITUAL THING because the physical doesn't repeat itself at all; the physical is always fresh, intact, new-born. Every millionth of a second the physical comes back to life. However, the spirit ("the content of the content of the content of the content of the content . . . of the consciousness") is eternal, pitiless, colossal, pharaonic, a bundle of repetitions, a lisping, boring, holiday drunk — "evra'body's wonnerful" — it's pontifical too, but especially, more than anything, it's an unmistakable SYSTEM OF AUTHORITY — for the impotent, of course.

And at last I fall asleep or doze off, or at least I think I do. Not even two minutes have passed, and I've woken up: my neck itches, I'm sweating like a pig, I cough half-heartedly, a flea climbs up my leg . . . Suddenly I hear noises! I really had gone to sleep! I was sound asleep, and somebody got into the house, taking advantage of my stupidity! It's not thieves because thieves have other tricks. What time is it? Ninethirty or so. It turns out I've slept over four hours. Who could be in this house? My attack of tachycardia doesn't keep me from getting as far as the bath. I make a noise, a lot of noise, to attract their attention. The cold water slides off my neck, soaks my pajama pants. And then I SEE MYSELF. Huge blue shadows — let's not kid ourselves, bags — under my eyes. Several days' growth of greyish beard. Dirty, sticky, yellowish hair. The threat of baldness. I've definitely gotten fatter. My hands are smaller than ever. My hips have begun to look like plump vegetables. I feel terribly old, crazed, broken-down and squalid — an usher reduced to picking up cigarette butts. I'm UNPRESENTABLE. I fix myself up as best I can. I pick out my only decent shirt, a black and blue plaid. I shine my shoes on the bedspread. I barely have the strength, and my heart is still playing ninepins with my blood without the least consideration. Calm down. Get a hold on yourself. You get hysterical over the slightest thing! I sit on the toilet for a while. Finally, I leave the bathroom, cross the hall and storm into the kitchen, feigning a concentrated interest in breakfast. I pour milk into a pan that's scorched with the milk from yesterday and the day before and the day before that, but while it's still heating up, I hear the unmistakable tapping — a terse, military sound — of the Chinaman's heels as he heads toward the kitchen. Good morning. I see you're getting up early now. Everything all right? Why did you buy ten cans of that foul stew? You don't look so good — kind of swollen up. Is anything wrong?

I hurl myself at the milk, which is boiling over with a sound like a train whistle. I offer to fix breakfast. No thanks, I ate breakfast hours ago. Now, listen carefully. Either tonight or tomorrow at the latest, I'm expecting the owner of the house. She's a GREAT friend of mine, and she already knows that you're here for a few days. You can stay as long as you like, but try not to get things too dirty. She hates to have maids in, so she does the cooking and cleaning — the things you're not used to — herself. Now Diego comes in. I'm glad to see him. I like his thick neck, like a column supporting his granite head. He's wearing suspenders with the Catalonian flag and a short-sleeved T-shirt that reads "From Fraga to Mao." This refers not to Manuel Fraga and Mao Tse-tung, but to the frontiers in Aragón and the Balearic Islands that will one day be Catalonian. Done. I put it where . . . ! He shuts up when he sees me. Good morning, Diego. You put what where? Oh, nothing. Diego looks at the Chinaman. Nothing. We put something DELICATE in the attic, says the Chinaman. Try to forget it. Don't go near there, and don't let anyone see it. Not even her? I ask shrewdly. No, don't even think of it, not her. I'll show both of you later, but right now, please, don't go up to the attic. I'll come every night and keep an eye on it. Ah! So it needs watching? A new proof of my quick wits. Correct! We're leaving now, but I'll be back this afternoon in case the owner shows up. See you later — are you sure you don't need anything? You're sort of withered-looking (he scrutinizes me). You look almost rotten . . . Oh, all right, some cornflakes. The Chinaman hides behind his round spectacles like a snail that pulls in its gelatinous antennae. Cornflakes? He walks over to the drinks cabinet in the pantry. Gosh! You haven't touched a drop! Don't worry; you can count on your cornflakes. They leave, and I tell myself: Gosh! What have we got in the attic? Adulterated olive oil? Cocaine? Montserrat Cologne? Parabellums . . . ?

The day drags on as slowly as time spent in prison. It's twilight now. The blackbirds are starting their daily battle in the garden: their sequences of oblique long calls against other sequences of more or less oblique and more or less long calls. I feel doubly threatened. DELICATE merchandise in the attic, imminent arrival of lady-owner. Fortunately, one balances out the other in the same way a headache makes a toothache more tolerable.

The day is dying, the ashtrays are brimming over with butt ends, the mosquitoes are circling around the lantern on the terrace, but there's not a trace of HER. I've watched an incredible program, felicitously baptized "You Be the Judge," that offered training for future members of the popular and very summary court martials that are upon us. The participants opted for the hatchet, the noose, the scaffold or the firing squad. The masses got enthusiastic about condemning and EVEN MORE enthusiastic about "saving" and "pardoning." Gesture of clemency, humiliation of "pardonee." Excellent intentions on the part of the people's delegates.

July 12th

We're eating supper in the garden. The Chinaman bought a box of cornflakes, and he's insisting I try them with milk and whiskey, You'll see how good they are. Once they've lost their sugary sweetness, cereals begin to taste like wet sawdust. It's an honest flavor, but it's also revolting. To get them down a reluctant esophagus, the Chinaman suggests gin mixed with vodka. We gulp it down, staring at each other bitterly. The Chinaman's insistence is a crude imitation of the "Ragpickers of Emaus." When the alcoholic miner (he's the only good guy, you have to admit) jumps off the wagon after being humiliated by a fellow worker, the village priest observes the scene from the tavern door. Better yet! In "Río Bravo" the alcoholic ex-Chief of Police picks up the alms thrown into the spittoon; his friend, the new chief of police, who's just as good as the priest in the Belgian movie, observes the scene from the tavern door. To get to the point, these doublings of the consciousness — me as a Belgian miner, me as an American ex-chief of police — furnish the scientific proof that THERE'S ONLY ONE CONSCIOUSNESS for all our separate bodies. Under the Chinaman's opalescent, neutral gaze, I chew my cornflakes and slurp my exquisite gin and vodka cocktail, satisfied and revolted in equal measure.

I touch on the occupant's delay. What exactly does "any moment now" mean? I shouldn't worry. It's odd that I worry. She's a bit unpredictable. She's one of the people who reach decisions. What does that mean? Well, that sometimes she reaches a decision apparently without knowing anything about the mechanics of reaching a decision (that is, the inexorable drama involved, since every decision is always a mistake, no matter

how you look at it). Her decisions are as unforeseeable as meteors. On the one hand, they're perfectly predictable, but on the
other hand, nothing in the world guarantees the prediction will
be fulfilled. Satisfied now? You're a good talker, Chinaman. It's
a leisure, I mean a pleasure, to listen to you. It's a shame you're
not the mouth of the Lord! I babble a bit and even trip myself
up, but the Chinaman bends his head over the ice, the liquid,
the glassware — he should be painted like that, presiding over
that family of transparent things — and then he fires: Look, we
can clean up this situation if you like (ah! delighted!). As I see
it, our accounts are balanced. You helped me get through a bad
situation, and I'm not interested in why you did it. I think I've
paid you back. Correct? (Don't say that word, for the love of
God!) I'm saying just what I think, and I'm fed up with being in
debt to . . . someone's who's insolvent (Insolvent? Me?). It's
really irritating to deal with your sort, people who hang on like
leeches to what they call "their freedom." The truth is, I'm not
interested in you. I detest your kind of selfishness: it only produces victims; so, as I see it, this little excursion has come to an
end (Fine then!) That doesn't mean you can't stay here until
you find a new inn, and there's no reason to act as if we don't
know each other. That would be too dramatic (You should talk!).
Will you stop interrupting me? You're just like a woman. Anyway, I fully intend to show you to my animal before you leave.

That brings me up short. I gulp down my drink. It's already
here? It's arrived? Are you an idiot? It's not arriving anywhere;
it's not an animal that ARRIVES. The Chinaman is gulping,
too, but it doesn't seem to have any effect on him. I'll show it to
you when you're . . . morally prepared. Ah, no! I won't stand for
it. I'm not putting up with any more humiliation! First the

toughs, then the money, then scrubbing the floor (because you felt like it, and you were plastered!), then in the police station, and now it turns out that everything was a contract, a debt, an account! Who do you think you are? Who do *you* think you are, you and that splashing around in the sewer you call "control" or "power" and I don't know how many other sordid things? A usurer, that's what you are (Thanks, friend!), and like every miser you'd love, *love* to reduce nature to three or four simple elements so they'd be easier to hoard. Green, white, and red things. No shades. No ambiguities. No doubts. Everything clear. Your feet on the ground. (Blah, blah, blah . . . !) Will you stop interrupting me? You're just like a . . . Well, they're not planted on the ground. They're planted on human flesh. You jump from corpse to corpse like the flies at the zoo, and all the while you're keeping your accounts — a dead dromedary, a rotten chimp, Señor Guardiola (who?) — and if you slip up one time, you'll drown in blood . . .

I wasn't really mad. I was speaking calmly, almost imitating the Chinaman's pedantic gestures, his circumspection. Well, yes, I was imitating him. Fine. You're right. I am a selfish person (Of the worst kind! he keeps interrupting me, but I don't pay any attention to him), but I like to think that only a selfish person can solve the single, most embarrassing question of all, a question of life or death. (What question?) Ah. I have no idea. I can't even imagine what it would be. If I could, I wouldn't need an answer, but I can picture it perfect-ly, its shade, its form, its face. (All right, like what?) Oh, I don't have the slightest idea about that either, but we could call it "the secret of the universe," ta-dah! Before dying the guy who tried so hard has an oblique hint about the secret of the universe. How stupid can you get. So, in order to get some sort of oblique hint just before you kick the bucket, you've got to spend your life playing the victim, pretending to make sacrifices, swearing you'll give up who knows what all and stinking of sanctity and gin and, if I do say so, sometimes even worse things, and all that spectacle, who's it for, if I may ask? You're just a gnat! It's not a sacrifice, not a renunciation, not a proof of *ascesis*, that's your kind of thing, you infamous bookkeeper — even if cadavers are what you count! The secret of the unifirst, the universe, will be revealed to whoever knows how to PLAY DEAD; I *live* like a dead man!

The Chinaman smiles beatifically and speaks to me as if he were a mother, just like a mother, the pig: You poor thing, you still don't realize that you're going to die, that there's no guarantee — oh, you probably KNEW it but thought you'd made a mistake, because you can never prove it, because nobody comes back here and nobody leaves there. You still don't believe it, do you? He fills big, fluted glasses with two parts gin to one part vodka, no ice and no water. Because we're going out just like we came in. ONLY ONE LIFE IS POSSIBLE, and in that life each of us, his whole world AND EVERYTHING ELSE IS A FANTASY. There's no voice but your own, no universe, no world but you yourself. Everything else is a nightmare, and so you seize the nightmare and give it whatever shape you like. You seize the Earth and make it into your own image. People, mothers, sweethearts, civil guards — all of them are products of your imagination; they're YOUR SOLE RESPONSIBILITY. If you don't like the mothers in your nightmare, kill them off. If you're crazy about the civil guards, make everybody wear a three-cornered hat and a moustache. I'm the world I give myself, and that's that.

No, I wasn't mad, not even vehement or nervous. We had both sunk into a suspicious calm so monstrous it was lulling us to sleep. We kept on drinking fast, just vodka now since we'd finished off the gin. Our voices were sounding more and more alike, and not without perplexity, I noticed how similar our arguments were. One from without, the other from within, one from above, the other from below, one from the species, the other from the individual, but we were both fascinated, stupid, peering into the same void, void, void. The Chinaman looked at his glass; I looked at the Chinaman. His spherical head with no neck, his occiput or whatever it is, like a heavy, leaden ball; inside it swam tropical fish with incredibly long tails. For the first time, I realized that, against all odds, the Chinaman was LUXURY GOODS and that I accounted for the garbage side of things. Take the world and give it whatever form you like with your hammer and your chisel (it would be cannon and cannon fodder), it makes no difference (No difference . . . !). That's the secret of the world you're talking about. Make the world into your own image: that's your only security, your only secret. What's it to me if five hundred million people die? said Stalin. And to the world? And to the secret of the universe? Grab the world, and mold it until it looks like you! Fine, let's go with that, but what happens if it doesn't work out, if it's just a smudge instead of a portrait, like yours, if I may say so, or if it's nothing at all, nothing whatsoever, not to mention the five hundred million who've scythed, uh, died. Then it doesn't matter. (What do you mean, it doesn't matter?) Because in that case, you're dead now or you were born dead — and how's that different from your dead man?

Silence. End of the vodka. To your health — and yours.
Look, the truth is, I ferper, prefer, my selfishness. (Of the worst
kind!) Yes, the worst. Why should I look at my reflection in the
world if I hate seeing it in the mirror, eh? And, apart from this
little detail, do you really think there's a world OUT THERE
waiting for you to straighten its hair and whisper sweet nothings
with your hammer and chisel? Of course! Or maybe I'm not
talking to you, but to the ghost your spirit has invented? I don't
understand this part; let's see: one fine day the mountain will
stop being a "mountain" in quotes, and it will tell you, nobody
but you, just what it really is, eh? I don't understand this part,
but do you really think that if a flowerpot falls on your head,
we'll all disappear along with you? One thing I do understand,
and I have to tell you: YOU BELIEVE IN GOD! If I understand anything at all, it's not that you believe in God, it's
that YOU ARE GOD, and that's much worse. Hypocrite!
Paranoid! Humanist! Fascist! At that very moment, as if it
were a performance put on by the National Subsidized Theater, we hear an unmistakable noise, the sound of somebody
dragging or kicking and pushing a too-heavy suitcase over a
parquet floor. Then, a door slamming. Shortly after, a fairly
shrill feminine voice. Her words came to rest on the fuzz of
my horrible drunken state like one of those yellow-dyed baby
chickens in a shoe box lovingly prepared by a little kid. Hi!
I'm here. Anybody home? Oof, is this place a mess!

July 14th

That's how it happens, how you have one of those meetings
that little by little, very, very gradually, form the Secret of the

Universe. To explain, we have on the right a pumice stone whose vaguely explosive origin has been forgotten even by the pumice stone itself, and on the left, a resplendent comet that drags its tail through the void with the arrogance of a soprano trailing her bathrobe behind her. The comet barely notices that an insignificant particle of cosmic mud has become part of the fiery wake of its trajectory, but this little bump makes it shift its course by a trillionth of a millimeter, and a jillion years later this detour leads to a collision with the north star. End of comet. It's a fantasy we've all toyed with. Well, then, the same goes for us. I was in the kitchen, quite entertained by the glass of water I held in my right hand. Watching the bubbling fountain produced by the effervescence of an aspirin tablet, I had plunged into a daydream about the endless sea, no doubt because the sun was pouring into the room, bringing out greenish tones in the bubbling water that were like both the ocean and bile. My appearance could not have been very reassuring, since I've absolutely let myself go for two days. I'm unshaven and unadorned, and — except for brief sallies to gobble up fruit and gulp down gin — I've scarcely left the bedroom, which is the best place to listen to their laughter. It's as if I were struggling to HELP ALONG my ridiculous appearance — fat, soft, swollen, big-assed, straw-haired — with the firm intention of not fixing myself up at all so that she will see me as I am, see me at my worst, that is see *me*, so that everything will be clear from the beginning. If my legs are thin and my belly fat, well, that's what my soul is like, let there be no mistake about that. There's nothing reassuring about it, I stress, because she's standing at the door with the light on her, God help me, still and perplexed and silent.

Absorbed as I was, I didn't hear her come in, and when I really saw her or conducted her from my eyes to my brain, I was confused by a reflection on the window and took her for a piece of furniture or an appliance. I should add that a red canvas bag with two white clasps and some lettering I either couldn't read or don't remember hung from her shoulder and another bag, made of plastic the color of a peeled mandarin orange, swung from her arm and revealed some stalks of curly celery. We observed each other from different universes, the comet universe and the pumice universe, and probably from different points of view, as well, because if I saw St. George with a white pleated skirt and short blond locks, she must have seen nothing but a vulgar intruder who had vaguely impinged on her attention two nights ago before she and the Chinaman disappeared up the stairs two steps at a time on the first cloud of intimate laughter — rather rude of them, I'd say — an intruder from the sordid world of her companion in laughter, from the world of deluxe crime.

With the spontaneity that on these embarrassing occasions gives us an edge over the Tibidabo automatons, we simultaneously abandoned — I — my glass of water with its bubbles in decline and — she — her bags. With this Egyptian ritual behind us, we could get on with our greeting. I'm not sure if her gaze — clearly suspicious but not at all fearful — showed a real interest in me (as mine, obviously, showed in her). I would guess that her scant curiosity was aroused more by practical considerations: was I there because I wanted to be, was I a fugitive? a guest? an Oriental servant? hiding out? This just confirmed what I'd already suspected: the Chinaman hadn't said a single word about me.

I tried to reassure her with my relaxed, worldly tone: Heavens! I didn't know you'd be back so soon, I mean, now . . . but my voice decided to go soprano on me and then gave out in a loud squawk. After nodding her head like parrots do when they look at the floor (there wasn't the slightest hint of concern in her eyes now, just indifference and things-to-do), she deposited the bags on the pearl grey tiles of the kitchen and headed toward the stairs, not without murmuring a "delighted" more in tune with her own nature than the effect of my existence.

With imperturbable resignation, I gulp my deoxidized aspirin, arrange the contents of the bags on the marble counter top — apples, cream cheese, Lu cookies, celery, cucumbers, carrots, four yogurts, the kind of feast athletic women with fragrant crotches go for — and get ready to leave with a tremendous sigh of farewell when a light bulb goes on and I have A VERY GOOD IDEA. I take the package of La Cigala rice (hmmmm), fill a pot up with water, apply the second match (out of sheer excitement I break the first like Michelangelo with his first piece of marble), and while it's heating, I yell in my most virile, ochre, accordion-like voice: Would you care for a cold celery and rice salad?

Ten interminable seconds pass, enough time for the question's absurdity, its desperate stupidity and humiliating servility, to sink in. I wait terrified, like a child who has seen the flash of lightning and is waiting scrunched up for the clap of thunder, which is what frightens him even though the REAL danger has already passed, but that's what kids are like. Finally from up above, through various layers of curtains, in a shrill tone that lasts from the first to the final syllable, a decisive, happy "And how!" descends on me. Amazing! I say to myself softly. She's Catalonian!

July 15th

I've gotten up my nerve to sketch out this first note now that my uproar, my whirlwind, has subsided. I have to tell myself that I'm here, evidently I am here, that I'm in this place just like the window over there, the chair, the note-book, the Mont Blanc that keeps an eye an me from its horizontal position while I betray it with this Bic, in short, that I form part of a family of things that have a certain relationship with one another, a certain familiarity, even friendship! Invisible threads which would be hard to break but harder yet to define. These threads are in my head, of course, joining window, chair, Mont Blanc and so on. But the strangest thing is that my head, at this point, lies in ruins, spread out over a hill exposed to the four winds. That's why I'm so anxious to understand these ties and relationships, to understand, in short, what joins things and holds them together like those landscape paintings in which the cow doesn't cancel out the rainbow but instead shows that it's ESSENTIAL.

Because of my penchant for disorder, maybe the easiest thing would be to begin at the end. So, what's the painter's secret? How does he relate the cow and the rainbow? Musical tonality! Cows and rainbows are accidents of the palette, and his palette is, quite simply, the color of his brain, that is, of his body, of the painter's body. Yellow cows and yellow rainbows. Or green cows and green rainbows. Or geometrical cows and equally geometrical rainbows. The painter's soul, or rather, his body, is a disposal that with one mouth devours everything there is and with the other emits pictures, one after the other like sausages, as homogenous and monotonous as sausage links. Sometimes nourishing, sometimes toxic. But always sausages. Anyway, my own body's tonality depends on my sense of smell. There's no doubt about that. So, in my first note I'll try to relate each piece of news by means of its smell.

I remember perfectly the odor of the first armoire, the one where leather bags, shoe boxes, American tobacco, English cologne and piles of *Cinémonde*, with those photos of Mylène Demongeot, were stored. I also remember the odor of the second armoire, crammed with technical reviews on glossy paper that hid the volume of *Common Cause*, with its collection of numbered corpses. The first odor, essence of virility and silver coins, had a positive effect on my olfactory system; it was the tutelary god of all my affirmative actions, including my wild dreams of glory, heroism, sacrifice, battle and confusion, an odor of gunpowder, incense and gasoline. But the second smell, compensating for the first, acted like a memorandum from underground, reminding me of what is swept under the thrones, the professorial chairs, the Persian carpets and the armchairs made of Australian leather.

Okay, then, formed according to both these *principles of animal direction*, a real man's man trained for destruction, I've been totally deaf to the scent of the feminine affirmative. I never had the chance to smell a woman's closet or a woman's room that wasn't part of either virile exploitation or domestic service. I'm actually quite familiar with the rooms set aside for housemaids, lady's maids, scrub girls and cooks, but it's a childish and negative model of femininity. Even today that buttery, loud smell transports me back to the happy world in which plaster virgins always have sylvan flowers at their lily white feet. Sweaty thighs, fat cheeks devoured by acne, arms like geese roasted in their own fat, all enclosed in airless rooms that were decorated only by photos with edges trimmed like doilies. This explains my detour, my corruption, my perversion! They were girls inclined towards liquids of every kind, not excepting tears, girls whose explosive good health turned to ashes in the desolation of the gynaeceum. They lost vigor due to metaphysical and sexual consumption. The work involved in a bourgeois household was ridiculous compared to the horrific labor demanded by agriculture, yet these girls were always worn out, melancholy and withered. Their Doric forms, filled out with all sorts of protuberances, just cracked open, emptied by the leech of the void, a blood-sucker born of absolutely NOTHING.

Here you have the crooked origins of the association between sex and slavery that was my inheritance: the sweaty shroud that was never a white sheet, the irreversible connections between uric acid and patchouli, between squash-heeled *alpargatas* and Myrugia beauty products, between fresh meat soaking in blood and skinned hands. Here too you have the origin of my irresistible attraction toward waitresses, prostitutes, women who drive taxis (not to mention the ones who drive buses!) and any woman who's a member of a labor union.

How did I manage to lift the heavy paving stone that had weighed me down since childhood? Thanks to the intervention of an essentially REVOLUTIONARY odor that has brought about a transformation in my entire being not unlike the revolution produced by the invention of coordinates and abscissae. Now I understand certain poetic metaphors, narratives, portraits, collections of songs, fashions and forms of religion that were totally foreign to me in the past.

I am, of course, talking about the AFFIRMATIVE odor of sex. Because the inhabitant, the real inhabitant of this house (I must have suspected it since I had rooted around in her room and her closets, unconsciously soaking myself in her revolutionary odor — hence my nervousness) smells of idleness and contemplation, of *Cinémonde* and of corpses scrupulously numbered by the official photographer of the Spanish army, but she doesn't smell of the exploitative order, also known as the real or even the real and true order. Everything in her is lies and artifice and destruction, glory and power without a hint of work and without a hint of submission to the male. It's a malignant, irresistible odor that opens the doors on a fantastic cerebral voyage.

I'm going to surrender my brain, that is my body, to this dream even if it's the last thing I ever do. I've been cheated, corrupted, exploited and humiliated by a subtle providence whose effects on the pituitary gland go unnoticed. Now I see the ocean of decay hidden under the goose step, hidden in the absurd gestures of the choirboys and in the afflicted mass that rocks cyrically at the feet of the politician. It's FEAR of the heir, fear of the protosuicide whose natural inclination to embrace the cross paralyzes the carpenter's hand, fear of fortune. I finally understand St. Joseph's sinister joke when he showed his son how to nail a beam!

Not very convincing. I'm getting back to literature. Getting back to litttteratttttture! Try again.

July 16th

Second sketch. But without litttteratttttture. Can I get away from literature? Second sketch. Parenthesis. In any event, I'm becoming more and more aware that my nucleus is in a state of fission. I'm the atomic bomb. Not just because of this irresistible ascent toward literature, but also and especially because of having lost confidence in the military aspects of my character, which had somehow — if nothing else — kept me alive over the last few months, affiliated with the guerrilla war on behalf of banality. Grey terrorism.

Right now I can hardly see what I'm writing. And do I have to keep on writing, sliding toward literature? Yes, I do for one very important reason: after the Jailhouse Vision I'm not at all sure everything that's happening to me is happening to anyone but me. And of course I have absolutely no desire to wind up BEING HER like I wound up being the Chinaman. Here at least we can tell each other apart, or rather we can MAKE each other OUT.

Well, then, she's just what I'd thought she'd be, but much worse. In fact, she's sarcastically worse, which is important because during the age between twelve and twenty-five this product appears completely differentiated, the idea (or the organic combination of its elements) being singular only *before* admitting moral, theoretic and creative intelligence. I am, of course, talking about girls, to be precise, about THIS girl. What makes a grown woman a delightful human being is the same thing that makes a man, adolescent or grown, a delightful human being, but a specific difference is manifested in girls and not in boys. From birth boys are docile and understanding about the grown-up world; they let themselves be flattered and corrupted. Girls, on the other hand, are its true negation and undoing. They can only be compared to certain gods and goddesses in ancient myths who live in isolation, dedicate themselves to the hunt and haven't the least talent for social life. They are real animals but without that unpleasant feeling of GENERALITY produced by animals in the narrowest sense of the word. It's as if every dog, every cat, every buffalo, every sea urchin had its own intimate secret to tell NOBODY ELSE BUT me. Paradise is poor compared to a girls' boarding school!

And yet you have to be careful. Hardly conscious of their animal strength, these beasts destroy you out of sheer caprice, thinking they're doing you a favor, and they become deeply boring when they are trying to be wicked. It's impossible to distinguish their idiocy from the most elevated sublimity. Their every act would be wonderfully lofty if it were carried out by an adult, but carried out by a girl, it's as silly as a goose's waddle. And just as inevitable. It's their equilibrium.

Even though I'm emphasizing the apparently numerical aspect of the product by drawing with agitated and crude strokes, it has absolutely nothing to do with Kantity. I'll give an example, a brilliant example: ever since I met her, I've been the same age she is, and I've in part changed into a teenager again, ah ah ah, now that I'm submitting her to my "unifying musical key" (UMK) and putting her into the "family of things" (*domesticating* her) so that I also participate in her body, that is, her soul. Scientific proof: if not, how could I know so much about her? Because, hey, I know EVERY-THING.

July 20th

I leave home at ten A.M., when the sun is still tolerable, thanks to the authorities' amusing idea of setting up the clock. The acacias — some stunted, the rest sickly, all twisted like weak imitations of the olive trees — tremble with the weight of light. Dozens of cats hide under the parked cars, dragging their bellies along the sidewalk and carrying sardine bones encrusted with dirt. I buy milk at the Corele Dairy, an establishment tended by an old woman as red as a geranium who yells Long live Spain! whenever I go in and by a nut who manages to look intent and distracted at the same time; he wears the kind of shorts colonial soldiers use, and he stands at attention in front of the old woman every time he has finished loading up the little iron delivery wagon.

I get two crumbly *croissants* that fall apart under the slightest pressure and return, trying not to make any noise. When I hear her get up (the blinds, the shower, sometimes the radio), I throw myself at the toaster, split the *croissants* with varying degrees of success, toast the halves, heat the milk, lay out the cocoa (we hate coffee, it tastes like licorice), the sugar, the cups, the plates, the spoons, the apricot jam (we hate orange marmalade, it reminds us of the preserves they make in Fraga) and hover uneasily like a Hebrew shepherd who hangs on every last detail of a sacrifice that will convince Yahweh of the great, immeasurable joy it gives him (the shepherd) to break his back at any task destined for HIS GOD. Would you like a little more blood? Would it be better with the eyes smashed in? Should I cut off the balls for you? Can I do anything else?

Attentive and admiring, I listen to her come downstairs.

She has a strong body, and she places her feet on the floor with the same aplomb as those women that academic painters sometimes show bearing enormous pitchers on their left shoulders. Then I remember the last, crucial detail (forgive me! forgive me!) and rush for an ashtray and cigarettes so I won't have to get up at the moment of communion. The valet's strategy demands great rigor to wipe out every trace of effort. And so when she comes into the kitchen with her hair wrapped up in a yellow towel, she finds me idle, almost bored, slightly peevish, looking vaguely out toward the garden, a bit philosophical. I've even had time to wash the pot.

Opening out over the soft, fine curves of her features, her smile reveals the hidden vehemence of a bird-dog excitedly whipping the hunter's boots with his tail. It's only an atom of obscenity, but blossoming in the very center of her luminous, glacial face, it rings out like a shot. In defiance of my expectations (I had bet on Mercedes, Mireia or Montse), her parents baptized her with the musteline name of Marta.

Yesterday afternoon I took advantage of an opportunity to sniff around her bedroom. I couldn't pay much attention to details because I was barely through the door when — immersed in the aroma of cowhide, urine and American perfumes — I stumbled over her sandals. A shock! My shoes aren't really shoes but canvas boots like the ones those interesting fellows the basketball players wear. They have eight holes per side, and the long string laced back and forth looks like an illustration on the art of navigation. There we were, the two of us: her insubstantial sandals composed of a rough leather sole, a cinnamon colored cross strap that is a kind of girth and two minuscule strips on the heel with an open buckle, immodest, lascivious, bacchanalian, naked with open buckles, revealing . . . and me, of course. Caught up in the comparison and convinced, like Van Gogh, that our shoes are the most compromising part of our attire, I felt my blood pound when I realized that our natures corresponded, respectively, to a Greek temple and a municipal slaughterhouse. I licked the inside of the heel: nettles, milk and mint.

Now when I watch her out of the corner of my eye slathering on butter, I take consolation in the thought that there's not such a great distance between the place the Greeks used for slaying oxen before roasting them and the place we set aside for the same purpose — without the roast. It's a technical difference. I mustn't cultivate my difference.

Have you been to Switzerland? It's Heidi all over. The only part that's worthwhile is Geneva. Do you know Geneva? It's beautiful! Full of Arabs. That boulevard by the lake looks like Morocco without the flies. They all have bottles of Coke and ice creams. The men hold on to each other's pinkies — so sweet! — and the women beat the children. It's great. I think Geneva is the only city I'd go to live. They have a cathedral that looks like an airplane hangar, and I absolutely froze when I saw the monument to Calvin. The watches are very cheap, but they're not amusing anymore. You have to wear several to make any impression. And this thing about them running on their own. The truth is, I don't like it, but then nobody listens to me. It's as if they belonged to somebody else. I'm thinking about the time my mother left me hers, and I had to wind it for a good while every night so it would run. Isn't that terrific? It was like feeding it. You get fond of them. Strasbourg (she says *Strasburk*) isn't bad either, but the Germans . . . all right, they're French, but it's as if they were German. And anyway, the French . . . oh, they're okay, but they're so silly, always running around with lizards on their shirts . . . Fine now. I'll give my hair a good rubbing, and I'm off. Here, take the towel, get to work! I don't understand why people hate the Arabs so; the poor things don't harm a soul. Of course, if I were an Arab woman, I'd go live in Geneva. Where I wouldn't live FOR ANYTHING IN THIS WORLD is Japan. All those people committing Hare Krishna . . . Great, now I'm really off. Hey, I love your boots. Would you hand me that nail file over there? Fine. See you tonight.

Yes, see you tonight. Sacrificial towel, humidity soaked in the odor of your ideas, Nenuco shampoo and all the nocturnal emissions, a bit rank now. See you tonight. But before the night falls, the Chinaman will come. Every day without fail, like a stone in a pond, he drops by. Every day from the very first, the Chinaman has come and shut himself up with her in her room. He doesn't even stay for supper. It's pretty sickening. The Chinaman arrives and fools around in the attic with his goods until he hears the front door open and her "yoo-hoo." Then he shuts himself up with her in her room. Afterwards, he takes off. It's truly disgusting. We hardly exchange a word: How's it going? Fine. Do you still believe in God? Of course, I have him right in front of me!

He arrives with bags full of stuff and leaves with them empty. This makes me think that he's still piling up material in the attic. Piling up material in the attic or feeding the animal. The animal's not what I thought. To be exact, he's not what the Chinaman wanted me to think. The animal *really is* in the attic. He's had the animal in the attic ever since he knew Marta was coming! Wait a minute, wait a minute. What is it Diego said? Ages ago? Oh, my sweet little notebook, you're the one that knows.

Yes, sir! On March 14th, Diego asked the Chinaman, Should I take him home? And then, What if I left him alone? What an idiot I've been! I was convinced they were talking about . . . He tried to fool me. He planned it so I'd confuse the animal with what's not the animal. Or did he? Is it the other way around? He's putting me off the scent, distracting me from MY PREY. He wants to palm off as the animal something that's not the animal at all. Oh, my God!

I can't be sure. The attic door is locked. I spent a long time with my ear to the door. Was it a grunt? a panting sound? Something is in there. Something alive or half-alive. Or were my brain and my ears and my guts playing hide and seek with me? Was I making noises myself? Was I grunting myself?

The most surprising part, however, is the smell. A sickening zoological fume that escapes through the crack in the door. I breathed it in deeply, there on my knees, and nearly fainted.

I'll talk to the Chinaman this very night. Or should I play dumb? What if my reaction to the false animal is just what he's foreseen? What if I deceive him by slyly pretending to take the false animal for the real animal and spy on him that way? What if I do something beastly?

July 24th

The breakfasts are getting spiritual too. A thick sexual atmosphere competes with the cocoa and apricot jam. I offer her a piece of toast, holding it out to her fingers with an insinuating gesture. Her rosy finger tips touch mine. An intense look of fire.

The plantigrade bellow suppressed in my chest puts my lung cage in grave danger. She lowers her eyes! Submissive to my fiery virility! While she chews the toast (without any real appetite, her desire is so intense that her whole digestive tract is convulsed), my virility bumps against the table and pushes it so hard it threatens to overturn the cup of cocoa. I try to control myself, but my saliva bubbles over. Marta is talking non-stop with the good intention of hiding her perturbed state: Well, in Cadaqués I was living with the Gabarrós in a gorgeous house on the top of the mountain, up on a cliff overlooking the sea . . . Another piece of toast? I beg, my eyes sweaty with lust. Once again her fingers dripping with jam advance vaginally toward mine. She sucks them while she's looking at me! I have to compensate for the mad leap of my virility by leaning both arms on the table and making a colossal effort. She can't stand it any more. Red as a beet, she gets up and goes out the front door. The kitchen smells of wood mushrooms and chestnuts after I unload. Relief and a quick clean-up.

But I'm furious all day and half-crazy in the afternoon: great suffering during those sessions of laughter with the Chinaman in her bedroom! I'll explode if I don't stick my tongue in her saliva-soaked mouth, if I don't suck her breasts, if I don't bite her thighs, if I don't introduce my right foot into her warm, viscous sex, before I fill it with this blood-swollen muscle that's been just impossible all day long. The roar of a tiger that has twelve deadly darts stuck in his spine, his belly, his hindquarters and, worst of all, his head, wounded scrotum of the spirit! I console myself by licking the sandals I've stolen and thrusting my head down to the bottom of the toilet in hopes I'll find traces of her smell.

(instead of a date: Marta 11th)

Great serenity. Great serenity. A measured tone. Concerto grosso. Ladies and gentlemen, as a result of the spontaneity with which the copulation was produced I remain in my former and previous state when I knew everything about her but couldn't say a single word, except now that I know everything about her I know nothing at all about her in spite of the fact that we're living through an experience of such demanding promiscuity that we don't even know day from night — watch out! — obviously our eyes see the light and SEE the dark so we don't even bother to raise and lower the shades anymore. For example, today (what does "today" mean?) I woke up half numb in the bathtub, where I must have gone with the intention of cleaning off the urine, mucous, semen, saliva, tears and blood; all of the fluids of my spirit flee as though terrified of the process (process!) I'm going through. Calm down.

On occasion, I think, we're separated or looking for each other in different rooms or waiting on the supposition that the other has gone out to buy bread and milk. During these lost moments, I grab this notebook in search of intelligible signs, a date, for example (and then I realize that barely two days have passed, or four, but what day is today?), without success because, ahhhh, just glimpsing each other on the far side of the door or seeing her sitting cross-eyed on a stool in the bathroom, our rapture is renewed, and we fall intertwined, joined together, looking for orifices under our clothes, if we're wearing clothes, or chasing each other or even hitting each other so hard we wind up with swollen noses and cut lips . . .

I don't want to deceive myself (Hi, I'm back), but I don't think this can last, this avalanche of flesh and hair, hours and hours of flesh and hair since, naturally, I'm exhausted, but this doesn't keep her from scratching, biting and pawing my livid member, half-asleep but threatening, in fact, there's no limit to these spiritual activities and, once you yield to it, to speculation I mean, a lifetime can pass without any other needs but filling your stomach and drinking water, which we do directly from the tap in the bidet, taking advantage of the opportunity to clean off the scabs and dried-up, organic crusts, since we don't even respect the intimacy customarily conceded to excrement and excretions, so great is our need to swallow each other up! if by chance we happen to fall near the toilet — a toilet! — and one of us or both of us raises up on our hind legs over the bowl to relieve a bladder or any other organ; it's an asceticism so absolute and Brahmanic, on the other hand, that if one of us, me for example, has to go out (for bread and milk, I can't remember anything else) so we won't starve to death, that one's sure to go in disguise, even if it's only pants and a sweater, since I now go barefoot to the Corele Dairy where EVEN THEY look at me like an unidentified flying object, greeting Long live Spain!, the mongoloid in shorts stands at attention, the old woman yells *Sieg Heil* and I feel an exalting sense of relief when I get back and throw down my clothes like a newspaper, but then: huge erection and where do I put it now? until I put it somewhere and faint away, yet it seems to me that during one of those almost losses of bodily consciousness while we were fighting like earthworms, the Chinaman was walking around the house and I think he even watched us for a good while with curiosity and then boredom, I'm not sure, as I say, it was only a fleeting impression between one bite and another or one lick and another or one pant and another or one howl and another, however, at some point when I had recuperated the faculty of speech, I asked Marta if she didn't remember something similar, I think I said, very slowly, do you think the Chinaman was looking at us a while ago? but either she didn't understand me or she knows the Chinaman by another name, but anyway the fact is she emerged from under the sofa, dragging herself, with the idea of opening a can of corn that had appeared from who knows where, an operation she tried to carry out by puncturing the can with a knife (great! we're down to knives now!) until the blade broke in two, and I didn't think any more about it until . . . My God! she's back again!

(date illegible)

Very interesting, very interesting. Her breasts, for example, are sometimes large, sometimes small. They grow and inflate until they reach the diameter of watermelons or wrinkle and shrink like green peppers. Her ass also grows out of all proportion, crossed by red lash marks, a window with wrought-iron grates open onto the world, or it's transformed into a little, rubber ball with colored stars printed on it. But the most flexible thing is her vagina; it's extraordinary. I've put my whole head inside it — a spiritual experiment repeated three times — without feeling crowded or dying of asphyxia. I was quite comfortable; in fact, there was space left for reading, even with eyeglasses although this was difficult on account of the acid excretions that burned my tongue, but what can I do because now nobody goes out for bread and milk, so I drink big sips of vaginal liquid when I'm on the verge of a fainting spell, a fit of weakness, then recuperation and afterwards: the erection, and where can I put this thing? Where can I nail it in now? I get confused, of course; I'm laid out, for example, in the bathtub, surprise, confusion, I had put it in the drain, where is she? I hear her panting here beneath me while I'm writing, between my legs! Is it you, is it you, Sweetiepie? Oh, it's . . . ! *(illegible)*.

(no date)

What's happening to me? Am I asleep? Silence. Time to kill, nothing's happening, let's see, nobody's home. Has it ended? No. She's not here. That's how it is. Unbelievable. She's AUTONOMOUS. Very curious. How can she . . . ? Better to sleep, better to sleep.

August 7th

Has the Chinaman taken her away with him? Has she gone
out to work? Is she unionized? Will she come back? I don't
know how long I've been stretched out at the front door, prostrate. I yawn, howl, scratch myself with my hind foot, rest my
head on the ground, perk up my ears if I hear a sound, if I smell
something. It's not possible, just not possible. Right now I'm
making myself over, pulling myself together. Let's look it in the
eye: from now on, every night, every morning, hour after hour,
so intensely, so painfully, every afternoon, every dawn, moderat-
ing it so I can keep on suffering this material need of her, this
hunger, this absolute, awful hunger that gnaws not at my guts
but, again, at my spirit, that is, my body and my guts. Although
I'm perfectly capable (I'm not crazy!) of imagining a life in
which every need is satisfied, my body, that is, my soul, was not
meant for such a life. It's become a mere RECEPTACLE where
the only thing that fits and that fills it up is another body, that
is, another soul, whose most noteworthy characteristic is that
IT'S NOT HERE.

I deduce the voluptuosity of childbirth from this model:
the uterus, the vagina, whatever, an inflamed muscle that
withstands great pressure. If it doesn't burst like a fig, that's
because it only hurts OUTSIDE the muscle so the expulsion
of the foreign body, even though it rips or crushes the gut,
doesn't mean liberation but just a transition from pain to
ecstasy. And so — since my MENTAL body is occupied by a
foreign body — I too feel my muscles swollen, my veins fat
with blood, my head inflamed with heavy fluids, but I can't
console myself like a pregnant woman since it's impossible

for me to EXPEL the foreign body, to transform the pain into rapture, since the body that occupies me only occupies me in the degree to which IT IS ABSENT.

The only possibility I see — unlike the newborn baby who, from now on, is a *really* foreign body — would be to insert the body that occupies me into my body until it disappears IN ME and so reestablish the equilibrium between internal and external pressure. It's what happens on planes and submarines when the oxygen whistle blows and saves the passengers from being suddenly crushed because of a sudden change in altitude.

But inserting her into my body means occupying the void that pricks me like a pincushion by brute force, that is, EATING HER, and that wouldn't solve anything at all because after digesting her and expelling her, I would experience the rebirth of her absence and all the pain. I would have exchanged a corporal and spiritual absence for, much worse, a total and metaphysical absence, that is, neither corporal nor spiritual, because Marta would have bid the world good-bye. And just for a momentary relief in the minutes spent quartering her, chewing her, swallowing her and perhaps, too, the minutes spent excreting her, and then? She'd be irrevocably lost . . . No, it's better to keep on being a dog. However, if things get VERY BAD, if it hurts too much, if there's no alternative . . .

August 10th

I'll get over it. I'm beginning to understand. Marta was a diversionary tactic. I'm very frightened. Because I know things. The more you know, the more you're afraid; if you know everything: sheer terror. But not knowing is impossible now.

I stumble along, finding out things, and suddenly I know a lot. So I'm very frightened. For example, I now know why Marta didn't come back until this morning. A terrible night without her — or was it days? Her absence, however, was the fruit of her obedience. Marta obeys the Chinaman. She obeys him. I can say it calmly. She's another calculation, another column in his eternal accounts. Is she a number? The number nine? Maybe he doesn't even give her the rank of species. She may only be a reminder of multiplication. Oh, there can be no doubt she's closely related to multiplication! The only thing that interests her is multiplication! But not the evangelical multiplication of the loaves and the fishes. Everyone else — yessirree, every last one! — believes in nothing but THE OTHER KIND of multiplication.

Fine. Let's slow down, take a break. So she wasn't here (she wasn't here before, but now she wasn't here at all, she was *gone*): a chronometrical calculation. And the Chinaman appears. Solitary house. Paleontological man. I didn't even recognize him at first. Have we gone cold turkey? he asks, but I don't understand a word. Don't you know what cold turkey is? Then I recognize him and feel a great rush of warmth. I'm suffering terribly, a replay of the famous Jailhouse Vision, and my Oriental friend shows up miraculously to soothe my pain. Where is she? I ask. Don't worry, she'll be back soon. She won't be long at all. And I see the needle and the spoon and . . . but I hadn't shot up at all.

Weak. No food. Worn out. I keel over. I must have hit my head because I smell something humid, a wonderful damp exhalation. The Chinaman props me up, that's clear. He fixes a glass of warm milk, a bit of whiskey; he's a great help. Come on, take a shower, and put some clothes on. Just like the Jailhouse Vision. Little by little, like one of the automatons at the Tibidabo, I do what he tells me. I see then that it's morning or afternoon. I see too that the Chinaman is fixing me an omelette. A spiritual hunger overwhelms me, and I devour the bread, the tomato, the cheese, the almonds, the peach. I drink over half a bottle of wine and feel much, much better. It's like going back, once again, going back. The Chinaman lets me carry on in silence, an imitation smile like a hatchet cut on his thin lips, his hands crossed on his knee. Everything planned carefully, I'm sure, even though I greatly doubt he's given much attention to the business, that is, to my business or to me as part of his business.

Now I'm used to his harangues, and I can see them coming from the way he concentrates until you can hear his cranial bones cracking and from the stupefied gaze that pierces the glass and the ice cubes. It's always the same. I've never had the slightest hint of intellectual ambition, he begins, nor the least bit of emotional anxiety. I overcame childhood earlier than usual. I despise artistic and amorous consolations. Artists and people in love are all the same; art and love are inflammations, Hindu inflammations. Rays of sunshine for people who are already dead. I'm not afraid to say these things because it's only as a member of the SPECIES that I feel naked and useless. I'm in part an obedient animal governed by biological rules. But I can also be a disobedient animal, and once CONSOLATION has been suppressed and once RESIGNATION has been suppressed and once COMPAS-SION has been suppressed, I can raise up the biological level of the species by my PERSONAL will. I can convert this species into a new species of disobedient animal, following the good example set by our first two parents in Eden, two disobedient animals that weren't artistic or amorous in the least; they were hardworking, sudoriferous and mammiferous, and they decided to stop talking to the other animals so they could just talk to EACH OTHER. Well, I too refuse to talk to artists and people in love. I refuse to talk to anyone governed by present-day biology. The only thing I'm betting on is my deification! I represent the best and highest and noblest points our biology has achieved. I refuse to get involved in *animal relations*! You don't understand what heights a human being can reach because you're a banal man. I'm following the only TRULY HUMAN tradition. From Satan on, the truly human tradition has been not to be an animal AT ALL.

For once he seemed stunned, stupefied, leaning over his glass and protected by a hundred pairs of spectacles, poor little thing. He got up for more gin and ran into the glass door. It rang out like a bell. Later when the night had fallen, a sweet, coolish night that hinted at bonfires and roasted chestnuts, he kept on talking in the pitch dark. Every ten minutes or so, I could hear a scratching sound and see his eyes dilated in the light of a match. He'd stare at the fire until it burned his fingers. The moon was hanging in the sky, huge and green and blasphemous. My attention wandered. I listened to him at times, but without paying much attention. I was distracted by the odor my fingertips still exuded. A narcotic smell of ammonia and freshly mowed grass that blew me away for another half hour. However, he got my attention all of a sudden — actually, he may have been repeating it automatically for quite some time — with a question that brought my daydream to an abrupt end. Aren't you, the Chinaman asked, an expert in animal questions? A lover of Nature? That form of DECADENCE? The regression of the species to the point of respecting and taking care of animals, minerals and vegetables? A traitor? People like you interrupt the really human work time and time again! Show respect for nature! Love the victim! Save (although it's just for a short period, a little while, a few hours) the condemned! You're just prolonging their death agony! But what do you know about the TRUE animal? I do know. I've studied it. But there's one thing I don't know yet. ONE specific activity remains an unknown quantity. I don't know how you can *avoid* acting like an animal in these circumstances! It happens to all of us. All of us do it. How can you avoid it? Don't accept it! Don't admit it no matter what! But it's essential to study it! And now I have a chance to study it. Now I have, under the microscope as it were, the ANIMAL THAT DIES. Pay attention, now, I mean the animal that dies, not THE OTHER, the one that doesn't know it's going to die and so neither lives nor dies, that appears and disappears like a snap bean. Listen to me. If the common animal knew it was going to die, it would lay claim to the law that makes it die and even though later, inevitably, it died, IT WOULD NO LONGER BE AN ANIMAL, but MORE than an animal and for that reason immortal. You can only be immortal if you invent death. So the real animal must understand that it only dies BECAUSE IT FEELS LIKE DYING, and then it's not an animal, but something more than an animal, and it can die *its own death*.

I had drifted off because I wasn't remotely interested in that delirium, that product of his brain, but I realized intuitively that we were getting closer to the explanation of my presence in that house and, more important, of Marta's absence. We were getting closer to the origin of that marvelous natural history, so now I did pay attention without really paying much attention. We've got to take advantage of the situation, he continued. We can't waste time because he doesn't have much time left, just a few days now, we can't wait long. It's hard to feed him now — nothing but liquids. His neck is swollen, and he's lost his hearing. He can't hear me any more. I need to make clear that it's his idea! He asked me! Get a doctor? Prolong things a few more years? Better to leave him alone! Chemotherapy, tranquilizers, watching it come as if he could see himself FROM OUTSIDE . . . ? But nobody would let him into their house; everybody wanted to turn him over, hands tied, to the hospital, the butcher shop, to that sense of moral satisfaction, to the care and compassion of the victims, to the last priesthood. I was able to help him. Another thing — and this is important — the law forbids this. Absolutely forbids it! So, do me a favor, and come with me, because we're going to see the animal, the real animal.

We got up without saying a word, rendering homage, at each of the successive doors, to the *after you — no after you* ritual, until we got to the top of the stairs. Until we got to the attic. Either the smell had become stronger or my olfactory system had taken on a life of its own, had turned into a monster with a sense of touch and now was setting off on its own to hunt down clots of smell in the air as if they were moths. The Chinaman not only opened the door, he also handed the key over to me with a courtly gesture. Keep it, he said. From now on, if you like, he's as much yours as mine. I peer in carefully, but see nothing. The room is dark. The first light of dawn along with the exasperating racket of the sparrows and blackbirds comes in through the window. Behind me, the Chinaman closes the door. My eyes begin to get accustomed to the dark, and little by little on their own they put together a whitish shape, a cloud that solidifies into a bed. I can hardly breathe. The sheets cover a body whose head rests on the pillow, face up. The Chinaman pushes me on gently, but I balk. I've seen all I want to see, at least for now. Is he dead? Not yet, but he doesn't have much time left. We have to hurry.

Now I see his cranium covered with wisps of hair like a halo. The odor is asphyxiating. This man is dead. No, he's not dead. Get closer. I'm very close now. I hadn't noticed his panting, but now as though my imagination were making room, it breaks out noisily. Every ten seconds or so, a labored, gurgling intake of breath. What's this poor man doing here? Man? Why do you say "man"? This is the unfortunate animal, the true animal, the sole and supreme animal, the great computer, the merciful one.

I shoved the Chinaman aside and left the room with my lungs about to burst and a sensation I hadn't remembered since childhood when I used to fish for octopus. Getting down the stairs wasn't easy. Once I'd reached the kitchen, I hit the floor, sick. The raw morning light illuminated the white furniture, the refrigerator, the dirty plates in the sink. According to the electric clock, it was nine-fifteen. I hadn't seen him follow me, but the Chinaman was there, in front of me, sitting on the table, holding a can of La Española olives from which he was removing the contents one by one. Slowly, interrupting the operation (a meticulous, surgical procedure), to submit the odd opinion or bit of curious information for my consideration. He himself came and asked me — you see? — to help him die. I only need the minimum, he said; he offered me a fortune! A fortune that's mine anyway! I feed him. As long as he could talk, we talked. Now we just look at each other. Twenty years without looking at each other, and now we look at each other!

I don't know how this idea came to me, an absurd, crazy idea, since it was totally impossible given his age and complexion, but I asked the Chinaman, Is it Cucurella? Is he dead all over of the same thing? Fortunately, he wasn't even listening to me; a tepid sadness was confusing his face and his numbers and his accounts. Now he can't hear me anymore, the Chinaman was saying. Soon the tumor will have consumed the medulla oblongata; one of his animals will devour another of his animals, and there'll be nothing left. But he's still conscious. The pain, the nausea, the fainting spells keep him busy, take up most of his day, but not ALL day. Suddenly he'll feel a few seconds of relief and come to himself again. If you can get him to look at you in those few, short seconds, then your salvation is assured. Now I have to be there when those eyes try to look, try to see.

Infected with his delirium, I was about to insist he tell me the identity of the dying man when I heard the front door, the firm footsteps, the bags being dragged along. I didn't feel a thing. Just indifference. She's here now, I told myself, but I didn't feel a thing. Just indifference. I told myself too that that indifference would soon disappear, and I embraced it with even greater love. She was in the kitchen. She didn't look surprised or happy or anything at all. She kissed us successively on the cheek, first the Chinaman and then me, and after that I found out she'd come from Madrid because the Chinaman asked, How was the flight? Pssssch, there was almost no line for the shuttle, but the flight was terrifying . . . the plane dove like a roller-coaster — imagine, I even said an Our Father! Then I was sorry since I don't believe in God, and he might get mad and make the thing crash . . .

I interrupted her, Do you know what this fellow has in the attic? Shut up! He's driving me crazy! The very idea of putting a dead man in my house! What hurt me most about her answer is that she called him "a dead man," that is, she considers him dead because for her he's ALREADY dead. It means that for her, anything that can't multiply is dead; she's only interested in multiplication. Then they disappeared up to the first floor, to her bedroom. They're still there. And I'm still here. Absolutely indifferent. Still.

August 12th

Although worn out and mistreated, I've had an *explosion of calm* following my attack of indifference. The effect of having death upstairs, present, always with us. Stretched out on my bedroom floor, after a light sleep from which I'm rudely awakened by a kick in the head (a very gentle kick that in my dozy state seemed like an octopus sliding over my head with its mouth open, although it was, in fact, Marta's leg that had slipped off the coverlet), I picture Great Unhappiness. Its habitual form is the sadness of the child they wake up and hurry off to school. I get as far as the bed and, curled against that soft, warm body, look at her face and the two pieces of blue ice that float above it.

It's essential to point out that I felt so abandoned, so torn away from my earlier carnality, that I started to talk without really knowing what I was saying, driven by the need to cover our former nudity with a veil of words — like Adam and Eve, who become aware of their nakedness when they're dressed up in words — until compassion, which had been playing hide and seek, wound up leading me to a cruel, even perfidious question of the "what's the point of all this?" genre, as though I assumed there must be some point or some point other than the one there is. To top it all off, I asked the question aggressively in a what do you want out of me? or what are you looking for? tone. She gave me the answer I deserved without hesitating, with the assurance of somebody answering a question about her gastronomical preferences: Well, a child, of course, and she looked at me with such an expression of *well, obviously, anyone knows that*, of *what a breathtakingly stupid question*, that I felt my heart crack.

However, I didn't stop looking at her eyes, perplexed as I was now by the loss of banality my question betrayed, nor did I stop looking at her tranquil mouth with its natural — that is to say, enigmatic and Mycenean — smile, her mouth which had just pronounced the only answer that was possible and also the one that was furthest removed from the intellectual and banal projects that I was made of, that was furthest, then, from everything about me: what I'd done with my life, what my life had done with me and what little was left to do — fast. So I kept on looking at that mouth, absorbed, cavilling over other trivia — the color of the bedspread (cherry-red and pear-green stripes), the Martini and Rossi song (*Wherever you are, whenever it is*) — until that very same mouth opened again, timidly and with an almost painful tenderness, to ask once more, Isn't it? And what could I answer? Without any conviction, resorting mechanically to tricks I'd already learned, to professional ruses, I responded that we were like two Egyptians who look into each other's eyes eternally to see if they can see something, a pointless activity that keeps them face to face like the positive and negative poles of a magnet, creating an energy field that modifies what crosses its path, but otherwise produces nothing. It's the same thing, I say, as spending day after day in front of a mirror, sunk in the contemplation of a body that's familiar but may always harbor a secret, a new wrinkle, a new protuberance, a new freckle, a new cancer. It's blindness, because as long as we're looking into each other's eyes, we can't see anything else, and we let the world go to waste, sell it cheap, for a pair of eyes. Marta, who up until this minute had been staring absorbed at one of her thighs with its golden sheen of hair, looks into my eyes. She seems disconcerted, as if she has taken a while to translate the question into a woman's language she can understand. But when she finally manages to strip what I've said of all its rhetoric, sparks fly: Oh, *now* I understand you, but, hey . . . what a pair of eyes! And she looks at me out of those Carolingian eyes encircled by lilies.

And what can I say to her . . . if it's true the real human species is composed of nothing but a handful of women and the rest of us are just superfluous, if we live off them vicariously like parasites and even take pride in a power only granted us out of pity. They take care of the funeral details, dress the corpse, console the friends and neighbors and see to the preparations for the funeral banquet, all with such corporeal solidity that sometimes we even confuse them with death itself. But that's a mistake. They're not death, they're the species, and the rest of us only manage to be individuals. Which now, in fact, induces in me — my God, what changes! — a serene, youthful feeling of comfort that eases me back toward a very distant past. She is multiplication, just multiplication, and I'm changing at such speed that I'm sloughing off layers of skin like wet sheets. My January notes seem immeasurably far away. But even then I foresaw this break with myself, this split! Is this what literature is like? Reading the beginning over and over again? Multiplying it? Have nine months passed? Am I going to give birth?

I was ugly, Marta continues, as a little girl. I was ugly. I was embarrassed to go to parties. Everyone was prettier than I was, or older or braver or better dancers or more endowed. I didn't dance. I'd sit in a chair and wait for somebody to come up. It was terrible and sad. I felt obliged to dance because the boys, poor things! had gone to all that trouble just to feel us up a little, but I simply didn't know how to dance. I didn't mind at all if they felt me up, that is, if they wanted to, but I was incapable of dancing, *in-ca-pa-ble*, I would have died first. So they couldn't feel me up after all since I couldn't go out on the dance floor, not that anybody wanted to anyway. That's why my friends were always the strays, the ones who were left out, the boys who only dared to talk. I thought they were marvelous, but I knew that everybody else thought they were dull, humorless, common, even stupid. She falls silent and reflects before laughing a splendid, fresh laugh. The truth is they probably were dull and common. Me too? I ask. Am I one of those unfortunate souls who talk so we won't have to dance? Well, only at the beginning, but the first time I saw you without any clothes on . . . you seemed so refined! Your body and all that, you see? And she laughs and laughs.

I don't think I'd cried since my Jailhouse Vision. Marta accepts my tears as normal, which is as it should be. She doesn't try to console me; she only says to herself out loud: I wish I were your aunt and you were little. I'd take you to the Tibidabo to see the automatons, and then I'd buy you a Mickey Mouse. She's holding my head against her breast. I see my tender, swollen belly covered with red down. At that privileged moment, I love myself, but almost immediately I remember the Animal choking in the attic and feel an icy contraction. My tears dry up, and my promising erection disappears. That dead man, always with us. Always present.

August 15th

I'm doing a lot of thinking now along literary lines. A lot. Through the filter of the dead man. Here's an example: like a crippled ship that makes for port guided only by its instinct (a rare phenomenon!), like an old mule that returns to the stable while its rider is asleep, I too return to myself WITHOUT MY BRAIN, urged on by the last vestiges of *amour propre*, eh? Or something like that. Variations on a theme: crushed by the storm, the vessel enters port driven by its instinct, independent of the pilot and the crew, helped only by the substance that gives life to its wooden timbers; and the horse, carried along by a nostalgia for the flesh, returns to the stable, its rider dead; and in the same way, I too return to my body without a brain, thanks only to the mutual love of the hydrocarbons. Horrible, isn't it? I could spend hours, playing arpeggios, separated from the other fiction that has remade me from without, on the spiritual side. In other words, I return without a brain to my body, moved by the substance hydrocarbons breathe in from the earth in order to be burned above the atmosphere and then to revisit the vast fields where, centuries ago, they were forests of ferns, an immense organic ocean, as though both body and brain had spent time underground and now wanted to dissolve into the air releasing great quantities of heat and light, but only one, only one intrepid hydrocarbon had passed the test, and so on and so on, and now the Orpheus and Eurydice bit, what a bore.

I could spend my whole life like this! Sheltered here, lost to myself, jumping from word to word, from idea to idea, like the classic Cabalist with his incredible stew pot full of signs, in search of the combination that will transform him into a god and, once he has become a god, let him shake off his enslavement to signs. What do you think? I've sometimes seen painters covering paper and more paper with one coat of color, unable to give it a form, but ecstatic over that flight, transported from a painful existence to the splendid, neutral life of pure tone and pure color. Hmmmmm. Then comes the bit about the pencil that's sharper and sharper but writes nothing.

Without any doubt, this return is the humus my future body can grow in. A scientific proof: I've gone back to reading as well. Led by Montaigne, of course. This has nothing to do with my former amusements, which were fruitless, angry and resentful. No. Now it's a great comfort. Yesterday I took a volume out of the library — although "library" is an exaggeration, it's more like a warehouse filled with books whose identical bindings show they formed part of a weekly installment plan. It had been ages since I'd read anything! Except for those verses of Laforgue that were to have such fateful consequences. I really did read those. The kind of reading you do, when you invent fancies, varnish each page and cover a notebook with numbers, all of that is the same as writing WITH STYLE. It's the refuge to which the foundering vessel returns, guided by the instinct of its wooden timbers, and so on.

Montaigne says that "to meditate on death ahead of time is to meditate ahead of time on freedom; he who learns to die does not know how to be a slave." A remark as banal as the others. But it's banal because of the translation. Montaigne uses prefixes that in my language have no *corporeal* life. For example, *préméditer* (to meditate ahead of time, not to pre-meditate) and *désapprendre* (forgetting, which is different from not knowing). Deprived of its *pré-* and its *dés-*, the sentence withers and dies like a jellyfish in the sun. Literary problems! The luxury of death! The scribe's delicious existence in his cell, lulled by the creak of the parchment, scribbling baroque fantasies with the help of God! Through the window, a bay tree, a swallow, and a pristine sky . . . And sometimes the chemistry of this delirium produces a miracle. There, in that place, in that little room together with death and delirium, the mouth of the Lord speaks.

But I can't surrender to this exquisite chemistry *yet*, even though the fervor of prayer is already taking up too much of my time now. And the other words, the ones that have nothing to do with prayer, make me smile. Like math. Like every kind of multiplication. For Montaigne, that citizen of a moderate, fertile land served by many rivers, death is a question of courage or cowardice, a kind of equestrian exercise. But it's not an enigma that valor can throw any light on; it's more closely related to charity, to our regression to the animal. And animals don't know the fear of death. But that doesn't mean they're brave.

I think that when, desiccated by the sand and the wind of the desert, the Egyptians decided to proclaim the immortality of the Pharaoh, they put an end to substantial fear and invented terror, the terror of irony. I can picture the languid men with long, black beards and a stench of goat who peopled the neighboring countries approaching these novelties with great curiosity: Have you heard that by the Nile there's a god that's immortal . . . ? The Animal is now putting a foot on the first burning stones of the pyramid, his pyramid. His soul is timid, the room is enormous and cold, the ornaments of the Masonic ritual are geometrical. Step by step he sinks deeper and deeper into pyramid time until he reaches the embalmed body and its architecture of coins, food and perfumes. The music, of course, is Mozart, but the text is blank. The fear that has allowed him to escape from death for all the years we call "his life" — that same fear now urges him on, one foot after another. I can find no explanation more powerful for this surrender to death or to the Chinaman, which is the same thing. The Chinaman is his DEATH INSURANCE.

When I go up to the attic to look at his face (the door is always open now, and the window as well, to air it out a bit), or when I put a little sugar water between his cracked lips, using the filigreed coffee spoon, I once again see man regressing to animal with an exhausting effort on the part of the muscles and the viscera, reversing the direction of the Sphinx, whose human part takes off from her animal part. Just as the Chinaman said, he opens his eyes sometimes and seems to recognize me, although I think he's too far away from us now. Still, in spite of every prognosis, there is something in his gaze that seems like a memory of the glory and the misery of being a man, of when he was a man.

He can't move his eyes (his whole face is deformed now by the pressure of the tumor), he can't move a single muscle in his face, but I think I hear, although I actually see it, a welcoming smile. My time is divided between taking care of the Animal and Marta's arrival, both joined in a family of ammoniacal, fetal and fecal odors. And, mysteriously, like siblings, they share a specific sense of humor, a humor also found in rotten fish: the cadaverine. It involves TNT, *herigslacke* . . . Stop! Literature rears its ugly head again!

August 16th

Like most of my contemporaries, I'm used to seeing solid gold in churches and museums; that is, in the dark or by artificial light. But I've been told that if it's exposed to the sun, gold takes on a greenish shade which, in great quantities, is dazzling. I'd exaggerate if I said that's exactly the quality of her hair, since there's a serious difference between a compact mass of gold and a framework of hair composed of multiple threads each with its own constitution and reflection. However, in the full sun, it can look green. Enough literature.

I didn't hear her come in today because I've become more and more involved in my diary and my reading. Recently I've been writing bits of literature before getting down what happens to this *I* that drags itself from page to page. She showed great surprise over my attachment to this diary. Me too! she exclaimed. I kept a diary when I was little so it wouldn't all be gone with the time, I mean the wind, and I still have it, from when I was twelve, during Viet Nam — how do you pronounce it? Do you want me to read it to you?

She leaves the kitchen, sluing her feet out a little, slightly palmiped, and comes back with two photos. Look, in these photos I'm as corny as I am in the diary, no? Marta takes it for granted that I can imagine exactly what the diary is like from seeing the photos and that seeing the photos is like reading the diary. Why would there be any difference? Aren't both things "Marta herself"?

All pictures of children are alike. They produce a disquieting impression of *Common Cause*. The children in these photographs are still alive, but nobody knows where they are nor who embodies them now. The dead girl in the picture lives shut up in adult pyramid Marta, embalmed and waiting for immortality. I was overwhelmed by a feeling of great sadness, and I embraced her violently as if I could tear the embalmed child from her guts. Barely taking off our clothes, we copulated on the kitchen floor, and I dug down in search of the Child Who Disappeared, lost in the labyrinth of time.

Later, while we were eating a salad in the garden, I felt once again the sense of warmth and well-being I've been experiencing lately. The only thing I missed was a cat, the childhood cat that got lost too. I said so. Why do you want a cat? she asked with her eyes open wide. I don't know. To scratch its head, I guess. Why don't you scratch mine? Another violent encounter, this time on the grass, right under the hysterical gaze of a neighbor who was hanging out clothes in the sun.

The twilight today was an intense shade of lavender, and the Chinaman's arrival caught us with her skirt rolled up and my pants around my ankles. It's true that when she pulled them up, Marta made a profoundly sarcastic face: I hadn't noticed! Look at these pants! What's wrong with my pants? What's wrong! Don't you think they're just a bit *evasés*? Later on she carted them off to her room, but I don't care. I understand why she's disgusted, even irritated with my pants. Once something has gone out of style, the traces of style expose its absurd pretensions. You have to keep up in order to HIDE your affectations. Fashion is a system of disguise. If I buy enough clothes, they'll take me for an elegant cretin. I've got to keep this in mind when I'm writing. If I don't write with style, it will seem as though I'm telling the truth, that is, that I'm the same as always, and that's a monstrous lie.

August 20th

Not a word about what the Chinaman told me today. Just his voice, branded on my memory. He started off with an air of distraction, as though he didn't know what he was going to toss my way. I think you said something about Cucurella? Didn't you ask me last week or so about Cucurella, about Cucurella's death? I thought you knew; it came out in the newspapers. Cucurella and I were in Africa at the same time, serving the flag. He was sent there by chance, but I volunteered. Anyway, we both left our most zealous executioners behind; we were both getting away from the systematic bludgeoning our fathers had subjected us to, and that meant we had something in common. We hadn't known anything but scorn and criticism and vindictiveness at home, all this at the hands of men who were brutalized by their evil victories, sated with murder and betrayal, who exploited their

servants and their children. When we were off duty, we used
to drink to the death of our fathers, the death of all fathers,
the death of the father of our country and the death of God
the Father. A stagnant hatred kept us on edge and (I'm convinced) on *the* edge of insanity. Cucurella had tried to kill his
father, but after that event, he suffered from violent attacks
of fury followed by nervous spasms during which he destroyed
everything he came across before hitting his head against the
floor. I protected him from his own madness, dragging him
away from the dives when the knives came out or holding
him back before he stuck a bayonet into the lieutenant of the
company, an abject professional torturer. I did everything I
could to keep him out of jail and away from the firing squad,
but I was perfectly aware that Cucurella wanted to get it over
with, and the sooner, the better. Moved by pity (I could still
feel pity then), I deferred his death as though it were up to
me to choose the appropriate time. And the time came without my consent, but I participated actively in it.

The lieutenant of the company was from Madrid, a tall,
thin guy. His eyes were sunk into sockets of greenish bone,
and his hair was absolutely white even though he wasn't thirty
yet. During our first month at the garrison, he devoted his
energy to humiliating Cucurella. Obviously he'd fallen in
love with him. During that month Cucurella found an extraordinary substitute for his hatred, and I think that's why
he fell into the lieutenant's hands. Attached by a web of
torture and sadism, they got closer and closer until nothing
but the blade of a knife could come between them. Then, at
the apotheosis of that relationship, when Cucurella was leaning over the lieutenant with a bayonet and nothing but my

presence kept him from nailing it into the lieutenant's gut, the reversal took place. It was so violent and unexpected that they didn't even know what was happening to them. During the second month, Cucurella drew away from my protection and began to join in the lieutenant's delirious parties. I think he began to shoot up that very month.

We ran into each other — it was inevitable in a place that small — drinking at the same bars or stumbling down the incredibly narrow streets of the market. I'd be on my own; he was always with his lieutenant. We'd greet each other disdainfully. But I started to get worried when I came on him, time after time, doing business with young Arabs of the worst kind. Not the usual sex slaves or small-time black marketeers, these were part of the abominable race of spies, stool-pigeons and hit men the government looks after in those African posts. Nobody I knew of who dealt with them had come out alive, and nobody but the naïve or the desperate believed they could get something out of those lepers. I knew all about it because I carried a safe-conduct.

By the third month, Cucurella had fallen into the arms of his madness. Then he made the biggest mistake of his life. He approached me and tried to convince me to do some business with him, that's the way he put it. An import-export business, to be precise. I asked if the lieutenant was involved, and he said, Of course, the lieutenant's essential. I agreed just so I could find out what kind of nasty trap the fellow was setting.

Although he was disgusting, I had to eat with the lieutenant, I had to drink with the lieutenant, I had to witness the moral downfall of Cucurella, who submitted so willingly to his executioner. In one of his many drunken brawls, the lieutenant begged Cucurella to let him put out his cigarette. Cucurella held out his right arm with the sleeve rolled up. I saw that it was covered with burns, some of them infected. I struck the lieutenant's cigarette aside, but Cucurella asked me with extravagant seriousness not to interrupt the investigations they were carrying out. He lighted another cigarette and handed it to the lieutenant, who, smiling benevolently all the while, stubbed it out on Cucurella's arm without giving me a chance to react.

Ten or twelve days went by like that, and they refused to tell me a thing about the business in spite of my insistent questions. But then on a Friday night, they told me to get ready for a little trip so we could take advantage of the weekend. We're travelling in Arab dress, but wear boots because we'll be on the sand, Cucurella advised.

We left on Saturday in an unmarked army truck that the lieutenant got hold of regularly by either bribing the drivers or having them arrested. We crossed over to Moroccan territory without any problem and drove deep into the interior where there's nothing but stone. Since it's a desolate, dangerous land, it didn't surprise me that the lieutenant gave the two of us pistols. When we got to one of those caravan sites that have been abandoned for years and now only serve as shelters for whorehouses and gambling dens or depots for stolen goods, we stopped.

Half a dozen Arabs were waiting for us inside. They had obviously come from the most impoverished rural areas — good Mohammedans and self-sacrificing fathers, who were selling themselves into slavery to save their families from hunger. They were lying on the floor, resignation writ on their faces, but when they saw the lieutenant enter, they got up and flocked together like sheep. Now I knew what this import-export business involved: crossing the frontier with a load of illegal immigrants, unhappy souls destined for the hardest, most repugnant work. I sighed in relief because, even though there was a certain risk, it was nothing compared to what I had imagined. Carried on a wave of youthful enthusiasm, I felt quite cheerful. I even slapped the lieutenant on the back. Every time I remember it, I feel like vomiting.

After collecting their fee — one hundred and ten thousand *pesetas* — they put the Arabs in the trucks and covered them with a brown tarpaulin. The men must have been suffering under there, even though the sun was low in the sky and we'd soon be assaulted by the intense cold of the night. We started on the way back, using an alternative route that wound along by the sea between sand dunes and canebrakes. Inexplicably, when we were still an hour and a half short of the frontier, the lieutenant stopped. Let's give these people something to eat, he remarked jovially. It was a sandy spot, whipped by the wind and illuminated by a huge, red moon. In the background, you could hear the roar of the sea.

The Arabs got out one by one and herded together again, looking at us out of their sunken eyes. Cucurella unloaded a bag full of lunch boxes and passed them out as though it were a soup kitchen. The Arabs thanked him for the supper with a nod and words of gratitude. Let's go up on that dune, Cucurella said, while they eat supper. You'll see better from there. I assumed, innocently, that he was talking about the nocturnal landscape, which was truly marvelous, with shreds of green mist over the sea and the breakers. While we were

climbing, I didn't suspect anything, but half an hour and half
a pack of cigarettes later, when I was stiff with cold, I began
to wonder. The Arabs were up against the truck, sheltered
from the wind. What are we doing here? I asked. Why are we
hanging around? My voice was swept away by the first howl,
a guttural, zoological sound warning me that I was finally
going to know real terror.

The Arabs who had sat down close together, waiting for
the order to start traveling again, were now standing up slowly.
Some of them squeezed their stomachs with both hands and
stumbled around as if they were drunk. Other screamed, ran
a ways toward our dune and then fell over writhing frenetically. What's this? I exclaimed, looking at Cucurella. His eyes
were shut; he was panting, caught up in an inexplicable delirium: Cyanide. Listen, listen to the sea.

From that moment on, I lost all perception of time, of
myself, of my sinister companions. I can't say if those death
throes lasted half an hour or an hour and a half. I remember
that one of the Arabs — perhaps one who was stronger, not
so hungry, not so poisoned — managed to reach us on the top
of the dune with his arms outstretched; whether to strangle us
or to ask us for help I don't know. Cucurella took out his pistol,
but the lieutenant stopped him: What are you doing? Don't
dare shoot him. If their skin is full of holes, they're not worth
half as much. A tremendous kick in the stomach sent the
Arab rolling down to the foot of the dune. He didn't move
again. You're crazy! As long as I live, I'll never forget
Cucurella's beatific smile of sexual satisfaction, Now we're
coming to the best part.

We descended. Cucurella and the lieutenant gathered

the corpses together, dragging them by the ankles. While Cucurella undressed the bodies, the lieutenant went through the pockets of the jackets and pants with a pedantic, military neatness, putting the different objects into carefully labelled burlap bags. The six bodies — thin, yellowish, naked, frozen in the light of the moon, which was like a drop of mercury over our heads — made up a scene out of a Gothic print.

Grab this! the lieutenant ordered, throwing me one of the shovels that were strapped to the fuselage of the truck. I followed him, bereft of will and understanding, to a hollow lighted by the headlights Cucurella directed from behind the wheel of the truck. Was it here? the lieutenant shouted, pointing to some Leucothoe bushes.

No, more to the left! Cucurella answered. Once they had agreed, we began to dig in the sand, the three of us, in a silence broken only by the whistle of the wind that made my teeth chatter. But I still hadn't finished my initiation into horror.

We weren't digging graves for dead men. Back then I still felt pity; I hadn't doubted for a minute we were burying the bodies. But on the third or fourth shovel-load, the lieutenant remarked jauntily: Look, here's one. We drew closer. From out of the sand that had been messed about, a dried-up foot protruded. It was unmistakable, the skeleton of a human foot, with skin hanging around it. Ah. It looks pretty good, Cucurella confirmed. See, I told you. Two weeks are enough, at least at this time of year.

By the time the moon had begun to drop, eight mummies were lined up. I must not have looked too different from them, because the lieutenant informed me, solicitous, that the real business had nothing to do with the money the illegal immigrants paid, but with selling mummies to American and European museums. Here, buried in the sand, it only takes fifteen days to make a mummy. There's not a worm, not a fly, not a beetle. The hyenas and jackals have disappeared. The wild dogs sometimes dig holes, but there's no enterprise without its risks . . . They dry out like autumn leaves, and they have a really exquisite waxen quality. You can pass them off as Peruvian, Aztec, Chinese, even Egyptian. The museum directors don't care whether you send them from Africa or from Auschwitz. They pay up to five hundred *pesetas* for the best ones. Today's crop is going to the anthropological museum in Chestown, California, Cucurella concluded.

I think it was the word "California" that woke me up. I took in the whole situation with such a flash of lucidity that for an instant I wondered if I hadn't lost my head too. Taking advantage of the fact that both the lieutenant and Cucurella were busy lifting up the mummies, which weighed no more than a pack of cigarettes, I shot them both in the back. I got the lieutenant in the neck, and he fell over like a sack, deflated, without a sound, but I missed Cucurella. He turned around without letting go of the mummy and looked at me with great serenity. He took a step in my direction. I still felt pity back then. He took another step. I kept my arm up and the gun pointing at his head. When he took the third step, I shot him in the neck. His blood, mixed with air from his lungs, burst out with a happy, cheerful bubble. I couldn't help laughing. I laughed for quite a while.

I got into the truck and drove until I was close to the coastal frontier, the frontier used most often for contraband and the opium trade and, therefore, the least scrupulous about registering entries and exits. I slept for a few hours in the cab of the truck until the sun warmed the roof and I was soaked in sweat. Before throwing it into the thick canebrakes, I cleaned the pistol carefully. Sunday afternoon I sank into a leaden sleep, spread out on the cot in my barracks. A few days later, the newspapers reported that two Spanish soldiers who were vacationing on the Mediterranean had fallen victim to the plague of bandits which is all that's left of the old, nomadic way of life. After putting up a gallant fight, they had been robbed and murdered. A lukewarm protest was tendered through diplomatic channels, followed by a punitive expedition that took the lives of a couple of shepherd families and then peace here and glory in the hereafter.

Not a single comment on the Chinaman's story, surely his way of telling me good-bye. And may Cucurella rest in peace, done in by a neck wound.

August 22nd

The Animal's liturgy, as far as it affects me, takes place late in the afternoon. At that time, in spite of the open window, his room is charged with organic effluvia in a ripe state. Since he no longer can control his sphincter, we've spread out diapers under the sheets, and we change them every day. The room is getting to be more and more like the Natural History Museum. Will the Chinaman let the flies eat the corpse?

Here's the ritual: Marta supports him by the heels while the Chinaman and I take hold of him under the arms and lift his body. In one movement, we swing him onto the wing chair, not without his letting escape a tiny moan because of the contraction his horribly swollen neck suffers. Marta pulls off the sheet and the diapers, all stained the color of algae. The stench is almost unbearable. Then we put the oilcloth, the spare sheet, and the clean diapers back on. I think he's actually aware of the cleanness and freshness of the bed, because every day without fail I discern something like a beatific smile on that twisted, livid face. However, it's hard to believe since the Chinaman injects him with morphine each and every day.

There's a certain order in this madness. The Chinaman is taking a serious risk — not just by denying him assistance, which is without any doubt the accusation the family would levy against him if any of them found out the Animal died without medical attention; he could also be charged with improper use of medication and even with trafficking in drugs. But he's not taking these risks because of money. In fact, I've stopped thinking that he is, in general, motivated by money. He's motivated by his own volition, and it weighs him down like a ball and chain. An old debt between the Chinaman and the Animal is being liquidated, a conflict from the past between two lovers who were separated by pride, a pride that's now flowing slowly toward the drain. From a couple of sentences the Chinaman muttered, I gather the Animal encouraged him, gave him help and support, offered him a model, an ideal; that's why he became an obstacle, a mistake, something to be extirpated. How can you grow and take care of yourself and *take yourself in hand* — I'm talking about the Chinaman, about his self-image, an image dependent on the exercise of his will — when you suspect that you've CLIMBED UP ON A STOOL to reach the height you desire? Years ago the Animal must have had that fraction of height the

Chinaman needed, must have been the stool that allowed
him to look in a mirror that was too high. Now he's pulling
away the stool to see if he has reached the right height. So
it's satisfying for him to take part in the Animal's dissolution.

Marta, on the other hand, takes it all in stride. For her,
keeping the house clean demands special attention to the
bathroom, the kitchen and the DEAD MAN. We hardly
speak while the liturgy goes on, but if Marta makes any remark, it's always of a technical nature: Why don't we try
Dodotis, they're more absorbent? or Don't you think it'd be
better to shave him with an electric razor — his skin is getting irritated. His skin! What skin? That membrane as tight
as a blown-up frog? But the fact is she's not part of OUR
history, OUR story. What she sees stretched out there, with
his eyes half open like the Christ of Basel, is on the other
side of life, and even though she can devote as much — or
more — energy to him as anyone, she knows instinctively
that it's a luxury or a perversion. All her GOOD HEALTH
protests against shows of medical and scientific virtuosity,
against imitations of life. She would have buried the Animal
at the slightest symptom, the first attack of nausea, just like
she'll bury herself as soon as she realizes that life has passed
her by; a few wrinkles, a little loose skin, will be enough.
She'll bury herself alive, and she won't be unhappy about it.

She combs the Animal's long, sticky hair with the same
satisfaction she'd feel combing the hair of an eight-year-old
daughter. She even pats his forehead and monstrous neck
with cologne. Isn't she still playing with dolls? Won't she
perhaps keep on playing with dolls in hell? But I'm shocked
by her exchange of looks with the Chinaman after a com-

ment that's both transparent and opaque, simultaneously luminous and blind. We were going down the stairs one after the other, with me in the middle. The Chinaman said over my head, Anything new, Marta? And then Marta, without stopping or turning around, Nothing. Isn't that good? If it keeps on like this for another week . . . The Chinaman insisted, but his voice was different, that is, it was his usual voice, but with a sinuous, youthful tone: Another week? You're still not sure, hon? It was exactly then that he piqued my interest. Why did he say "hon?" He never uses those expressions, those sordid expressions that are somehow AFFECTIONATE. Something very important must be going on for him to talk like that.

I felt the same revulsion as if he had addressed me as "young man" or used any of those nauseating expressions ("to the delight of," "a lavish feast," "Hi, Cap," "his lovely wife," "the black-tie brigade," "irreproachable behavior") commonly employed by base souls. In any event, Marta, who had now gotten as far as the front hall, finished up with the most disturbing of all, a Be paaaaaatient! with the "a" drawn out just like that, "paaaaaa-tient," an intolerable, sinister sound — let's get to the point — a CONJUGAL sound. Between the two of them. And the association of ideas is transparent anyway. The Animal, his excretions, a general surgical atmosphere, eh? and Marta with her physiological disorders, her feminine peculiarities, eh? Another kind of operating theater, you might say.

At that moment, I jumped back, way back. I imagine, intuit, the plan, the strategy (why should we kid ourselves? I see the sword falling not just on the Animal), but I still don't dare deduce the consequences. For the time being, I'm not taking it too seriously (let the dead bury the dead, life is for the living, ah hah). I hum it to myself unconsciously because if I took it soil — I mean, ser — iously, I couldn't bear it. Or could I? Actually, I could. The unfortunate thing is that I'm preparing myself, after so much humiliation, to accept it, to relate — even "domesticate" — it, never to forget my transitory condition (!), not to drag things out, not to wait — that's clear — ANOTHER week. This is my conclusion. Oh, Lord! Her head, her neck, her shoulders, her arms, her hands, her breasts, her belly, her genitals, her legs, her feet, all those THINGS they talk about on the radio . . . Oh, Lord! All those things, all that *spirituality* . . . ! Is it always going to be the same? Eternally repeating out of sheer fatigue, if not an erection, repeating YES, since this seems to be the only word that ever reaches Your ears, Your monolexic, monaural ears!

(last entry in the notebook, no date)

Sin is compulsion! Obligation! It's resignation itself. Speaking with *scientific* precision, that's what sin is. If my acts aren't free, they're sinful, infected, revolting. Everything we do because we can't help it, because of submission and humiliation, is a sin. There's a lot of sin in this world. If I don't want to take a shower, but I do take a shower, I commit a venial sin. But I'm not sinning if I WANT to kill, and I kill! The Indian wasn't sinning. He wouldn't be sinning even if he finished off half the city. I've freely decided to kill, and I kill; therefore, I haven't sinned, I'm innocent, I can explain, I can make myself understood, I can give death a meaning. My INSTINCT made me do it. Let them kill me like a wild beast then, but an innocent beast! Well and good; but if somebody kills because it's his duty, then he commits a sin.

That's the way I put it, just like that. Of course, she didn't understand, or anyway she pretended that she didn't understand. What are you talking about? You're acting very strange! I'm talking about killing! Please, you're scaring me! Marta frowned but without any anger, both of her hands were on her neck as if she either wanted to strangle herself or had just broken her coral necklace. It's awful seeing an innocent person frightened, but she hadn't left me an alternative. You're scaring me! Stop talking like that! She didn't move her legs, which were pressed together under her blue canvas skirt. From time to time, I got a brief glimpse of one of her shoes. Hush! Don't say anything else crazy! You're a nut! But I wanted her to understand me: I'm sorry I'm frightening you, but you have to understand. It's not bad to kill or steal or lie or take a walk or a bath. Evil doesn't lie in what people do or don't do, poor ephemeral, acephalous mosquitoes that we are. Evil lies in denial and betrayal. You don't want to kill, so you have to convince yourself that you want to in order to do it freely. Like the Animal who's being killed by the Chinaman, put up for death at the request of the interested party, right? That's what both of them want. When you CONVINCE an animal that it wants to die, then it's free and it can decide to die. But as long as it doesn't know, as long as it doesn't go along with things, it dies out of a sense of duty and that's a sin. All animals die in sin. All of them are self-condemned. Only men want to die and die freely, and for that very reason, WE DON'T DIE, but animals are condemned — they don't exist!

Marta looked at me with her Antarctic eyes, her fingers

wound up in her little coral necklace. That's enough now! What's the matter with you? Have you started drinking again? Do you want to scare me? Well, I'm scared! She didn't understand. She didn't understand anything at all. I need your collaboration. I need you to collaborate, to put your ideas in tune with mine, to flee from your instinct (may it be damned a thousand times, it preserves you FOR NOTHING WHATSOEVER!) and seek refuge in your BODY'S BRAIN. If you get that far, it's not going to be hard for you to understand that you even want to kill a part of yourself and that you'll kill it out of love . . . At that second, she screamed. A perfectly predictable scream, the scream of newborn babies that drove the French soldiers crazy on the Maginot Line. You're a murderer! Naturally, I'm a murderer. I'm a humiliated man; so I'm a willing murderer! I defend sterility!

And then, by magic, the Chinaman appears holding on to the door jamb. For the first time, I can see an expression of haste in his eyes, or in his glasses, that's not the least bit reassuring. What's going on here? I didn't know you were home. What have you done to Marta? He says he wants me to kill I don't know what; he's gone crazy! What? He says he wants me to kill I don't know what; he's gone berserk! You were upstairs, you were upstairs with the Animal. What were you doing upstairs at this time of day? And who does she have to kill if I may ask? She has to, Marta has to kill, I want to be sterile! You probably are. Yeah, well, but she . . . Not her; that's why she went to Switzerland, but then she decided not to pay attention to me. It doesn't matter. Marta has to freely Marat another animal, the poor, unfortunate animal who's been forced on her like a monster with two bodies, with two souls or, worse yet, with two sins and two humiliations, and she's got to do it fast because that animal is growing and clinging to her guts like a vine; it devours her, it possesses her just like that hulk of an Animal, and soon it'll be too late because that animal will FORM A CONCEPTION OF DEATH! — we form it so fast — and then there's no way it can be killed. Yes, I'm performing an ORAL ABORTION on myself, that's what I'm doing.

Did I cry then as I did in the Jailhouse Vision? Self-pity? Self-abortion? Things have changed so much I can't be sure now. I know that Marta finally understood and that she was holding my head in her arms, kneeling on the floor, saying, Poor thing, poor thing. Between the two of them, they lifted me up and sat me on the kitchen table, just like a child. That's when my dismissal got underway. In the Chinaman's changing features, as flexible now as an octopus's skin, there was a new mask, created, hammered in, not on top of but underneath the other, with darkly distant eyes, a gold tooth and even — good God! — a moustache. His voice had also gotten richer, with liquid "l"s and "e"s, unmistakable ornaments of the Valencian dialect. His soul was more cast down, more humiliated than mine, and this consoled me even though I was already liquidated.

Now, let's go up to the attic, he was saying, the three of us together, to get this over with once and for all, and then you're going to leave this house. But he said it so kindly that I found myself thanking him on the way from the kitchen to the stairs. Climbing those interminable steps, I saw my days pass by in the form of sheets of paper. And I was getting myself together, gathering myself together.

In the attic, you couldn't smell anything organic. It was a dry smell, like leather or burlap, stamped by the lance of African sunlight that plunged from the window onto the bed. The Animal had escaped from his immortality, and he was now a man who had died under the auspices of the highest poetry and the most elevated ideas. A monument. Now I realized that his features were smooth, his chin bluish, frozen at an arrogant right angle from the pillow. His dried-up lips had drawn in toward the inside of his mouth, revealing a gold tooth. On either side of his chiseled nose grew a few long, curly hairs that disappeared into a grizzled brown beard. His eyes were neither open nor closed, but half-open. The pupils had congealed like fish eyes. His hair, combed back, covered his nearly transparent ears.

From the right side of the bed, the Chinaman watched him with great solemnity, as if he had taken off a hat, or as if the two of them had exchanged signals from beyond. Suddenly, stepping forward in an almost military fashion and without hesitating, he leaned over the cadaver and kissed it on the forehead. When he did this, seeing the contrast between the two profiles, I finally recognized the secret personality of the Animal, who was now a dead man. The nose, eyes, cheekbones, mouth and hair of the two coincided like two silhouettes cut out around a wine glass. Now, said the Chinaman, I've just been born; that's how it is. And, in fact, there had been a pact between them, a lifelong pact, starting after birth, a pact written during the hours and the days of apprenticeship, a pact that had perhaps been forgotten later on because of pride and mutual envy, but a pact that was indestructible because it was written in their common blood, and the veins are the highways of man.

I couldn't hold myself up any longer even though I was still starting a sentence, surely one of reconciliation and fare-well, surely one that began: *Through your mouth, Lord, I have received the father* . . . but it was pointless now. The scene was illuminated with such a blinding light that my words produced no sound. This was, at last, the mouth of the Lord that links father and son. It sealed a door that made me a stranger twice over: a stranger to the dead and to the living, a stranger to what the Chinaman was leaving behind and to what the Chinaman was receiving. I was certain that I no longer had a meaning in that sentence written by time, the sentence that joined three of the bodies present* and whose inheritance, protected now by Marta's resolution, did not belong to me in any way.

The afternoon silence covered each figure with a sheet of intense beauty, the clarity of a dead man withdrawing into himself, the clarity of the heir like a candle on the tomb, the clarity of the vessel whose presence is the joy of mankind, their confirmation and their enduring honor. I was out of things. Expelled by the multitude. Lukewarm. Sterile. Spewed out. So irrelevant that I barely had to move my feet to reach the street. I was swept along in a transport of the soul rather than being moved by the wind. The tops of the acacias swayed like Palm Sunday fronds, but not for me. Almost without effort, I found myself once again on the Avenida del Tibidabo, which was deserted in the August heat, enclosed in the glass bubble that the half-melted asphalt gave off. I would have

---

* Play on the term *cuerpo presente*, which is used to designate a body laid out for viewing at a wake.

circled the plaza aimlessly like the crippled ship that makes port guided only by its instinct if it hadn't been for a strange sensation that had begun to disturb me when I left the house and that was only now becoming intolerable.

I stood still and made a painful effort to concentrate in order to figure out what irksome element held me together or drew me back to myself even though all my animals — brain, liver and heart — wanted to make off on their own, leaving me in pieces. How could I possibly still be stuck together? The Judas trees, whose lavender flowers are the glory of April, trembled in the light. It seems impossible, but the Lord also condemned the fig tree because it didn't produce fruit when he passed by — even though it was out of season. Sitting on a bench in the plaza in the shade of the flowering Judas, I tried to understand why the leaves moved to the rhythm of my heart and lungs and what we had in common. Time passed, along with women and children and stupefied workers and buses and desperate dogs.

Before nightfall, just before nightfall, I felt an intense pain under my arm that came from staying so still, but when I raised it to let the blood circulate, something fell to the ground. At first I had trouble recognizing what it was, but then I felt as though I had stumbled over my own tomb. In what extraordinary delirium had I searched the house until I found it? Which of the body's spirits kept me from leaving it behind? I can't say, but there it was with its crumpled covers, like answers without a question. We were still separate and joined together. I've kept up with my notebook, and I may keep up with it for a long time. We're both off for a stroll in these welcoming streets among a kindly humanity. We wander up and down the Ramblas, lulled by the Oriental tapestry of its colors and smells. With curiosity we approach the Ensanche, where the economic anthill sleeps on, locked in a spell cast by a geometrician. We climb the Tibidabo to look at ourselves in the desperation of the sea. Every minute we want to embrace every inhabitant of the city as did the old philologist with that whipped horse, our brother. We look impatiently for Leandro Bonet, but without any luck so far. We share ephemeral perceptions with Andalusian drunks as well as the exaltation of the thinker, battered in body and soul, left without hope by love and philosophy. We commemorate the great men of the past, buzzard breeders, dog trainers, book thieves, and strong chatty women, classical figures. We've gone back to the Boa and even bought drinks for new girls from Málaga who are there with their boyfriends. We read! We've gotten thin and gotten our hair cut in the barbershop on Tallers. Sometimes we walk by the liquor store and tell ourselves that one of these days we're going to drop in and say hello to Diego. I owe it all, all, to my notebook, because I've never heard again from Marta or the Chinaman. With this notebook I explain over and over, hour after hour, the event that sent us back to the world. Soon, when our body recovers its acidic, tepid voracity, when it wipes out the specialist in banality from the family of relations, then from the pages of this notebook I'll draw the faith I need to write a book. A modest book that's full of hope. This book.